## STOLEN KISSES

"Don't you kiss me, Jarrod Blackstone," she warned.

He smiled, but it didn't reach his eyes. "What makes you think I'm going to kiss you?"

"That look on your face. It's just like last time—"

"I knew it! You can't forget about it either, can you?"

"Haven't given it another thought since you promised you wouldn't do it ever again." A ripple of need ran through her, undermining her resolve. "You are a man of your word."

"What if I did it again, Abby? What would you do? Would you wrap your arms around my neck and press yourself close like last time?"

"You're imagining things. I never did—"

"That's it, isn't it? You liked it when I kissed you. You wanted more. That scares you more than anything."

"Ridiculous," she said, trying to duck under his arm.

"Then don't run away." He caught her and pulled her back. "You're afraid that if you admit you care for me, you might have to give up your dream."

She drew in a sharp breath, feeling exposed—and cornered. She shook her head. "You and I—we can't ever be."

Books by Teresa Southwick

*Winter Bride*
*Reckless Destiny*
*Blackstone's Bride*

Published by HarperPaperbacks

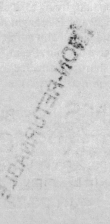

# Blackstone's Bride

## TERESA SOUTHWICK

**HarperPaperbacks**
*A Division of HarperCollinsPublishers*

**HarperPaperbacks**
*A Division of* HarperCollins*Publishers*
10 East 53rd Street, New York, N.Y. 10022-5299

This is a work of fiction. The characters, incidents, and
dialogues are products of the author's imagination and are not to
be construed as real. Any resemblance to actual events or
persons, living or dead, is entirely coincidental.

ISBN 0-06-108371-2

HarperCollins®, 🔥®, HarperPaperbacks™, and
HarperMonogram® are trademarks of HarperCollins*Publishers,* Inc.

Cover illustration by Aleta Jenks

First printing: November 1996

Printed in the United States of America

Visit HarperPaperbacks on the World Wide Web at
http://www.harpercollins.com/paperbacks

❖ 10 9 8 7 6 5 4 3 2 1

*To Maureen Child. Line by line you kept me on track.*
*And Cheryl Arguile, for making sure I stayed true to my characters.*
*Last, but by no means least, to Christopher Boyle, my brother and number one fan. Your support means more than I can say.*

# Blackstone's Bride

# 1

### Blackstone Ranch—Santa Barbara County, California—1886

*"Damn it! I smell smoke."* Jarrod Blackstone reined in his roan and looked around. His foreman, Gib Cochran, stopped beside him.

In this wild, rugged country, a man learned to listen with all his senses. No sight, sound, or smell could go unexplained. The threat of fire struck fear in every rancher, especially after all the rain that winter. Vegetation had grown waist high in some places, but was dry and brown now. One spark and a little wind could start a wildfire that would consume every last blade of grass. A blaze could burn for weeks, until it reached the ocean, destroying grazing land, cattle, and lives.

They were about a hundred yards from the house. The birds still chattered and bees continued buzzing. That told Jarrod that the faint smell of smoke was nothing nature need worry about. So he knew it came from the ranch buildings.

"You didn't forget to bank the fire in the bunkhouse again, did you, Gib?" he asked.

"Nope."

"I was afraid of that." Jarrod's horse shifted nervously as he looked closer. Pointing a gloved finger, he said, "There. It's coming from the main house."

Beyond the thick oak grove in front of him, smoke rose, gray and unmistakable against the rich, dark blue haze of the mountains behind it.

"Yup. No mistake. That's where it's comin' from all right."

"I left the stove cold," Jarrod said, uneasy. "Haven't had a fire in the front room since . . . " He recalled the last time and frowned.

"You expectin' anyone?" Gib asked, scratching the silver stubble on his chin.

"Who'd come all the way out here?"

"No one. And if they did, they wouldn't make themselves at home. Unless maybe they was lookin' for help—or trouble."

"Yeah, that's what I thought," Jarrod said, lifting his pistol from the holster strapped to his thigh. He spun the cylinder to make sure he had a full load. Gib did the same.

"Ready, boss?"

"As ready as I'll ever be," Jarrod answered. "Let's go." The thick undergrowth muffled the sound of horses' hooves. It was late afternoon and nearly dark beneath the dense ceiling of interlacing tree branches. There was still enough spring left in the air to make it chilly as the sun went down.

They approached the rear of the three-story, white-shingle-covered house. The top floor was an attic, the middle contained bedrooms, and the bottom held the main living area. That's where the intruder would be, but from here Jarrod saw nothing amiss.

He pulled back on his reins and held up his hand, signaling Gib to stop. Jarrod quickly dismounted, and the other man followed suit. Together, they circled around to the front of the house. Three columns held up the roof over the porch, where two slat-backed rockers sat with a table in between. A wagon hitched to a couple of chestnut horses stood several feet away. Other than that, everything looked the same as it had when he'd left that morning. As they moved closer, Jarrod saw there was writing on the side of the wagon proclaiming its owner: HOLLISTER FREIGHT CO. In the wagon bed stood a canvas-covered object.

Jarrod relaxed his grip on his pistol and holstered it. Wasn't likely that anyone from the town of Hollister was dangerous. When redheaded Abby Miller walked out onto the porch, he changed his mind about that. She was trouble of a different sort.

"Howdy, Firecracker." Gib grinned.

Jarrod groaned. He hadn't seen Abby for a while. Not since Dulcy had left.

"Good day, Gib, Jarrod." Her voice was husky. "I've got a delivery for you. From Chicago."

He nodded. "I'll have Dusty and Slim unload it."

"Thanks."

"Looks like ever'thin's fine here. I'll rub down the horses and stable 'em, boss."

Jarrod nodded, although he wasn't so sure everything was fine. It never was when Abby showed up.

"Nice to see you again, Gib," she said.

"Same here." He nodded once, then walked away.

In any other woman, Jarrod would have thought that smoky, soft voice was practiced and meant to tease a man. But not Abby. She was a no-nonsense, get-the-job-done sort of woman. He'd never known her to flirt, at least not in front of him. He couldn't say what she did in Hollister, which was where she lived, worked, and spent most of her time, when she wasn't at Blackstone Ranch trying to deliver some newfangled contraption someone else had ordered and didn't want.

He stopped at the bottom porch step and looked up at Abby. Dressed in a long-sleeved, plaid cotton blouse, brown split skirt, and boots, she leaned back against the middle porch column. They were not quite eye-to-eye and she looked down her nose at him. He noticed it was a pretty little nose crisscrossed with freckles, but he still didn't like that she was looking down at him.

Jarrod stepped up to the bottom step, then stared straight into eyes as blue as the Pacific on a clear summer day.

He frowned. "What did you bring this time? Some contraption that'll turn cow pies into perfume?"

Far from being intimidated by his gruffness, she smiled at him. Her eyes twinkled, again reminding him of the ocean as the sun's rays turned the peaks of the swells into diamonds.

"Are you still angry about that painting? That was a long time ago, Jarrod."

"It was fruit, Abby. What am I supposed to do with a flat canvas full of apples, pears, and bananas?"

"Hang it in the parlor like I suggested."

"I didn't want it."

"Maybe not, but your wife did. My responsibility was to deliver it to its destination. You could have sent it back to Hollister with me."

"You would have charged me to haul it back."

"I had no choice. It's my job."

"So what *did* you bring me this time?" He almost didn't want to know. Every time she showed up, his life turned upside down.

"It's the bookcase you ordered. There's something else—"

Just then the front door opened and slammed shut. A small boy stopped beside her. Jarrod hadn't the least notion how old he was. He'd never been around kids much. This one's blond head came to about Abby's waist. He was blue-eyed and scrawny. He had his thumb in his mouth, and his other hand clutched his privates as he hopped from foot to foot.

"Are you my uncle Jarrod?" he asked.

Stunned, Jarrod couldn't get a word out. A pained expression crossed the child's face. "Gotta go," he said. As he bounced, he looked around for the necessary.

Jarrod pointed through the trees. "Over there," he said.

The boy took off running.

"What's going on, Abby?" he asked suspiciously.

Before she could answer, the door opened again. A girl came out and stood beside Abby. She was slightly taller than the boy and there was more than a little resemblance between them. Same color hair, but hers was curly, and she had green eyes.

"Where's Oliver?" she asked.

"He went to the outhouse." Abby put her hand on the child's shoulder. "This is Katie."

Two of his sister Sally's children were named Oliver and Katie. The door opened again. An older girl and a boy slightly younger stepped outside. The brown-haired, green-eyed girl stood close to Abby, as if for protection. The boy's hair was the exact color as his sister's, but his eyes were gray. He kept himself slightly apart.

All four of them were thin. Jarrod didn't remember ever being that skinny as a boy, but that had been a long time ago. He wondered about their ill-fitting, threadbare clothes. Sally wouldn't dress them in playthings to travel. More likely, they'd be in their Sunday best.

"What's going on?" Jarrod asked.

Abby looked at him nervously, although she was trying to hide it. "I did bring you something else," she said. "But this time I think you'll be pleased. They tell me you've never met. Jarrod, may I present your nieces and nephews."

"Where's Sally?" he asked. He hadn't seen his sister in fourteen years. Why hadn't she let him know she was coming? He had a bad feeling as he glanced at the three of them. "Where's your mother?"

Abby's eyes clouded as she looked at the oldest girl. "Lily?"

The child's hands anxiously twisted together. "She's dead, Uncle Jarrod. We buried her three weeks ago. Before she died, she wrote you this." She reached into the pocket of her patched calico dress and pulled out an envelope. Then she stepped shyly to the edge of the porch and handed it to him.

He opened it and scanned the paper. Instantly he recognized Sally's neat, artistic handwriting. He read quickly, barely absorbing the essentials. Sally's no-good husband was dead. She begged Jarrod's forgiveness for not listening when he had tried to warn her about Reed Donovan. When she knew she was dying, she had to make sure her children would be provided for. She wanted them raised as Blackstones on the family ranch, as she and Jarrod had been.

He looked at Abby. Of all the deliveries she'd made, this was the worst. Shock, grief, and unreasonable anger boiled up inside him. He knew it was unfair, but the need to lash out at someone was overpowering.

He fought it as Abby and the children stared at him, waiting.

The silence dragged on, and Katie started to whimper. Abby squeezed the girl's shoulder reassuringly. "Say something, Jarrod."

"I can't."

"They're your family. The resemblance is unmistakable. Tom has your eyes. They've got Blackstone written all over their faces."

"I can see that."

"On the way from town, they could hardly wait to meet you. Lily showed me a picture of you that her mother gave her." She half turned to the girl. "Show him, Lily."

The girl hesitantly stepped toward him again, and Jarrod's chest tightened when he saw that she was the image of her mother. He took the old tattered tintype from her and recognized the likeness of himself taken when he was twenty and Sally six years older. She had left not long afterward.

He couldn't believe that his sister, always so full of life and mischief, was gone. He'd never see her again. There were things he wanted to say to her, and now he never could.

At the sound of running footsteps behind him, Jarrod turned to see Oliver coming as fast as he could go on his short, spindly legs. The boy stopped beside him and tugged on his pant leg.

"What?" Jarrod asked.

"Mama said you'd take us to the Specific Ocean. Will ya?"

"Not today."

"Then when?"

"Can't say."

The boy stuck his thumb in his mouth and spoke around it. "When's Mama gonna get here?"

Jarrod didn't know what to tell him. Surely he knew his mother was never coming back. Was he old enough to understand?

"How old are you?" he asked Oliver.

The child left his thumb in his mouth and held up his other four fingers. When he turned five, he would have a better use for that thumb, Jarrod thought wryly.

Jarrod knew nothing about bringing up children, and even less about helping them deal with the death of their mother. He knew they were blood relations, even before Abby had pointed out the obvious to him. He knew all about them from Sally's letters. Lily, thirteen and on the verge of young womanhood. Tom, eleven, staring at him with hostile gray eyes. Katie, six, cute as a button, with her curly blond hair and green eyes. He wondered at the purple circles beneath them. And last was Oliver, only four years old. The dark stain on the front of the boy's pants told him that the child had not found the necessary in time. He wasn't old enough to grasp the fact that his mother was never coming back.

Jarrod was having trouble with that one himself. How could he explain it to the little guy?

But the most immediate question was: With a ranch to run, how the hell was he supposed to look after four children?

When the silence continued, Katie started to cry. "Don't you want us, Uncle Jarrod?"

He felt horrible. When she walked to the edge of the porch, he instinctively opened his arms, pulling her up against him as sobs wracked her tiny body. Her thinness surprised him; she weighed hardly anything.

He awkwardly patted her back. Although he liked

youngsters well enough, he had no experience comforting a small child, or an older one either. She continued to cry, and when she buried her face in his neck, he swallowed hard, twice. The lump in his throat wouldn't budge. He wasn't sure if it was her grief or the trusting arms around his neck that moved him. But the fact that she went to him at all felt good.

"Don't cry," he said, tightening his hold on her. "Everything's gonna be fine."

She lifted her head. "You won't send us away?"

"Oh—" Abby made a small noise somewhere between a gasp and a stifled sob. "Of course he won't send you away, sweetie. Lily, will you take them in the house and help Oliver change? Supper's ready. We'll be in shortly."

"Yes, ma'am," she said, taking Katie from Jarrod. The others followed Lily inside.

As soon as the door closed, Abby rounded on him, eyes flashing. "You *aren't* going to send them away. Are you, Jarrod?"

"Of course not. But I need some time to get used to this."

"Unfortunately, you don't have time. Those children lost their mother a few short weeks ago. They need to know they have someone who will take care of them. You could look a little happier to see them." Her disbelief, annoyance, and discouragement were evident as her body tensed.

"Now hold on, Abby. It's not every day a man finds out his only sister has passed on, much less that she left her four kids to him. This is a hell of a shock. Just give me a minute."

"I'm sorry. I wasn't thinking," she said softly. "This must be a terrible blow. I can only imagine what it would feel like. If the shoe were on the other foot, and it was my brother, Clint—" She stopped and swallowed. "I'm sorry for your loss."

He nodded and the muscle in his cheek jerked once as he clamped his jaw tight. When he trusted his voice, he asked, "How did she die? Did the kids tell you anything?"

She took a deep breath. "Lily said it was sudden. One

day she was fine, the next she was hurting, and she didn't
eat after that. The pain got worse and she wasted away."

"Seems you know a lot."

Abby shrugged. "It's a long ride from town. They needed
to talk to someone."

"Did Sally have a doctor?"

"They didn't say anything about one. I'd guess not. Did
you notice their clothes, and how thin they are? I don't
think there was much money."

Jarrod heard the disapproval in her voice and knew she
was wondering why his sister's children were wanting when
he had so much. He didn't know why, but he felt he owed
her an explanation.

"Since she left here in 'seventy-two, my sister wrote me
twice a year. Once on my birthday and again at Christmas. I
knew about every one of the kids being born. Other than
that, all she ever said was that things were fine."

"You never went to visit her?"

"I've got a ranch to run. For God's sake," he said defensively, "there are hardly enough hours in the day to do what
needs to be done around here as it is. Besides, I never had
reason to suspect things weren't the way she said. Which
brings us back to those kids. I don't know anything about
raising children, and I don't have the time to see that it's
done the way Sally would want."

"Maybe not, but you're all they've got. And you're better
than nothing."

"Thanks," he said wryly.

"You know what I mean. They're just children, Jarrod,"
she said softly, sympathetically. "You've lost your sister, but
they've lost their mother. Think about what they're going
through."

Jarrod knew she was right. It didn't sweeten his temper
any, but he did his best to tamp his anger down. For the
kids' sake.

He took a deep breath. "Guess I'd best go inside and get
acquainted."

She nodded. "You'll do fine. Good-bye, Jarrod. Good luck."

"Where are you going?"

"Back to town."

He glanced through the oak grove and saw the rays of the setting sun. "You can't get there before dark. It's too dangerous to travel at night."

"It's a chance I'll have to take."

"Why didn't you wait until morning to deliver the kids, if you couldn't get out here and back before dark?"

"I thought I could. They're nervous and upset and needed to be settled as soon as possible. I figured I'd have just enough time. But when we arrived and the house was empty, I just couldn't leave them here alone."

"So now that I'm here, you're going to dump them in my lap and hightail it back?"

"Yeah."

He took her arm. "I don't think so. This is the last time you drop something on my doorstep and leave. Besides, what kind of host would I be, not offering you a place to stay for the night? I don't want to come across what's left of you when the coyotes get finished. You can leave at first light. Not before."

Abby felt the strength in the hand gripping her upper arm. He didn't hurt her, but she couldn't break his hold without struggling, and probably not even then. She wouldn't give him the satisfaction of seeing her try.

She met his gaze directly. "Please release me, *Mister* Blackstone."

Something flickered in his gray eyes, a flash of respect, she thought. Or maybe it was more personal than that, but it was gone before she could tell. She didn't want to know anyway. She just wanted to go back to Hollister. Jarrod Blackstone made her nervous. He always had. Not because of his intimidating size. He wasn't the only man several inches over six feet she'd come across. It wasn't even because he was handsome as sin.

She was uneasy around him because of the fluttery feeling she always got in her stomach when he was nearby. Her palms grew sweaty and her knees weak. A man who could do that to her was a man to stay away from. Besides, even if Jarrod Blackstone hadn't made it clear that he had no use for her or any other woman, she had no time for that sort of thing. Knowing his feelings like she did, his insistence that she stay the night came as a surprise.

When he didn't let her go, she looked at his fingers, then back into his eyes, and lifted a brow.

Amusement flashed across his face as he loosened his grip and dropped his hand.

"Thank you," she said, resisting the impulse to rub her arm.

Those gray eyes of his, fringed by dark lashes, were piercing, unnerving. It was as if he could tell what she was thinking and found it funny. His jaw was strong, square, with an indentation that made her want to touch it. A high-crowned black hat covered his brown hair, but the collar of his plaid shirt touched long strands that needed trimming. They were wavy, she noticed, and her heart skipped a beat.

"You're welcome," he said in a deep voice that caused tingles to skitter up her spine and over her chest. "Now, about staying here for the night. Are you going to argue that some more?"

She wanted to. It annoyed her that she couldn't. He was right about the danger of traveling at night. It also irritated her that he ordered her to stay, as if she were one of his ranch hands. He seemed accustomed to having his commands obeyed without question. How she would have liked to defy him. But only a fool would travel through that rugged land in the dark, and she was no fool.

"I'd like to—thank you for your invitation."

"Good." He started into the house, then turned back to her. "I can see why Gib calls you 'Firecracker'. And it's got nothing to do with that red hair."

"Look, Jarrod, I appreciate your hospitality. But if you think that gives you the right to make fun of me, I'll just take my chances with the coyotes."

"That wasn't a criticism. I was—"

Just then a shriek came from inside the house. Abby turned, but Jarrod was past her in a flash. His boots thumped on the wooden floor as he hurried through the living room. Abby was on his heels as the wailing rose in volume.

In the kitchen, Katie sat on the floor, sobbing. Tom, with his arms crossed over his thin chest, had his back to the pump handle in front of the window. He looked at them with a mixture of guilt and defiance on his face. Oliver and Lily sat in ladder-backed chairs at the oak table, the food on their plates hardly touched. Their eyes were wide as saucers as the adults entered the room.

"What's going on here?" Jarrod asked, going down on one knee beside the little girl. He picked her up and held her as she struggled to control the crying.

Oliver took his thumb out of his mouth. "Tom socked Katie in the arm and pulled her hair."

Jarrod looked at his oldest nephew. "Is that true?" When Tom's only response was a shrug, he asked, "Why did you hit your sister?"

"She's a baby."

Jarrod handed the little girl to Abby. "Will you take care of her?"

"Of course. But what—"

He turned back to the boy. "Tom, I'd like to see you in my study."

Abby felt the child in her arms tense then start to tremble, obviously afraid of what would happen to her brother. What had happened to frighten her so? She had no reason to fear Jarrod. At least not yet. Couldn't he give Tom a break? They had just met, after all.

"Jarrod, they're all upset. This hasn't been easy. Maybe you should—" The words on her lips died at the look he gave her.

"Not five minutes ago you told me these children are my responsibility."

"That's true, but—"

"We might as well get a few things straight." He stared at Tom and said, "Come with me, son."

The boy straightened his shoulders and lifted his chin, trying to appear brave. But in those gray eyes so like his uncle's, Abby saw that he was only scared and very young. Jarrod took his thin arm in a firm, but gentle grasp. They left the room, and a moment later a door down the hall closed.

"Wha's Uncle Jarrod gonna do?" Oliver opened his mouth wide enough to be understood around his thumb.

Abby put Katie in her chair at the table and pulled her plate close. "I'm sure he's just going to have a talk with Tom."

She hoped that's all he was planning to do. She had always thought him to be a fair man, but what if he believed that sparing the rod spoiled the child? These children were tired and cranky. For them, the journey had been heart-breaking and long, not to mention uncertain. Granted, Tom had been a bit hostile and standoffish with her. But that was understandable. He'd been through a lot. They'd all been through enough already. Surely Jarrod would take that into account. Wouldn't he?

Abby nervously hovered over the three other children, then paced to the kitchen doorway to listen. She'd give anything to know what Jarrod was saying to the boy, and almost wished he would shout so that she could hear something. But in the hall, only silence greeted her.

When Lily and the other two were finished eating, they gathered plates and utensils and took them to the dry sink by the window. As she waited for water to heat on the stove, Abby wandered back to the doorway and stood, listening. Still no sound.

"When's Tom coming back?" Katie wanted to know.

"Your uncle is just talking to him, sweetie."

"My brother didn't hurt me that much," she said. "Was Uncle Jarrod real mad?"

"I'm sure he wasn't." She hoped he wasn't. She bit her lip and glanced at the doorway.

The more time that passed, the more her curiosity was pricked. For a man who claimed to know nothing about children, he apparently had a good deal to say to Tom. If the two of them didn't come out of that room soon, Abby figured, she would  push her way in. When Katie and Oliver insisted on helping with the dishes, she welcomed the distraction and gave them towels to dry the forks, knives, and spoons.

Finally, she heard the door down the hall open. A few seconds later Tom appeared. The other three children all spoke at once, besieging him with questions. Abby studied him closely. He hadn't been crying. In fact, he seemed downright cheerful. She was as interested as everyone else about what had taken place.

"What happened?" Katie asked, worry wrinkling her forehead. She seemed to accept some responsibility for what happened.

"Did he wallop you?" Oliver asked.

"Was Uncle Jarrod real mad?" Lily wanted to know.

Abby was near to bursting with curiosity herself. "Tom? Tell us. Say something."

"If you'll give me a chance, I will."

"What did your uncle say? You were in there with him for a long time. He didn't wallop you, did he?" she asked, repeating Oliver's question, though she didn't believe Jarrod would have done so.

"Nah. We just talked."

"What about?" Abby asked. They all gathered around Tom, who sat down at the table to finish what was left of his dinner.

"I tried to tell him Katie started it, but he said that I mustn't ever hit girls. No matter what."

Abby wasn't sure why that should have surprised her, but it did. "He said that?"

Tom nodded as he ripped off a bite of bread with his teeth. "When I tried to tell him she's just my sister, he said that was no excuse. She's still a girl and you never hit girls, not ever."

"I think I like Uncle Jarrod," Lily said, grinning.

"Me too," Katie chimed in.

"Me too," Abby added, a little surprised.

Tom glared at the three females. "Don't go gettin' ideas. Or I won't do the other thing he said."

"What was that, Tom?" Abby asked.

"He said we men have to take care of you women 'cause we're stronger."

"Did he say anything else?" Abby stifled a smile at the boy's serious tone. She wondered if it was the same one Jarrod had used.

"Yeah. He said 'cause we are stronger, we can't hit back." He glared at his sisters. "Don't you go takin' advantage of this."

"He didn't raise his hand to you? Not at all?" Abby asked.

"Nope. I thought he was goin' to. He said he'd be understandin' until I knew what was expected. Once I did, he was sure it wouldn't be necessary. We just have to learn one another's ways. 'Just."

"Adjust?"

"Yeah. That was it."

Abby was ashamed it had even crossed her mind that Jarrod would strike the boy. It probably wouldn't have except she sensed Katie's fear. Again she wondered what these children had been through. Pushing the thought away, she put her hands on her hips and smiled at them. "Didn't I tell you everything would work out fine?"

"Yes, ma'am." Tom stuffed the last of his bread into his mouth. Before chewing and swallowing, he said, "Almost forgot."

"Don't talk with your mouth full, Tom," Lily reminded him.

He sent her a look fit to kill, but didn't say another word until he'd swallowed his food. When he'd washed it down with a drink of milk, he looked at Abby. "He said for me to tell you he'd like to see you in his study."

"Me?" She asked.

"Yes'm."

"What could he possibly want to talk to me about?"

"He didn't say. But he's waitin' in there."

# 2

*As soon as Abby left the room,* Lily raced to the doorway and watched until she disappeared into the study. She hurriedly turned back to the others. "It's time for a family meeting."

"How come?" Oliver wanted to know.

"We have some things to decide."

"Like what?" Tom asked.

"Like what if we don't want to stay here with Uncle Jarrod?"

"I like him," Katie piped up.

"Me too," Oliver added.

"He didn't even holler at me for hittin' Kate," Tom said defensively.

"I like him too. But we just got here. I'm not saying things won't work out," Lily said. "I just think we need to think about what to do if they don't."

She motioned them all into the farthest corner of the kitchen, away from the door. Her gaze constantly darted in that direction. "We need to have a plan—just in case."

"In case what?" Katie asked.

"In case Uncle Jarrod isn't as nice as we all think." Lily had been scared when Uncle Jarrod had taken Tom into the study. Real scared. Like she used to be when Pa had come home, loud and mean. Lily wasn't sorry when Mama had told her he'd died and was never coming back. She was only sorry he wasn't the kind of father she would miss. Mama had said that not all men were like him. She also said her brother Jarrod would be good to them. But Lily was in charge of them now. She wasn't taking any chances. Uncle Jarrod seemed all right, but what if he got mean, like Pa?

"Tell us the plan, Lily," Oliver said.

She scratched her nose. "I don't have one yet. You got any ideas, Tom?"

He shook his head. "He seems all right to me, Lil. Maybe we should hold off on this."

"We met him less than an hour ago. You can't tell anything yet." She thought for a minute. "How about this? If we decide we can't stay here, we'll run away."

Katie's curls swung from side to side and her eyes widened with fear. Katie hadn't slept the night through since Mama had died. Oliver was the lucky one. He still thought she was coming back.

"But where will we go?" Katie asked, her lips starting to quiver.

"Yeah. Where?" Oliver asked. Then his eyes lit up. "I know. Abby would take care of us."

Lily smiled and brushed the hair off his forehead. "I bet you're right. That settles it. If we don't like it here, we'll run away to Abby. Agreed?"

"I don't need anyone to take care of me," Tom said. "I'll just run away and be a cowboy."

"I like Abby," Katie said, her curls bobbing up and down now. "I agree."

"Me too," Oliver said.

"Take your thumb out of your mouth," Lily ordered her youngest brother. He shook his head and the hair fell into his eyes again.

She glared at him. "Brat. Never mind. We have more important things to do now."

"What, Lil?"

"Uncle Jarrod wanted to talk to Abby, and I'd bet anything it's us they're gonna talk about."

"I bet you're right." Tom's eyes narrowed. "When I was in there with him, I saw a window that looks out on the back porch. Betcha if we're real quiet we could stand outside and hear what they're sayin'."

Lily smiled at him, then looked at the two younger children. "You two stay here."

"No," Katie said stubbornly. "I wanna hear too."

"Uh-huh," Oliver added, shaking his head. "Wanna go too."

Tom met his older sister's gaze. "If we don't let 'em, they'll tattle for sure."

"I know." Lily sighed. She speared first one then the other with a hard look. "Can you be quiet as mouses?"

"Yes," Katie said, nodding hard.

Oliver nodded.

"All right. Not one word, not one sound out of anyone. Is that clear?" Lily asked.

"Yes," they all said.

Abby walked into the room and stood in front of Jarrod's desk. "Tom said you wanted to see me?"

"That's right."

He leaned back and laced his fingers together over his stomach as he looked at her. This was the first time he'd ever been alone with Abby. He'd never realized how pretty she was. Maybe because he was usually mad at her for delivering some item he had no use for or papers he didn't want to see. Or because she sassed him back whenever she had a mind to. He liked that about her, even though he didn't want to.

By the time he was not much older than Tom, this land had taught him to heed his instincts. Now, his gut told him to keep his distance from Abby. Under the circumstances, he had to admit he was glad of her company. The truth was, he would rather face a rabid wolf than be alone with these four kids.

"Sit down, Abby," he said, indicating the spindle chair in front of his big desk.

"Thank you," she said, gracefully lowering herself into the seat. For some women, that was a learned gesture. For Abby it was just naturally feminine, if for no other reason than she was always too busy to practice being a lady. She folded her hands in her lap and looked around the study. "I've always liked this room."

"You've seen it?" he asked, surprised. She'd never been inside while he was there.

She nodded. "When Mrs. Blackstone was here, she invited me in for tea every time I delivered something. Once, she took me on a tour of the house."

"I think that's why she was always ordering from catalogs."

"What do you mean?" Wisps of red hair curled around her face and she tucked a strand behind her ear.

Jarrod realized he'd never seen her hair fixed any way but in a braid that hung down her back. It was that way now except for the strands that had escaped. He wondered what her hair would look like without being tied back. Would it be as wild as he thought? Wild and free like the land . . . That was a dangerous direction for his thoughts. He turned his attention back to Abby's question.

"Dulcy never adjusted to the isolation of the ranch."

"Blackstone Ranch *is* the farthest from town."

Jarrod knew that better than anyone. "She was trying to bring civilization to her."

"And every time I came out here, she asked me to stay for a bit. You think she ordered things so that she could have company?"

"That was part of it." He sure as hell hadn't been enough for her.

She looked down at her hands, then back at him. "I liked her, Jarrod. I'm sorry I was the one who brought you the divorce papers. But even if I hadn't, the result would have been the same."

"I know."

"You never had children."

"We wanted them—in the beginning. Then she changed her mind."

Because she'd changed her mind about him. Their dream of having children died when she left. Now all he had was the ranch. It was all he wanted. He glanced up and saw Abby staring at him, an expression on her face that looked a lot like pity.

He frowned. "That's over and done with," he said sharply.

She shifted in her chair. "I didn't mean to bring up the past. What did you want to see me about?"

"The children."

One auburn brow rose. "Oh? What does that have to do with me?"

"Do you have any suggestions about what I should do with them?"

"Why would I?"

"You're a woman."

"So?"

He clamped his teeth together. She was going to make this difficult. He should have expected as much.

"Just because I'm a woman doesn't make me a mother. I have never had a child, although I practically raised my younger brother. But I don't understand why you think that the mere fact that I'm a woman means I would know what to do with four motherless children."

"They seemed to take to you."

"I was kind to them. It wasn't difficult. They're nice kids. They didn't know a soul in Hollister, so the stage driver brought them to me. They were frightened. If they took to me, it was because they hadn't much choice." She frowned. "All except Tom."

"What did he do?" Jarrod asked.

"Nothing outright," she said quickly. "Thanks to you, I think the girls are in no danger from his temper."

"He told you about our talk." He smiled in spite of his effort to remain serious.

"Yes. The others were curious about what happened."

He suspected that she was too. She had tried to intercede for the boy. He had wondered about that. "Did you think I was going to take my belt to him?"

"The thought never crossed my mind," she said, her gaze dropping to her lap.

"Liar."

Blue eyes met his. "All right. It's just that you looked so serious, I wondered what you would do to him."

"Did I pass the test?"

She grinned. "You did with Lily and Katie."

"How about with you?" he asked gruffly. For some reason he couldn't explain, it mattered to him what she thought. His gaze narrowed on her, and her cheeks flushed a becoming pink.

"Why would you care what I think?"

"Because I'd like your help."

"With what?"

"The children."

"I'd like to, Jarrod. But Hollister is too far away for me to do much."

"Yes, you made it clear the ranch is the farthest from town. But they do need looking after." He thought for a few moments. "Lily is thirteen. That's old enough to—"

"You can't do that to her!" Her voice rose and the note of outrage in it was unmistakable.

Jarrod was intrigued. In about ten seconds she'd gone from sympathetic to blazing mad. His words had been the fuse that set her off. Firecracker. The nickname fit like a custom-made pair of boots.

"Why not, Abby?"

"Lily is a child herself. She's too young to be responsible for three other children and a house. She lost her mother. Don't take her childhood away from her too."

A whole range of emotions crossed her face: anger, pain, loss, regret. She'd let it slip that she'd raised her younger brother. He had a feeling she'd been forced into a position of responsibility at a young age. He was sorry about that.

But he suddenly found himself with four children and a ranch to run. What did she expect him to do?

"Abby, I don't see as I have a choice."

"There are always choices."

"Do you have another suggestion?"

She thought for a minute. "You need a wife."

He winced. Firecrackers were unpredictable, sometimes went off in your hand. And hurt like hell. If she had tried, she couldn't have picked anything he wanted to talk about less.

"I had one. That was one too many."

"Sorry," she said, rubbing her forehead. "I keep bringing up a sore subject."

"It's not sore, just closed."

"But it would be an answer."

"Not for me."

He'd put away the hurt right after Dulcy left. He closed that door and he wouldn't open it again.

"All right. But there's got to be another solution." There was a scraping noise out on the porch.

"Did you hear that?" he asked as she looked at the window.

"I thought I heard something," Abby answered.

He glanced in the same direction. They listened for a few moments, but there was no sound. "I don't hear anything now."

"Me either. Must have been the wind."

"I suppose so. Now, back to the problem at hand. How am I going to manage a ranch this size and raise four kids?"

"You could hire a housekeeper," she said. "Someone to look after the house and the children."

A reasonable idea; he'd thought of it himself. There was just one drawback.

"Housekeepers don't grow on trees in this neck of the woods. How do you propose I find one?" he asked. An idea suddenly occurred to him. Couldn't hurt to ask. "You interested in the job, Abby?"

"Me?" Surprised, she pressed her hand to her chest and stared at him for a moment. "You're serious, aren't you?"

"Dead serious."

She shook her head. "I already have a job."

"You seem to like them. Are you sure you won't—"

"No. My life's in town."

"All right, then. Do you have any suggestions? This won't be easy."

"No, but it's not impossible. That's where I can help. I know almost everyone in town. I'm sure I can find someone suitable for you."

"I'd have to meet her first."

She nodded. "When I find someone, I'll bring her here to the ranch for you to meet."

"All right." A thought occurred to him. Since he wasn't the one who would be with her all day, his opinion wasn't the most important. "The kids have to meet her too, and like her. If they don't, that's the end of it."

"Good point. I'll do my best."

"Thanks, Abby. I appreciate this."

"You're welcome. I'm glad to help."

Jarrod's heart was a little lighter. He wasn't sure whether it was because she would come up with an answer to his problem, or because he'd have an excuse to see her again. He found that thought a downright pleasant change. The next time she came out to the ranch, she would bring him something, or rather someone, he actually wanted and could use.

"I don't understand why Abby won't be our house-keeper," Katie complained. She settled herself more comfortably between Lily and Tom in the center of Lily's four-poster bed. Oliver sat in his brother's lap and sucked his thumb.

"You heard her. She's already got a job, dummy." Tom glared at his sister. "Besides, we don't need anyone. Why can't we just take care of ourselves?"

In her room, Lily had called another family meeting after Uncle Jarrod and Abby had gone to bed. As they huddled together on the mattress, the lantern on the table beside it sent all four of their shadows bouncing on the wall, making her nervous.

This house was so big. Lily had never seen so many rooms in her whole life. They all had a bedroom to themselves, even Abby. Tom's was next to her own, connected by a door. Katie was across the hall, beside their uncle's room, and Oliver had the one closest to the head of the stairs. In case he had to make a run for it to the outhouse.

They should have been asleep. Lily kept listening for a sound in the hall. They had to be quiet and make this fast.

She looked at her brothers and sister. "Uncle Jarrod wants someone to look out for us. We all heard him say that."

"So why can't Abby work here instead of town? She said she wanted to help." Katie frowned.

Lily thought for a moment. "I'm not sure. Something funny's going on between her and Uncle Jarrod. They're like two cats circling each other with their backs up."

"Maybe they don't like each other," Katie said. "But I like Abby."

Lily smiled at her sister. "Don't worry. Uncle Jarrod won't hire anyone we don't like. He told Abby so. Remember?"

Katie nodded. "I remember."

Tom snorted. "You don't believe that, do you? Why should he care about us?"

"'Course he cares," Katie said, kneeling on the bed with her hands on her hips. "I can tell he likes us."

"Don't say I didn't warn you," Tom said.

Lily tapped a finger to her lips. "Maybe she would change her mind if she can't find anyone to be our housekeeper."

Tom's eyes narrowed as he stared at her. "I know that look, Lil. What do you have in mind?"

"Everyone listen carefully," she said.

Abby rolled over in the soft bed. Not quite awake, she tried to figure out what had disturbed her. She'd fallen asleep to the pleasant chirping of crickets mixed with the mournful call of coyotes. She was puzzled.

Moonlight streamed through the lace curtains at the window, spilling pale silvery light into the room. A yellow-and-blue quilt covered the four-poster oak bed that matched the dresser on the wall across from it. This house had enough bedrooms to sleep half the United States Army, and all of them had been empty until now.

She heard unidentifiable sounds down the hall and wondered if it was one of the children. Abby threw the covers back and jumped out of bed. She grabbed the quilt and wrapped it around her, covering her chemise and pantalettes, went to the door and yanked it open. Looking around, she noticed the door to Katie's room was ajar. Then she heard Jarrod's deep voice as he spoke softly to the little girl. Apparently, he wasn't as sound a sleeper as she was, Abby realized, since he'd gotten to the child first.

Abby moved forward and stopped in the shadow of the doorway. She started to ask if she could help. The words died on her lips as she observed the scene. Dressed only in denims, Jarrod sat in a rocking chair near the window, with Katie curled against him in his lap. Her light-colored curls rested against the sprinkling of dark hair on his bare chest as the girl trustingly snuggled in his arms. Abby couldn't bring herself to disturb them.

"Go back to sleep," he said to the child.

"I can't." Katie sniffled. "I saw Mama."

"It was a dream."

Something caught in Abby's chest. Her heart ached, not only for Katie, but for all the children.

"A mean man took Mama. I thought he was gonna take me too." Her voice rose in fear and panic, one notch short of a wail.

"Shhh," he said. Jarrod's arms tightened around her. "I won't let anyone take you."

"What if he's bigger'n you? What if you can't stop 'im?"

"If he's stronger than me, Gib will help."

"You mean Mr. Cochran? The man me and Oliver met after supper, down at the bunkhouse?"

"Yup."

"What if he's stronger'n Mr. Cochran?"

"Then Slim will help. You met him too, along with Dusty Taylor. Remember?"

She nodded. "He's awful skinny. What if he can't stop 'im?"

"Then we'll get Dusty."

"What if all of you can't keep him from taking me?"

"If all of us together can't do it, then we'll follow his trail. We'll ambush him, tie him up, and bring you home safe and sound."

"Really?"

"Really," Jarrod answered emphatically.

Abby couldn't help smiling at the awe in Katie's voice. The child sounded surprised that any man could do all he promised. Abby suspected there hadn't been any heroes in her short life.

"Where's Mama now, Uncle Jarrod?"

The lump was back in Abby's throat, nearly choking her. Tears burned her eyes. She'd lost her own mother, although not as young as Katie. But that loss at any age cut deep.

"The angels took her to heaven." There was a husky quality to Jarrod's voice, but it only broke once.

"Do you think she's happy?"

"I know she doesn't hurt anymore."

"Do you think she misses me?"

"No doubt about it."

"I sure do miss her. Why did the angels take her?"

"I don't know." He sighed. "I guess it was just her time."

"How do you know when it's time?"

"We don't. It just happens."

"What if you're not ready to go? I miss Mama, but I don't want to leave Lily, and Tom, and Oliver. And you."

"I don't think God would take someone who's not ready to be with Him."

"Really?" she asked, twisting in his arms so that she could look at his face.

"Really."

"That means Mama must have been ready." She thought

for a few moments. "Mama worked awful hard. Maybe she wanted God to take her so she could rest."

"Maybe so—" He stopped and cleared his throat.

Jarrod had a wellspring of patience that Abby would never have guessed at if she hadn't seen and heard it for herself. He claimed to be inexperienced with children, but his instincts seemed to be working just fine.

It was quiet for a few moments, then Katie piped up again with, "Lily said you and Abby act funny around each other."

Abby's gaze darted to Jarrod's face to see his reaction to the statement. One corner of his mouth lifted in a half smile.

"Lily said that?"

"Yes, sir. *Do* you and Abby act funny around each other?"

He thought for a moment. "Nope."

"Then why did Lily say it?"

"To others it might seem like we're acting strange. But that's the way Abby and I always are."

Abby felt awkward eavesdropping, but even more so now that their conversation had taken this turn. She started to go to her room, but Katie's next words stopped her.

"Do you like Abby?"

She was curious about the answer to that one herself. The rocker creaked as Jarrod shifted his weight. "Do *you* like her?" he asked.

The quilt slid a little, letting in a draft of chilly air as Abby put her hands on her hips and glared at him. Why couldn't he just answer straight out?

"I like Abby a lot," Katie answered, yawning broadly. "So do the others. All except Tom."

"Why?"

Her thin shoulders lifted in a shrug. "He's dumb. 'Cuz Abby's real nice. She took us over to the restaurant in Hollister and bought us fried chicken for lunch."

"That *was* real nice."

Katie nodded. "And she got us each a licorice whip

before we left town. Said it was a long trip and it takes a long time to eat licorice. I don't think it does. Do you, Uncle Jarrod?"

"Does what?" he asked, distracted.

"It didn't take me hardly any time at all to eat my candy. It took a long time until we saw the ranch."

"Yeah. Hollister isn't real close by."

"I don't care. I like it here, Uncle Jarrod."

"I'm glad," he said, stifling a yawn.

"Are you sleepy, Uncle Jarrod?"

"Are you?" he asked.

There he goes again, Abby thought, not answering questions.

Katie nodded. "I'm pretty tired."

"Then I'll put you back under the covers."

He stood up with Katie in his arms, her small bare feet and spindly little legs visible below the hem of her nightgown. He put her down, pulled the blankets up underneath her chin, then pressed his knuckles into the mattress on either side of her, bracing himself.

He hesitated for a moment, then leaned over and kissed her forehead. The sight of gruff Jarrod Blackstone putting that little girl to bed made Abby smile. It was just about the sweetest thing she'd ever seen.

He touched Katie's nose. "Don't let the bedbugs bite. Y'hear?"

"There are bugs in the bed?" Katie squealed. She sat up, pushed the blankets down, and stood up in the middle of the mattress.

Jarrod sighed and sat on the bed, rubbing the back of his neck. Katie crawled into his lap and looked suspiciously at the sheets.

"Do they really bite, Uncle Jarrod? Do they hurt? Why are there bugs in the bed?"

He stood up and carried her back to the rocker. "It's just an expression, Katie."

"What's a 'spression?"

"It's something people say that means something else."

"Why don't folks just say what they mean?"

"Y'got me."

"What does that 'spression mean? The one about bedbugs?"

Abby clamped a hand over her mouth to keep from laughing.

"It just means sleep well," he said.

"How can folks sleep good with bugs in their bed? Don't the bugs crawl all over 'em? That'd tickle pretty good. Right, Uncle Jarrod?"

"It would if there were really bugs. But there aren't really bugs. Because it's just—"

"A 'spression. Right, Uncle Jarrod?"

"Right," he said. His voice was tight, as if the edges of his forbearance were ragged.

Abby knocked softly. Jarrod looked up at her as she walked into the room.

"Hi, Abby," Katie said. "Why're you wearin' that quilt?"

"I don't have nightclothes."

"Are you wearin' clothes under there?"

"Yes."

"Your drawers?"

"Yes." Her cheeks grew hot.

Jarrod chuckled. "What are you doing up?"

"I heard noises," she said truthfully. He didn't need to know she'd been there for some time watching and listening.

He shifted in the rocker. "Sorry we woke you. Katie had a bad dream."

"You must be a light sleeper. I didn't hear her call out."

"I wasn't asleep yet. Had a lot on my mind. It's been quite a day."

"Me and Uncle Jarrod are talkin' 'bout 'spressions. Do you know what that is, Abby?"

"I sure do, sweetie pie." She squatted down in front of the rocking chair and tweaked the little girl's foot, which rested on Jarrod's knee.

Abby had the most absurd urge to put her hand on his thigh, just to see if it was as rock-hard as it looked. Another heated blush flashed across her face. Thank the Lord it was too dark for him to see.

Abby cleared her throat. "Are you having trouble sleeping, Katie?"

"A little. I had a bad dream. Uncle Jarrod and me been talkin' 'bout it."

"Among other things," he said wryly.

Abby glanced at him, then said to the little girl, "How about if I talk with you for a while so your uncle can get some sleep?"

The child's blond curls swung from side to side as she declined the offer. "You're not big enough or strong enough. If the bad man comes for me like he did for Mama, I want Uncle Jarrod. He's big. And he'll get Mr. Cochran and Dusty and Slim. They'll tie the man up so he can't get me. Right, Uncle Jarrod?"

"That's right." He met Abby's gaze. "It's a long story. You might as well go back to bed and get some sleep."

Katie sat forward suddenly and put her hand on Abby's arm. "Watch out for the bedbugs. Don't let 'em bite."

"I won't, sweetie." Abby stood and walked toward the door, reluctant to leave him, and not really sure why. She stopped and glanced at the two in the rocker.

Katie plucked at the bodice of her thin cotton night-gown, then turned her head and studied him. "Uncle Jarrod?"

"Hmmm?"

"You have hair on your chest."

"I know." There was a chuckle in his voice.

"Why?" she asked.

Abby waited for him to answer with a question.

"I'm a man."

There's news for the *Hollister Gazette*, Abby thought. He was a man, all right. That same darn fluttery feeling came again, right smack in the pit of her belly. She rubbed first one, then the other sweaty palm down the sides of her pantalettes, and leaned against the door frame as her knees threatened to give way.

"Tom doesn't have hair on his chest," Katie innocently commented.

"He's still a boy. Wait till he grows a bit, he'll look just like me."

"Like a man?" the child asked.

"Yup."

Jarrod slid a glance to Abby. Though she couldn't be sure, she swore his eyes twinkled, as if he knew what all this talk about him being a man did to her insides.

Gosh darn him, anyhow. Why couldn't he just be businesslike, the way he usually acted? She was comfortable with that Jarrod. This one made her nervous.

Annoyed, she walked across the hall. She went into her own room and shut the door as if demons from hell were chasing her.

Jarrod Blackstone was a dangerous man. At least he was to her. And probably to every other unattached woman within two hundred miles of here.

Why in the world had she agreed to find him a housekeeper? That meant she would have to arrange it and transport her out to his ranch. That meant she'd have to see him again soon. She shook her head. When she left here tomorrow morning, she didn't want to set eyes on him, at least not without a whole town full of people between her and him.

Abby crawled back into bed, pulled the quilt over her head, and rolled on her side. She wanted to tell Jarrod she'd changed her mind and he'd have to come into town and find a housekeeper all by himself. But she had already promised. More than anything, she hated people who broke their word.

# 3

*Abby overslept the next morning.* She had wanted to be up and gone at first light. Instead, thoughts of Jarrod had kept her awake until just before dawn. Sunlight poured through her window, but she was too tired and cross to appreciate it. Now she would have to face Jarrod Blackstone.

The gentle, patient way he'd handled his niece during the night was far too fresh in her mind. The scene brought back memories of her own father, and renewed her determination to find him. She had dreamed too long about living with her father again to let anything stand in her way. Especially her softening feelings for Jarrod Blackstone. With luck, he was off doing all those chores that kept him too busy to find his own darn housekeeper.

Using the pitcher of water and the basin on her dresser, Abby washed up. After dressing, she tried to fix her hair. Without a comb and brush, there wasn't much she could do. Finally, she grabbed her hat from the bedpost and went downstairs. At the bottom of the steps she stopped and looked around.

Abby had fallen in love with this house the first time she'd seen it. The wooden floors and French doors in the living room and parlor gave it an elegant, yet surprisingly cozy feel.

She remembered when the living room suite was delivered, shipping weight two hundred pounds, three dollars per pound from Chicago to Sacramento by rail, then on to Hollister by wagon. The large sofa, easy chair, and two large parlor chairs were made of three-tone green velour. They were overstuffed with hardwood frames, fancy binding, and rococo brass ornamentation. The pieces were arranged before the hearth in the front room with three beautifully carved oak tables, shipping weight sixty pounds.

Abby wondered how it would hold up with four active children. She'd never lived with furniture so fine and had no idea. Still, the kids had the land to explore. She supposed they wouldn't spend much time inside.

With her hat in her hands, she went to the kitchen. Before she entered, she heard the sound of voices.

"But I'm hungry, Lily," Oliver said.

"My stomach's about wearin' a hole in my backbone too, Lil." Tom said pleadingly.

"Me too," Katie added.

"What do you want me to do?" Lily asked. "I've already checked. There's no food in the kitchen. Remember when Abby fixed us supper last night? She had to rummage through the bunkhouse."

"Then let's go down there," Tom suggested.

"We can't do that," Lily answered. "It wouldn't be right to go through other folks' food. And don't tell me to ask Uncle Jarrod, Katie. You know as well as I do that he's not here."

Abby sighed. She wanted to get on the road. But again, she couldn't go when the children were hungry and alone.

She walked into the room. The four of them sat around the table with dispirited expressions on their faces.

"Good morning," Abby said. "Did everyone sleep well?"

"All except Katie," Lily answered.

"Yes, I know." Abby rested a hand on the top of the little girl's ladder-back chair.

"She hasn't slept through the night since Mama died," Lily explained.

Tom made a face at his younger sister. "She's a baby."

"Am not," Katie said, thrusting her bottom lip out.

The circles beneath her eyes were darker this morning. Abby wondered what kind of shape their uncle was in after staying up with her. Instantly, an image of Jarrod Blackstone's bare chest flashed through her mind. The memory of his broad shoulders made her insides flutter. He was definitely a man.

"Oliver's the baby," Katie said.

"Am not," he piped up.

"You're the youngest—"

"That's enough." Abby looked at the four faces around the table. This was all new to them; they were understandably upset. But someone had to take control before things got out of hand.

"You need some breakfast," Abby said.

Lily nodded. "But we didn't know if we should get some or not."

"Of course you should."

Just then they heard the sound of boots on the back porch. The kitchen door opened and Jarrod came inside, carrying several burlap bags. He glanced around, looking uncomfortable.

"Mornin', everyone," he said.

A chorus of greetings hailed him. Katie jumped up from her chair and ran to meet him. He set the bags down and stared at the little girl beside him.

"What did you bring, Uncle Jarrod?"

"Food," he said.

"Why isn't the kitchen stocked?" Abby wanted to know.

Jarrod's gaze met hers. "I take my meals in the bunkhouse with the ranch hands," he explained. "No need to stock the house too."

He seemed pretty chipper for a man who'd sat up with a little girl for half the night. Abby wished she looked even half that good. But she noticed that a shadow of beard covered his chin and jaw. He hadn't shaved yet this morning, and he seemed the sort of man who would unless something had unsettled him. Finding out you were the guardian of four children could do that. Had he overslept? Abby hoped she wasn't the only one.

"No need to stock it until now," Abby reminded him.

"Until now," he agreed. He slid a look to the little girl peering into the sacks, then picked the bags up and moved them to the worktable beside the iron stove. "I brought bacon, flour, sugar, coffee—"

"The children shouldn't drink coffee," Abby cautioned.

"I like it," Tom said. He sent her a challenging look.

Abby met his gaze. "Maybe so, Tom. But you're too young to have it."

"Who're you to tell me—"

"Hold on. That's no way to talk to your elders, son," Jarrod said. He looked around at all of them. "The most important thing right now is food, and lots of it."

He's right, Abby thought. These children needed fattening up.

"The only thing I didn't bring is eggs," Jarrod added as he placed the food in the cupboards. "I don't suppose anyone would want to gather some for me."

"I will," Katie said.

"I wanna," Oliver chimed in, running over to his uncle with his sister on his heels.

Both children looked up at Jarrod. He was so tall Abby wondered if they could see his face. Their heads were tipped so far back, Abby held her breath, waiting for the youngsters to topple over backward.

Jarrod hunkered down to their level. "Can you do it without breaking them?" Both children nodded solemnly. "All right, then. Go on down to the bunkhouse and ask Gib to show you where the hens are."

"Oh, boy!" They raced out the back door, Katie first because her legs were just a little longer than her brother's.

Suddenly the door opened again and Katie ran back inside and stopped in front of Abby. "I forgot somethin'."

Abby bent down. "What?"

"I forgot to give you a hug."

Abby held the little girl against her. When small arms encircled her neck, Abby didn't mind the fingers that caught in her hair. It would take a heart of stone to resist this child's inborn sweetness. Katie stepped back and accidentally yanked on Abby's braid. The minor discomfort was lost in Katie's generous show of affection. The little girl ran over to her uncle and repeated the gesture. Moved by Katie's actions, Abby sniffled and turned away.

"You better hurry." Jarrod's husky voice raised goose bumps on Abby's arms. She looked in time to see him tap Katie's chin kindly. "Oliver will find all the eggs."

Blond curls bounced as she shook her head. "No, he won't." Katie raced out the door again.

Jarrod looked at Abby uneasily, then at his oldest niece. "Lily? I hate to ask you this, but do you know how to cook?"

She nodded. "Mama taught me a long time ago. After Pa died she had to work. She needed me to take care of Tom and Katie and Oliver."

"Don't need takin' care of," Tom grumbled.

Abby's heart went out to Lily. The girl hadn't said a word in complaint, but Abby knew how hard things had been for her. Wanting to play, to be with girls her own age, but forced to help out at home because she was the oldest. Abby understood, as no one else could who hadn't gone through the same thing.

A pained expression crossed Jarrod's face at Lily's words. "If I had known how bad things were, I'd have done something. I want you to believe that."

Lily nodded. "I do. Mama was proud. She didn't want charity from anyone, at least not for herself. If it was something for us—"

"I'm gonna go help find eggs," Tom said. "We'll starve if we have to wait for them two."

"Those two," Jarrod corrected.

Tom started for the door. As he passed, Abby put a hand on his shoulder to stop him.

He shrugged off her hand. "Don't touch me."

"Why not?" she asked, surprised at his vehemence. Katie had said he didn't like her, but the look in his gray eyes was downright hostile.

"You're a girl," he responded, wrinkling his nose.

"He's definitely family," Abby said, glancing at Jarrod as she tried to make a joke to cover her hurt feelings. "He states the obvious just like you." Then she turned back to Tom.

"What?" he asked, his tone sullen.

"I was just going to remind you to watch out for your brother and sister."

He stared at her for a few moments, then nodded. "Can I go now? Before those two squirts find all the eggs?"

"Git," Jarrod said. "Don't scare the hens," he called out just before the door slammed. He looked at Lily. "Why don't you go with the others?"

"I thought you wanted me to cook. I should start making biscuits. When they come back with the eggs—"

"I'll start breakfast," he said. "Abby will help. Right, Abby?" he asked, and glanced at her questioningly.

She'd wanted to get on the road, but how could she refuse to help? "Can't let a man make biscuits, can we?" She smiled at Lily. "You run along."

The young girl beamed at the two of them, then turned and ran out the door as if afraid they might change their minds. Far from doing that, Abby was more convinced than ever that she had to keep her word to Jarrod. The feelings he stirred in her were strange and unsettling, but she couldn't take the safe path for herself and abandon these children. Especially Lily. She deserved to be a child until it was time for her to be a young woman.

As she stared outside, Abby heard a clang and crash behind her. She turned and studied the play of muscles across Jarrod's back as he stoked the stove and stirred up the fire. He cut the slab of ham into pieces and tossed them into the cast-iron frying pan.

He glanced over his shoulder and caught Abby staring at

him. When she closed her mouth, he grinned. "You gonna stand there? Or are you gonna make those biscuits you promised?"

"I didn't promise exactly. I said a man couldn't be trusted to make biscuits. I really should get on back to town."

"You can, after you eat."

The sound of sizzling meat was followed by a delicious aroma that made her mouth water. "I shouldn't," she said, but the words lacked conviction. "My job is waiting for me. And it's a long drive."

"You must be hungry. You need to keep up your strength."

She was starved, and the bacon smelled heavenly. She swallowed. "Not that hungry. If I could just have some jerky and hardtack, I could chew on that while I head back."

"Stay, Abby. Breakfast won't hold you up long." Gray eyes met her own. "I'd like to talk to you."

"What about?" She was weakening. Darn it. He was awfully hard to say no to.

"Things. The kids."

He didn't seem like the sort of man who asked for much, and that made it impossible for Abby not to give in. She sighed. "Right after breakfast I *have* to get back."

"Is Whittemore a hard man to work for?"

She grinned. "He'd like folks to think he is, but he's a faker."

"How did you happen to go to work for Hollister Freight?"

Abby pulled a bowl from the cupboard, then measured flour into it. "Mr. Whittemore was a friend of my mother's. I needed a good paying job. He did me a favor. He's told me more than once that he didn't think I could handle it when he hired me. But I've never given him cause to regret his decision."

Jarrod knew from first-hand experience that she was tenacious. And conscientious. Not many people came to mind who would take the time to bring four kids all the way out to the ranch, then stay because they were all alone. He hoped Abby's kindness hadn't jeopardized her position.

"Will Whittemore give you a hard time when you get back?"

"I don't think so."

"Good." He jabbed a piece of ham with a fork and flipped it.

"So what about the children?" she asked, stirring the biscuit mixture.

Where did he start? In less than twenty-four hours his life had turned upside down. The welfare of four children was his responsibility, a fact that had kept him up half the night. He was tired. And not just on account of Katie.

After she had finally settled down, he'd tried to sleep. Every time he came close, a vision of Abby's wild red hair and big blue eyes jolted him awake. He couldn't forget the curve of her slender shoulder when her quilt had slipped down. Or her charming embarrassment when Katie had asked if she was naked under the blanket. It surprised him just how much he wanted to touch and explore what he couldn't see. He couldn't remember a time that a woman had tempted him this sorely. He'd spent the remainder of the night trying to push those thoughts from his mind. But it was daylight now, and he had far more important things to worry about.

"Did you notice the clothes they're wearing?" he asked. "At first, I thought they were play clothes. Sally would have taught them better than to travel in something other than their Sunday best." He put the frying pan on the worktable beside the stove and looked at Abby. "The condition of their clothes today is worse. I think they did wear their best for the trip."

"So they need new clothes," she said practically.

"Just where am I supposed to get them? I don't sew, even if I had material."

"There's a dressmaker in Hollister. I'm sure she could make them some things. Or you could buy ready-made at the mercantile."

"I can't get away from the ranch. We're rounding up new calves for branding. Spring is a busy time around here."

"Most folks are busy. It's catch-up time after the winter," she reminded him.

He studied her profile while she vigorously mixed the biscuit dough. She had fine cheekbones and her skin was smooth and soft. Her looks made a man want to touch her and see for himself if she was as silky as she seemed. Only her freckles kept her face from being flawless. The turned-up tip of her small nose was pink, and a scattering of caramel-colored dots dusted the bridge as a result of her time outdoors spent driving the freight wagon. Jarrod put the ham slices on a plate. "Since you're coming back when you find a housekeeper, why don't you pick out what you think they'll need and bring it with you?"

"What about sizes?"

He shrugged. "Do the best you can. I've got an account with Don Shemanski at the mercantile. I'll give you a letter of credit and you can get the things there."

"In the meantime?"

"I don't know. Guess we'll just see what we can find around here and cut it down. Gib is pretty handy with a needle when he has to be."

"I'll bet he is," she said, smiling fondly. Abby looked at him. "What are you going to do with the kids today? Have you made any plans?"

"Hadn't thought about it."

"You could take them out to see the land. Show them around. Give them chores. Make them feel a part of things."

"I just told you, I'm busy."

"Too busy to spend time with them on their first day here?"

"Yeah. We're spread thin as it is. I have to ride out to San Augustine Canyon and bring in the cattle."

"You can't put it off for one day?" She stared at him.

"No." It was all Jarrod could do to meet her honest,

direct gaze without flinching. "Gib will stay here and watch out for them."

"I see."

Why did those two words put him on the defensive? For some reason, it seemed very important that she understand his situation. "I'm the boss," he explained.

"I understand, Jarrod. You have to work to take care of their outward needs, like fattening them up and putting clothes on their back. Gib's a good man. He can handle their inside needs, the ones that will turn them into well-mannered, upstanding adults someday."

The look on her face was innocence itself. But she made him feel guilty all the same. He had a feeling that was her intent. "That's not fair."

"Maybe not. But neither is what happened to those children. They're hurting, Jarrod. They're your flesh and blood. They need you. Do they have to be cattle to get your attention?"

"The truth is, I've never been around kids. I'm not much good with them." Or grown-ups either, for that matter. If he was, Dulcy wouldn't have left.

"The man I saw comfort a frightened child last night was very good. Sally didn't send them to you because of your experience. She did it because you're her family and she knew you'd take good care of them. She wanted you to teach them the same values the two of you learned growing up here."

"Some values I learned. My own sister worked herself to death. Her children are thin and wearing clothes that we'd use for rags. I never knew."

"How could you?"

He folded his arms over his chest and stared at the ceiling, knowing he would have to live with the guilt of his neglect for the rest of his life. "You were right. I should have gone to see Sally. I should have checked on her and the kids. I meant to, right after she wrote me that Reed had been shot to death in a saloon for cheating at cards. I knew that man was little better than worthless. I should have gone—"

"But you thought there would always be time," she said softly.

It wasn't a question. He looked into her eyes and knew she understood. "Yes. She was young. I thought she would have more tomorrows. I thought I'd get another chance to tell her I loved her."

"She knows, Jarrod." Abby put her hand on his forearm. "She may not have had a lot of material possessions, but she sent you something more precious. Her children. I think that says a mouthful about how much she loved you."

"Never thought about it that way."

"Here is something else you should think about. This is your second chance—an opportunity to help her."

If that didn't beat all, he thought. Abby Miller, the woman he'd verbally sparred with more than once, offering him comfort. He had the most foolish urge to fold her into his arms and give her a hug. Was he taking lessons from Katie? Or was it lack of sleep that was making him think like a damn fool?

Whatever the reason, he kept his arms folded. He'd been burned once by a female. He didn't want to share even the most innocent intimacy with Abby Miller. Thinking like a damn fool was one thing. Acting like a damn fool was entirely different.

But he found that it was easier to reason himself into not holding her than it was to ignore what her touch was doing to him. He lowered his arms to his sides and her hand dropped.

He walked over to the cupboard and pulled out some plates. "The past doesn't matter anymore. The present is what I have to deal with. That means feeding those kids and putting clothes on their backs. To do that, I have to work this ranch and make it pay."

She nodded. "I'll find you a housekeeper, Jarrod, as soon as I can."

She seemed determined, and he knew that she was stubborn. If anyone could find him someone to help out with the kids, it was her.

\*   \*   \*

Oliver raced into the kitchen and looked excitedly up at Lily. "Abby's comin'!"

Thank goodness, Lily thought. Abby had left them five days before. Lily had prayed she would keep her word to come back, but was afraid to hope.

"How do you know?" She set the skillet on the stove and brushed her hands down the sides of her apron.

"Uncle Jarrod's here. Said he passed her on the road. Said we needed to clean up proper."

"That means Abby brought someone with her?"

The boy nodded emphatically.

"Where are Tom and Katie?"

Just then the kitchen door opened and the other two came inside. They all gathered around Lily.

She looked at each in turn. "Tom, you know what to do?"

"Yup."

She bent at the waist and said to Katie, "You have to do what you do best. Remember?"

"Ask questions. Right, Lily?"

"Right." Lily smiled at her younger sister.

"Oliver? Do you have to go to the necessary?" His straight blond hair slid into his eyes when he shook his head.

Lily smiled. Everything was going to work out fine.

The back door opened and Uncle Jarrod walked inside. He saw the four of them standing in a huddle and smiled. "What's this?"

Lily glanced at him over her shoulder. "Oliver said Abby's coming and she has someone with her."

"That's right. She'll be here in about ten minutes." He took a basin from a shelf beneath the window and pumped some water into it.

"What do you want us to do, Uncle Jarrod?" Lily asked.

"We need to put our best foot forward and make a good impression. Can you clean up Katie and Oliver? Make sure they're presentable?"

"They're muddy from playing by a waterfall we found, but I'll do the best I can."

He frowned at Katie and Oliver. "Do you know how to swim?" When they shook their heads, he said, "Don't go there alone again. Do you understand?"

"What if Lily or Tom goes with us, Uncle Jarrod? We can go then, right?"

"Do you know how to swim?" he asked the two older ones. They nodded, and he said, "Right, Katie. Now you run upstairs and change into clean clothes."

Lily took the two little ones by the hand and led them up the stairs.

Abby pulled her team to a stop, pushed the brake handle forward, then wrapped the reins around it. "This is Blackstone Ranch, Bea. What do you think of it?"

The white-haired woman beside her looked around and nodded approvingly. "Very impressive. It's quite a large house, isn't it?"

"Yes. It's very comfortable," Abby answered.

"And four children," she said.

"They're wonderful children, Bea. You're going to love them."

Abby had told the other woman the whole situation. Beatrice Peters was fifty-five years old, and very young at heart. They had known each other since Abby was a little girl.

"I'm sure I will. I've missed being around youngsters."

"I know."

The front door opened and Jarrod Blackstone stepped out on the porch. He had changed from the plaid cotton work shirt she'd seen him in earlier. Now he wore a long-sleeved white one with the cuffs neatly buttoned. His hair was still damp from combing it. Lines of fatigue around his eyes told her that Katie still wasn't sleeping through the night. She couldn't help feeling sorry for Jarrod, but she was sure Beatrice Peters was the answer to his problems.

As Abby stood to climb out of the wagon, Jarrod quickly walked down the porch steps.

"Hello, Abby." He held his arms out to help her down.

"Jarrod," she said, then cringed at the huskiness in her voice when she said his name.

She hesitated before putting her hands on his wide shoulders. When he circled her waist with his hands, she assured herself that he couldn't possibly know how hard her heart was pounding. After he set her on the ground and turned to help the other woman, she took a deep, steadying breath. How could she have told Bea this place was comfortable?

"Ma'am," he said, lifting Bea down.

Abby cleared her throat. "Jarrod, this is Beatrice Peters. Bea, Jarrod Blackstone."

"Mr. Blackstone." The older woman smiled warmly at him.

"A pleasure to meet you, Mrs. Peters."

"It's *Miss* Peters, Mr. Blackstone."

Jarrod frowned at Abby. She knew what he was thinking. A woman who had no children of her own wouldn't know the first thing about this job. Abby was convinced that Bea was perfect for it. If Bea wasn't, then she would have to keep looking. That meant another trip to the ranch. Another face-to-face meeting with Jarrod.

That was out of the question.

She wouldn't allow anything to sway her from her goal. She was leaving to find her father. Not even her attraction to Jarrod Blackstone could stop her.

"I've known Bea for a long time. The children will love her," Abby said.

Jarrod looked skeptical, then turned his gaze back to the other woman. "Before we see whether or not that's the case, Miss Peters, may I ask what your qualifications are?"

"I'm a retired teacher, Mr. Blackstone."

"I see. So you would be able to give them schooling in addition to your other responsibilities?" There was a spark of interest in his voice.

"That's right," she said briskly. "And I'm no stranger to hard work. Each summer, I've been employed at the boardinghouse in Hollister to tide myself over." She reached into her reticule and pulled out several folded papers. "These are letters of introduction and recommendation from Mrs. Edelman, who owns the boardinghouse, and Mr. Cooper, the president of the school board."

Jarrod took them from her, then gestured to the house. "Won't you come in?"

Abby noted that there was a decidedly more welcoming tone in Jarrod's voice. She was irritated that he thought she would bring just anyone off the streets of Hollister. "Are you sure you don't want a letter of introduction from the mayor first?" Abby asked, shooting him an angry look.

"I don't think that will be necessary," Jarrod answered.

"Now, Abigail, don't be impertinent. Mr. Blackstone is merely being cautious and thorough. After all, the welfare and safety of these children are his responsibility. Isn't that right, Mr. Blackstone?"

"That's right."

"And one can't be too careful where children are concerned. Isn't that also true, Mr. Blackstone?"

"Absolutely, Miss Peters. And won't you please call me Jarrod?" he asked in an amused tone.

"I'd be delighted, Jarrod," Bea said, her light blue eyes twinkling.

A realization dawned on Abby as she looked at the older woman, who was smiling coyly up at Jarrod, fluttering her lashes. Well, call me stupid and slap me silly, Abby thought. If Beatrice Peters wasn't smitten with Jarrod, she would eat her hat. That confirmed her theory. He was definitely dangerous to every single woman within a two-hundred-mile radius, *and* under sixty years old.

"I think Lily made some lemonade," he said.

"That sounds lovely," Bea answered. "The drive out was very dusty. My throat is bone dry."

Jarrod opened the front door and indicated that they should precede him inside. Bea went first. When Abby followed, she made sure to keep the other woman between herself and the handsome rancher. Bea wasn't as effective as a whole town full of people, but she was some protection,

Abby thought. At least with Bea there, she didn't have to be alone with him. Of course, with four children underfoot, they were hardly likely to be alone.

"Where are the children?" Abby asked. It was odd that there had been no sign of them.

"They're upstairs," he said.

She found she could hardly wait. They had been in her thoughts constantly since she'd left them five days before. She wondered how they were adjusting. Were they homesick? Were they left alone to fend for themselves all day? Was Lily overwhelmed by responsibility? Had Jarrod managed to find some clothes? She had some things for them in the back of the wagon that she'd bring in after they met their new housekeeper.

Jarrod led them through the house, pointing out rooms as he went. After they had gone through the whole downstairs, he took them into the living room. "Please make yourselves comfortable," he said.

"It was a long ride," Abby replied. "I think I'll stand."

"Where *are* the children, Mr. Blackstone?" Bea asked, sitting in the big easy chair beside the fireplace. "This house is very still for having four youngsters in it."

"They're good kids," he said. "Well-behaved and self-sufficient. Respectful of their elders. Quiet. Clean. They take real good care of themselves."

"So why do you need a housekeeper?" Bea wanted to know.

"I have to be away from the house a lot of the time, and I'd feel easier if there was someone here with them."

"I understand completely."

A door slammed shut upstairs. Then footsteps thumped on the stairs just before all four children filed into the room.

"Hi, Abby," they said at the same time. All except Tom.

"Hi," she answered. "How are you?"

"We're fine," Katie said. "Right, Lily?"

"Right."

Abby studied each in turn. In just five days there was more healthy color in their cheeks, more life in their eyes.

All except Tom. Oh, he looked better. She saw more energy in his rangy body. But there was a definite trace of animosity in his expression, too. He didn't think he needed taking care of, she reminded herself. He was bound to dislike anyone who hired on as housekeeper.

Abby noted that their clothes were the ones she had first seen them in, but she would take care of that soon. She looked carefully at each of them and was satisfied that they were well.

"This is Lily," Jarrod said, standing behind the girl, his hands on her shoulders. "The others, in order of age, are Tom, Katie, and last, but *not a baby*, is Oliver. Children, I'd like you to meet Miss Peters."

"How do you do?" Lily said. The others mumbled greetings.

"It's a pleasure to meet you all," Bea said.

Jarrod cleared his throat. "Miss Peters is going to be our housekeeper."

# 4

*Katie stepped out of line* and stood in front of her sister. "But we don't like her. Right, Lily?" Jarrod felt Lily's shoulders tense, then she turned her sister around and put her hand over her mouth. "Hush, Katie."

The child wiggled until she could talk. "But you said—"

"I said you should be polite. You're being rude to Miss Peters."

"Sorry, ma'am," Katie said, hanging her head.

Bea shifted in the green velour chair. "No harm done, child."

Jarrod saw Katie's bottom lip thrust forward in a pout. Being corrected by her sister had obviously put her in a snit. But why had she decided so quickly that she didn't like Bea? And to say it straight out that way. Katie was direct and said whatever popped into her head. Maybe she just saw something the rest of them didn't.

He glanced at Abby, standing beside Bea's chair. There was understanding in her eyes as she looked at Lily and Katie. She was the one who had pointed out to him that it was unfair to put Lily in the role of parent when she was still a child herself. If Abby had chosen well with the woman she'd brought them, Lily wouldn't have to take responsibility for her brothers and sister any longer.

Abby should be pleased that he'd said the woman would be the housekeeper. Instead she looked like something was eating her as she studied the two girls.

Abby folded her arms over her chest. "Katie? What did you mean you don't like Bea? You just met her."

Jarrod wanted to know the answer to that himself.

"She's old," Katie answered.

Jarrod studied the woman and tried to see what Katie meant. He couldn't find anything wrong. He thought her age perfect. Not too old to keep up with the kids, but old enough that there wouldn't be gossip about her living under his roof. She had worked in the boardinghouse, and she was a teacher. What more could he ask for?

He shouldn't have blurted it out to the kids that she would be the new housekeeper. The only reason he could figure for the slip was lack of rest. But his gut told him the woman would do a good job. If she accepted the position—and he had no reason to think she wouldn't—he ought to be able to sleep the night through real soon.

He looked down the line of children. "Does anyone else have anything to say? Lily?"

"Miss Peters looks very nice," Lily said doubtfully.

Abby smiled. "She is. She was my teacher when I was in school."

"Is she gonna make us do lessons?" Tom wanted to know.

"Absolutely, young man. An idle mind is the devil's workshop." Bea looked over the spectacles on the end of her nose. Her tone was firm, but not unkind.

Katie shot an angry look at her older sister and brother. "I want to learn to read and write. Mama wanted us to. Lessons are good. Right, Uncle Jarrod?"

"Right, Katie. Miss Peters is going to help out around here. And give you your lessons."

"She can't take Mama's place," Tom said angrily.

"I would never try," the older woman told him.

Abby stepped forward quickly. "Jarrod, you did say that the children must approve of whoever you decide to hire."

"That's true."

He was almost sorry he had said that. This was not going at all as he had hoped. The kids seemed to resist the woman, and he couldn't see why.

"I have an idea," Abby said looking at the children. "What if you spend some time alone with Miss Peters? Get to know her. She should get to know all of you too. Then you can better tell how you feel."

"But, Abby, Uncle Jarrod." Katie stepped away from her sister and turned to look at both of them. "We already know how we feel—"

"That's a wonderful idea," Lily said quickly. "Uncle Jarrod, you and Abby can go do something while we get to know Miss Peters."

"Is that all right with you, Bea?" Abby asked the woman.

"Perfectly. It makes a great deal of sense."

Beatrice Peters hadn't taught school all those years without learning a thing or two about children. These four were definitely up to no good. She sat in the big easy chair beside the rock fireplace and studied them.

Right after Jarrod and Abby left, Tom had disappeared to his room and returned a few minutes later. He waited in front of her now with his hand behind his back. "I have something for you," he said.

The scamp had looked at her with nothing less than hostility since he'd first come downstairs to be introduced. Now he was smiling like a cherub. Why did children always think their elders had less brains than the good Lord gave a rock? She met his angelic expression with one of abject innocence, and braced herself. "What have you got there, young man?"

He yanked forward a bouquet of yellow dandelion weeds. "Here," he said, thrusting them at her.

She took them from him. "How very thoughtful. Thank you, Tom." She made a great show of smelling them. "Did

you know that these leaves are edible?" she asked as Tom
sat on the stone hearth, very close beside her. She eyed him
with a good deal of suspicion, but was distracted when
Katie came closer.

The little girl rested her elbows on the arm of the chair,
thrust her chin into her hands and tipped her head to the
side. "Ed Bull? Who's that?"

"Not a who, dear. Ed-i-ble means you can eat them. They
make a fortifying soup, and tasty too."

"You don't like soup. Remember, Katie?" Lily stood
beside Oliver, looking a little nervous. Bea realized the girl
hadn't been able to meet her gaze since she had come
downstairs.

"I liked Mama's soup," Katie corrected. Her green-eyed
gaze turned to Bea. "Did you know the angels took my
mama to heaven?"

"Yes, dear. Abby told me," Bea said softly.

"I have bad dreams about a mean man coming to get me.
Mama went because she was tired, and that made her ready
to go."

"Katie hasn't slept all night since Mama passed away,"
Lily said. "Poor Uncle Jarrod gets up with her constantly."

"That's why he wants me to come stay," Bea said. "What
do you think about that?"

Lily glanced up quickly, then back down at her hands. "I
think you probably wouldn't like getting up with her every
night."

"Why don't you let me worry about that. Is there anything else I should know?" she asked.

Katie thought for a minute, then piped up, "Oliver wets
the bed. And he has accidents—"

"Do not."

Bea looked at the boy sitting cross-legged at her feet,
thumb in mouth. "I'll bet the outhouse is just too far away.
Isn't that right, Oliver?"

He nodded without removing his thumb.

"What else?" Bea asked, looking at the young faces. She
glanced beside her at Tom, who quickly moved his hand

away from her skirt and stuck it in his pocket. "What about you, young man? Do you have anything to add?"

"I can take care of myself. Don't need a housekeeper."

"Your uncle disagrees, and if you think we can all get along together, I'll be taking the job. What do you say?"

Lily smiled thinly. "We'd like that. Right everyone?"

There was a chorus of weak assent. Then Bea looked at Katie. "But I think there are some things we should straighten out first. Dear, you said you didn't like me. Have you changed your mind?"

The little girl thought for a minute, glanced over her shoulder at Lily, who shook her head slightly, then looked back. "No'm."

These children had made up their minds before meeting her. Why?

"You're honest, child. I like that." Katie beamed. "But what is it you don't like? Perhaps if we talk about it, we can—"

A loud croaking noise interrupted her at the same time she felt something wiggle around in the pocket of her skirt. Aha, she thought, the dandelions were a decoy, a way to get close to the real objective. The children glanced at each other expectantly.

If they wanted screaming and carrying on, they were barking up the wrong tree, Bea thought. She reached into her pocket and pulled out a medium-sized frog. She held him up, letting his legs and webbed feet dangle as she looked him over carefully, then pronounced, "He's a fine fellow. Thank you, Tom. I like him better than the dandelions."

The boy's gray eyes widened with something close to admiration. "You do—"

"Did you know that frogs eat insects? He'll have a feast this year. After all the rain, there will be a bumper crop of mosquitoes and flies. And aren't you glad he'll be around to do that? He will certainly make our life more comfortable. Don't you think?"

Bea stroked her finger along the frog's back, and the

children's jaws dropped. Oliver's thumb fell out of his mouth.

She extended the frog. "Katie, would you like to hold him?"

The little girl squealed and jumped away. "No'm. I don't even like bedbugs. Does he bite? Uncle Jarrod says bedbugs don't, it's just a 'spression. But I don't wanna find out. And I don't wanna hold him," she said, jamming her hands behind her back.

"Oliver?"

He shook his head. "Gotta go," he said, and raced from the room.

"Anyone else?" she asked the others.

Lily and Tom shook their heads. Bea put the frog on her palm and he croaked loudly. Without warning, he leapt from her hand and Lily and Katie squealed. Tom laughed. The animal poised in the middle of the wool carpet, seeming almost at home on the patterned rug done in shades of white, goldenrod, and bright emerald-green. Only the bubble beneath the frog's chin puffing in and out at an alarming rate told Bea he was nervous and frightened.

"Tom," she said, spearing the older boy with a stern look. "Catch the poor creature before he hurts himself and take him outside where he belongs. Put him back where you got him. And don't harm him. Do you understand?"

He nodded. "Yes'm."

"Good." When he was gone, she looked at the two girls. "Would either of you young ladies care to explain to me what's going on?"

"Not me," Katie said. "I was just s'posed to ask questions. That's what I do best," she said proudly. "Right, Lily?"

When Lily turned the shade of a sun-ripened tomato, Bea's suspicions were confirmed. A conspiracy was definitely afoot.

Lily looked down, then reluctantly lifted her gaze. "It's not you, Miss Peters. We've been planning this for anyone Abby brought."

"But why, child? Your uncle obviously wants and needs help."

"We know that. But we decided we want him to hire Abby as our housekeeper."

"Why not come right out and ask your uncle to do that?"

Lily shook her head. "He already did and she said no."

"How do you know?"

"We overheard them talking."

"Did anyone ever tell you eavesdropping is underhanded and not a very nice thing to do?"

"Yes'm," Lily said. "But when Mama was alive, she always told us things were fine, to protect us. We knew different. We felt it was better to know what was going on, so we started listening in."

"I see." Bea's heart went out to the children. She wanted to see them get what they wanted for a change. "Why did Abby turn down the job?"

"She said she already has one and her life is in town. I think she and Uncle Jarrod don't like each other."

"Is that so?" Bea asked, making her own assessment of what Jarrod and Abby felt. "So you plan to play this little game with everyone Abby brings to meet your uncle. Why? What if I decide to accept the job in spite of your shenanigans?"

"Uncle Jarrod said he wouldn't hire anyone we didn't like."

Bea nodded in understanding. "So the plan is to scare everyone off. That's not fair to Jarrod."

"We figure Abby will feel sorry for him and be our housekeeper." Lily hung her head. "Are you gonna tell Uncle Jarrod what we did? He'll probably send us away to an orphan home."

Bea snorted. "I doubt that. Jarrod Blackstone takes his responsibilities seriously." She studied the girls for a moment, then said, "Let's discuss this with the boys when they come back and we'll see what we can do."

Abby sat on a swing hanging from the sturdy branches of two huge oak trees. It was early afternoon, but the foliage was so thick, only dappled sunlight penetrated. A warm breeze blew the hair around her face as she gently moved back and forth. Abby didn't remember seeing the swing the last time she'd been at Blackstone Ranch.

She looked up at Jarrod, who leaned one broad shoulder against the thick tree trunk as he watched her with an unreadable expression on his face.

"Did you make this?" she asked, indicating the thick, sturdy hemp ropes holding her up.

"Yes."

"For the children?"

"Why would you think that?"

"It looks new. Just seems to me you would have made it for them."

"I did. When Sally and I were young, we had one. The ropes and seat rotted a long time ago. I just thought the kids might like it."

Abby felt a glow close to her heart. It couldn't be easy taking on four children. He had never been around any, yet he was trying to do his best for them.

A sudden yearning for her own father sliced through her. Sam Miller had gone away when Abby was a bit younger than Lily. To find a better life for the family, he had explained. Abby had been inconsolable. She had missed him terribly but hadn't seen him since. Every year or so he sent a letter. One day soon, she planned to find him. From the moment he'd left, she'd dreamed of uniting the family again.

Mama was dead, but she and Clint still needed their father. Abby closed her eyes as she swung gently and promised herself that she would make it happen. Right now she was too busy working. All the money she could spare went to put Clint through college. Come hell or high water, she would make her mother's dream for Clint come true. Afterward, she would find her father and go live with him. As soon as her brother came around to her way of thinking, they would all be together again.

"There's not much for kids to do here," Jarrod said, breaking into her thoughts. "No one to play with."

Abby looked at him. "It was thoughtful of you to make them the swing."

"I had to do something to keep them occupied."

There was an edge to his voice that made her wonder. "Has there been a problem?"

"Nothing big. Tom's been getting into mischief."

"He hasn't hit Katie again, has he?"

He smiled. "No. Just teasing the animals, stuff like that. I'd ignore it, but I have the feeling it's getting worse."

"Have you talked to him?"

"Of course. So has Gib. But so far it hasn't stopped him."

"What are you going to do about it?"

He shrugged, bent over to pluck a blade of grass, and twirled it through his fingers. A stray dark curl blew across his forehead. The lines around his eyes seemed deeper, whether from worry or lack of sleep, she didn't know.

"When I talked to Tom that first day, I told him we needed time to adjust, that I didn't want to have to tan him. But I'm beginning to think—"

She stopped swinging and stood up. "Are you sure that's the answer?"

"I don't know what else to do." He looked completely bewildered.

"Try giving him some of your time first."

"What makes you think I haven't?"

"Have you?"

"Some, but—"

"Have you taken the time to at least eat breakfast and dinner with them?" He started to answer and she pointed at him. "The morning I was here doesn't count."

"Then no, but I get up before daybreak—"

She sighed. "Jarrod, please tell me you've tucked them into bed at night."

He let out a long breath. "You don't understand, Abby. It's easy for you to judge me when you're standing on the outside looking in. You have no idea what I'm up against running a ranch this big, and now having to worry about four kids." He ran a hand through his hair. "They found the waterfall where Sally and I used to go. But the two youngest can't swim. What if they disobey me and drown?"

"Jarrod, I—"

"They're into everything. They're just playing, but it's dangerous. Accidents happen to grown men who know to be careful. When I have to be away, I never know what I'll find when I come back."

Abby felt terrible, especially when she looked closer and noticed the dark circles under his eyes, the weary slump of his shoulders. Now she knew it had been worry and lack of sleep that carved the lines around his eyes and forehead.

"Is Katie still waking up?" she asked gently.

He nodded. "Like clockwork. She has the same bad dream every night."

Abby didn't have the heart to stay mad at him, especially when he looked so worn-out. "She's been through a lot. When she feels secure, the dream will stop. Maybe if you put her in Lily's room—"

"I thought of that. It didn't help. She just woke all of them up. At least if I go to her, no one else is disturbed. The days seem to be more peaceful that way," he said wryly.

"If you don't spend time with them, how would you know?"

"The hands take turns staying behind to keep an eye on things."

He was right. She hadn't the vaguest notion what he went through. But surely with a little common sense he could get through until Bea had the household under control.

"I have a suggestion," she said.

"What?"

His gray eyes narrowed as he shot her a wary look. Why that expression caused her heart to beat a little faster, she couldn't say. But for some reason, it made her see what she had been trying hard to forget or at least to ignore in the days since she'd been here. He was a fine-looking man. A fact that kept jumping into her mind even though the distance between Hollister and Blackstone Ranch separated them.

She turned until her shoulder brushed his arm and they stood side by side, staring at the front porch. "Take Tom with you when you leave in the morning."

"What do you mean?"

"Whatever you have planned for the day, take Tom with you. My guess is the mischief is his way of getting your attention. So give him what he wants. Sooner or later he's got to learn about the ranch."

"He's just a boy. I leave before sunup."

"It won't kill him. He'll go to bed earlier. Tom's a boy who's getting bigger every day. Why, I swear he's grown a foot since I last saw him. Makes me wonder if the clothes I brought from the mercantile will fit."

"So you think all I need to do is give him some notice and spend some time with him?"

"That's right. It doesn't have to take you away from work. Include him in what you're doing. Explain things. Teach him."

"Might slow me down some."

"Might. But at least you'll have him where you can see him. You won't have to worry about what he's up to while you're gone."

He nodded absently and gave Abby a small smile. "There is that."

The fact that he didn't dismiss her idea caused Abby to warm to her topic. That smile on his face caused her to warm to him. She started talking faster. "It's always been my belief that you catch more flies with honey than you do with vinegar."

"Hmmm."

"While you're about it, he'll learn how to be a man." She recalled Katie's disbelief when Jarrod told her he wouldn't let any harm come to her. Chances were good that Tom had never had a decent man to look up to. "Show him how to be a good man, Jarrod."

"Abby Miller, did you just say something nice to me?"

"Good Lord, no. Whatever gave you a crazy idea like that?"

He stuck his hands in the pockets of his denims. "Beats the heck out of me."

In spite of her vehement denial, Jarrod knew she had just paid him a compliment. That surprised him some, since more often than not she was hot under the collar about something he'd said or done. He was surprised how much her favorable opinion meant to him. It felt good to talk to her about the kids and the things that had been bothering him. He hadn't wanted to resort to tanning Tom. Her notion of letting him tag along, of teaching him, well, maybe it was a good one.

The ranch would probably be Tom's someday. Jarrod figured it wasn't likely he'd ever have a son of his own to leave it to, since he didn't want a wife.

He glanced at the house. "Do you think they've had enough time to look Bea over?"

Abby shrugged. "Maybe we should give them a little longer. What do you think of her, Jarrod?"

"She's just what the doctor ordered."

"I'm glad you feel that way." She looked up at him and smiled. Her eyes sparkled with pleasure at the praise.

She was real pretty when she smiled, he thought. Although she was real pretty when she frowned. And when she looked like she wanted to shoot him too. He rubbed a hand across the back of his neck. This kind of thinking was dangerous. If he wasn't careful, he could get to like Abby Miller a lot more than he already did.

"I hope the children approve," Abby said.

"Yeah. But why wouldn't they?"

"No reason that I can think of," she said. "And from the looks of you, I brought her just in time."

"What does that mean? From the looks of me?"

She shook her head at him as if he was dumb as a post. "You've got bags under your eyes big enough to store grain for the winter."

"No," he said, resisting the urge to touch his eyes. "I don't look that bad."

He felt that bad, but he didn't think it showed. Shoot, he'd put on a clean white shirt, combed his hair, and generally spruced up. It bothered him that he didn't look his best. Hell, it annoyed him that he even cared about how he looked to Abby.

"It's all right. There's not so much damage that a few good nights of sleep won't fix it right up." She flipped her long red braid over her shoulder and started toward the house. "Trust me. Bea will see that you get it."

"They're comin'," Katie said, turning away from the window she'd been looking out.

Bea glanced at each of the children in turn. "Do you all know what you're supposed to say?"

They nodded. The front door opened and Jarrod and Abby walked into the living room. Bea studied the younger woman and noticed a becoming pink in her cheeks that she'd never seen before.

Something told her it had nothing to do with the sun, but everything to do with one handsome rancher. Her hunch had been right. She couldn't blame Abby. Why, if she were thirty years younger, she'd set her cap for Jarrod Blackstone. She noticed the attractive indentation in his strong chin and revised that. Twenty-five years younger and the man wouldn't stand a chance.

"Jarrod, did you have a nice walk with Abby?" Bea asked.

He tossed a quick gaze at the redhead beside him. Something flickered in his eyes that Bea was sure he wasn't even aware of.

"We didn't get farther than the swing in the yard. But it was all right, I guess." He looked from Bea to the children who were sitting beside her, lined up on the stone hearth.

Jarrod cleared his throat. "Miss Peters—"

"Please call me Bea," she reminded him. "I gave the children permission."

"All right. Bea—I'd like to formally offer you the position of housekeeper."

Bea folded her hands in her lap and stared at him over the spectacles on her nose. "I'm afraid I must decline your offer, Jarrod."

"I don't understand," he said, shocked. The way the woman had them lined up beside her, and given her consent to use her first name, had convinced him they were as familiar as an old pair of boots. "Do you like Bea?" he asked, glancing at each of them.

"Yes, sir," Katie answered and sat down. "I like everyone."

Bea cleared her throat. "It's not that."

"Then what?" Abby asked in dismay.

Bea felt sorry for her. She had worked so hard to find someone for Jarrod. Under different circumstances, she would have loved this job. But there was something more important at stake.

"She's too old," Tom said.

"Tom, it's rude to say things like that in front of someone else," Abby said.

"Yes'm," he responded. He couldn't quite hide a small grin.

Bea was certain the two adults were too stunned to notice. That was good. "His sentiment is correct, although bluntly put. As much as I hate to admit it, I don't believe I have the stamina to keep up with four children."

"Lily, do you have anything to say?" Jarrod asked. "You have the biggest stake in this."

"I think Tom is right. Bea's nice and all, but this bunch," she looked down the line at her brothers and sister, "well, they're a handful. I think we'd be too much for her, and I'd hate to see her health do poorly."

"Oliver? Do you have anything to say?"

He took his thumb out of his mouth. "She's got mean eyes."

"It's unanimous?" Jarrod asked.

"What does that mean?" Katie asked. "Is that like Ed Bull?"

Jarrod shook his head quickly as if to clear his ears. "I

don't know about that. But unanimous means you all agree."

Four heads nodded in unison.

"I just don't understand. You knew there were four of them when you came all the way out here. Did something change your mind?" His eyes narrowed. "Did they do anything?"

"Good heavens no. Tom picked flowers for me and brought me a pet. They couldn't have been more well-behaved. They're just as you said, clean, well-mannered children. But I think it's just not going to work."

"We could try having you here for a week or two. Just to see."

Bea had expected him to take no for an answer. The poor man was even more desperate than she'd thought. "I don't know—"

"What about a trial period of two weeks? The kids will all help out and be on their best behavior. I'll pay you—"

"No, Jarrod. If I take this job, I will lose my employment in town. I can't afford to do that unless I was certain this would work out. I am sorry."

Lily stepped forward. "I know someone who would be perfect."

Jarrod frowned. "Who?"

"Abby." Lily looked at her sister and brothers. Only Tom didn't seem to agree.

Abby put her arm around Lily's shoulders. "It means so much that you want me. As much as I'd like to, I can't take the job."

"Why not?" Katie asked.

"The same reason as Bea. I work in town." She looked at Jarrod, her eyes troubled. "I'm sorry."

"Not half as sorry as I am," he said.

# 5

*Jarrod yawned and rubbed a hand* across his face, feeling the stubble. He was too godawful tired to bother shaving this morning. A week had passed since Bea Peters had turned down his job offer. Abby had brought another candidate out to the ranch. While the children were getting acquainted, he and Abby waited in the oak grove beside the swing that had pleased her so the last time she'd been here. This time she paced. Jarrod didn't have the energy. He sat, his back braced against a tree trunk.

"What do you think?" Abby asked, glancing at the house as she stopped briefly beside him.

"I'm too tired to think. What do *you* think?"

She sighed. "I thought Bea would be perfect. My opinion isn't worth the powder it would take to blow it to kingdom come."

In spite of the deep weariness filling every muscle and bone in his body, Jarrod smiled. He watched the sunlight that peeked through the thick tree branches ignite her red hair. Firecracker, he thought. When you lit one, it sizzled and sparked and looked real pretty. Made a person smile in anticipation, waiting for the excitement. Abby was like that. Shimmer and sparkle. He'd have bet his last nickel no one could make him smile, as tired as he was. But she had.

A firecracker explodes, he reminded himself. One could be dangerous if a person didn't know how to handle it. Best not to get too close.

He blinked his eyes and shook his head, trying to clear the cobwebs. When he started thinking like that, he knew lack of sleep had turned his mind to mush.

Abby started pacing again. "No matter what happens, Jarrod, I want you to know I did my best." She stopped for a moment and stared at the house, puzzled. "I talked to nearly everyone in Hollister. Bea wasn't the only one I thought would do. But now no one seems interested."

"Except—What did you say her name was?"

"Mary Jane Watkins."

"Yes, Mary Jane. I really do appreciate you bringing her out here. I know it's pretty far out of your way."

She shrugged, downplaying his thanks. "I had to come almost this far anyway. A delivery at the Encinas Ranch. Lydia finally got that bedroom suite she ordered from Chicago."

"Something's been puzzling me," Jarrod said.

"Keeping you up nights, from the looks of it," she said smartly.

He ignored her and asked, "How do you manage to get heavy stuff off the wagon?"

"I'm stronger than I seem?" When he gave her a doubtful look, she laughed. "There's usually someone around to do the strenuous lifting. If not, I just wait until there is."

He glanced at the house. "So, tell me. How do you feel about Mary Jane Watkins?"

Her lips thinned for a moment, then she turned her big blue eyes on him. Once more they reminded him of the Pacific Ocean. A man could drown in her eyes. Maybe he could get some rest then. He shook his head again to clear it of those thoughts.

"I think she's too young," Abby said.

"How old did you say she was?"

"Seventeen. Why, she's hardly older than Lily. How is she going to get them to mind what she says?"

"Still, they thought Bea was too old, that they'd run her ragged. Mary Jane likely has a lot of energy." Enough to deal with Katie at night and still ride herd on the kids during the day, he thought.

She nodded doubtfully. "Maybe."

"You don't think so?"

"I'm not all that certain she truly wants the job. She hemmed and hawed then asked if Dusty Taylor still worked here."

"What are you thinking?" Jarrod breathed deeply of the fragrant spring grass as he rested his back against the thick, rough bark of the oak tree. He was too tired to stand up and pace with Abby. And way too worn-out to figure out what she meant.

"I think she's looking for a husband."

"Did she tell you that?"

"Not straight out. But I got real tired of hearing about what she's putting in her hope chest, what she still plans on putting in. Why is it that just because I work for the freight company, folks think I should know what things cost?"

"Don't you?"

"Of course not. I have a good idea what it costs to ship them, but not what the manufacturer charges."

"Do you have a hope chest, Abby?" he asked.

She sent him one of those looks that made him glad she wasn't holding a pistol on him. "Why would I?"

"To make a home when you marry."

"I haven't thought about that."

He tipped his head to the side and studied her. "How old are you?"

"A lot older than Mary Jane," she shot back.

"I really want to know. How old are you?" he asked again.

She turned away and folded her arms over her chest. "Twenty-five."

"And you haven't considered marriage? A family?"

She shook her head. "Too many other things to think about."

"Like what?"

"My brother Clint, for one. He's in college back East."

"What does that have to do with you?"

She glanced over her shoulder. "You're not planning to drop this any time soon, are you?"

"Nope." He grinned at her in response.

"I send him money to help pay for his schooling. It was our mother's wish that he be the first Miller to graduate from college. I plan to see that happens."

"How much longer does he have?"

"A year."

"So you could be thinking about a hope chest?"

"Could be. But I'm not."

"Why?"

She turned on him and planted her hands on her hips. "You're the nosiest man I ever met, Jarrod Blackstone."

"Not nosy. Sleepy."

"And prying into my personal life helps?"

"I'm being neighborly. And asking questions keeps me awake."

"Don't let me keep you from nodding off. I'll wake you if anything exciting happens."

Interesting, Jarrod thought. Most women were like Mary Jane Watkins. Looking for a man to marry them. Not Abby. He had a feeling there was more to it than just helping her brother. But it was none of his business.

"Do you think we should go see what's going on in there?" she asked, nibbling on her thumbnail as she stared at the house.

He was pretty sure that question was a deliberate attempt to steer him clear of asking her anything else personal. That was all right with him. If he wasn't so damn tired, he would never have pried into her life in the first place. He didn't want to know about Abby Miller, or any other woman for that matter.

"I don't know if we should interrupt them. What do you think?" he asked.

She tapped a finger against her lips thoughtfully. "This time I think we should wait."

"Done," he said, letting his eyes slip closed.

Abby glanced over her shoulder when a few minutes had passed without Jarrod asking her a question, or saying anything at all. His head was tilted back, resting against the tree. She smiled when she saw that his chest rose and fell gently, telling her that he was asleep. Her gaze was drawn to the neck of his shirt, where a few masculine chest hairs peeked out. How she wished she could erase the memory of what he looked like wearing nothing from the waist up.

His mouth, relaxed as he dozed, drew her attention. It had a nice shape, not too full, but not thin and stern. She couldn't help wondering how his lips would feel against her own, and her heart beat a little faster at the thought.

This preoccupation with notions of Jarrod Blackstone annoyed her. What business did he have snooping into her life the way he had? If she didn't think about getting married, that was her own business. She had her reasons. Good ones.

She glanced at the house again. With luck, she was wrong about Mary Jane Watkins, and Jarrod would have his housekeeper. Then her promise, and any real or imagined obligation to him, would be fulfilled. She wouldn't have to see him here on the ranch again. If he came into town, which was rare, any chance meeting between them would be far from intimate.

The front door opened and Mary Jane walked out on the porch. Her straight golden-blond hair lifted in the breeze as she looked around.

"Jarrod?" Abby turned to him. He didn't budge. She bent down and put a hand on his shoulder. The muscle was wide beneath her palm and she felt the warmth of his skin clear through his shirt. Quickly, she shook him and pulled her fingers away as if he had burned her. "Wake up."

"Hmm?" He stretched like a bear coming out of hibernation. "What?" he asked sleepily.

She wished she didn't have to wake him, but she had

promised she would if anything exciting happened. "Mary Jane just came out of the house."

He sat up and blinked, then ran a hand across his face. The rasping sound of whiskers drifted up to her. She held a hand down to him, to help him up.

He hesitated a moment, then took it, swallowing her palm in his much larger one. She braced herself and pulled with all her might. As he got to his feet, she felt the weight of him. It had been nothing more than a polite gesture on her part, she realized. If he hadn't cooperated, she didn't possess the strength to actually move him.

Abby took a deep breath. "Let's hope she has good news."

"Yeah."

Side by side, they walked from beneath the shady oaks and stopped at the bottom porch step. "How'd it go?" Abby asked.

"All right, I guess." Mary Jane tossed a strand of hair over her shoulder.

"Where are the kids?" Jarrod wanted to know.

The young woman cocked her thumb over her shoulder toward the door. "Inside. Having a family meeting. They're great kids."

Abby smiled at Jarrod, relieved that the girl liked them. One less thing to worry about. "Yes, they are."

Jarrod stuck his fingers in the pockets of his denims. "Do you think you can handle them and the housework? Now that you've seen the place, I mean?"

Mary Jane nodded. "I've got a younger brother and sister and helped Ma with chores. I think I can do a good job for you, Mr. Blackstone."

"So you'll take it? If the kids agree?" he asked.

"Yes, sir." She glanced down the hill toward the outer ranch buildings. "Dusty Taylor around anywheres?" she asked a little shyly.

Jarrod shook his head. "I sent him to look for strays in the canyon."

"Will he be back soon?" she inquired, sliding him a look from beneath her gold-tipped lashes.

"Can't say for sure. But my guess would be no. Probably not till close to sundown.

"Shoot," she said. "I was hopin' to say howdy."

"Slim Logan's in the barn working on the bridles and harness," Jarrod offered helpfully. "He'd be pleased if you went up to say hello."

She smiled coyly and nodded. "Thanks, Mr. Blackstone. I think I will."

She skipped down the steps and headed in the direction Jarrod indicated.

Abby looked at him. "Do you think that was wise?"

"What?" he asked, watching the girl's back.

"Encouraging her to see one of the hands?"

"Why not?" he asked. "She'll be living here at the ranch soon."

"Just seems like you're letting yourself in for a pile of trouble if any of them, or all of them, take a shine to her."

He turned his gaze back to Abby and lifted his shoulders in resignation. "Short of putting a bag over her head, or locking her up, I don't see how I can keep them away from her."

Abby frowned. "It would have been a lot easier if Bea had taken the job."

"I agree," he said, stifling a yawn. "But right now, beggars can't be choosers."

"I suppose." She looked at the closed door. "Do you think we should join the children?"

"They're having a family meeting."

"You're family," she reminded him.

"I'm not so sure they consider me family. Besides, I don't want to influence them."

Considering he was tired enough to sleep under a tree with oak bark for a mattress, that was awfully generous of him, Abby thought. She wondered if she would be as understanding if their situations were reversed. It was a shame he had never had any children of his own. Then again, maybe the good Lord knew what he was doing, knowing that Sally's kids would need a father. But he wouldn't have to

father them much since the housekeeper would be the one
spending time with them.

She sighed. "Maybe they do need a few minutes by themselves."

He slid her a lazy grin. "Another trip, another compliment. Careful, Abby. Folks might get to think we like each
other."

"Can't have that," she agreed. "Still, you're understanding."

"Not really. Just practical. The kids are the ones who
have to spend time with the housekeeper. Not me. It's not
like choosing a wife."

She shot him a sharp look as he yawned again.

Lily looked at her brothers and sister. "What are we
going to tell Abby and Uncle Jarrod?"

"I liked Mary Jane," Katie said.

Tom made a fist and stuck it in his pocket. "You can't
tell him that, dummy. Not if you want him to hire Abby. I
don't need—"

"Tom's right," Lily said. "Besides, Katie, you like everyone."

"But I like Abby best."

"Then we have to figure out what's wrong with Mary
Jane so Uncle Jarrod won't give her the job." Lily sat down
and rubbed her back. It had been aching off and on, though
she didn't know why. She was tired and out of sorts too.

"She's not much older than you," Tom said helpfully.
"Don't s'pose it'd do any good for me to remind 'im that I
don't need no one to take care of me."

"You do a good job of reminding all of us, Tom. Don't
reckon we'd forget," Lily said.

"You don't need looking after because you're with Uncle
Jarrod all the time," Katie reminded him. "He looks after
you all day." She looked at him enviously.

"Yeah," he said smugly.

"You like bein' with 'im?" Oliver asked.

Tom shrugged. "It's all right. Better than hanging around
here and having Lily boss me."

"Stop it, Tom. That's not helping us figure out what to say," Lily snapped.

"I could say I didn't like her," Katie offered. "I could say she was mean."

"They wouldn't believe you," Lily said. "And we don't want to lie. She was very nice."

In fact, Lily decided if things were different, she would like to make friends with Mary Jane. She wasn't *that* much older. Maybe when their plan had worked and Abby was at the ranch, she might have time to make her acquaintance.

"We told Uncle Jarrod that Bea was too old. Why not just say Mary Jane's not old enough to handle the likes of us?" Tom asked.

"That's probably best," Lily agreed. "Anything else?"

"Her teeth kind of stick out. Like a horse," Tom added, causing Lily to glare at him.

"She's too skinny," Katie offered. "If the mean man comes for me at night, she won't know what to do."

Lily smiled. Perfect. Uncle Jarrod would especially want someone Katie would like, so she would sleep all night. He was about done in from getting up with her.

Lily reminded herself that they were doing this to get him to hire Abby. It would be best for all of them, including Uncle Jarrod. He would only be tired a little while longer.

"All right. Everyone know what to say?" Lily asked.

They all nodded.

Abby poured herself some coffee from the pot she'd just made and sat wearily at Jarrod's kitchen table. It would be dawn soon and she had to get back to Hollister. Whatever had possessed her to stay the night? No one had asked her; she had offered. The words had come out of her mouth before she could stop them. Then Gib Cochran latched on to the idea like a dog to a favorite bone. He'd said he could take Mary Jane Watkins back to town since he was going in for supplies anyhow.

Abby was so tired. She hadn't spent more than an hour

or two up with Katie during the night, but after settling the child, she hadn't been able to sleep again.

Thoughts of Jarrod Blackstone kept her awake.

That was when she'd figured out what made her stay. It was the pleading expression in Jarrod's gray eyes. She was sure he hadn't been aware he looked like that. No matter how she tried to harden her heart against his situation, she just couldn't abandon him. Or the children.

"Abby?"

The deep voice sent shivers down her arms even as it drew her gaze to the doorway where Jarrod stood. Dressed in denims, with a long-sleeved plaid shirt rolled to his elbows, he looked ready for a day's work. She was ready to crawl back into bed.

"Morning," she said. "Hope you don't mind me helping myself to coffee."

"Lord, no." He crossed the kitchen and pulled a cup from the cupboard. "Do you have any idea what a pleasure it is to have it already made?"

She took a sip of hers and shook her head. "Mr. Whittemore has coffee made when I get to work, but I swear it's strong enough to tan leather." She glanced at him as he sat down across from her. "If I were you, I'd reserve judgment on how pleasurable that coffee is until you've sampled it."

"I'll just do that." He blew on the steaming black surface, then sipped. "Won't be tanning any hides with this. It's real tasty."

"Thanks."

He held the cup between his hands as he looked at her. "I'm almost afraid to ask, but did you get up with Katie last night?"

She nodded. "How did you know?"

"You look tired this morning."

"I am. By the way, I'd just like to take back what I said about the bags under your eyes. Mine feel like they'd hold a five piece living room suite, with an ornate sideboard thrown in."

"You don't look that bad."

Abby shot him a look. "That bad?"

"Not bad at all."

She told herself she didn't care what he thought of her appearance. Her only reason for staying last night was to help him out because she felt guilty that the kids hadn't taken to Mary Jane. If she could just find someone to work for him, everything would be dandy. She could do her job in town and he could get a good night's sleep.

"You didn't hear Katie, did you?" she asked quickly. "I tried to keep her quiet."

"No. By the way, thanks for the best night's sleep I've had in days."

"You're welcome."

"How long did it take you to get her settled down?"

"'Bout an hour and a half," Abby answered nonchalantly, even though he had disturbed her rest more than the child.

"That long?" he asked skeptically.

"We talked for a while," she said, feeling defensive. She knew he wasn't criticizing her, but she felt compelled to explain. "She seemed upset about Mary Jane."

"Why?"

"Katie worried about whether she had a job. If she would have a place to live, food to eat, clothes. She's just chock full of questions in the middle of the night, isn't she?"

"I'm sorry, Abby," he said sympathetically, although he couldn't suppress a chuckle.

She shrugged it off. "Don't worry about it. I just wish Mary Jane hadn't turned down the job."

"Me too."

"Why are you up at this hour?"

He grinned. "I've got a ranch to run. There's only so much daylight. Gotta make the most of it."

"Of course." That was stupid, she thought. Whenever she was around him, her mind seemed to seize up on her and not function properly. Certainly he had work to do. So did she. But trying to get him a housekeeper so he could run the ranch without having to worry about the kids was going very poorly.

Abby studied him. That grin of his would melt butter, she thought as her heart skipped a little. Straight white teeth stood out in contrast to his tanned face. His jaw was freshly shaven and his hair neatly combed. He was just about the best-looking man she'd ever laid eyes on.

He made her feel all the more bedraggled because he looked so darn good.

"Speaking of daylight, I've got to get back to town." She started to get up, but his large hand on her arm stopped her.

"Can you give me just a few minutes? There's something I'd like to talk to you about."

There was that pleading look in his eyes again. When he turned that on her, she was almost helpless to refuse him.

"All right. Just let me refill my coffee," she said, lifting her cup.

"Let me get it for you," he offered.

"No, thanks." She stood quickly, needing to put some distance between her and Jarrod. If she was going to hear him out, she had to do it from a few feet away, or she had a feeling she wouldn't hear much of anything at all.

She poured herself more coffee and rested her back against the counter beside the stove. "What's on your mind?"

"Boarding school."

Her hand holding the cup stopped halfway to her mouth. "What about it?" she asked.

"I'm thinking it might be good for the kids."

She started to say something, and he held up a hand.

"Now hear me out. You have to admit, finding a house-keeper is proving to be harder than you'd thought."

"Well, yes—"

"The kids seem mighty picky. Now don't get me wrong, I want them to be happy with whoever I hire. But I thought you did a fine job both times of choosing ladies suitable for the job. It seems the kids are a handful."

"But, Jarrod—boarding school?" She set her cup on the counter. "Maybe there are other relatives—"

"No." He frowned. "What else can I do, Abby? Spring and early summer are a real busy time here on the ranch. I'm short several hands."

"But think about the children—"

"I am, damn it. How can I do the work of two men and make sure the kids are okay too? Besides being up half the night with Katie."

He had a point. But Abby's heart cried out against sending the children away. After her father had left, she had missed him terribly. She didn't know what she would have done without her mother and Clint. These children needed to be with Jarrod. He was family; he cared about them. The idea of Lily, Tom, Katie, and Oliver being with strangers who would see them as nothing more than a job tore at her. She had to make him see that whatever time he had left over from ranching would be far better than the indifference they'd suffer at boarding school.

"I understand what you're going through, Jarrod."

"No, you don't." He looked up at her face just as she tiredly rubbed a hand across her forehead. "Maybe you do, at least partly. But there's more to it."

"There sure is—four young lives," Abby added.

"How can they get schooling out here? What if one of them gets hurt while I'm working? No one's here to teach them right from wrong," Jarrod replied.

"It wouldn't bother you thinking about Tom with people who don't care what he's gone through? What if he starts looking for attention the wrong way and gets tanned because of it?"

"That doesn't set well, but—"

"What about Oliver? Do you think strangers will have patience with him when he's had an accident?"

"There are good schools. I'll check—"

"And Lily. She'll be a young woman soon. Do you want to stifle her in an all-girls school?"

"It wouldn't be that bad. There are vacations and—"

"And what about Katie? Could you stand wondering if someone hears her when she's afraid at night? What if no one goes to her and she's left alone crying? Wouldn't that bother you, Jarrod?"

"Hell, yes!" He stood up and glared at her for several moments. "I just don't see as I've got any other choice."

"There's always another way."

"Not this time."

Abby walked across the kitchen and rested her hands on the top of the ladder-back chair across from him. She gripped it, squeezing so tight her knuckles turned white. "What would Sally say about you sending her children to boarding school?"

When a look of sorrow and pain clouded his eyes, she hated herself for saying that to him. But there were four young lives at stake.

"That was low, Abby," he finally said in a hoarse voice.

"I know. I'm sorry. But she sent them to you for raising, because she wanted the best for them."

"What makes you think I'm best?" A dark look shadowed his face.

Abby sympathized with whatever memory was eating him, but he was an adult. Her concern was the children. "Because you're family."

"The ranch takes all my time. Family or not, there's nothing left over for them. I'm not the best person for the job."

"Sally grew up here. She knew what it takes to run this place. She also knew how much time is necessary to raise four kids and work a job. She still sent her children to you."

"My sister was ill. She wasn't thinking straight. I'm the wrong man."

Abby wouldn't be sidetracked from what she felt was right because he thought he was unfit. So he had problems. Everyone did. Life was putting one foot in front of the other no matter what. "You were willing to try if you had a housekeeper," she reminded him.

He shot her a look. "But I don't have one."

"Give me a little more time, Jarrod. I'll get you some help."

Abby heard a loud creak that sounded like someone on the stairs. Jarrod met her gaze. "Do you think we woke the kids?" he asked.

She moved around him to the doorway. "I'll check." Abby walked down the hall and rounded the corner to look at the stairway. No one was there. Sighing with relief, she returned to the kitchen.

"They're still asleep. Must have been the house settling."

He nodded. "Now where were we?"

"You were just about to agree to letting me have more time to find a housekeeper before you send the children to boarding school."

He smiled. "Was I?"

She nodded. "Yes. Because you know it's the right thing to do."

"Do I?"

"Yes. Because you're a very wise man."

"Am I?"

Abby grinned at him before answering his question. "Yes, indeed. You're smart enough to know you don't know everything about raising kids."

"I don't know *anything* about it. But I do agree that boarding school should be a last resort."

"So you'll give me more time?"

"Any wise man would," he said. "You've got another week."

Abby was so relieved, she didn't care that he'd only given her a week. She'd changed his mind. Jubilation bubbled up inside her until it overflowed.

"Jarrod Blackstone, I could hug you."

He held his arms wide. "Okay."

Too exhilarated to think about what she was doing, Abby threw herself against him and looped her arms around his neck, squeezing him tight.

He wrapped strong arms around her and returned the pressure. When she leaned back slightly and caught the intense look in Jarrod's eyes, she knew his teasing mood had changed.

"Abby Miller, I could kiss you," he said, echoing her own words and giving them an intimate twist.

Her eyes widened and she held her breath as he lowered his mouth to hers.

# 6

*Abby's heart fluttered* as hard and fast as the wings of gulls taking flight over the ocean. Jarrod's lips touched hers. The sensation was soft, warm, wonderful. Jarrod Blackstone was not the first man who had ever kissed her, but he was the first who didn't make her want to rub the back of her hand across her mouth afterward. Her knees wobbled and a shiver of excitement skittered over her arms and down her legs. If she hadn't been wearing boots, her toes would have curled.

When he traced her lips with his tongue, Abby instinctively opened to him, her heart pounding. He slipped into her mouth, stroking her, sending tingles through her. This was what she had been afraid of from the beginning, but at the moment she couldn't find it in her to care. The sensations were too wonderful.

She was filled with disappointment when he pulled his mouth away and stared down at her, gray eyes cloudy. His breathing was quicker than it had been moments before, as was hers.

His dark look had faded, replaced by one of amusement.

"What's so funny?" she asked.

He smiled. "Who said anything was funny?"

"You did."

"I haven't said anything at all," he answered.

Her eyes narrowed. "You were about to. I can tell by that smirk on your face."

She didn't think that kiss was the least bit funny, and it was on the tip of her tongue to tell him so. But his expression told her that it had meant little or nothing to him. That scared her, because it meant more than nothing to her. A lot more.

Abby stepped away from him and let out a short, quick breath. She decided she had two choices. Either ignore what had just happened, or make light of it. Maybe do the latter first, then ignore the whole thing from then on.

He rubbed a hand over his cheek. "I'm not smirking."

"My mistake," she said, then shook her head. "Fancy that."

"What?"

"A hug *and* a friendly kiss from Jarrod Blackstone."

"Friendly? Interesting choice of words." One of his dark brows rose questioningly. "You sound surprised."

"You don't seem the huggin', kissin' sort of man." She forced a lightness into her tone.

"What sort do I seem?"

"I don't know. The brooding type. The kind who hardly ever smiles."

"Me?" he asked. "Why, I can be as neighborly as the next man."

"Yes, sir, you just proved that." Abby smiled, then cursed inwardly when her mouth trembled. She quickly turned away, not wanting him to see her reaction. "It's about time I started back to Hollister."

"Reckon so." He hesitated for several moments. "Abby?"

"What?"

"I'd like you to see the new foal I've got in mind to give Tom."

She whirled around. "You're giving him a horse?"

"Sort of." He tucked his fingertips into the pockets of his denims. "He watched the mare foal a couple days ago and really took to it. Can hardly tear himself away from the animal to do chores."

"Really?"

"Yeah. I think he'd sleep in the barn if I let him. He's got a birthday coming up pretty soon, and I thought I'd give it to him then. He'll have to learn to take care of it, train it, but it'd be his."

She swallowed past the lump that grew in her throat and studied him.

He frowned. "What's wrong?"

"Nothing. I was just trying to decide if you're the same man who just a few minutes ago was talking about boarding school."

He grinned sheepishly. "Yeah, one and the same."

"My my."

Jarrod grew restless under her scrutiny. "Do you want to see the foal or not?" he asked, a note of irritation creeping into his voice.

"I have to get on the road."

"Might just as well wait till the sun comes up. Won't put you behind too much, and it'd be a whole lot safer too."

As much as she wanted to put some distance between herself and Jarrod Blackstone, she couldn't resist the temptation of his offer.

"I'd love to see the horse."

"Follow me."

"Lily, wake up."

Katie climbed up on her sister's bed and sat beside her. When Lily didn't move, she poked her shoulder. "Lily? You gotta wake up," she said, leaning close and speaking loudly into her sister's ear.

Lily groaned and opened one eye. In the early morning light she saw Katie.

"Are you all right?" she asked.

Her sister nodded vigorously.

"Then why are you waking me up?"

"I need to know somethin'."

"What?" Lily asked, sitting up as she rubbed her eyes.

"Is boarding school a place where they teach you about boards?"

"Of course not," Lily said, annoyed. "It's a school where you live all the time."

"Do you learn to read and write there?"

"Yes."

"But it's away from home?"

"Yes."

"Uh-oh," Katie said, looking serious.

"Where did you hear about it?"

"Abby and Uncle Jarrod."

"When?" Lily was waking up fast.

"Just now. They're talkin' in the kitchen. What's a last resort?"

"That's when you've made up your mind about something because there's nothing else you can do."

Katie sat cross-legged on the bed and leaned her elbows on her knees. She rested her chin in her palms and looked glum. "Uh-oh. We're in trouble now."

"What's this all about, Katie?"

"Uncle Jarrod told Abby that he's sending us away to boarding school 'cuz he's not a good person."

"What did Abby say?"

"That Mama wanted him to raise us here on the ranch where she grew up."

"Abby's right."

Lily remembered her mother telling her about Blackstone Ranch and what a wonderful place it was. She'd gone on and on about Uncle Jarrod and how much they'd all like him and what a fine man he was. Mama couldn't have been wrong. She wanted them to stay at the ranch. Lily figured it was up to her to see that they did.

She looked at her sister. "Did they see you, Kate?"

The little girl shook her head. "That one stair made a noise and Abby came to look, but I ran back up and hid so she wouldn't see me."

"Good. I'm calling a family meeting. Go get Tom and tell him to meet us here in my room."

"What about Oliver?"

Lily thought for a minute. "He'll be cross later when he's tired, but he's part of the family." She nodded. "Oliver too."

"All right, Lily. I'll tell them to be quiet as mouses like always."

"Good girl." Lily jumped out of bed. "Tell them to get dressed. You too, Kate."

"All right," she said, then tiptoed from the room.

They didn't have much time.

"Where you s'pose Tom's been all mornin'?" Dusty Taylor pulled his gloves off and stuck them in the rear pocket of his denims. The dark-haired, blue-eyed cowboy brushed the back of his hand across his forehead to wipe away the sweat. "Figure he's lost interest in that foal already?"

Jarrod stared up the hill at the house. "I've been wondering the same thing."

He stood beside the other man, checking the section of fencing they had just repaired. Any minute, he'd been expecting his nephew to come and look at the new horse, same as he had every day since seeing it born. But there hadn't been any sign of him. Come to think of it, he hadn't seen any of the kids all morning.

"I need a break," Jarrod said, starting toward the house.

"I'll go with ya. Make sure them young 'uns ain't up to mischief."

Jarrod couldn't shake the feeling that it was too quiet. The kids hadn't been with him long enough for him to decide whether or not that was good or bad.

They walked up the rise to the house and through the back door into the kitchen. The room was dark and empty, the only sign of life the cups he and Abby had drunk coffee from early that morning. The silence was strange, unnatural. He was learning more about kids every day, and the one thing he could count on from them was noise.

Katie never stopped asking questions. Oliver never walked anywhere, he ran. Tom and Lily laughed and wrestled. He shook his head as he felt the cold stove. The other thing he knew about them was that they ate about as much as the U.S. Army. The fire Abby had made for coffee was cool now. It was way past time when Lily would have cooked breakfast for herself and the others.

Jarrod looked at Dusty. "Something's wrong. I don't think the kids are here."

"Where would they go?"

"Can't say."

"Wouldn't they leave you some word if they was goin' off to play?" Dusty asked.

Jarrod shook his head, at a loss. He couldn't say what they would do. A wave of guilt crested over him. Abby had told him to spend time with them, get to know them. He hadn't. But maybe he was jumping the gun and they were here.

"Let's check their rooms."

In minutes they had searched everywhere. The children were gone along with their clothes.

Jarrod pushed aside the knot of worry and tried to concentrate. He looked at Dusty. "Where could they have gone?" he asked. Maybe they had gone off to play and just hadn't thought to let him know. "There's a waterfall not too far from here. My sister and I used to go there. Lily said they found it. Maybe they all went there."

"Maybe so." The young cowboy ran his hand through his hair. "Leastways we know they're on foot."

"And if they haven't gone to the waterfall—"

"We'da noticed if mounts was missin'. They can't have gone far."

Jarrod nodded. "But there's no telling when they left. Abby was up with Katie during the night, so they were here then. Far as I know, they were asleep when Abby went back to Hollister at sunup. They must have taken off after that."

"So they been gone two, three hours?"

"Four at the most," Jarrod answered.

Plenty of time to get lost out there in the back country. Fall into a gully. Have a run-in with a wild animal.

Jarrod rubbed the back of his neck. "We have to look for them. Damn, I wish Gib was here. He's got a nose for tracking. He won't be back from town till tonight or tomorrow."

Dusty nodded, then followed him downstairs. "I'll get Slim. We'll saddle up. There's sure t'be signs of 'em."

"Those four would leave a trail a blind man could follow."

Dusty chuckled. "Ya got that right, boss."

"We'll find them," Jarrod said, more to convince himself than the other man. "They couldn't have gone far."

"When're we gonna eat, Lily? I'm hungry." Katie grabbed her belly.

"Yeah, Lil. How much longer we gotta hide out?"

"Do you think Abby's gonna be real mad when she finds out we hid in the back of her wagon?" Katie wanted to know.

Lily thought about that. She shook her head. "Not too mad. Maybe a little at first, but when we tell her why we did it, she'll understand."

"I didn't want to leave the ranch," Tom grumbled.

"Mama wanted us to stay together," Lily reminded him. "Just because you always get to go with Uncle Jarrod doesn't mean you can forget about us."

"Aw, I wasn't tryin' to. It's just I didn't get to say goodbye to the baby horse. The foal," he corrected himself. "'Sides, my stomach's makin' so much noise someone's liable to hear and Katie's questions are about to drive me crazy."

"I don't ask too many questions. Do I, Lily?" the little girl demanded. "How much longer do we have to stay in here?"

Lily lifted the canvas covering them and looked at the rear wall of the Hollister Freight Company. "I've already told you a hundred times. Until it's too late for Abby to take us back to the ranch. We agreed. Remember? We need time to talk her into keeping us."

Oliver took his thumb out of his mouth. "I want ham and biscuits *and* milk," he said, then popped his thumb right back where it was. He took it out again and added, "*And* I gotta go."

"Oliver, can't you hold it?" Lily asked. "Please try."

"Okay," he said.

Oliver wasn't the only one, Lily thought, growing more uncomfortable herself. It would have been worse if they'd had food and water. But they hadn't, and she felt bad enough. They would have to go soon. But how could they all get to the outhouse without being seen? Even two at a time they were likely to draw attention. She couldn't think of any other way to do it, because Katie and Oliver couldn't be trusted to go by themselves.

Lily peeked again and tried to tell from the shadows how late it was. Just a little longer, she decided. Without a lot of daylight left, Abby would have to keep them for the night. They had to hold out a while longer, just to be sure.

Leather creaked as Dusty Taylor eased out of the saddle. Jarrod had just returned from his own look-see. The two had split up, each taking a section of the ranch to search. Jarrod had chosen the area closest to the house, checking the waterfall, where he found no trace of the kids, and crisscrossing as far out as he thought they could get. He kept reminding himself that Oliver was with them. He was four, and had those short, spindly legs. The children couldn't get far.

"Any sign of them?" Jarrod asked.

The ranch hand shook his head. "Nothin'. That's real puzzlin'. No way they could be on foot and not leave a trail, even if they were tryin' to be careful."

It was early afternoon. They had been searching for several hours without success. Jarrod was perplexed about where they could have gone without leaving a trail, or why they would have left in the first place.

He looked at Dusty. "You got any other ideas?"

"Let's think on this a minute—"

"I've been thinking," Jarrod shot back angrily. "I've

wracked my brain thinking until I'm about to go crazy. If you can't come up with something . . ."

Dusty stared at him long and hard. "There's no reason t'think anythin's happened to them."

Jarrod looked into the distance and let out a long breath, wondering how the other man had read his mind. "I'm sorry. I didn't mean to bite your head off. It's just—"

"Worry. No need t'explain." Dusty hooked a thumb in his gun belt. "Now, as I was sayin', we gotta think about this. You said they was sleepin' when Miss Abby left."

Jarrod thought back to that morning. "We were having coffee. Abby had been up with Katie, and made a pot while she waited for sunup."

"And?"

"We were talking."

"'Bout anything in particular?"

"Why do you ask?" Jarrod said sharply.

"Just wondered," Dusty answered. "You got a look on your face. Seems like there's somethin' on your mind."

Jarrod rubbed the back of his neck. "I mentioned that I was thinking about boarding school for the kids."

"How'd Miss Abby take to that notion?"

Jarrod raised an eyebrow. "You don't know Abby Miller very well or you wouldn't have to ask that question. She blew up."

Dusty grinned. "Yeah, I heard Gib call her Firecracker."

"We thought we heard someone on the stairs, but when Abby checked, no one was there, so—" His eyes widened. "What if they heard us talking about sending them away?"

"Might give 'em cause to take matters into their own hands."

"That still doesn't explain why we can't find a trace of them."

"Don't it?"

Jarrod thought for a moment. "Abby's wagon. They hid in the back."

Dusty nodded. "That'd be my guess."

If they were with Abby, then they'd be all right. As the

tension in his gut eased off a bit, Jarrod smiled. "How'd you get to be so smart?"

Dusty chuckled. "If you wasn't so worried, you'da figured it out same's me."

"I'm going after them. Chances are, Abby discovered them and she's on her way back right now."

"True enough," Dusty agreed.

Until he saw with his own eyes that all four kids were safe and sound, Jarrod wouldn't rest.


"If it hadn'ta been for you, she'da never caught us." Tom glared at his younger brother.

Abby bit back a smile as she stared at the two boys in front of the outhouse. Earl Whittemore had given her quite a shock when he'd looked out the freight office window and said, "Didn't know you'd brought those two boys of Jarrod's back with you."

She had raced to his side and seen for herself the two sneaking up the rise to take care of their "business."

"I hadda go, Tom. Lily said I could," Oliver reminded his brother. Then he stuck his thumb in his mouth and wrapped his other arm as far as it would go around Abby's leg. He pressed his little body against her, and she put a hand on his shoulder reassuringly.

"Tell me what's going on. What are you doing here?"

Tom glared stubbornly at her, his mouth a straight line.

"Not talking? Are your sisters still in my wagon?"

Oliver's head snapped up as he looked at her. "How'd you know?"

"How else would we get here, stupid?" Tom said, taking his frustration out on his younger brother.

"Tom, I understand how you feel, but I want you to stop treating Oliver so badly. Sooner or later you'd have had to come out."

"But not before sundown."

"But why—"

Just then the two girls came up the rise from behind the outhouse and stopped short when they saw Abby.

Abby lifted an eyebrow. "So now everyone is present and accounted for."

Katie ran over to her and grabbed the leg Oliver wasn't holding. "You're not mad, are you, Abby?"

"I'm not sure, sweetie. Why don't you tell me what's going on. Does your uncle know where you are?"

Lily shook her head. "He'll probably be glad we're gone. He won't have to worry anymore about what to do with us."

The resentment in her tone got Abby's attention. "What are you talking about?"

"Boarding school. Katie overheard him say it was his last resort."

Now Abby understood. "So you stowed away in the back of my wagon?"

Katie asked, "What does stowed away mean?"

Abby put her arm around the little girl staring up at her. "It means taking a ride without permission."

Katie's eyes widened. "Are we goin' to jail?"

Tom snorted. "'Course not."

"Don't be too sure about that, mister," Abby said, shooting him a look. "What you've done is very serious. Not just to me, but to your uncle. He's probably worried sick about you."

"If he cared enough to worry, why would he send us to boarding school?" Lily asked.

"He hasn't definitely made up his mind about that. And after this stunt, I'm not so sure he isn't right."

Abby stared from one child to the next, but not one of them would meet her gaze. "How did you find out that he was thinking about it?" she asked.

"Katie overheard the two of you talking this morning," Lily explained.

Now Abby understood. That creaking on the stairs had been a blond, curly-haired little eavesdropper. She looked sternly at Katie. The little girl buried her face in Abby's leg. Abby turned the most severe look she could muster on each of the others. "You should have talked to your uncle before running away. He's going to give me more time to find a housekeeper."

"You mean we're stayin' at the ranch?" Tom took two eager steps forward, then seemed to catch himself.

"That's right."

"Hot damn!" he said.

"Tom, watch your language," Lily said.

"You've been spending too much time with Gib Cochran," Abby added.

"Sorry. I'm sorta glad we get to stay. I wanted to see that there baby horse, 'n' all," he said, rubbing his nose. "I mean foal."

Abby squinted into the distance as the glare of the sun descending behind the mountain caught her in the eyes. "Before I take you all home with me, I have one more question."

"Asking questions is what *I* do best," Katie said proudly.

"Indeed it is," Abby said, smiling down at her. "Why was it so important to stay out of sight until sundown?"

Lily shrugged. "That's easy. We had to make sure there wasn't enough time for you to take us back to Uncle Jarrod."

"How did you keep me from finding you in the back of the wagon?"

"That's two questions," Katie corrected.

Lily grinned. "We fell asleep."

"What made you so sure I'd take you rascals in?" Abby asked.

Oliver took his thumb out of his mouth. "'Cuz you love us."

Katie held onto Abby's leg, but leaned back to study her. She tilted her head to the side and asked, "Abby, you got somethin' in your eye?"

Abby sniffed. "No, sweetie. Why?"

"'Cause you're blinkin' and there's water in there," she said, pointing at Abby's eyes. "You cryin'?"

She cleared her throat. "I never cry. Especially over thoughtless children like yourselves. Tomorrow I'm going to take you back to your uncle. It means I'll have to take more time off work. Mr. Whittemore may not like it."

"Who's he?" Lily asked.

"The man I work for. If he doesn't like it, I could lose my job." Abby noticed the four of them exchange a knowing look. What were they up to?

"Are you mad at us, Abby?" Katie asked.

"I should be."

"But you're gonna take us home with ya? Right, Abby?" Oliver asked.

"Right."

"'Member the last time we was here and you took us to that place for fried chicken?" the little boy asked.

Abby suppressed a grin as she nodded. "Would you like to go there again?"

"Yes'm. I'm hungry *and* thirsty."

Abby ruffled his blond hair, then brushed it off his forehead. "Let's get you all cleaned up, then we'll go there."

Jarrod rode into Hollister about an hour after sundown. He was tired and hungry. His temper was frayed real thin.

He left his horse at the livery with orders for a good rubdown and an extra ration of oats. It wasn't smart to push an animal as hard as he had. A healthy mount could mean the difference between living and dying. When he laid eyes on the kids, they might be sorry the ol' roan hadn't dumped him on the trail. With an effort, he reined in his anger. One thing he'd found out today—he didn't like worrying.

He planned to put an end to it real soon. Standing in front of the livery, he stared down the main street of Hollister and wondered where to start looking.

The freight office. Just so happened, it was right next door. With the place all dark, it didn't take him long to figure out no one was there. The next building down was the sheriff's office. Light spilled through the window onto the boardwalk. When Jarrod looked inside, he saw Zach Magruder hunched over his desk with paperwork.

Jarrod opened the door and walked in. "Evenin', Zach."

The sheriff looked surprised, then pleased. "Don't that beat all. Jarrod Blackstone. What the blue blazes are you doin' here in town?"

"Wish I could say it was a social call, Zach. But the fact is, I'm looking for some kids—my nieces and nephews. You seen 'em wandering around?"

"Not wanderin'. Seen 'em with Abby Miller not too long ago over at the Hollister House Restaurant."

"Are they all right?"

Zach laughed. "The way they were puttin' away Henrietta's fried chicken—yeah, I'd say they were doin' just fine."

"Glad to hear it." Relief washed over Jarrod and he let out a long breath.

"Something wrong?" the sheriff asked.

Jarrod paused in the open doorway. "Not yet."

**7**

"*Don't you ever do that again.*" Jarrod stood beside the table in the restaurant and pointed at each of the children in turn.

Abby had never seen him like this. Lines of worry cut his face from nose to mouth. There was no teasing glint in his cold gray eyes. He looked dirty, tired, and angry.

"Take it easy, Jarrod," she said, pushing her chair away from the table. Around them, people had stopped eating and talking. They stared at Jarrod Blackstone.

He turned to her. She'd been wrong about his eyes. They weren't cold at all. Spitting fire was more accurate. "Abby, you stay out of this."

Lily stood and moved between Abby and Jarrod. "Don't blame Abby, Uncle Jarrod. She didn't know anything about this until she found us a little while ago."

"I'm not blaming her. I just want to know what the hell is going on. What do you mean sneaking off like that? I've lost a day's work looking for you. Not to mention Dusty and Slim. And I've been—" He gritted his teeth as he ran his hand through his hair.

Abby put her hands on Lily's shoulders and moved her out of the way. "Jarrod?"

"What?" he asked.

"Just tell them you were worried sick about them. *Then* give them a talking-to they'll never forget."

He sighed and his shoulders relaxed a bit. He stared at her for a moment, his mouth a straight line, then said, "Abby Miller, you're developing an irritating habit of being right."

He turned to the children and opened his arms wide. "Come here," he said gruffly.

Katie and Oliver were the first to reach him, and he scooped them up, one in each arm. Lily put her arms around his middle and hugged him. He smiled at her.

Around them, other diners put down their forks and knives and nodded approvingly as they applauded.

Jarrod grinned. "Sorry to interrupt your supper, folks. Don't pay us any mind. Please go on eating."

He looked back at Tom, who stood within the circle but didn't touch his uncle. "That foal missed you today."

"Did she?" he asked, his eyes lighting up. "I missed her too. She okay?"

"Fine."

Tom tipped his head back to meet his uncle's gaze. "I didn't want to leave the ranch, but Lily said Mama wanted us all to stay together."

Jarrod put the two youngest down. "Finish your dinner."

"Did you miss us, Uncle Jarrod?" Katie asked.

"Yup." The lines appeared again between his eyebrows. "No one's told me yet why you ran off without even a by-your-leave. Dusty and Slim and I have been looking everywhere. Then I get here and you're laughing and talking and having a grand old time—"

"Why don't you have something to eat with us, Jarrod?" Abby said. "You must be hungry. When you're fed and watered, you're bound to be in a better frame of mind."

"There's nothing wrong with my temper," he said sharply.

"I think there is. You've lost it," Abby said.

"Hogwash. A good day's work and a long night's sleep is all I need," he snapped.

Katie put down her fork. "Why are you talkin' so loud, Uncle Jarrod? Is it because you can't find your temper?" she asked.

He sucked in a breath between his teeth. "I have not lost my temper. Is it too much to ask why you all took off the way you did?"

As he glared at Abby, the bell over the restaurant door rang loudly. Everyone turned to look as Gib Cochran and Bea Peters walked in together.

The older man took off his hat, then nodded to people at a table in the corner. Spotting Jarrod and the others, his gray-black brows went up in wonder. Bea noticed the group at the same time and glanced at Gib, surprised. Not any more surprised than Abby was to see the two of them together. She stifled a grin.

The older couple walked over and said hello to the children.

"Howdy, Firecracker," Gib said, nodding to Abby. He looked at Jarrod. "Didn't know you was plannin' t'bring the kids into town."

"I didn't," Jarrod said through clenched teeth.

Oliver ran over to the foreman and grabbed his leg. "We comed all by ourselves."

"Did ya now? And just how did you do that?" Gib asked, giving Bea a curious look.

Katie joined her brother. "Can you guess how we did, Mr. Cochran?" When he shook his head, she said, "We hid in the back of Abby's wagon. Tom didn't think I could be quiet," she went on, wrinkling her nose at her brother. "But I was. We made it all the way to town and Abby never heard us."

"Only because you were asleep," Tom said sharply.

"Children," Abby said in a firm voice that got their attention. "Are you all finished with your dinner?" When four heads nodded, she handed Lily a key and continued, "I want you to go upstairs in the boardinghouse to my room. Do you remember the way?"

"'Course we do. Right, Lil?" Tom asked his older sister. "We're not babies like Oliver."

"I'm not a baby," Oliver said indignantly.

"That's enough. Everyone go upstairs. Your uncle and I need to talk."

Katie pulled on Abby's skirt to get her attention. "Are you gonna find Uncle Jarrod's temper for him?" she asked.

Abby bit back a smile. "Yes. And I need peace and quiet, because it's a very difficult thing to do. Can you go upstairs and be good while I do?"

The little girl's curls bounced as she nodded vigorously. "I'll play with Oliver so he'll be quiet too."

Abby glanced at her older brother. "Tom? Take him to the necessary, please."

The older boy frowned at her. "You can't tell me—"

"Tom," Jarrod said in a tone that allowed no disobedience. "Do as Abby asked."

"Yes, sir."

When they were gone, Abby turned back to Jarrod and breathed a sigh of relief. "Now we can talk."

"We'll join ya," Gib said.

Bea Peters touched his arm. "I don't think we should, Gib. They have some things to discuss regarding the children."

"I'm fond of those young'uns," Gib said. "Maybe—"

Abby could have sworn Bea elbowed him in the ribs. But as smooth as molasses over hotcakes, the older woman said, "We'll just have supper by ourselves so you young people can talk privately."

Just before they turned away, Abby saw her shoot Gib Cochran the look she used to give her students. The one that said, *I know you're not dumb as a post, so why are you acting like it?*

A young boy came out of the kitchen. Abby recognized Joe Schafer, who worked at the restaurant. He started to put the dirty dishes in the bucket he carried.

She touched his arm. "Joe? Would you ask Henrietta to put together a big plate of chicken, mashed potatoes and gravy, and green beans and biscuits, for Mr. Blackstone?"

He glanced up at Jarrod, then back to her. "Sure thing, Miss Abby."

She turned back to Jarrod. "Now sit down, so we can find your temper."

"I haven't lost it," he snapped. But he sat, and Abby took the chair to his right.

Joe made another trip for dirty dishes, and Abby shook her head, still amazed at the pile of plates, forks and knives, napkins, crumbs, and chicken bones. The kids had been starved and hadn't eaten anything all day. They'd been in too big a hurry to conceal themselves in her wagon without being seen.

"You want to know why the children ran away?" Abby caught and held his gaze as she clasped her hands together on the white tablecloth. "They overheard us talking about boarding school. The idea didn't strike their fancy."

"I remembered hearing that creak on the stairs, and figured that's what happened."

"That's what happened, all right. Katie wasn't as sound asleep as I'd thought. She crept downstairs, listened to part of the conversation, and assumed you had already made up your mind."

He took his hat off and rested it on the chair beside him, then pushed his fingers through his dark hair. "Wouldn't you know it would be the one time she didn't ask questions?"

"They jumped the gun."

"Why?"

"Because they don't want to be sent away. You heard what Tom said. Sally wanted them raised together. As much as they pretend not to like each other, they don't want to be separated, and they'll do what they have to so that doesn't happen."

Jarrod looked at her as a thoughtful expression pulled his dark brows together. "They've got Sally's gumption. Sure didn't get it from that no-good she married."

"They've had a rough time. It'll take them a while to feel like they belong."

"Guess I didn't help any with this talk of boarding school. Then coming in here loaded for bear when I saw they were with you and fine as could be."

"They'll understand that you're not mad. That you acted the way you did because you were worried."

"How do you know that's all it was? After all, I can't find my temper."

"Call it a hunch."

One corner of his mouth turned up. Abby knew he wasn't going to let go of his irritation anytime soon. For good reason. He'd probably been half out of his mind with worry all day. She wished she could have prevented him going through that, and searched for a way to make him relax.

She grinned. "Katie thought boarding school is a place you go to learn about boards."

"She's really somethin'." He laughed. "The kids sure have taken to you."

The merriment smoothed away the lines of worry and fatigue, transforming his face. Her heart skipped and fluttered. He was looking at her now in a way that made her uncomfortable, as if to say they weren't the only ones who had taken to her. She tried to think of a safe subject.

"They don't do what I say. At least not all the time. Tom especially."

"I noticed that. I wonder why."

She shrugged. "It doesn't matter. The important thing is that he's really taken to you."

"Thanks to your advice. He's eager to learn. In fact it was because of Tom that we started looking for the kids."

"What do you mean?"

"We got curious, then suspicious when he didn't show up this morning to see the new foal."

"He wasn't happy about it either."

"If I'd known for sure they were with you, I wouldn't have lost my temper," he said with a grin.

She smiled back as his compliment warmed her all over. So much for a safe subject. "There was no way to get word to you, the ranch being so far out and all. I was going to bring the children back in the morning. Those clever little rascals stayed hidden until they knew it would be too late for me to take them home and they'd have to spend the night."

"What did they hope to gain?"

"Time."

"For what?"

"To talk me into keeping them," she said.

"Would you have? Taken them in, I mean?"

She sighed. "I have no right to them. Besides, I'm just as busy as you are. How would I watch over them?"

He studied her. "You care about them. Don't you, Abby?"

She squirmed under his scrutiny, wondering why he was asking this. "Oliver informed me that I love them."

"Do you?"

"I'm awfully fond of them, Jarrod. Who wouldn't be?" Just then the kitchen door swung open and Henrietta Schafer brought a plate piled high with food. "Here ya are, Jarrod. Ain't seen you in a coon's age. Where ya been keepin' yerself?"

She was a small woman, not even five feet tall. Her deep, lisping voice had seemed oddly out of place to Abby when they'd first met. But she'd found that the tiny woman had a heart twice her size. Abby had become terribly fond of her.

Jarrod smiled at the woman, who stood watching him with hands on her hips. "Hello, Hettie."

"No one but you ever calls me that."

"Don't know why. Henrietta's just too big a mouthful for a little bit of a woman like you."

She grinned. "Flatterer."

He nodded toward the kitchen door where Joe had disappeared. "That son of yours sure is getting tall in a hurry. How do you keep him in pants?"

Hettie grinned. "Hasn't been such a hurry. And I'm gonna forget that it's been months since you've been to Hollister and just say, thank you, sir. Joe takes after his daddy, thank the Lord, and will likely hit six feet."

"He's a nice boy, Henrietta," Abby said. "You should be real proud of him."

"I am. And speakin' of young'uns, hear tell you got yourself a houseful, Jarrod. Real sorry to hear about Sally."

"Thanks, Hettie." He scooped a pile of mashed potatoes and gravy into his mouth and swallowed. "They're a handful, that's for sure."

"Especially with you bein' a bachelor 'n' all." Henrietta looked from Abby to Jarrod, then back again, and lifted an eyebrow.

Abby wasn't quite sure what she was trying to say, nevertheless it made her uncomfortable.

Jarrod put his fork down and grabbed a chicken leg. "Abby's helping me find a housekeeper."

"That so?" The other woman looked at her again.

Darned if she didn't feel her cheeks flush warmly. "I'm not having much luck," Abby replied. "Jarrod needs someone right away. You don't happen to know of anyone, do you, Henrietta?"

The other woman glanced at Bea Peters, sitting in the corner with Gib. A strange look flashed across her face and was gone before Abby could assess it.

"Nope, can't say's I do." Then she thoughtfully tapped a finger against her lips. "Wait a minute. Might be I just spoke too soon. Could just be someone here in Hollister can help you out."

"Who?" Abby and Jarrod asked together.

Standing between them, Henrietta placed a hand on each of their shoulders. "Hold your horses, you two. Let me check out the lay of the land first." She looked at Jarrod. "You gonna stay in town tonight?"

He nodded. "The ranch is too far to try and make it back tonight, after dark. Especially with the kids. You got room for all of us here in the boardinghouse?"

The other woman nodded. "We'll make do. Not to worry."

"What are you thinking of, Henrietta?" Abby asked.

"Since you're in town anyways, you can meet the person I'm thinkin' of."

Abby smiled at Jarrod. "That would be wonderful. Don't you think?"

He nodded. "If the kids approve, I can take her back with me. Save you a trip back out to the ranch."

Abby nodded, but her smile faded as a vague sense of disappointment stole over her. That's what she wanted, wasn't it? To stay as far away from Jarrod Blackstone as she could? Especially after the way he'd kissed her. Had it really been only fourteen hours ago? When she thought about his mouth against her own, her skin felt hot and her breath caught.

A very good reason to be happy that he was saving her a trip out to his ranch. Henrietta Schafer was a good judge of people. If she had someone in mind for his housekeeper, there was a better than even chance that person would work out fine. As hard as she tried to make it otherwise, that thought didn't make her want to run down the main street of Hollister shouting "Yahoo."

This time tomorrow, all her problems with Jarrod Blackstone would be over.

"Bea Peters, you want to tell me what in tarnation you got up your sleeve?" Henrietta put down her coffee cup.

The two women sat at the table in the restaurant kitchen. Bea smiled at her friend, then took a sip of the strong black brew. She liked drawing out the suspense. It wasn't often she knew something Henrietta didn't, and God help her, she wanted to enjoy this moment as long as she could. "I don't want to say too much, Hen. You know how hard it is for you to keep secrets."

The smaller woman slapped her hand on the oak table and snapped, "What makes you say that?"

"Everyone in town knows it's true. You're better than the *Hollister Gazette* for spreading news."

Henrietta sniffed scornfully. "It's nothing more than idle conversation. What am I supposed to do with my customers? A body's got to make 'em feel welcome. Gotta chat some."

"I'm merely saying you should think before you speak."

"All right. I promise. Now what are you up to?"

Bea smiled. "Jarrod Blackstone's children want Abby to be the housekeeper. I'm giving them a helping hand."

"You know as well as I do that Abby has bigger fish to fry."

"That's what she thinks. I think she shouldn't spit in the eye of fate."

Henrietta traced the handle on her cup. "Are we talkin' about something besides a new job for Abby? Somethin' to take her mind off that foolish notion she's got about goin' t'find her pa and live with him?"

"Could be."

"You shouldn't meddle in things, Bea. They have a way of comin' back on a body."

"People who live in log houses should be careful with fire, Hen. You're enjoying this as much as I am."

"That's not true," Hen grumbled. "I can't enjoy it as much as you because you won't tell me exactly what's goin' on."

Bea knew she looked like the cat licking cream from her whiskers. But she had worked too hard to ruin things now by giving Hen too much information. "You just do as I told you tomorrow, and you'll see what I've got in mind."

Jarrod stared across the boardinghouse hallway that separated him from Abby. It was dim where they stood. The only light came from lanterns mounted on the walls at either end. Their rooms were in the center of the hall.

"Are you sure you don't mind having Lily and Katie with you tonight?" he asked.

She shook her head. "The boys wanted to stay with you. And neither room is big enough for all of them. Seems splitting up for the night is best."

"I hate to impose—"

"Forget it. I love having them. Besides, you paid for dinner. The least I can do is keep the girls."

She ran her tongue over her full bottom lip, reminding Jarrod how sweet it had felt to kiss her. His heart quickened, sending blood to points south. He'd tried to fight his involuntary reaction. But try as he might, the sight, sound, smell, and touch of her seemed to bring him alive again. He had thought he was dead inside. He wanted to be; it was easier to feel nothing.

Unfortunately, the steady throbbing between his legs reminded him painfully that parts of him were still living. The undeniable fact was he wanted to kiss her again.

"If you need anything during the night. . . " he said, letting the sentence hang.

She lifted her gaze to his and her eyes widened as she studied him. She took a step back, pressing herself against her door.

Stupid bastard, Jarrod thought. She saw what he was thinking and didn't want any part of him. He had to learn to hide his feelings better. He had gotten good at it with Dulcy. Now he was out of practice. Soon it wouldn't matter. When he had his housekeeper, he wouldn't see Abby Miller, at least not like this.

He sighed and glanced down the hall at the light, then back to her. "If Katie bothers you and you want me to sit with her, just let me know."

"I'm sure she won't. Just get some rest. So you can find your temper," she said, smiling.

"Yeah. I guess I've got to make it up to them."

"No. Just be honest. You were worried. You got angry. Because you care."

"You think they'll understand that?"

She lifted her brows in thought. "Probably. If not, buy them a licorice whip."

He grinned. "So you *do* think I have something to make up to them."

"No. I just think the way to their hearts is through candy."

"What about the way to your heart?"

She looked down and took a big breath. "I already told you I'm not looking for that."

"I thought every woman was looking for that."

"Not this one." She met his gaze then. "I think it's time we said good night."

He nodded. "'Night, Abby. Don't let the bedbugs bite."

"Jarrod," she said, turning the knob. She glanced back at him. "Whatever you do, don't say that to Oliver."

He grinned. "I usually only make a mistake once."

She went into her room and he stared at the closed door.

If he let her, Abby Miller could tempt him to make another mistake. He wouldn't let her.

The following morning, Abby got the girls ready and Jarrod did the same with the boys. Right after breakfast, Henrietta Schafer herded them into her cramped parlor. A gold brocade sofa and two matching wing-back chairs stood in the center of the room with various oak tables and accent pieces scattered throughout. She had been a good customer to the freight company.

In front of the window that looked out on Main Street, all four of the children stood next to Abby, boys on her right, girls on her left. The two youngest each clung to her legs on their respective side. Jarrod was beside Tom, with his hand on the youngster's shoulder. They all watched the young woman Henrietta had arranged for them to meet. Abby thought they seemed nervous, which was surprising. They had gone through this procedure enough times that she would expect it to be easy for them.

The small woman made introductions. "Children, Abby, Jarrod, this is Nita Gibson. She's Annie Shemanski's cousin, here from Kansas to visit."

Jarrod nodded politely. "A pleasure to meet you, ma'am."

"Likewise."

Abby guessed that Nita Gibson was in her early twenties. She was slim, blond, had big brown eyes, and was strikingly pretty. At least Abby thought so. She glanced at Jarrod and wanted to wipe the appreciative male smile off his face.

She turned her gaze on the newcomer and saw her taking Jarrod's measure as she batted the longest eyelashes Abby had ever seen on a body, man or woman. Apparently, Kansas ladies were susceptible to the Blackstone charm too.

Nita Gibson was most definitely a lady, with her full dark green linen skirt, crisp white blouse trimmed with lace at neck and wrists, and a fashionable matching hat that dipped low on her smooth forehead, making her eyes look huge. She was a stunner, and Abby felt ill-dressed, plain, and dowdy by comparison.

"So, Mr. Blackstone, I understand you're looking for a housekeeper?" Nita asked.

"Yes, ma'am. My sister passed away and I have her four youngsters to care for."

"I find it hard to believe a man like you isn't married," she said.

"I was."

Nita's gloved hand fluttered between them for a moment, then she place it on her chest, flustered. "Your wife passed away. I'm sorry. No one told me. I didn't mean to bring up painful memories."

Jarrod shook his head. "No, ma'am. She's still alive, far as I know. Things just didn't work out."

"I've got chores to do in the kitchen," Henrietta said. "Why don't you folks sit down and visit awhile. Take all the time you need."

"Thanks, Hettie," Jarrod said. "Appreciate you introducing us to Miss Gibson."

"Call me Nita, please."

Abby called after the smaller woman, "I'll see you later, Henrietta."

Jarrod sat beside the woman on the sofa. "So, Nita, how long are you planning to stay in Hollister?"

"Permanently. If I can find work."

Or a husband, Abby silently added.

Lily cleared her throat. "It must be a lot different than Kansas."

Nita laughed. "Indeed it is."

"Are you sure you'll like it enough to stay on?" Abby asked. "After all, it wouldn't be good for the children to get used to you, then have you up and leave."

The blond toyed with the wisp of hair near her cheek as

she looked at Jarrod. "I'd never do that to them. Children need stability, especially after their loss. My condolences to you, Mr. Blackstone."

"Call me Jarrod."

"Thank you, Jarrod," she answered shyly.

Abby snapped a look at him. She had known him for years before he got that friendly with her. He'd just met this woman, and invited her to use his given name. He'd done the same with Bea. Only that hadn't bothered her. She didn't want to look too closely at why it did with *Miss* Nita Gibson.

Abby released a big sigh. "Miss Gibson—"

"Please call me Nita. And if I may call you Abby?"

Abby nodded grudgingly. "The ranch is pretty far from town."

The woman laughed, a sweet, musical sound that grated on Abby's nerves. "I'm a farm girl. Where I come from, the nearest town is several hours away. That's nothing new for me."

"That's good," Jarrod said, standing. "Why don't you spend a little time getting acquainted with the children?"

"I'd like that. How about you?" she asked, looking at the four youngsters.

They all nodded.

Jarrod took Abby's elbow. "C'mon with me to the mercantile. I'll buy you a licorice whip."

They walked out onto the boardwalk, and the spring sunshine warmed Abby's shoulders. Too bad it couldn't reach the part inside her that was chilled, she thought. She pulled her hat down to shade her eyes. Beside her, Jarrod stared thoughtfully at the building where the children were.

"What did you think of her?" he asked.

"She seems like a lovely woman." As much as Abby wanted to say otherwise, she couldn't.

"I thought so too. Wonder if she can read and write," he mused.

"When you grow up on a farm that far from town, it's not likely there was a teacher anyplace nearby."

"Hmm. From the way she talks, she seems genteel and I'd guess she's had some book learning. If not, I could always do some lessons with the kids in the evenings."

Abby's eyes narrowed on him. "What about all the work you have on the ranch?"

"Can't do it after dark anyway."

"I thought you were too tired. All of a sudden you've got the time and the energy?"

"If I don't have to get up with Katie during the night, I'll have plenty of energy."

Abby wanted to ask him plenty of energy for what, but held her tongue. "Katie slept straight through last night," she said defensively.

"Good. Maybe she's beginning to get more comfortable here."

"At least with me." Abby folded her arms over her chest and looked at him.

A half smile lifted one corner of his mouth as he studied her. "Something eating you, Abby?"

"'Course not," she said, a little too quickly.

"I thought you said you liked Nita."

"For all I know of her, I do."

"You don't seem very enthusiastic about her."

Abby shrugged. "You're excited enough for the both of us."

With a knuckle, he pushed his hat back and stared down at her, hands on his hips. His eyes sparkled with amusement. "I'll be damned," he said, shaking his head.

"What? Why?"

"You're jealous."

She snorted. "You're crazy."

"Nope. You're jealous of Nita Gibson. I'm flattered."

"That's the dumbest thing I ever heard."

"Then what's bothering you, Abby? There's not one good reason I can see not to hire her. Here and now," he said.

She put her hands on her hips and glared at him. "Can't you tell when a female has something on her mind besides a job?"

"You think she's dishonest?" he asked. But Abby saw the look in his eyes and knew he was baiting her. She *was* jealous, and the fact that he knew it irritated her.

"No, I don't think she's dishonest," she snapped. "And why in the world you'd think I care whether or not the two of you make cow eyes at each other is beyond me."

"Then you have some doubts about her. I'd like to hear them. Not that you've ever been shy before about telling me what you think."

"I don't know," she said, glancing over her shoulder at the boardinghouse behind them. Abby couldn't help wishing that the kids had liked Bea Peters and she was already working for him. "Nita just seemed too prim and prissy to take care of four children. Even if she did grow up on a farm."

"How do you think the kids took to her?"

Probably the way Jarrod had, like ducks to water, Abby thought. But she said, "I couldn't really tell. They were pretty quiet. You never said what you thought of her."

"She seemed all right to me," he said. A typical male understatement, given the way his eyes lit up at the sight of her. "Guess we'll just have to wait and see how the kids feel."

# 8

*Henrietta shot a glare* at Bea Peters as they shared a piece of fresh corn bread in the boardinghouse kitchen. "Nita Gibson is a smart, sweet, lovely girl. How did you know those kids wouldn't take to her?"

Bea smiled that know-it-all look that made Henrietta so mad she could spit. "They have already decided to reject anyone but Abby. I saw that right away when I went out to the ranch."

"So why put Nita through that?"

Bea laughed. "She knew all about it ahead of time and was delighted to play along."

"How come you didn't see fit to tell me?" Henrietta was truly affronted now. Bea could tell a total stranger what was going on, but not her?

"You and Jarrod are thick as thieves. I know you, Hen. You're susceptible to his, shall we say, exceptional good looks."

"And you're not?" the smaller woman shot back, not bothering to deny it.

"I can't imagine a woman still able to draw a breath not being susceptible. But since I'm old enough to be his"—she hesitated a moment—"very attractive older sister, I suppose I'm no exception."

Henrietta put her chin in her palm as she picked at the corn bread on her plate. "I've always thought if I were a foot taller—"

"And twenty years younger—"

"That too." She heaved a big sigh. "My Clyde's been gone ten years now. That's a long time to warm a bed by yourself."

"Neither one of us is suitable marriage material for Jarrod Blackstone. We are straying from the topic, Hen," Bea said in her best teacher's voice.

"You're right. So the kids have decided ahead of time not to like anyone they meet?"

"Precisely."

"How are they gonna convince Jarrod to hire Abby?"

"Just about now, Lily is going to suggest it to him."

"And how is he gonna convince Abby to take the job?"

Bea smiled. "I've put the word out. No one in Hollister will take that job. Desperation gives a man a silver tongue."

"I hope you're right, Bea." Henrietta shook her head. "Abby Miller is as stubborn as they come."

Jarrod stared at the four children sitting on the sofa in Hettie's parlor. "What did you do to make her turn down the job?"

"She didn't take it?" Lily asked eagerly. Then she demurely folded her hands in her lap. "We didn't do anything to her. Maybe she doesn't like boys."

"How can you know that?" he asked.

"Ask Tom and Oliver. They're the ones who said it."

Jarrod turned his gaze on his nephews. "Well?"

Tom glanced at Oliver and rolled his eyes when his younger brother popped his thumb in his mouth. He concluded that made him the spokesman for both of them.

"It's hard t'explain, Uncle Jarrod," Tom said, squirming as he put his hands between his knees.

"Try," Jarrod said through gritted teeth.

"It's more of a feelin' me 'n' Oliver got."

"What kind of feeling?"

"The way she was dressed 'n' all, so fine and ladylike. We just sorta think she don't have any use for boys. Bet she doesn't know nothin' about horses."

"She could learn," Jarrod said. "Horses and boys aren't so different. I could talk to her again and try to change her mind. Girls? What about you? Do you think you'd feel comfortable with her?" he asked, looking at Katie.

Her forehead wrinkled thoughtfully before she shook her head.

"What do *you* think is wrong with her?"

"She snorts when she laughs."

Jarrod let out a long steadying breath. He was trying real hard not to lose his temper again. "I thought she had a very nice laugh."

"You weren't here the whole time." Katie stuck her bottom lip out. She hadn't missed the exasperation in his tone.

He ran his hand through his hair. "You have met three very suitable ladies. I don't understand what the problem is."

"There's no problem, Uncle Jarrod." Lily looked at him calmly. "At least nothing that Abby couldn't handle."

Jarrod walked into the Hollister Freight office and looked around. Earl Whittemore sat behind a paper-cluttered desk in the corner of the room. Barrels, wooden crates, and odds and ends were scattered around the rest of the space.

"Earl?"

The company owner, a big man with a belly hanging over the waistband of his pants, looked up. "Well I'll be. Jarrod Blackstone. What brings you in here? Don't recollect an order for you."

Jarrod shook his head. "I'm not expecting anything. I came to see Abby. Is she here?"

The other man gestured toward the rear of the building. "Out back. She took it into her head that the storage shed needed straightening. I never argue with Abby when she makes up her mind about somethin'."

"Is there ever a good time to argue with Abby?"

Earl laughed and his belly shook like hotcake batter slapped on the griddle. With his thumb and forefinger he smoothed his thick mustache over his lip and down the sides of his mouth. "Got a point there, Jarrod. Still, I can't hardly complain. Abby's the best worker I ever had."

"She's conscientious and stubborn. I'll give her that."

"What'd you want to see her about?"

"Come to offer her a job."

"The hell you say." Earl looked mighty curious. "Doing what?"

"Housekeeper."

Earl nodded. "Heard tell Sally passed on and y'got her kids with ya. Sorry t'hear that, Jarrod. I can see why you need some help. But Abby?" He shook his head skeptically.

"It's a long story, Earl. But I aim to do my best to take Abby away from you."

"I don't think ya can. But you're welcome t'try." The big man grinned good-naturedly.

"Thanks."

Jarrod opened the back door. He spotted Abby instantly, just a few feet away, standing in the shade of the shed. Head tipped back, she drank from a dipper and water trickled down, spotting her cotton shirt. Where moisture soaked in, the material was almost transparent. A droplet clung to her full bottom lip and she licked it away.

Jarrod watched her, holding his breath. He'd never seen any woman quite so stirring in his whole life. Not even Dulcy.

Abby *was* a firecracker.

There was something warm, wild, and wanton about her, tempered with a genuine sweetness. The kids sensed it. That's why they took to her. A part of him had taken to her too. That made it all the harder to ask her what he had to. As much as he wanted to turn tail and head in the opposite direction, he didn't see as he had much choice.

He closed the door and her head snapped around.

She seemed surprised to see him. "Jarrod."

"Hello, Abby." His voice sounded huskier than usual, even to him.

"Is something wrong with one of the children?"

"Why would you think that?"

"Can't think of any other reason you'd come looking for me."

"They're fine. But I am here on account of them."

"What is it?" she asked.

"I'd like to offer you the job of housekeeper. Again."

"But I already told you why I—" Comprehension dawned in her eyes. "Nita Gibson didn't work out."

"That's right. The kids asked for you again."

She smiled, pleased. "Really?"

"Really." He rubbed the back of his neck.

"What was wrong with Nita?" She couldn't quite hide the pleased expression on her face.

"She turned the job down flat. But the kids found fault with her. They said she doesn't like boys, probably doesn't know a thing about horses, and she snorts when she laughs."

Abby laughed, and the sound was cheerful, contagious. Jarrod chuckled along with her.

She wiped her eyes, then turned serious. "There's only one choice, Jarrod. I think you should try Bea Peters again."

"I tried. She turned me down."

"Why?"

"Said she'd taken a job in the boardinghouse." He shook his head. "Everyone says the same thing. Four kids are a handful."

Abby put her hands on her hips as her eyes narrowed. "I just don't understand. There's nothing wrong with those children. They're high-spirited, normal kids."

"Maybe we'd have saved ourselves a lot of time and trouble if we'd just listened when Lily said you'd be perfect."

She shook her head. "I can't work for you, Jarrod."

"I know it's not on account of the kids."

"Of course not. My reasons haven't changed. I have my job here in town."

"I pay well," he argued, then caught himself. Getting Abby mad was the fastest way to make her dig her heels in. He was tired and discouraged, desperate for help. He needed Abby.

"It's not enough. I told you I help out with my brother's schooling."

"I know, but—"

"In addition to the freight office, I sometimes get work in the boardinghouse, and the mercantile. Sometimes even in the Watering Hole."

"The saloon?" His voice rose a notch as outrage set in.

She nodded. "Just cleaning up. And only if I really need the money."

He didn't like the idea of her working there at all, not for any amount of money. The idea of her anywhere near those drunken cowboys with wandering hands made him mad as hell. "That's no place for you."

"Who do you think you are, telling me where I can or cannot earn a decent wage?"

"The saloon isn't fit for a woman. You'd be better off on the ranch. I'll pay you more than you're making here in town."

His hopes died when she stubbornly shook her head and he saw the angry glint in her eyes. "I don't think so, Jarrod."

"Then I guess my only alternative is to check into boarding schools."

She sniffed. "You won't send those kids away."

"How do you know?"

"The look on your face when you saw them with me in the restaurant last night."

"What does that have to do with anything?"

"You were worried sick. I think that showed you how much you care about them. It's a good bluff, but there's no way on God's green earth you're going to send them away."

He hated that she was right. Again. He threw up his hands. "Okay. You win. Boarding school is out of the question. Won't you reconsider?"

"There's no way I can work for you."

He frowned. "What aren't you telling me? Spit it out."

She looked down at her boots for a moment, then met his gaze. "Have you thought about the gossip? A man and woman living under the same roof without benefit of vows? What would folks say?"

"I'd stay in the bunkhouse. Besides, since when are you so concerned about what folks say?" He decided to toss her a challenge. "Nita Gibson was willing to risk it."

Her mouth thinned. "So hire her."

He moved beside her, near enough to see the dark blue ring around the pupil of her eyes, close enough to feel the warmth of her skin and smell the womanly scent of her.

"Dammit, Abby, the kids don't want her. They want you. And so do I." He cleared his throat. "I mean, because I know how much you care about them."

"No." She shook her head and backed up a step as the pulse in her throat fluttered. "It's not that simple. Here in town there are more opportunities for me to earn money. The ranch is just too far from everything."

She wasn't the first woman to tell him that, he thought bitterly. He should have known. Her life was in town; the ranch was too isolated. He nodded grimly and backed away.

"I'm sorry, Jarrod."

"Forget it. I won't bother you again."

"You didn't bother me."

"Good-bye, Abby. I'm taking the kids back to the ranch." He turned and started down the alley between the freight company and the mercantile.

"Jarrod, wait—"

He didn't stop or look back.

Abby sat on her bed in the boardinghouse. It was way past dinnertime, but she wasn't hungry. The sun had set several hours before, but she didn't light the lantern on the bedside table. She just stared out her open window as the curtains moved in the cool breeze drifting through.

Tears lurked dangerously close behind her aching eyes. Jarrod had hired a wagon and left Hollister with the children.

She had waved to them on their way out of town, but only Katie waved back.

After finishing work, she'd gone straight to her room. She had done the right thing. Turning down his offer was best for everyone, especially the children. She just hadn't realized how much saying no would hurt.

A knock sounded on her door. She didn't want to talk to anyone, so she kept quiet.

There was another knock, louder this time. "Abby, we know you're in there."

We? The voice belonged to Henrietta, but who was with her?

"Abby?" That was Bea Peters. "Let us in, child. We want to talk to you."

Abby kept quiet, hoping they would go away. A person was entitled to a little privacy. Several moments passed and she thought she heard the sound of retreating footsteps. She sat up straighter, listening carefully.

"Abigail Miller, you open this door right now." Bea Peters's stern voice came through the wood. Probably carried out onto Main Street too, Abby thought. "Quit pouting and open this door. If you don't, we'll shout through it, loud enough for everyone to hear."

Pouting? She did *not* pout!

Abby bounced off the bed and unlocked the door. "I'm not in the mood to talk right now." She looked up at Bea, then down at Henrietta. "Would you mind leaving me alone?"

"Yes, we would mind." Bea brushed past her into the room and went straight to the lantern. She lit the wick, then dropped the glass chimney to protect the flame and send light dancing through the room.

Abby blinked at the brightness. "Then say what's on your mind. I'm tired. I want to get some sleep."

"It doesn't take a genius to see that you're upset."

Henrietta stepped into the room. "You didn't come down for supper. Never known you to miss a meal."

"What's wrong, Abby?" Bea asked.

"You tell me. You seem to know what's going on around here."

"Don't you take that tone with me, young lady," Bea huffed. "Obviously you're annoyed with me. Stop acting like a spoiled child and tell me what's wrong."

Abby put her hands on her hips. "All right. I'm angry because you've been meddling in my life."

"You know about the children's plan?"

She glared at the older woman. "They had some help, Bea. Why didn't you tell me what they were up to?"

"It's complicated," she said.

"You let me walk all over this town, talking to everyone I could think of, knowing that those children wouldn't approve of anyone."

"They're very fond of you, my dear," Bea said kindly. "Did Jarrod ask you to take the job?"

"Yes. I had to turn him down."

Henrietta sighed loudly. "I don't understand you, Abby. Fine-lookin' man like that offers you a good job and you turn him down flat."

Bea pushed the spectacles up on her nose. "That's why the children and I came up with this plot in the first place. They wanted you and were prepared to do anything to get you. I had my own reasons for helping."

"How would it help if no one took the job?" Abby asked.

"We decided if Jarrod found out he couldn't get anyone else, he would ask you and you would say yes."

"And you were in on this." She looked from one to the other. "You two are unbelievable."

"What are you talkin' about?" Henrietta asked.

Abby sighed. "I can't understand how you let that man turn your heads, just because his looks—"

"Wouldn't strip paint from the side of a barn?" Henrietta offered helpfully.

"There!" Abby pointed at her. "You can't see anything but—"

"The way he fills out a pair of jeans?" Bea said, her eyes twinkling.

"I'm shocked at both of you," Abby said, but now she was having trouble staying mad at these two man-hungry meddlers.

Bea stared sternly at her. "Abigail Miller, you look me straight in the eye and tell me you aren't the least bit attracted to Jarrod Blackstone." She wagged her finger. "Don't you fib, young lady. I could always tell when you were fibbing."

"Well. . ."

Henrietta grinned. "Tell me when you're around him your skin doesn't feel hot. Haven't you ever felt that way?"

"Yes," Abby admitted. "But I just figured it was the start of a bad case of poison oak."

"You're fibbing," Bea said.

Abby threw her hands up in the air. "All right. I think he's nice."

"Nice?" Henrietta asked. "Earl Whittemore is nice, but he wouldn't be my first choice for a buggy ride in the moonlight. But Jarrod . . ." She smiled.

"All right. You win. I did notice that he's not hard on the eyes. But I still can't accept the job."

Bea's eyes narrowed. "It's precisely because you're attracted to him that you won't take it. Isn't that right, Abby?"

"Partly, I guess. But you both know I have plans. It wouldn't be fair to him, or the kids, for me to take the job. It would be dishonest, and they've been through too much for me to do that to them."

Bea sighed. "When are you going to give up this foolish notion about finding your father? You're not getting any younger, Abby. It's time to get on with your life."

"It's not foolish. Why, just last month I got a letter from him."

"And how long has it been since the one before that?" Henrietta asked.

"A year. Maybe a year and a half," Abby guessed.

"It's been at least two and you know it."

Abby winced. She didn't know anyone else had noticed.

What she didn't tell them was that she'd been just about ready to give up. That last letter had renewed her determination to find him.

"Does he have an address yet?" Bea asked.

"No. It was from San Francisco, a post office box. He said he's still moving around and that's the best way to contact him. He always checks his mail when he's in town. He said he thinks this new job will work out. He's planning to save some money. That means he's putting down roots. When he does, we can be together again."

"He hasn't asked you to join him?" Bea asked.

Abby looked down. "Not yet. But he will. Things are looking up for him."

"Child, I remember the day after he left you. You walked into my school and I knew there was something wrong. You kept saying over and over that he would come back. It's been thirteen years. You have to face the fact that he's gone for good."

"Bea's right," Henrietta said. "It's time to put that behind you."

Abby knew they meant well, but that didn't stop the anger that welled up inside her and spilled over. "It's none of your business. Either of you," she said, glaring at them.

Bea huffed. "I'm an old woman who cares about you."

"Me too, child." Henrietta met Abby's gaze. "I mean that it's my business because I care. Not that I'm old."

Bea glared at the other woman. "What Hen is trying to say is that we'll meddle whenever necessary, if we think it's for your own good."

It was obvious that she couldn't stop them, and Abby let go of her irritation. "It's over. Let's forget about it."

Henrietta smiled. "You must be starved. Why don't you come down to the kitchen and I'll fix you a plate of stew. I think there's some biscuits left over too. 'Less Joe got into 'em. I swear that boy never fills up."

Abby's mouth watered at the mention of food. Henrietta made the best stew in the whole world.

"All right. I'll come down." She pointed a finger at each

of them. "I want a promise from you. No more interfering. Deal?"

"Absolutely," Bea said.

Henrietta nodded.

"Are you looking for your temper again, Uncle Jarrod?" Katie stood on the other side of the tub, resting her elbows on the brass rim as she regarded him solemnly.

"No, Katie. I'm not ready to look for it yet."

Oliver stuck a soapy thumb in his mouth. He was in the bubble-filled tub. It struck Jarrod that he might as well have been in there with Oliver. He was wet from the waist up after two hair washings and one body scrubbing. He was getting ready for the second.

Oliver had taken it into his head to be a cowboy. He had wanted to help them with the branding, like Tom, and everyone had ignored him. He decided he'd just do it his way. After rustling around in the barn, he'd proceeded to brand everything in sight that he could get his hands on. With white paint.

It was in the corral and on the fence, the chickens, the horses in the barn. He was damn lucky one of the animals hadn't hurt him. The stuff was everywhere, including Oliver. In his hair, on his face, hands, and arms, his clothes. Fortunately, he hadn't gotten to the house before Jarrod noticed what he was up to.

It had been two weeks since Abby had refused his job offer. He hadn't had a decent night's sleep since he'd followed the kids to Hollister. He had to do the work of two men during the day, then take care of the kids at night. There weren't enough hours in the day to do what needed doing when things went smoothly. Now this, he thought, slamming the sponge into the soapy water. Both children jumped and their eyes grew wide.

He had definitely lost his temper. And he wasn't ready to look for it.

"Katie, where's Lily?" he asked.

The little girl shrugged. "I dunno."

"Look for her. I need her help." When the little girl hesitated, he added, "Please."

"I'll help, Uncle Jarrod."

"You're not quite big enough for this job. You can help me by fetching Lily. Will you see if you can find her?"

She nodded and her blond curls bounced around her head. "I'll be back."

Jarrod looked down at Oliver. His hair was wet and slicked back. He'd soaped it twice and there was still white paint visible in the wet, dark blond strands. It might just have to grow out, he thought grimly.

Since Jarrod had discovered Oliver branding the side of the barn and hollered for him to stop, the boy hadn't looked at him. After seeing the far-reaching effects of Oliver's endeavor, Jarrod hadn't trusted himself to speak. He was beginning to cool off now.

He plucked the sponge floating in the murky water. After soaping it good, he said, "Oliver, you have to take your thumb out of your mouth so I can wash your arm."

He did, but continued to look down.

The one thing Jarrod hated about finding his temper was facing the results of his behavior after he'd lost it. He didn't worry about it with Gib and the hired hands. It was part of the job, went with the territory. But the kids were a horse of a different color. He had a right and a responsibility to teach the kids right from wrong, to show them when they'd done something bad. But how the hell did he smooth things over without undoing the lesson?

He sure as hell couldn't do it if he didn't say something to the boy. "Oliver, do you know why I wouldn't let you help with the branding?"

He shook his head.

"Did you see the fire, and how the irons in it turned red-hot?" Oliver nodded, and he continued. "If you don't know what you're doing, those can hurt you real bad. Gib, Dusty, Slim, and I have all been doing that for a lot of years. We work together. We know how to do the job without getting hurt. Do you understand what I'm saying?"

The boy shook his head again.

Jarrod sighed, then drew the soapy sponge over the child's chest. He was pleased to note that he'd filled out a lot since his arrival. At least something was going right.

"What don't you understand?" He waited, but Oliver wouldn't look up. "Are you not talking because I yelled at you?"

He nodded.

"Are you afraid of me, Oliver?" Negative shake. Well, that was something. "Did I hurt your feelings?" A nod. Now they were making some progress. "Because I yelled at you?" He shook his head. Jarrod's shoulders slumped. "Oliver, I'm sorry I yelled. I'm sorry your feelings are hurt. But you're gonna have to talk to me so we can work this out."

The child scratched his nose but didn't look up.

"I can't guess what you're thinking. You gotta tell me straight out, son." Jarrod touched the boy's chin with his finger, nudging it up until their gazes met. "What's wrong?"

Oliver's chin quivered. "Tom was helpin'."

"Not with the branding. Tom was doing what I told him to do, watching and staying out of the way."

"I saw him pick up one of them metal things."

"That was a brand and it wasn't hot. I asked him to fetch it for Dusty."

"Oh."

"Do you know why I got so mad, Oliver?"

"Because I branded the horses in the barn?"

That's when Jarrod had hollered. "It wasn't because you painted them. That will grow out and go away. It won't harm the horses any. But you went in their stalls. If you had scared them, they might've kicked you, or bitten you." He stopped for a moment, taking a deep breath. "You could've been hurt. Or worse."

A spark of interest brightened Oliver's eyes. "Were you worried?"

"Hell—I mean, heck yeah, I was worried."

"Okay, then." He smiled.

Jarrod blinked. "Okay?"

Oliver nodded, spreading a few drops of water. "Abby s'plained it to us. She said you get mad when you're worried about us, 'cuz you love us. She said if you didn't love us, you wouldn't get mad. So it's okay."

"I see."

As easy as that, Jarrod thought. All he'd done was talk to the youngster, man to man. He grinned. Taking care of the kids wasn't so hard. If he could be at the house more, he wouldn't need a housekeeper to look after them.

According to Oliver, Abby had explained things to him. She had an answer for everything. Unfortunately, the answer she'd given to his job offer wasn't the one he'd wanted. If she had been there today. . .

"Uncle Jarrod?" That was Katie. She sounded upset. The back door banged open and hit the wall as she came running inside. She ran into the bathing chamber. "Uncle Jarrod?"

"What's wrong? Did you find Lily?"

She nodded. Worry darkened her green eyes. "She's cryin'."

"Is she hurt?"

"I dunno."

"Why is she crying?"

"She said there's blood." Her lip trembled. "She says she's dying. I don't want Lily to die like Mama."

# 9

Jarrod pulled *Oliver out of* the tub and wrapped a towel around him. He went down on one knee in front of Katie and gripped her upper arms. "Where's Lily?"

The little girl sniffled. "By the swing. Behind the tree."

"You stay with Oliver. Dry him off and help him get dressed."

"Is Lily gonna die, Uncle Jarrod?"

"No." He forced a smile. "Be a big girl and help your brother."

"Don't need any help," Oliver said, then poked his thumb back in his mouth.

"You two stay out of trouble. I'm going to find Lily and see what's the matter."

"Yes, sir," Katie said.

Jarrod walked out the back door and down the steps. The swing wavered slightly in the breeze. Just beyond it he saw a small bit of Lily's calico skirt peeking out from behind the thick, gnarled trunk of an oak.

"Lily, what's wrong?" he asked, moving beside her.

She pulled her knees up to her chest, wrapping her arms around her legs. Bending her head forward, she refused to look at him. Her shoulders shook and gasping sobs echoed beneath the canopy of trees.

Jarrod hunkered down beside her, wanting to make it better. "Katie said you're bleeding. Honey, you need to tell me where so I can help you."

She shook her head. He couldn't see her face, but her neck was red. If only Abby were here. She never seemed to lose patience.

Frustrated and annoyed, he gripped her shoulders. "Dammit, Lily. Look at me."

She lifted her tear-streaked face and turned red-rimmed eyes up to his. Except for her blotchy cheeks, she looked all right to him. "I'm dying, Uncle Jarrod."

He quickly scanned her from head to toe. She looked fine, at least what he could see of her. "Don't be silly."

A fresh batch of tears filled her green eyes. She started to say something, then shut her mouth.

"Lily, you have to talk to me. If you don't, how can I help you?"

"You can't. No one can. I'm dying. Just like Mama."

Jarrod couldn't believe that was true. He couldn't detect any blood on her clothes or her skin. If she was bleeding, it was someplace he couldn't see. Someplace private. A light dawned in his thick male brain.

"Lily, I have to ask you something. Was the blood on your drawers? Between your legs?" He forced a calmness to his voice.

Lily gasped, turned bright red, and buried her face against her upraised knees.

"I'll take that as a yes." He let out a long breath as he looked up at the interconnecting branches of the oaks above him. He searched for the words to explain to her what was happening to her body. "Honey, did your mama tell you about what happens to a girl when she becomes a woman?"

"I'm not gonna live long enough to become a woman." Her words were muffled and unsteady.

"You're not dying. I swear."

She was silent for a moment, then tipped her head to the side as she stared at him through one eye. "How do you know?"

"Have you had your monthly?" Of course she hasn't, you knothead, he told himself. If she had, she wouldn't be hysterical now. He just didn't know how else to start this conversation. If he had ever doubted before, this just proved once again how much he needed Abby.

"What's that?"

"When a girl becomes a woman, her body prepares to have babies." Oh, Lord. This was a can of worms he didn't want to open in the worst way. "When she's married, of course."

"I don't understand." She was looking at him straight on now.

"That's because I'm not telling it real well. Don't you worry, though." He took a deep breath. "There's nothing wrong with you that's not supposed to be happening."

Never in his born days had he ever thought to have a conversation like this.

"What's a monthly?" she asked

"It's like a bird building a nest."

"Huh?"

"Have you ever watched a mama bird gather sticks and bits of whatever she can find? She picks out a real nice, safe tree and puts all that stuff together into a little nest, then lays her eggs in it?"

"What does that have to do with a monthly?"

"I'm getting to that." He ran his fingers through his hair. "A woman's body becomes like a nest—a safe, warm place where a baby can grow."

"Why am I bleeding?" she asked, starting to tear up again.

"Don't cry, honey. There's nothing to be afraid of. The blood is just your body's way of building a place for a baby. When you bleed, it means there's no baby this month." Thank the Lord. That was another whole conversation he didn't want to have.

"When will it stop? Will I bleed to death? I don't understand." She started to cry again.

Jarrod pulled her against him and wrapped his arms around her. "It will stop in a few days. Believe me. Just don't cry. This is normal. You're becoming a woman."

"I don't w-want to be a woman. I don't want to bleed. I want my m-mama." Her body shook with uncontrollable sobs. "I w-want Abby."

In her room, Abby had just finished washing up for supper. She set her hand towel beside the pitcher and basin on the pine dresser.

There was a loud knock on her door. She opened it, surprised to see Jarrod with Lily beside him.

"What's wrong?" Abby asked, holding the door wide.

"Nothing—" Jarrod said.

"Everything," Lily blurted out.

They both spoke at the same time as they entered the room. Lily stood beside the bed with her uncle next to her.

Abby shut the door, then looked carefully at Lily. "What is it, sweetie?"

"I'm bleeding. Uncle Jarrod says there's a nest inside me, but I'm not having a b-baby." She sniffled.

Abby shook her head and looked at Jarrod. "What did you tell her?"

"She started her monthly and thought she was dying. I just explained what's happening to her."

"Oh, Lily." Abby put her hand on the girl's knee. "I'm so sorry you were afraid."

"I told her there was nothing to be frightened of, that she's just becoming a woman."

"Just?" Abby's eyebrow rose as she looked at him. "That's a very important event in a girl's life."

"Yeah, but nothing to get hysterical about—"

"If you're not prepared for the changes and don't know what's happening to you, I'd say it's plenty of reason to get hysterical." Her eyes narrowed on him. "But you're a man. You just don't understand these things."

"Something I'm real glad about."

"Why don't you leave us alone for a little while? We women will take care of this."

"No need to ask me twice. I'm goin' to the Watering Hole. Been a long time since I had a beer. I figure I earned one today. Maybe two."

"Where are the other children?" she asked.

"At the ranch. Gib's with 'em. I was in a hurry. Wasn't time to get everyone ready."

Abby studied him, and a feeling of pity twisted in her chest. A lesser man would have gone to the Watering Hole long before this. With the responsibilities he had, a lot of men would have stopped for a beer, then kept right on going.

Like her own father, she thought. She told herself that was a completely different situation. He'd gone for the good of his wife and children. As soon as she could, she planned to join her father and put her family back together.

Poor Jarrod. She wasn't surprised that Lily's change from a girl to a woman would send him to the saloon. He deserved a break.

"You go on then," she said to him. "I'll talk to Lily, and when she's feeling better, I'll find you."

He nodded. "Thanks, Abby."

"Don't mention it."

When he was gone, Abby put her arm around Lily and pulled her close. "Do you understand that you're going to be just fine?"

Lily nodded.

"All right, then. Let me tell you what's going on inside your body." She took a deep breath as she gathered her thoughts. "One of the ways a girl becomes a woman is when she starts her monthly. That means once every month, your body makes a place ready to take care of a baby just like your uncle told you."

"How does a baby get inside there?" Lily asked, lifting her head to look at Abby.

This was very important, and Abby figured she should tell her straight out how that all happened. "When a woman loves a man, they get married and share a bed together. They kiss and cuddle, and when the time is right, there's a physical union."

"What's that?" Lily asked, frowning.

"The part of him that makes him a man, joins with the part of her that makes her a woman." Abby was trying to be matter-of-fact, but she couldn't stop the blush that warmed her cheeks.

Lily wrinkled her nose in distaste. "Have you ever done that with a man?"

"No."

But ever since Jarrod had kissed her, her imagination had sure taken on a mind of its own. She had never wanted to do the things with a man that she was explaining to Lily, but she had wondered lately what it would be like with Jarrod. The way his kiss had made her feel told her that a physical union with him would be something special. Something a woman could get used to. If that woman was planning to stay, she thought. Which she wasn't.

She told the girl how babies are made, feeling a deep sadness that Lily's mother had been robbed of this special moment with her daughter. It also made her see how much the children needed womanly guidance. She was warmed and humbled that they wanted her.

Lily sighed. "I never knew it was so complicated."

"Do you feel better now?"

She nodded and smiled, a small, tentative expression. "I'm glad you explained everything to me, Abby."

"Me too. I'm just sorry you went through such a bad time." She gave her a hug. "Are you hungry?"

"Starved."

"Let's go find your uncle and we'll have some supper."

As Jarrod walked down the main street of Hollister with Abby beside him, he glanced over his shoulder at the front of the restaurant they had just left. "Are you sure Lily will be all right with Joe Schafer? I'm not sure I liked the way he was looking at her."

"And how was that?" she asked in a light tone.

"His eyes got this funny sort of eager puppy look. Did you see the way he kept dropping things when he was clearing the table? If he keeps that up, Hettie won't have a dish left in the place."

"Something tells me he only does that when Lily's around."

"Then, for the sake of all those breakables, maybe I should go get her out of there," he said, stopping in midstride. He turned as if to go back in the direction of the restaurant.

Abby grabbed his arm. "For heaven's sake, Jarrod. They're washing dishes together. What could happen?"

"A lot," he said, looking down at her. "There's water, soap, he'll brush up against her arm . . ." His expression grew intense. "I was a fifteen-year-old boy once. I know about these things."

"Do you?"

"You bet I do. Why, there was that time with—" He caught himself and sighed. "Why does she have to turn into a woman now?"

"You needed another challenge. Relax. Joe's a nice boy. Besides, Henrietta is there. She'll watch out for them."

He nodded thoughtfully. "You have a point. Hettie Schafer might be no bigger than a minute, but I wouldn't want to tangle with her when she's riled."

They turned away and started walking again. It was a right pretty evening. Cool, but not cold, and a soft breeze stirred up the smell of jasmine and roses from Hettie's garden behind the boardinghouse. He drew in the fragrance, relaxing for the first time since he'd last been to town. Maybe that had more to do with being near Abby than it did geographical location. He looked at her when she stopped walking again. The street was deserted. This time of day most folks were home with their families.

She sat down on the wooden bench outside the dark, closed mercantile. "So what did you want to talk to me about, Jarrod?"

The way the moonlight turned her hair to glowing copper almost made him forget why he'd asked her to walk with him in the first place. After the day he'd had with Lily, he didn't think anything could distract him from his purpose. He got her out here because he wanted this matter of a housekeeper settled.

He sat down beside her, close enough that their shoulders brushed, and ignored her womanly fragrance. If he let himself get caught up in the way it enveloped him, he might never get to what he had to say. Turning his mind to it, he decided the best thing would be to just say it straight out.

"Abby, I want you to be my housekeeper."

Her whole body tensed. "We've already discussed this—"

"I'm prepared to offer you twice as much as the largest amount of money you've ever earned in one month in Hollister."

She sat forward, pulling her back away from the wood-sided building. Her glance met his and her eyes were wide and shocked. "Jarrod, that's a lot of money."

"And worth every cent to me."

"Is Katie sleeping all night?"

"No. Why?"

"Lack of sleep must be making you delirious."

"Let me tell you about my day and maybe you'll understand. You already know about Lily." He leaned forward and rested his forearms on his knees. "Oliver had himself quite a morning."

"What did he do? He's all right, isn't he?"

"He's right as rain, except for the white paint all over him. He was watching us brand the cattle and wanted to help. I told him he was too little, so he took it into his head to brand the barn, the chickens, the horses in the barn, and everything else he could reach."

"With paint?" Her voice held a note of amusement.

He wasn't telling her this to be funny. He was throwing himself on her mercy. "Yes, with paint," he said, annoyed.

"Very inventive," she said, and laughed.

"He managed to get most of it on himself." He shook his head at the memory.

"You're lucky he didn't try to build a fire by himself," she said, turning serious.

Jarrod had thought the same thing. "Exactly why I need someone to be with the kids when I can't."

"I don't know—"

"If that's not enough to convince you, while I had Oliver in the tub trying to get him back to the color he used to be, Katie ran in and said Lily was crying because she was dying."

"I'm so sorry you all had to go through that. But I don't see—"

"If you had been there, it wouldn't have happened."

"Maybe not the paint. But I can't stop Lily from becoming a woman."

"I realize that. But *I* couldn't reassure her. She wanted you. It wouldn't have taken hours to calm her down. You'd have talked to her right away."

Abby stood up and turned her back to him, staring out at the hills bathed in moonlight. He felt her hesitation. It was obvious that she cared about the kids. Something was preventing her from accepting his offer that had nothing to do with the money.

"What is it, Abby? Why are you torn about taking the job?"

"What makes you think I am?"

"If the answer was yes or no, you'd have let me know it by now. The salary is not in question since you didn't turn me down flat when I told you how much I'm willing to pay. Something else is making you hesitate to take the job. Why don't you tell me what it is? Maybe I can help."

She folded her arms over her chest, but still didn't look at him. "I don't think there's anything you can do, but I suppose it's only fair to explain."

"I'm listening."

"Are you aware that my father left my family about thirteen years ago?"

"I heard something about it."

Jarrod hadn't paid much attention at the time. Gossip spread fast in a town like Hollister, but it didn't get the animals fed, the fences mended, or grain stored for the winter. He didn't put much stock in idle talk.

Abby sighed. "He left to find work, a way to provide a better living for his family."

"That must have been real hard on all of you."

"It was." Her tone held a whole world of hurt.

"What happened? What did your mother do?"

"She went to work for Mr. Whittemore. He was real good to us, let Clint and me help out too. We did whatever we could to bring in money. But Mama missed Pa. She never complained or let on that she was lonely, but it was hard on her. Then she died." She drew in a long, shuddering breath. "Just before she did, I made her a promise."

"What was that?" he asked.

"I told her I'd find him. I'd do my best to reunite the family."

"Have you heard from him since he left?"

She nodded. "Every couple years I get a letter from a post office box in San Francisco."

"Is that where he is?"

"I don't know. From what he says, he travels around to find work."

"What kind of work?"

She shrugged. "I'm not sure."

"I'm sorry about what you and your family went through, Abby," he said, not unkindly. "But I don't understand what this has to do with whether or not you'll take the job."

"I promised my mother two things, Jarrod. Number one, I'd see that Clint is the first Miller to finish college. And number two, I'd find my father." She turned to him and her eyes glowed with purpose. "I'm going to look for him, Jarrod. As soon as I'm sure Clint has enough money to finish his education, I'm going to go to San Francisco and track him down so we can be together again."

Jarrod had more questions than he figured she had answers. He didn't think much of a man who would leave his family to fend for themselves. He figured after thirteen years, Sam Miller had no intention of coming back to Hollister. But when he looked at the determination burning in Abby's eyes, he couldn't say that to her. He didn't have the heart to destroy her dream.

At least now he could understand why she was so high on family, why she'd been so hot-tempered about him keeping the kids with him on the ranch. He could picture the girl she'd been, just a little younger than Lily, but still the oldest of two. Taking on responsibilities because her mother carried the load of supporting them. She had missed out on her childhood and didn't want that to happen to Lily.

"It'll be a while until you have enough money for Clint. Right?"

"Not if I take your job." She sighed. "And when I've saved enough, I have to go. Do you understand?"

"I know how you feel, Abby. Having a goal, a dream, is real important. But what does that have to do with the job?"

"It wouldn't be fair to the kids. Just about the time they get used to me, I'll have to leave."

"We still need you. Right now. I'll take whatever time you can give."

"You mean—"

"I mean I'd like to try and talk you out of looking for your pa. You don't want to hear this, but a man who'd leave his family isn't worth all the fretting you've done."

"It's not your decision to make," she said stiffly.

"I know. I said I'd *like* to try and talk you out of it. I'm not that big a knothead. But you've been honest with me. And I still want you as a housekeeper. More important, the kids need you."

"I don't know—"

He sighed. "I can't worry about the future past tomorrow. That means, Oliver's hair might need some trimming to get the paint out, Katie needs a good night's sleep as much as I do, Lily needs a woman around the place, and Tom . . ." He frowned.

She tipped her head to the side, studying him. "What about Tom?"

"He says he can look after himself just fine. I don't know why, but that makes me think he needs someone even more than the others."

"I know what you mean. I've tried to be his friend, but it will take time."

He grinned at her enthusiastic tone. "Does this mean you've accepted my proposal?"

"It means I will come to work for you because the children need me. On one condition."

"What?"

"You must remember that I'll have to go. It'll probably be sooner than I thought because of the generous amount of money you're paying me."

"When you're ready to go find your father and live with him, Abby, just give me a little notice so I can try to replace you."

Maybe even try to talk you out of it, he thought. Abby was his friend. He hated to see her break her heart over a childhood fantasy.

"What if you can't find a replacement? Finding someone sure wasn't as easy as I'd thought, and I'll still have to go. I don't want any misunderstandings when the time comes."

"There won't be," he assured her. "If I have to look for another housekeeper, I won't make the mistake of getting the children's approval." He stuck his hand out. "Do we have a deal?"

"Deal," she said, placing her small hand in his.

As he closed his fingers around hers, a jolt of awareness shot up his arm. His gaze lifted from their joined hands to her face. Why had he never noticed before how creamy and smooth her skin looked? Made him want to touch it, find out for himself if it felt like silk or satin. He knew for a fact that her lips were soft as clouds and intoxicating as fine brandy.

He wanted to kiss her again, to see if she still tasted as sweet. He just plain wanted her. But her eyes widened apprehensively as he stared at her. He had finally convinced her to work for him. Getting personal might scare her off.

He released her and jammed his hand in his pocket. "How soon can you be ready to leave?"

"I have to let Mr. Whittemore know I'm quitting."

"I'd like to be there when you do."

"Why?"

"To see how he takes it when he finds out he was wrong." He smiled. "Can you come back to the ranch with Lily and me tomorrow? Do you think Earl will give you a hard time about leaving on such short notice?"

She shook her head. "He'll understand. Since I don't have much to get in order, I can leave in the morning."

"Right after breakfast?"

"I'll be ready."

# 10

*Katie and Oliver ran into the* kitchen and hugged Abby. Standing by the stove stirring eggs, Abby was nearly knocked off balance by the sneak attack. "Whoa, you. What's that for?"

"I'm so glad you're here," Katie said, looking up with shining eyes.

"Me too," her brother seconded.

"I've been here two weeks. Aren't you used to having me around?"

"No'm," they both said together.

"So I can look forward to this every morning?"

"Yes'm."

Lily walked in, followed by Tom, and the two sat down at the table. "We're all happy you're our housekeeper now. Even Tom, although he won't admit it."

Tom's only reply was a snort.

"That makes me feel good. Soon I'll just be like an old piece of furniture."

Abby filled plates with fluffy eggs and set them in front of the children just as Jarrod entered the room. "What's this about furniture?" he asked.

"Abby says pretty soon she'll be like an old piece of furniture around here," Lily explained. "We worked too hard to have her here. We'll never think that way. Will we, Uncle Jarrod?"

"Nope," he said, slathering butter on a biscuit.

"Do you think Uncle Jarrod is a fine-looking man?" Katie stopped playing with her scrambled eggs and stared at Abby.

Abby felt Jarrod's gaze on her. Since she'd moved to the ranch, he hadn't once joined them for breakfast. Why today?

"I'd be curious about the answer to that myself," he said, amusement lacing his voice. There was an edge of challenge there too.

Abby ignored the warmth that she knew was making her face red and looked him straight in the eye. "Yes, Katie. I think your uncle is a fine-looking man. One of the finest I've ever laid eyes on."

She drew her gaze from his and scanned the rest of the children at the table one by one, until she came to Lily, who had gasped when her sister asked the question, then stared at her hands in her lap. She hadn't looked up since.

"But why on earth would you wonder something like that, Katie?" Abby asked.

The little girl set her fork down. "Ever since Lily came back from Hollister, all she can talk about is that Joe Schafer and what a fine-looking man—"

"Boy," Jarrod snapped. "Besides, that was two weeks ago. You're not still mooning over him. Why, he can't have more than a whisker or two on that baby-smooth face."

Lily looked up, her eyes glistening with angry tears. "He shaves every third day. He told me so. I'm not mooning over him. I just think he's nice is all." She glared at her sister. "Katie, I'm never telling you anything again," she cried, jumping up and running from the room.

Katie stuck out her bottom lip. "Didn't mean anything by it. She had no call to get so riled." One big tear rolled down her cheek and plopped on the front of her calico dress.

Abby went to kneel beside her. "Don't cry, sweetie."

"But why is she actin' that way?"

"'Cause she's stupid," Tom said.

Oliver took his thumb out of his mouth. "She should be a cowboy."

Abby looked up when Jarrod coughed, and the twinkle in his eye told her he was doing his best not to laugh. Then his mood changed and he looked seriously at his youngest nephew as he said, "Cowboys don't cry, Oliver. That's a fact. But what's ailing Lily isn't something that riding a horse or herding cattle can fix. Her getting upset that way is just part of growing up."

"What do you mean?" Katie asked.

Abby glanced at Jarrod. "He means that your sister's becoming a woman. She's noticing boys."

"This is one time I'm glad that Blackstone Ranch is the farthest from town," Jarrod grumbled.

"Don't you like Joe Schafer, Uncle Jarrod?" Katie asked, frowning at him. "Who is he anyway? Does he like Lily? Is she gonna marry him?"

"Hold on, Katie." Jarrod got up from the head of the table and went to the stove to pour himself another cup of coffee. He turned back and said, "Lily is just beginning to look. As if she was buying a new dress. She's too young to even think about getting married."

Katie put her elbow on the table and rested her chin in her palm. "How come you're not married, Uncle Jarrod? You're not too young. Abby said you're a fine-looking man. Don't you want to get married?"

Just swallowing his coffee, Jarrod started to cough again.

Abby stifled her own amusement. "I'd like to know the answer to that myself," she said, echoing his words when she'd been the on the receiving end of one of Katie's blunt questions.

Tom put his fork down with a clatter. "Aw, Kate. Don't you never get tired of askin' questions? Can't a man get any peace around here?" He stood up. "I'm goin' to the barn to see the new foal." He grabbed his hat from the peg by the door. "You're welcome to come with me Uncle Jarrod."

"I'll be along directly," Jarrod said. Then Tom nodded and walked out.

Oliver took his thumb out of his mouth. "I'm goin' with Tom." He jumped up and ran to the door.

Before he could escape, Abby was beside him. She bent down and looked at him. "Don't forget to use the necessary while you're out there."

"Yes'm," he said solemnly. Then he was gone.

Katie, sitting alone at the table, started to sniffle. Jarrod looked at Abby, then crossed the room and went down on one knee beside the little girl. "Don't cry, Katie. Lily will get over it. She won't stay mad."

"That's not why I'm cryin'."

"Then what is it?" he asked.

Katie shook her head, sending her blond curls bouncing around her head.

Abby sat down on her other side, in the chair Oliver had just vacated. "I'd like to know too, sweetie. What's wrong?"

As she sniffled, her little shoulders lifted. "Does this m-mean we can't go to Hollister for the Fourth of July?"

Abby rubbed her forehead, trying to figure out how Katie had made the jump from fine-looking men to the Independence Day celebration. She finally gave up. "What are you talking about?"

The little girl looked from her to Jarrod. "Lily said Joe told her about it. Every year there's a town picnic with games and such. And fireworks," she added wistfully.

"That's true," Jarrod said as Abby nodded.

Katie twisted her hands in her lap. "Tom said you wouldn't take us. I told him he was wrong. Was he, Uncle Jarrod? What with the way you feel about Joe Schafer 'n' all."

"Why would Tom say that?" Jarrod asked.

"'Cause Hollister's too far away." She looked quickly at her uncle. "I told him that wasn't so. Missing one day of work wouldn't matter. But that was before I made Lily cry. Now we can't go. And I won't g-get to see the fireworks."

Jarrod gently lifted her chin, forcing her to look at him.

"Don't cry, Katie. Things will work out fine. I promise. Are you finished with your breakfast?" She nodded and he said, "Then you go on upstairs and try to make things up with your sister."

"All right," she said, and gave him a quick hug before leaving the room.

Jarrod stood up and ran a hand through his hair. "I don't understand, Abby."

"What?" she asked, looking up at him.

"Am I a slave driver?"

"Good heavens, no!"

It was on the tip of her tongue to add that he was one of the kindest men she'd ever known, but she decided against it. She had only been there a short time, and already she was jumping to his defense as if it was her right. She was nothing more than his housekeeper, a paid employee. She reminded herself that he needed her help with the children, not a wife. After all, he'd readily agreed to let her go whenever she wanted to. If she worked things right, that could be soon. It wouldn't do at all for her to let any tender feelings for him become more than friendship.

But when he looked at her in a certain way, like he had when he'd questioned her just a moment before, she wanted to put her arms around him.

"Why would you think something like that, Jarrod?"

"Have I made them feel that they couldn't even ask for the simplest thing, like going into town for the celebration?"

"It's just that they've seen how hard you work, and what it takes to keep the ranch going. You don't really think you've been unkind to them?"

He shook his head. "No. I guess they've had so little fun, they just don't figure it's in the cards for them."

Abby sighed as she looked at the doorway where Katie had disappeared. "You could be right. Do you want to take them into town for the festivities?"

He put his cup on the table and sat down. "I would if I didn't think Joe Schafer had some notions about Lily."

"What are you talking about?"

"He's the one who brought the whole thing up to her. It doesn't take much to see that he wants her there. Lily's a little girl and he's—"

"Shaving every third day," Abby interrupted with a smile. Slap me silly if he isn't acting like an outraged father, she thought. It was just about the sweetest thing. He'd taken to caring about those kids as if they filled up some part of him that had been empty and waiting.

He returned her look with a sheepish grin. "You think I'm making too much of this?"

"Maybe not. Let's think about it. What could happen?" She laced her fingers together. "People from all over come into Hollister for the picnic and games. So I'm sure Lily and Joe will find all kinds of places to be alone."

"When you say—"

"And even if they can find somewhere that isn't crawling with folks, I expect Lily will want to miss out on something because she's had so many Fourth of July picnics and they come up so often during the year."

He rubbed a hand on his chin. "Hadn't thought about it like that—"

"And Joe, being the wrong sort of boy he is, will probably just throw her over his shoulder carry her off, and do wrong by her. My guess is no one will notice either, when he carries her off, I mean. She'll be quiet as a little church mouse. That settles it. Going to town could be real dangerous. Might be best to skip—"

"Abby, I get your point. We'll take the kids into town for the Fourth."

There was a squeal of delight from the hall right outside the kitchen. Katie ran into the room and threw herself into Jarrod's arms. "Thank you, Uncle Jarrod."

He picked her up and put her on his lap. "Were you eavesdropping?"

Her forehead wrinkled. "You mean what birds do when they're flying over—"

"No. It means listening to what people are saying when they don't know you're there."

She studied him solemnly, as if she thought he was cross with her. But Abby could see the glint of humor in his gray eyes and bit her lip to stifle her own laughter.

"Yes, sir. I did listen to what you and Abby were sayin'. Are you mad, Uncle Jarrod? Does that mean we can't go like you said?"

"No. We're going to Hollister for the Independence Day festivities."

She frowned. "Don't know exactly what that is, but I hope it means fireworks."

"That's exactly what it means. Now, you can go upstairs and tell your sister. Maybe that will perk her up." Jarrod set her on the floor.

"I s'pect so. If she gets to see that fine-looking Joe Schafer." Katie made a face at that idea, just before she ran out of the room.

This time Abby listened and heard the little girl's footsteps going up the stairs.

She smiled at Jarrod. "You just made two girls very happy."

His gaze met hers and the humor vanished. A dark, intense expression replaced the tender one he had used on Katie. "What about you, Abby? Are you happy? Did you want to go to town?" He lifted her braid, rubbing the red strands at the end between his fingers. "Firecracker," he whispered. "I'll bet you like fireworks as much as Katie."

She suddenly felt warm all over and wanted to be anywhere else but here, a whisper away from Jarrod Blackstone. She forced herself to stay put and look him straight in the eye.

"I love the Fourth of July. It's even better than Christmas."

One corner of his mouth lifted in a wry smile. "Why's that?"

She thought about it for a minute before answering. "Because I'm never disappointed."

He dropped her braid and brushed the back of his knuckles across her cheek, making her stomach flutter. "I think you understand the children because you're just like them."

"I'm a grown woman."

"That you are. But just like them, you grew up without expecting fun."

"Until now. I mean the children," she said, feeling the heat rise to her face. Good Lord, she hoped he didn't think she had meant she was looking for grownup womanly sort of fun with him. Because she wasn't. "I mean now that they're here, I expect you'll see that they have fun."

"I know what you meant. And I thank you."

"For what?" she asked, puzzled.

"You put a lot of faith in me even though I don't deserve it."

Abby wondered at the shadows she saw in his eyes, but didn't ask. If he wanted to talk about it, he would. He had already earned her respect by giving the children a home. Faith? Phooey. He couldn't help being the man he was. "Why did you have breakfast with the children this morning?" she asked, and hoped, for her own sake, that it wasn't going to be a regular occurrence.

"One of the first things you said to me was that I should spend time with them. Have you changed your mind about that?"

"Of course not." Only now that the children were in her care, it meant he'd be spending time with her too. Stupidly, she hadn't counted on that when she agreed to be his housekeeper. She had only thought about how tired he looked and that he needed help with the children. Besides the fact that he'd made her a generous offer that would assure Clint's future. "I was just curious."

"Gib and I are repairing the barn roof, and I didn't have to ride out at the crack of dawn. I decided it would be a good time to see how the kids are doing with you."

"Are you satisfied?"

"Yes."

"Good. I wouldn't want you to think all that money you're paying me is a waste."

He frowned. Why should that bother him? she wondered. She *was* his employee. That's all she ever would be.

She stood up. "I'd better clean up these dishes. Will you give me a half hour, then send Tom and Oliver in for lessons?"

"Consider it done."

Sitting behind the desk in his study, Jarrod put his pen down and rubbed his tired eyes. It had been a long day, even though he'd stayed for breakfast with the kids that morning. Working on the barn roof wasn't his favorite chore, just a necessary one. Still, he'd rather be using a hammer outdoors than adding up figures in the ledger.

In the living room, Abby was reading to the children before bedtime. She had borrowed books from Bea Peters to bring to the ranch with her, and felt this nightly ritual was an important part of their education. Her pleasant voice was frequently interrupted by laughter. He gazed longingly at the door, then sighed and picked up his pen again, forcing himself to ignore the temptation to join them, and instead focused on the columns in front of him.

Another peal of merriment and high-pitched squealing drifted to him, drawing his gaze to the door again. He tossed his pen down and stood up, then left the room and followed the sound.

In the living room, Abby sat in the wing-back chair by the fireplace, with Oliver in her lap. Katie stood beside her and gazed at the book. Lily, cross-legged on the hearth, stared dreamily into space as Abby read. Tom sprawled in the middle of the floor with his back to everyone. Lighted wall sconces brightened every corner of the room. No one noticed Jarrod standing there.

Oliver pulled his thumb out of his mouth and pointed to the book. "His name is Oliver too, and he's an orphan just like me 'n' Tom, 'n' Lily, 'n' Katie."

Abby closed the book, keeping a finger in it to mark her place. "Do you know what an orphan is, Oliver?" There was a softness in her voice.

He nodded. "A kid with no folks."

"That's true. But you're not alone like Oliver Twist."

"He went with the pickpockets."

"Because he had nowhere else to go. You have folks, sweetie. A family to love you. Your uncle Jarrod—"

"And Gib and Dusty and Slim," Katie added.

"And Abby," Oliver chimed in.

"That's right," she said.

Jarrod heard the hesitation in the words. She wasn't staying, and didn't want them to become too dependent on her. Too late for that. It felt right to have her here. He had to admit the kids had been smart to hold out for Abby.

But she'd made it clear the situation was temporary. When Abby left, it would be hard. Harder than he wanted to think about. But they would go on the best they could.

"What's a pickpocket, Abby?" Oliver asked.

Jarrod walked farther into the room. "It's a person who steals things out of people's pockets."

Everyone called out greetings to him. When Abby smiled her approval at his arrival, he couldn't help returning it.

"I don't see how someone could lift something out of my pocket without me knowing," Lily said.

"It's definitely a skill that requires practice," Abby commented, brushing Oliver's blond hair off his forehead. Meeting Jarrod's gaze, she put her arms around the little boy almost as if she was using him for a shield.

Against what? Jarrod thought. Him? That was silly.

Jarrod looked around at the children. "Why don't you try? See if you can do it without getting caught."

Abby grinned. "That sounds like fun. I have something in my pocket that you might like to pick. What do you think? Anyone want to try?"

No one answered.

"Let's see what Oliver Twist had to learn." Jarrod walked over to Tom, who had turned around as soon as he'd heard his uncle's voice. Pleased by Abby's approval, he decided to pursue a game of pickpocket. He was becoming more comfortable with the kids, and the way they had just welcomed him to their midst, he guessed they felt that way too. After ruffling Tom's hair, Jarrod said, "Let's see if you can be the Artful Dodger."

"Have you read the book?" Abby asked him. She sounded surprised.

He shook his head. "I've been listening to you read."

A becoming pink crept into her cheeks. "I'm sorry. I didn't realize we were disturbing you. We can go upstairs—"

"Didn't say you bothered me. I enjoyed hearing the story. Let's see if these young 'uns have been listening. C'mon, Tom. Up and at 'em," he said, holding his hand out to the boy.

Tom grinned and grabbed it.

"I wanna be his mark," Katie said, jumping up and down. Jarrod grinned at her. "I see you've been listening. But Abby already said she's got something in her pocket worth picking. Let's see if he has a knack for being a criminal."

"Aw forget it," Tom said. "I bet she ain't got nothin' good."

"How do you know?" Abby said, trying to hide the hurt his words had caused.

He didn't think the children saw, but Jarrod wasn't so easily fooled. And he wouldn't let Tom off the hook in a hurry.

"She's right, Tom. How do you know? Take a chance."

"I'll try, Uncle Jarrod," Oliver said, squirming out of Abby's lap and scampering up to his uncle. "If Tom doesn't wanna do it, I will."

"I'll do it." Tom snorted. "You'd get caught for sure, baby."

"I'm not a baby," the little boy said, his voice rising.

"Of course you're not, Oliver," Abby soothed. "Tom knows it's not true. He just likes to call you that because he's the oldest boy."

Tom snorted again, but didn't say anything.

Abby stood up and walked around the room, whistling as if she was strolling Main Street in Hollister browsing and glancing in store windows. Jarrod angled his head in her direction, indicating Tom should make his move. The boy frowned, looking indecisive, but finally moved into step behind her. He stalked for a few moments, then reached a hand into the pocket of her green cotton skirt. When he latched onto something and tried to pull it out, it got stuck in the folds of her skirt.

Abby grabbed his wrist. "Gotcha."

"No fair," he said. "You knew I was there."

She looked at Jarrod. "He's right. I think he should get the licorice whip anyway."

The boy's gray eyes grew round. "That's what it is?"

"Yes," she said, pulling out several. "I have one for everybody. It was supposed to be a surprise before bed-time."

"Don't want none," Tom said.

"Any," Abby corrected as she handed the candy out to the others.

"Can I have Tom's?" Oliver asked.

"May I," Abby said. "And if Tom truly doesn't want any, yes, you may have his."

When Tom shook his head and turned away from her, Oliver took both eagerly, stuffing one in his mouth and the other in his pocket.

Katie took her treat and ran over to Jarrod. "It's your turn, Uncle Jarrod."

"My turn?"

"To play pickpocket."

"But Abby just handed out treats. She doesn't have any-thing for me."

"How do you know? You have to pick her pocket and find out. You have to play Dodger so we know if you've been listening."

He glanced at Abby. "I'm game if you are."

She looked like she'd rather walk barefoot through fire. "I think it's time the children were in bed," she said.

"But it's still early, Abby," Katie complained.

"Will you tuck me in?" Oliver asked, yawning.

"Of course, sweetie," she answered. "Lily, you too."

"But I'm too old to go to bed the same time they do."

Abby shooed the two youngest to the bottom of the stairs. "You don't have go to sleep. Read if you want to. But you need to rest."

"Oh, all right," Lily said, stomping through the room. "Good night, Uncle Jarrod." She stopped to kiss his cheek.

"Sweet dreams," he said. He moved beside Abby and watched until the three disappeared from sight, shaking his head in wonder at how easily she handled them.

"I'll be up in a few minutes to check on you." Abby turned from watching the others go up. "Tom? You too. It's getting late."

"You got no right to tell me what to do," he said angrily.

"Tom," Jarrod said, a warning in his voice.

Abby put her hand on his arm. "I've got to deal with him," she said.

She was right. Jarrod knew he couldn't be there all the time. He would have to trust her to take care of whatever came up with the kids in his absence.

She moved to where the boy sat on the sofa, dangling his legs. Lowering herself beside him, she said, "Tom, I said it's time for bed. I expect you to complain a lot like the others, then do as I ask."

"You're not my ma. Ya got no call to tell me what to do." He glared at her, his arms folded over his chest.

"That's where you're wrong," she said.

"Oh, yeah? You're just hired on, like Gib and Dusty and Slim. That's all you are. The others might need you to tell 'em what t'do, but I don't. Don't need nobody."

"Anybody," she corrected. "You probably could survive without me, but your uncle wants better than that for you. You're right about one thing, he is paying me. To see that you're taken care of. That means you'll do as I see fit."

"You can't make me," he shouted.

"Wrong again," she said, taking his arm. "We can do this the easy way or the hard way. The choice is yours."

"You can't make me," he said again, but there was less

confidence in his voice this time as he looked up to meet her
gaze.

Her eyes narrowed on him as she tightened her grip.
"You've been wrong twice now. Care to try for three?" she
asked, pulling him to his feet as she stood.

For several tense moments he glared at her, judging if
she could really carry out her threat. Finally, he yanked his
arm away. "Good night, Uncle Jarrod," he mumbled as he
passed him on his way to the stairway.

Jarrod truly admired the way she dealt with the children,
using just the right amount of toughness and tenderness.
What would he do without her?

"'Night, Tom." Jarrod let out a long breath when he was
gone. "Could you have done it? Taken him upstairs, I mean."

"I'm glad I didn't have to find out. He's put on some
bulk since he got here."

"I have a feeling you'd have managed it somehow."

"I'd have given it my best shot." Frowning, she glanced
at the stairway. "There's an anger in him I don't understand, Jarrod."

He rubbed a hand over his face. "I know. He's fine with
me and the other men. We've all become real fond of him.
But the way he is with you—It's a puzzle. The other kids
seem okay."

"They are. As far as I can tell. I expected that things
would be slower with Tom, but he seems to be getting more
hostile, and I don't know why." She sighed.

"He's growing up too. Like Lily. Maybe this is just his
way."

Frowning, she shook her head. "At least I'm still taller
than he is. Not for long, though. I remember when Clint
started sprouting, when he was just a little older than Tom.
Couldn't keep him in pants, at least ones that weren't high
water."

"You raised him by yourself, didn't you?"

"After our mother died."

"So I was right this morning when I said you understood
the kids because you hadn't had much fun."

"Doesn't matter. Can't miss what you never had." She shrugged. "I'll go tuck them in and hear prayers."

Long after she'd gone, Jarrod thought about her. He wondered again how he'd managed without her. And he wasn't just thinking of the children. Every day that passed with her under his roof made it harder to keep his hands off her. Still, he knew she didn't want his tender feelings. So he turned his musing in a different direction.

It didn't take much for him to figure out that Abby Miller's life had been filled with responsibility and not much else. Maybe that's why she was so determined to fulfill her promise to get Clint through school, then take off after her father. Trying to get back what she'd lost.

He couldn't fault her, but that didn't mean he had to like it. He paused, his eyes narrowed in thought.

An idea struck him, and took hold.

# 11

*Two weeks later,* Jarrod had breakfast with them again. This time Abby knew about it ahead of time since she was in on the surprise planned for Tom's birthday. After eating, Abby and Jarrod followed the children, who had raced to the barn, where Jarrod had sent them. It was the middle of June, and she savored the warmth and the clear blue sky overhead. This was her favorite kind of day.

"Do you think he suspects anything?" Jarrod asked her.

"Not that I can tell. But he doesn't show what he's feeling much."

"I noticed. Maybe this will help."

Abby increased her pace, anxious to see the boy's face. "I can't wait. Hurry, Jarrod."

"I'm practically running now," he said, laughter in his voice.

Abby wasn't sure who would enjoy this more, Jarrod or Tom.

After entering the barn, it took several moments for her eyes to adjust after the brightness outside. Standing just inside the door in a shaft of sunlight, Abby smelled the pungent odors of hay and horses. She heard the children as they patted the necks of the stabled animals.

Katie ran up to them. "Why are we here, Uncle Jarrod?"

"Gather 'round, everyone," he said. After they did, he cleared his throat. "Today is Tom's twelfth birthday."

Lily gasped. "Oh, Tom, I forgot. Happy birthday."

Everyone extended good wishes as Tom stuck his hands in his pockets and poked at the straw on the floor with the toe of his shoe. Abby swore his neck turned red, but dim as it was and with his head down, she couldn't tell if the color rose to his cheeks.

"I have something for you, Tom," Jarrod said.

The boy's head snapped up. His eyes were the mirror of his uncle's, gray and filled with excitement. "You didn't have to, Uncle Jarrod."

"I wanted to. Follow me." He led them through the barn and back to the corral beyond, where the newest foal frolicked beneath the watchful eye of her mother.

Katie pointed to the frisky little horse. "Why does the horse have a red ribbon around his neck, Uncle Jarrod? Won't that hurt him? Is it too tight?"

"No. And that's a she. Right, Tom?"

The boy nodded, his gaze following every move of the baby horse. He had come to a dead stop when he'd seen the ribbon, but hadn't said a word. As if he was afraid to hope, even though that ribbon told him the horse was a present and he was the only one having a birthday.

Jarrod stood beside Tom, who had climbed up two white slats on the fence and rested his arms on top. His uncle imitated the pose. "Tom, the baby foal is yours. Happy birthday, son."

Abby swore Tom went so still he even stopped breathing. Then he slowly looked at Jarrod, his eyes huge. "You mean it, Uncle Jarrod?"

"I wouldn't have said it otherwise."

Abby came up on the boy's other side. "What do you think, Tom? Are you excited? Are you surprised?" She felt like Katie with all her questions. She couldn't stop. Her feelings just rose to the top and spilled over at seeing the boy's dream come true.

"I can't believe it," Tom said, forgetting his hostility. He shook his head and whistled. The foal skidded to a stop and lifted her head, listening. Tom did it again, and she trotted over, then sniffed at him through the fence boards.

Oliver took his thumb out of his mouth and climbed up beside Jarrod. "Is Tom gonna be a cowboy now, Uncle Jarrod?"

"If he wants to."

"Do ya, Tom?" the boy asked.

"Yup," Tom said, gently rubbing the baby's nose.

Oliver looked at Jarrod. "I wanna be a cowboy too." He stuck his thumb back in his mouth and precariously held onto the fence with one hand.

Jarrod plucked him from the slats and settled the boy on his forearm. "You sure that's what you want to be?"

The youngster nodded, his head and arm going up and down with the movement.

"All right, then, I'm going to tell you a secret," Jarrod said.

"What?" Oliver asked around the finger in his mouth.

"As much as they might want to, cowboys can't suck their thumbs."

"Why?" Oliver asked, suspicion gathering in his blue eyes. They had all tried to get him to stop, and he sensed another lecture.

"They need two hands all the time."

"What for?"

"Riding. Roping."

"Really?" Oliver asked.

Jarrod nodded solemnly. "It's dangerous too. If a cowboy was riding hell-bent for leather and his horse stepped in a gopher hole, why, the jarring he'd take would not only shake loose his common sense, it could make him bite that thumb clean off."

To keep from laughing, Abby clamped her teeth tightly together. Not only was Jarrod's serious air tickling her, but also the sheer genius of his tactic to break the boy's habit without turning it into a big deal.

Oliver glanced cross-eyed at the four fingers visible in

front of his face. He lowered his hand. "Is Tom gonna ride his new horse?"

"Not today," Jarrod said. "She's not big enough. But eventually he will. He'll take care of her the way he's been doing. Today he gets to name her."

"What are ya gonna call her, Tom?" Oliver asked.

"Don't know yet."

Jarrod set Oliver on the ground. The boy started to put his thumb in his mouth, but stuck it in his pocket instead. It was all Abby could do not to clap her hands and jump in the air.

"A name's real important," Jarrod said, putting his hand on Tom's shoulder. "No harm in taking your time."

"Yes, sir."

"Another thing," Jarrod added. "I want you to have a new saddle. Couldn't get it in time for your birthday, but it's part of your present. We're going into Hollister the day before the Fourth of July so we can pick out something."

Tom looked like he was about to explode from happiness. He only hesitated a split second before he threw his arms around Jarrod and buried his face against his uncle's shirt. "This is the best day of my whole life. Thank you, sir," he said. There was a husky note in his voice that made Abby swallow hard.

"I wish it was my birthday," Katie said wistfully.

"Me too," Lily said.

Abby put an arm around each of the girls. "It will be soon enough."

"The day's just begun," Jarrod said, patting Tom's shoulder. Abby liked the way he didn't seem embarrassed by the boy's show of affection.

"Do you have another surprise that I don't know about?" she asked.

He nodded. "We're going to declare our own holiday."

"Like Independence Day?" Katie asked.

"Yes," Jarrod answered.

"Are we gonna have fireworks?" Her eyes lit up with excitement.

"No," he said seriously. "We can't take the chance of fire out here. That'll have to wait until we go to town."

"What are we gonna do?" Tom asked.

"That's up to you. What we're *not* gonna do is work."

"Can we go fishin'?" the birthday boy wanted to know.

Jarrod grinned. "I think that's a fine idea."

"I'll fix a lunch for you to take," Abby said.

"Make enough for six," Jarrod said, casually resting his elbow on the top rail of the fence.

"Good idea. Tom's growing so fast he can eat enough for two," she answered.

"No. You're coming with us, Abby."

Katie clapped her hands. "Oh, good. We're all going together. I've never been fishing. Does it hurt the fish?" she asked suddenly.

Tom walked over to her. "Nah, they like it when their mouth gets stuck on that sharp hook."

Katie looked stricken. "Do I have to hurt the fish, Uncle Jarrod?"

"I hope not," Lily said. "Because I won't put a worm on the end of a hook."

"Worms?" Katie said, green eyes growing wide.

Jarrod raised his gaze heavenward and sighed. "Let's call it a picnic. No one has to fish if they don't want to." He looked at them and said, "If you do, you'd best go dig up some worms. A real good spot is out there in the shade under the oaks."

"Yes, sir," Tom and Oliver said together, then raced away.

Jarrod looked at the girls. "You two might want to go swimming." When they nodded eagerly, he said, "Then gather up some towels and clothes to change into."

"Yes, sir," they answered, and ran off.

Jarrod looked at a frowning Abby. "What's wrong? Lessons can wait and so can chores."

"I agree. I don't disapprove of a holiday. In fact I think it's a wonderful idea for you to spend time with the children, especially Tom."

"Then what is it?"

"I can't go with you."

"You need a day off just as much as the rest of us."

Abby didn't know what a day off was. She was almost afraid to see what it felt like. But that wasn't why she hesitated.

"This should be a family day. Being the housekeeper, I'm not part of that."

He snorted. "That's the biggest bunch of bull—"

She knew he was right. Still she wavered. "I don't want the children to get too attached to me. Next year I'll be gone. I don't want Tom's birthday to roll around again and have them be sad because I'm not here."

Abby knew she was being selfish. *She* was the one who would be sad. The children would miss her for a while, but eventually they would forget about her. She would never forget them, or Jarrod.

"All the children want you to go."

"Except possibly Tom."

"He's so happy, I don't think he'd object." He moved in front of her, close enough for her to catch the scent of shaving soap on his skin. "The point is, you're here today. Enjoy it."

She thought for a moment, letting his words sink in. She decided he was right. When she had to go, it would be hard on everyone, including her. Until then she would care for them and give them everything she had to give every day. There was no reason to be miserable.

"What you're saying makes a lot of sense, Jarrod. I wouldn't want to spoil this day for them. If you're sure it's best."

"I'm not sure of anything. But I figure tomorrow will take care of itself. Besides, you need some fun as much as the kids do."

"I don't know. There's laundry to do, and cleaning. I have those vegetables to put up. And—"

"Keep protesting if it makes you feel better. But I'm warning you, one way or another, you're going on that picnic with us."

Her eyebrow lifted in surprise. "Just how do you know?"

"I'll kidnap you if necessary." The serious expression on his handsome face convinced her he would do exactly what he said.

"Then, of course I'll go along."

"Good."

That one word caused her heart to flutter. If word ever got out that there was more to Jarrod Blackstone than looks, she thought, he'd be hip deep in women.

She got the feeling that the outing was more for her benefit than the children's. Another sharp tug in her chest reminded her that she'd best be careful of Jarrod Blackstone. Like all those other females, she was already half in love with him. A little nudge would push her over the edge.

It had been a good day, Jarrod thought as he poured water in the basin on the oak dresser. Abby was settling the children for the night, and he had removed his shirt to wash up before bed. As he dried off he looked in the mirror and studied the room behind him.

A pleasant breeze from the open window billowed the lace curtains and cooled the skin on his bare chest. This was the largest bedroom, and one that his parents had shared before him. Dulcy had changed the furniture, ordering the big four-poster bed and matching oak dresser and armoire all the way from Chicago. Abby had delivered it from Hollister Freight and admired the hell out of it, he remembered.

He liked it too. One thing he could say for Dulcy, she had good taste. In furniture if not in men.

He pushed that thought away, refusing to spoil a nearly perfect day. It had shown him how good things could be.

A movement past his partially opened door drew his attention, and he wondered if the kids were all right, or up to mischief when they should be asleep.

He quickly moved to the doorway and peeked out. Abby was at the end of the hallway, just starting down the stairs. "Abby?"

She turned to him, then glanced at the closed doors to the children's rooms. Apparently she decided she didn't want to chance disturbing them with a conversation the length of the hall, because she walked to him. The light from his room spilled into the hall, but his height shielded her, throwing shadow over her face.

"Jarrod, did you want something?"

"Are the kids asleep already?"

She nodded. "If I'd known that a day by the stream swimming and fishing could do that, I'd have tried it sooner."

"They were pretty tired?"

"Exhausted. Even though Oliver napped while you carried him back, he couldn't keep his eyes open as I tucked him in. Didn't even have time to suck his thumb. His first step to becoming a cowboy."

Jarrod leaned a shoulder against the doorjamb. "He has latched onto the idea."

"And played right into your hands. You're a sly one, Jarrod. Did you see how hard he tried today to remember not to keep his thumb in his mouth?"

Her sudden smile made his breath catch for an instant. With that red hair, she was a beautiful combination of fire and sunshine. "He did give that little arm a pumping every time he put it in and pulled it out." He stared into her eyes, thinking that was a safe place. The clear blue depths pulled him in until he could hardly catch his breath.

"You gave the children a wonderful day, Jarrod. Especially Tom. I've never seen him so happy."

He nodded. "What about you, Abby? Did you have fun?"

"Oh, yes. Once I let go of thinking of all the work waiting for me, I had a wonderful time."

"Even though you let that worm escape?" he asked, raising an eyebrow.

"I did not *let* him escape. He slipped out of my fingers and I simply couldn't catch him."

"The world's fastest worm," Jarrod said dryly.

"That's right. I had no idea how quick those little devils

could be." She lifted her chin slightly, daring him to contradict her.

"It had nothing to do with the fact that you didn't like touching them or hurting the fish?"

"Absolutely nothing."

"So it really was an accident when you fell in the stream? Not just a way to get out of holding that fishing pole?"

"Of course not. My feet went out from under me. And I'm glad it happened. I was hot."

Not to mention soaked from chest to ankle, he remembered. Droplets of water had splashed into her face, clinging to her thick lashes and sparkling like diamonds. They were no match for the glitter of delight in her eyes. Her surprised squeal and merry laughter at her condition were contagious. They had all laughed with her. His attention had been drawn to her full, rosy lips, the most kissable mouth he'd ever seen.

If only his gaze hadn't strayed from there. But he hadn't been able to resist glancing lower, at the way the soaked material of her blouse plastered to her rounded breasts. He could almost see the naked, rosy-tipped peaks.

He couldn't let her struggle out of the water, so he'd held out a hand to her. The feel of it in his own—soft, delicate-boned, and feminine in spite of the calluses she'd earned from hard work—had made him want to wrap his arms around her and kiss every last bead of water from her lashes, her nose, her cheeks, her neck. And lower.

He went hard again, just as he had then. She wasn't the only one who had been hot.

Jarrod took a step toward her, stopping when their bodies were only inches apart. Her eyes widened as she stared at him. Could she see that his mood had changed from teasing to temptation? But she didn't move away. He cupped her cheek in his palm, savoring the satin feel of her skin for a moment, then lowered his mouth to hers.

She smelled like a field of wildflowers and tasted of cake and coffee. Sighing at the sweetness of it, he circled an arm around her small waist and pulled her loosely against his length. For a moment her palms rested stiffly on his bare chest. Then she relaxed and leaned into him. Her sudden surrender and the nearness of her womanly softness fueled the fire in his blood.

Tracing the seam of her lips with his tongue, he sought to deepen the kiss. A sigh escaped her as she opened her mouth, letting him slip inside. Very slowly, she slid her arms up his chest and around his neck. He stroked the honeyed recess of her mouth, eliciting a small moan. Shivers rippled through her, sending waves of male satisfaction crashing through him. He was glad she was affected by him. God knows he hadn't been able to get her out of *his* mind. "Let me love you, Abby."

"Hmmm?" she said dreamily, her mouth still pressed to his.

It was high time they figured out exactly what was between them.

He had wanted her since the first time she had spent the night under his roof. He was about to go crazy from wanting her. He could tell she liked kissing him; her rapid breathing was a match for his own. Surely they wanted the same thing.

Jarrod lifted her into his arms and stepped through his doorway.

She pulled her mouth away and stared at him, her chest rising and falling rapidly. "What are you doing?"

He nuzzled her neck and felt her stiffen. "I care about you, Abby, and I think you care about me. Let me show you—"

"I—I wasn't thinking straight, Jarrod. Please put me down."

The demands of his body kept him from hearing her. He took another step into the room and felt a sharp pain as she pulled the hair on his chest.

"Ouch! What'd you do that for?"

"I said put me down."

He did. She backed away from him toward the door, straightening her clothes. Her breathing was erratic, but he wasn't certain whether it was from passion or anger. The fire in her eyes answered the question.

"Wait, Abby—"

"No."

In one stride he was beside her and gripped her arm.
"You have to admit that there's something between you and
me."

"I don't have to do any such thing." She tried to pull
away, but he held on. "I can't feel anything for you. I
won't."

"You can control your emotions as easy as that?"

"Yes."

"You're not being honest with yourself." He ran a
hand through his hair, and it didn't sweeten his mood
when he saw it was shaking. "Or you're luckier than I am,
then."

"This can't happen again, or I'll have to go," she said, a
warning in her voice. "Job or no job."

"You wouldn't. What about the children? Your brother?"

Pain darkened her blue eyes, and he hated himself for
using her soft heart against her. He was a selfish bastard.

"I'd never deliberately hurt those kids. And I think you
know it. I like you, Jarrod. I think you know that too. That's
exactly why this can't ever happen."

"Would you feel differently if you weren't leaving?"

She said nothing, just bit the corner of her lip.

Jarrod dropped his hand from her arm.

"Do I have your word that you won't do anything like
this again?" she asked.

He slowly nodded. "I'm sorry for you, Abby." He sighed.
"And for me."

Abby walked briskly down the front porch steps and down
the rise toward the bunkhouse. She needed air and thought
the pleasant night might clear her head and the fire inside
her.

But a voice in her mind warned her that it would take
more than a nighttime stroll to make her stop wanting
Jarrod Blackstone.

There was a lantern hanging on the bunkhouse wall. In

her agitated state, Abby didn't see the figure sitting on the steps until she heard Gib Cochran's voice.

"Howdy, Firecracker."

Startled, she stopped and looked. With her hand pressed to her thundering heart she said, "Gib, you scared me."

"Didn't mean to. You must have a powerful lot on your mind. Wanna set a spell?"

She hesitated, then decided it couldn't hurt. His company would be soothing even though she had no intention of talking about what had just happened between her and Jarrod.

She sat down on the top step. The light hanging above them on the wood-sided wall turned the gray in his beard to gold.

"How are you, Gib?"

"Fine, thanks for askin'. This is real pleasant, if you don't mind my sayin' so. Haven't set this close to a pretty lady in a month of Sundays."

"Don't tell Bea Peters that."

He laughed. "She's a fine woman, she is. Don't rightly know why no man ever snapped her up."

"Maybe she didn't want to be," Abby said, glancing back toward the big house.

"That sounds like the voice of experience talkin'. You out here like a she cat heading for higher ground so's you don't get snapped up?"

"Who in the world would want me?" she asked, trying with all her might to make her voice light, joking.

"Jarrod," he answered simply.

She laughed. "I'm his housekeeper. He's my boss. There's nothing—"

"Horse pucky," he said. "You gonna tell me true or you gonna sit there and spin tales like you do for them kids? 'Cause I'm not buyin' what you're tryin' t'sell."

Abby sighed. She had a powerful need to unburden her heavy heart to someone. It might as well be Gib Cochran. "I'll tell you what's on my mind, but you have to swear on your mother's life that you won't say a word to another soul."

"Who do I look like? Henrietta Schafer?"

Abby laughed. "No. And as long as you don't replace her as the town gossip—"

"Hollister's awful far away. You need to let it all out pretty quick, I'm thinkin'."

"Jarrod just kissed me."

He slapped his knee and grinned like a fool. "Is that all?"

"No, I kissed him back, and he took me into his bedroom and he would have—If I hadn't stopped him we probably— It was my fault as much as his and I wanted—" She stood up as warmth flooded her cheeks. "I can't do this."

He gently tugged on her arm. "Sit down. You think I don't know about that sort of thing?" He chuckled. "Don't know what you're in such a snit about. I seen sparks fly 'tween you and that hard-headed rancher first time I ever saw you together. Why d'you think I started callin' you Firecracker?"

"I thought it was because of my hair."

"Not hardly." He shook his head. "Maybe I'm gettin' old, but I don't see what the problem is."

"The problem is that I should go away. Tonight. Or tomorrow at first light."

"You're not makin' sense, girl."

"I think Jarrod has feelings for me. I can't return them."

"You just said you kissed him back—"

"I did," she cried. "I liked it so much. Don't you see? I can't get involved with him because as soon as I earn enough to make sure my brother's future is secure, I have to go."

"Where to?" he asked, his voice hard and his eyes like coals.

"To find my father." She drew in a deep breath, grateful that he didn't say anything until she finished her explanation. "Ever since he left my mother to find work, I knew someday I had to look for him and reunite my family. Pa and Clint and me, together. The way it should be."

"What if he don't want you to live with him?"

"Why wouldn't he?" she asked sharply.

He shrugged. "Don't know. 'Cept he knows where you

are. If he wanted a family, wouldn't he have sent for you before this?"

"Not necessarily. He might not have enough money. He might think we're angry at him and don't want him back."

"So you're gonna find him and convince him otherwise."

"I have to, Gib."

"Honey, you're runnin' on fire and dreams. They both turn to ashes right quick if they got nothin' to go on." He nodded toward the big house, where she could still see Jarrod's light in the upstairs window. "There's a man up there with flesh and blood needs. I think you're the woman who can fix what's ailin' him."

"What makes you say that?" It didn't change what she had to do, she told herself. She was just curious.

"You're the first since Dulcy that he's shown any interest in. I never seen him look at her the way he does you."

"You're imagining things."

"Nope, I ain't. But he's a proud man. Doesn't take to failing. He won't easily give in to another woman."

"That proves my point. His only interest in me is of the—" She hesitated, trying to figure out how to phrase it delicately. "It's of a carnal nature."

Surprising her, he chuckled. "It is that. You're a fine-looking woman and he'd have to be deaf, dumb, and blind not to notice." He sobered just as quickly. "There's more to it than that. I ain't sayin' he even knows how he feels, bein' a knothead from time to time. But no matter what you think, you ain't just his housekeeper."

"Gib," she said, "I want you to know I'd walk barefoot through hot coals before I'd hurt Jarrod and the children. That's why I resisted taking this job in the first place. But until my family is back together, I can't think about anything else."

"I hear ya." He sighed. "And dang it, I ain't one to stomp to death a body's fancy, 'specially when they been carryin' it around as long as you have. Just want t'see you happy, is all. I hope ya are."

"I will be."

# 12

*Jarrod walked out of the* Hollister telegraph office, hoping the wire he'd just sent wouldn't rear up to bite him in the behind. He'd known Luke Brody for a long time, done business with him. The man knew San Francisco like the back of his hand. If Luke couldn't find the information, then he would find someone who could. Jarrod had thought long and hard about it, and in the end decided he'd have no peace if he didn't try.

He stood on the boardwalk and looked around. Hollister was alive with Fourth of July activity and excitement. The mercantile displayed an American flag, waving in the warm summer breeze. The upstairs girls at the Watering Hole had made a banner and tacked it onto the railing, letting it hang down from the second floor. Henrietta Schafer had a sign in the restaurant window advertising a breakfast special, for the holiday only. Abby was there now, planning the day with the children.

Abby.

Just her name brought out tender feelings in Jarrod. She'd been skittish around him ever since he'd kissed her. He didn't blame her, but couldn't find it in him to regret anything that felt as good as that kiss. It had made him want more. And he'd eat his hat if she hadn't felt that way too, although she'd refused to admit it. He was only sorry their easy friendship was strained now. If he'd thought it through, he wouldn't have taken her into his room. Problem was, he hadn't been thinking. At least not with his head.

He missed talking to her the way they had before. The damnedest part was, he still wanted her. Although nothing was likely to come of it, and that was probably for the best.

At least he knew where he stood with her. She hadn't changed her mind. She was still leaving.

He glanced over his shoulder at the telegraph. Time would tell, he thought.

As he stepped from beneath the overhang into the dusty street, sunlight warmed his shoulders. Gonna be a hot one today, he decided. Best see what everyone was doing. Abby would need help keeping track of the kids.

Jarrod entered the nearly empty restaurant. Abby sat alone at a table near the swinging doors of the kitchen. He crossed the room and stopped in front of her.

"Mind if I join you?" he asked, removing his hat, then spinning it through his hands.

"Of course not."

He took the chair across from her as she picked up her coffee cup and sipped. "Where are the children?"

"Katie and Oliver are with Annie and Don Shemanski," she said.

"Are you sure Annie doesn't mind?"

Abby laughed. "I'm not even sure she knows. With six of her own, two more are hard to notice. They're like a line of little ducklings, and Katie and Oliver fell into step at the end."

"Maybe we shouldn't impose."

Abby shrugged. "Annie invited them. Two of her children are just about the same ages as Katie and Oliver. The kids took to each other, and she was glad to have them occupied. They're supposed to meet us for lunch by that big oak in Hollister meadow."

He nodded his approval. "What about Lily?"

The kitchen doors swung open and Henrietta Schafer bustled through. "Don't you worry, Jarrod. She's with my Joe." She set a picnic basket on the table. "He'll take good care of that pretty little niece of yours."

"I don't mean to be critical, Hettie, but how can you be so sure?"

Abby grinned at the other woman. "He's a little nervous."

Hettie nodded knowingly. "Good. Shows he cares. I can guarantee that Joe will do his best to bring Lily back safe and sound. It's all any man can do."

"He's still a boy. And it's not safe and sound that worries me, Hettie. It's the two of them being—"

"Alone?" she asked, one eyebrow lifting.

"Yes."

"Shoot," the woman said, waving her hand dismissively. "Abby took care of that."

When he looked at Abby for an explanation, she smiled smugly. "I sent Tom along with them."

He nodded thoughtfully. "What if they give him the slip? There are so many people in town today, it wouldn't be all that hard. What if—"

Henrietta patted his shoulder. "Relax, Jarrod. If you don't watch out, you're gonna give yourself heart failure." She winked at Abby. "You gotta take care of yourself. Remember, you got that cute little Katie growin' up before your eyes. What are you gonna do when the boys come sniffin' after her?"

"Send Oliver along," he said emphatically.

She chuckled. "You learn fast. Mind if I take a load off?" she asked, looking from Abby to Jarrod, who shook his head and pulled out the chair beside him. "It's been a long day, and it ain't even noon yet."

Abby put her hands around her coffee cup. "Thanks for fixing lunch for us, Henrietta."

"Don't you give it another thought. Least I can do for them kids. I swear, never seen young'uns so worked up. They may be too excited to eat that fried chicken I fixed 'em. You'd think they never had a holiday before."

Jarrod frowned. "I'm not sure they ever did."

Or Abby either, he thought. At least not a carefree one. She'd been looking forward to this day as much as the kids. Maybe more.

He glanced from Abby to Henrietta. "I think it's about time we got out there to enjoy the festivities. What do you say?"

"I'd say you're right." Abby answered with a smile.

Hettie looked at them. "Which of the festivities you two gonna do 'fore havin' this mouth-waterin' picnic lunch?" she asked, angling her head toward the basket on the table.

"I thought I'd go down to the meadow and get in on the egg toss Mr. Whittemore is organizing," Abby said.

Jarrod didn't miss the fact that she had pointedly left him out. Hah! She was in for a surprise. He had agreed to take this break from the ranch as much for her as for the children. She was going to have fun. And he damn well intended to watch her do it.

Hettie stared at Abby. "You're gonna need a partner in that there egg contest. Earl won't let ya even sign up if ya don't come as a pair." She glanced at Jarrod. "What about you? Got anythin' better t'do?"

"Nope."

"I'm sure Jarrod won't have any trouble finding a partner, especially one of the female persuasion," Abby said. Her tone was casual, too unconcerned.

"You think so?" he asked, enjoying the way Abby's eyes turned dark blue. Was it anger? Jealousy? He'd put his money on the latter and he couldn't help grinning at the thought. "Any suggestions?"

Abby's mouth thinned before she answered. "Just go on down there to the meadow. I expect the ladies will swarm around you like flies."

"What about you being my partner, Abby?" he asked. "Seems like the easiest solution. We could just go on over as a team and—"

"I can't," she said, cutting him off.

"Don't see why. Unless you're afraid. *Are* you afraid to pair off with me?"

"Of course not. It's just that Robert Harmon never gets picked for the games. I sort of promised him if I was around we could—"

Hettie put her hand on Abby's and squeezed. "Sweet of you to think of that boy. He's simpleminded, but his feelin's surely do get hurt easy."

"Then you understand why I can't disappoint him." She looked at Jarrod. "I'm sorry—"

"Hold on," Hettie said. "Robert's sick. Come down with chicken pox three days ago. Doc says he can't be around folks till the spots are gone. Annie is beside herself. Her Matthew was playin' with Robert the day before he took sick."

"Oh, Lord," Abby cried. "Katie and Oliver are with Matthew. I need to—"

She started to stand, and Jarrod put his hand on her arm. "Where are you going?"

"To find the children."

"And do what? Pull them away from their fun? It'd be easier to catch a tumbleweed in a tornado. Besides, harm's already done now. Just leave them be," he said.

"I suppose you're right."

"Looks like you still don't have a partner for the egg toss," Jarrod said to her. As hard as he tried, he couldn't keep from smiling. "If I were you, I'd take advantage of my offer."

"Why's that?" she asked.

"You could do worse. I've got good hands and my aim is true. Wouldn't want you to miss out on the fun, just in case everyone's taken." He softened his tone deliberately, letting his words take on an intimate meaning. He knew her thoughts had taken the same turn when a pretty pink flush crept into her cheeks.

"Don't you worry about me, Jarrod. I'll find—"

"For pity's sake, Abby," Hettie said. "You could do worse than Jarrod Blackstone. Time's a-wastin'. Sit here jawin' long enough and you'll miss out altogether. Just don't let that pretty face of his distract you." She winked then chuckled as Abby's blush deepened. "I expect a blue ribbon this year, missy."

"We'll see what we can do, Hettie." Jarrod stood and grabbed the picnic basket, figuring action would goad her into joining him. He put his hat on, pulling it low on his forehead to shadow the twinkle he knew was in his eyes. "You ready to go, Abby?"

She shot him a look saying she knew she'd been railroaded, and stood up. "Ready as I'll ever be. We'll see you at the meadow, right Henrietta?"

"Nothin' could keep me away. Soon's I clean up here, I'm closin' for the rest of the day."

"So long, Hettie."

Wanting to touch her even in the most innocent way, Jarrod took Abby's elbow as they walked outside. She stiffened but didn't pull away.

Cradling the raw egg in her hand, Abby stood at the end of the line, across from Jarrod. She was still smarting some from his high-handedness. Who did he think he was, backing her into a corner she couldn't get out of? And the suggestiveness in his voice! In front of Henrietta, of all people. As they waited for the game to start, he laughed with Earl Whittemore. She looked at Jarrod's handsome profile, then at the egg in her hand. He thought he was so smart, maneuvering her into this game with him. Before she thought it through, she drew her arm back and heaved the egg at him.

He turned and his eyes widened just before it smacked him in the chin. She smiled with satisfaction as the broken shell and dripping yolk clung to his square jaw. With a swipe, Jarrod wiped some of the slimy goo from his face. "Why the hell did you do that?"

"Why didn't you duck?"

Earl Whittemore chuckled. "I'm not sure whether or not to disqualify you for that, Abby."

"I think you should, Earl," someone down the line said, chuckling as Jarrod glared at Abby. "I don't want to compete against her. She's got a pretty good aim and ain't never forgiven my Emma for makin' her haul that chifforobe clear out to our place. Then my wife changed her mind about the thing and Abby had to take it back into town."

Eli Catron, the blacksmith, hooted. "Hell, let 'em stay in the game. They ain't no competition if Jarrod can't handle what Abby throws."

Laughter rose from the spectators as Jarrod took her arm. "I'd like to speak to you, Abby."

"I was just funnin', Jarrod. I didn't mean anything—"

"The hell you didn't," he said, his voice low and angry as he wiped his face.

As he led her across the meadow to an oak tree on the far side, Abby looked into his eyes, gray and stormy with anger. Had she gone too far? She hadn't thought beyond her need to wipe that gloat off his face. She'd put egg there instead, and a good portion of the population of Hollister had seen her do it.

After pulling Abby to the far side of the wide oak trunk and away from the amused glances of the milling crowd, Jarrod pressed her against the bark of the tree. He stood in front of her, tall and strong, and as imposing as the inflexible oak behind her. She had about as much chance of moving him as she did that tree.

"What did you want to speak to me about?" she asked, trying to ignore the flutter in her stomach.

"I've never met a more contrary female in my life."

"Me?"

"For Pete's sake, Abby, that egg didn't slip out of your hand, and everyone knows it. You let fly, hard as you could, right at my face."

"So?"

"Why?" he asked, his breath coming fast and harsh, the way it had when he'd kissed her. The thought made her pulse race.

"You let Henrietta Schafer think there's something of a personal nature between us."

"She knew I was joking."

"She knew no such thing. It'll be all over town before you can say hogwash and horsefeathers."

"No one will believe her. And what if they do? Who will it hurt?"

"Me. The children. I don't want them to get any ideas about us, Jarrod. After that kiss—"

He pointed at her. "That's it, isn't it? You're still sore because of that kiss." He raked a hand through his hair. "Dammit, Abby, what's it going to take to get you to admit that I matter to you?"

"Of course you matter. We're friends—"

"The hell we are. It's more than that and you know it."

"I don't know any such thing."

"You do or you wouldn't have thrown that egg in my face in front of the whole town. You don't have the guts to own up to it. This is more than just being mad because I teased you in front of Hettie."

"A lot you know about it." Anger welled up inside her. She knew she was being unreasonable, but for the life of her, she didn't understand why and couldn't stop herself. "Teasing wouldn't bother me. I'm mad because you talked like a man who's sparking me, and you said it in front of Henrietta. Everyone knows she's the town gossip."

"So what if she tells them we're sparking?"

Her eyes grew wide. "We're not, that's why. If you can't see that, I'd have to say you've been out in the sun too long without a hat."

Shaking his head, he moved closer and braced his palms on either side of her, trapping her between him and the tree. "There's nothing wrong with me. Except you."

Abby didn't like the intensity in his eyes or the closeness of his body. He was too big, too masculine. Too much for her addled state of mind.

"Don't you kiss me, Jarrod Blackstone," she warned.

He smiled, but it didn't reach his eyes. "What makes you think I'm going to kiss you?"

"That look on your face. It's just like last time—"

"I knew it! You can't forget about it either, can you?"

"Haven't given it another thought since you promised you wouldn't do it ever again." A ripple of need wavered through her, undermining her resolve to ignore her weakness for him. "You're a man of your word."

"What if I did it again, Abby? What would you do? Would you wrap your arms around my neck and press yourself close like last time?"

"You're imagining things. I never did—"

"You did, Abby. I liked it too. A lot."

"Don't say that." She bit the corner of her lip to stop the trembling.

"I'm a man of my word, and that's the Lord's honest truth. So why are you scared?"

"I'm not."

"And I've seen snow in July," he scoffed. "Is it because of the way I make you feel? Do I make you want me, Abby?

"Don't be silly." Her whispery voice robbed the words of the sting she'd intended.

"That's it, isn't it? You liked it when I kissed you. You wanted more. That scares you more than anything."

"Ridiculous," she said, trying to duck under his arm.

"Then don't run away." He caught her and pulled her back. "You're afraid that if you admit you care for me, you might have to give up your dream."

She drew in a sharp breath, feeling raw and exposed— and cornered. "What if you do matter to me? What if I say it? Nothing changes."

"Everything changes."

She shook her head. "You and I—we can't ever be."

"Why not?"

"Because you don't want a wife and I don't want to get married. Ever. Where does that leave us?"

"At least our cards are on the table. It's better than hiding behind anger."

She leaned away from him, feeling the rough bark of the tree as she pressed against it. "Why is it so important for you to know? Why do you have to be right, Jarrod? Because you were wrong about Dulcy?"

He jerked back as if she'd struck him.

She wished she could call back the words as soon as they were out. "I'm sorry. I didn't mean to say that."

"Yes, you did." He rubbed a hand over his face. "I suppose I had it coming. And you're right. I'm not good at failure."

She pulled air deep into her lungs. "Then let it go. I told you from the start that I can't stay. Don't make me hurt you." Her voice caught for a moment. When she was sure she could control it, she looked at him. "I couldn't stand to hurt you, Jarrod."

He sighed deeply and his head fell forward for several moments. When he looked at her again, one corner of his mouth lifted in a sad smile. He dropped his arms, freeing her, although she couldn't have moved even if a pack of ravenous wolves were after her. Then he reached out and stroked a wisp of red hair near her cheek.

"Sweet Abby. All fire and spirit. And honesty." He shot her a wry look that put her at ease.

The want and the need were gone, tucked away as if they'd never been there. But she knew as long as she lived, she would never forget how he had looked at her. It had touched something deep inside her, a pocket of longing she hadn't even known was there. She couldn't forget, but she had to set aside her feelings. It would have to be enough that her friend Jarrod was back again. Not the man who wanted more from her than she could give.

"Anyone ever tell you you're too damn honest, Abby?"

"Only you." She smiled at him, and breathed a sigh of relief when he smiled too.

They stepped out from behind the tree and saw Katie running toward them. Her hair hung wet and limp on either side of her face. The embroidered bodice of her dress was soaked as well.

"Uncle Jarrod! Abby! Look what I got." Breathless, she stopped and held out the blue satin ribbon.

Jarrod went down on one knee and took it from her. "What's this for?"

"First place!"

"I mean what did you do to get it?" he asked, grinning.

"I bobbed for apples. Tom said it's 'cause I got a big mouth, but he wasn't really mad when he said it. See, Abby?" she said, taking it from Jarrod to show her.

"It's a beauty, sweetie."

"Do I truly have the biggest mouth?" she asked Jarrod. Without waiting for an answer, she asked, "What's that stuff on your shirt, Uncle Jarrod?"

"Egg," he said.

Katie looked sympathetic. "If your egg broke, I guess you didn't win. I'm sorry you didn't get a blue ribbon." Her face brightened. She took the strip of satin from Abby. After looking longingly at it for several moments, she held it out to him. "Here, Uncle Jarrod. You can have mine."

Abby glanced at Jarrod. She thought he couldn't have looked more pleased if someone had given him a first-rate parcel of land. "Thank you, Katie. That's mighty nice. But you won it. Wouldn't be right for me to take it. I've got to win my own. Means more if you do."

"I did feel awfully proud." She looked at him. "You could hold it for me."

"I'd like that," he said, and stuck it in his pocket.

Katie took Abby's hand, then Jarrod's, and stood between them. "Come with me. They're getting ready for the three-legged race. Maybe you can win your own ribbon."

"You game, Abby?" Jarrod asked.

She nodded. It was hard to keep from being swept along with his excitement, his enthusiasm. Harder yet not to enjoy being a part of this family, being with Jarrod.

"Before we get in the race, let's see what everyone else is doing," Jarrod said.

Katie tugged them along. "Tom tried to catch a greased pig." She giggled. "He looked so funny. He almost had it once, but it got away and he fell in the dirt."

In the meadow, tables were set up with pies lining the edges of both sides. Along with Joe Schafer and Paul Shemanski, Tom stood waiting. He was covered with dirt and axle grease from head to toe. His gray eyes looked like two pale circles in his filthy face.

When Abby and Jarrod stopped in front of him, he looked from them to his ruined clothes and back again as if he half expected a tongue-lashing. Abby noticed a jagged rip in one of the knees of his trousers.

When she glanced at Jarrod, she saw that he was grinning at the boy, who had an identical expression on his face.

"How bad does the pig look, son?" Jarrod asked.

"Not as bad as me," Tom admitted. He pulled a green ribbon out of his grimy pants. "I couldn't hang onto the pig, but I got this for being the dirtiest."

"Good for you," Jarrod said approvingly. "I guess you're fixing to eat pie now?"

"Yes, sir. They got strawberry and peach. My favorites."

"At least you don't have to worry about getting any on your clothes," Abby said. "Who will notice?"

"Ain't I somethin'?" Tom asked, looking down proudly.

"You sure are." Abby smiled at the pure pleasure on his face.

Katie jumped up and down. "Is this the best Fourth of July you ever had, Uncle Jarrod?"

He picked her up. "Yes. And do you know why?"

"Why?" she asked, sliding her arm around his neck.

"Because of you, and Tom, and Oliver and Lily."

"And Abby?" Katie asked.

When his gaze met Abby's, his eyes had darkened to pewter, the shade of clouds before a storm. "And Abby," he agreed.

"When are the fireworks gonna start?" Katie asked, tugging on Jarrod's pants as he and Abby danced. "You told me after dinner, and we finished that hours ago."

"It hasn't been hours. And they'll start when it's good and dark," he told her, loosening his hold on Abby.

He knew how anxious the little girl was, but he was mighty content for the moment. Katie might like the fireworks, but music and holding a woman in his arms were his favorite part of the festivities. He wasn't quite ready to let Abby go. They were good together, he thought. She felt good, just right against him like this. He was surprised she had accepted his invitation. Pleased, but surprised.

After their angry words earlier, he was sure she would never get that close to him again. But the sight of her dancing with other men had put the jealousy shoe on the other foot. He'd had to try. Now here she was in his arms.

"But Uncle Jarrod, it's dark now," Katie protested.

He glanced beyond the light created by the lanterns hung on the trees. The sky wasn't the inky-black that was the best time to see the explosives. As the strains of fiddle, guitar, and squeeze box created a slow tune that surrounded them, he adjusted Abby in his arms. "Katie, you won't be able to see the fireworks unless it's dark enough."

Abby smiled up at him, then looked at Katie. "Why don't you look for Lily and Joe? See what they're doing."

"If I do, will the fireworks start sooner?"

"No, but it will feel like it," she said, then winked at Jarrod.

"Oh, all right," the little girl said, and grudgingly turned away.

Beside them, Earl Whittemore laughed as he danced with his wife Jane. "That little girl of yours is a pistol, she is. Never seen a young'un get so all-fired excited over fireworks. And ours used to get pretty worked up over 'em."

Jarrod grinned. "Yup. She's been looking forward to it so long, I hope she's not disappointed."

"She won't be," Jane said. "Are you and Abby having a good time?"

"Can't remember ever having such a good time on the Fourth," Jarrod said, looking down at Abby. "Not since I was Tom's age, I think."

Abby's eyes sparkled so brightly, he didn't need to see fireworks. He was glad they had talked. The air was cleared even if things hadn't been settled. For now, it was enough that they had recovered their friendship.

From behind, someone tapped on his shoulder. He was about to tell whoever it was to go to hell. He hadn't finished dancing with Abby and he had no intention of giving her up.

"Hi, Joe," she said.

Jarrod half turned so he could see the boy. "Evening, son."

"Mr. Blackstone? Could I speak to you for a minute? Alone?" he asked, glancing at Abby. "Sorry, Miss Abby. But this is something that needs to be between menfolk."

"Is it Lily? She's all right, isn't she, Joe?" Abby stopped dancing and pulled out of Jarrod's arms. "If anything's wrong—"

"Don't fret, Miss Abby. I'd never let harm come to Lily. She's over there," he said, pointing to the far side of the clearing, where Katie stood talking to her older sister.

Jarrod relaxed and saw Abby do the same.

"I just need to talk to Mr. Blackstone about somethin'."

Abby nodded. "I'll go see the girls, and leave you men to your talk."

Jarrod watched her walk away, admiring the proud set of her shoulders, her trim waist, the flirtatious sway of her skirts—

"Mr. Blackstone?"

Reluctantly, he pulled his gaze from Abby and looked at Joe. Jarrod and the young man walked off the dance floor and over to the side, where they could talk without being jostled. "What is it, son?"

"Thought you should know somethin', sir. Gives me a real bad feelin'."

"What's that?" Jarrod heard the uneasiness in the young man's voice and gave him his full attention.

"Stranger's been followin' me and Lily and Tom all day."

"That so? You sure about this?"

"Yes, sir. Thought it was coincidence at first. Then every time I'd look up, he was there. He was followin' us. No doubt about it. Lily noticed him too."

"Joe, you didn't leave Lily alone at all, did you?" Jarrod kept his voice calm, but he didn't like this. He could handle someone asking about him, but he wouldn't let anyone get near the children.

"No, sir. Especially after I noticed him. I made sure if I wasn't with her, Tom was."

Jarrod clapped him on the shoulder, thankful that Abby had been right about the boy being capable and smart. "Good."

"Who do you think he is?"

"I couldn't say."

"I don't get it. Why would he follow me 'n' Lily?"

"Can't answer that either, but I'm going to find out." He looked at Joe. "I'd take it as a favor if you and Lily kept this to yourselves. No need to upset the other kids."

"Yes, sir. Whatever you want."

Jarrod started to walk away, then stopped. "I'd be obliged if you'd watch out for Lily till the fireworks are over."

Joe met his gaze, and Jarrod knew he was looking at a man. "I planned on it, sir. Nothin' will happen to her."

"Thanks, Joe."

"No need t'thank me, sir," he said, then walked to the group at the edge of the clearing.

Jarrod gazed at the people milling around, searching in vain for a stranger.

When Abby rejoined him, she asked, "What did Joe want?"

He almost sidestepped her question, wanting to spare her the worry he knew would spoil the rest of her evening. But he decided two pairs of eyes were better than one, so he repeated what Joe had told him.

Uneasily, Abby scanned the crowd. "What if he's dangerous, Jarrod?" she asked, gripping his arm.

He squeezed her hand reassuringly. "Don't borrow trouble. We'll gather up all the kids and keep them with us for the fireworks. Afterward, I want you to take them back to the boardinghouse."

"What are you going to do?"

"Look for this fella and find out what he wants."

When the first explosion sent colored sparks into the air, Katie covered her ears and squealed loud enough to wake the dead. "Ooh! Did you see that, Uncle Jarrod?"

"Sure did, honey."

Katie sat in his lap and jumped up with the next boom. She clapped her hands. "That was a good one. Wasn't that a good one?"

"It was dandy," Jarrod assured her.

With Oliver sitting on her outstretched legs, Abby was beside Jarrod on the blanket. Tom, Lily, and Joe were on his other side, keeping nearby, as he'd told them to.

Abby was close enough that her shoulder brushed Jarrod's, near enough that he could smell her womanly fragrance in spite of the smoke in the air. Another time, he might have deliberately rubbed up against her just to watch her breath catch and to see where that might lead. But tonight his attention was on the crowd, watching for a stranger.

Katie covered her ears again, then pointed when gold shards lit up the black sky. "Oh, that's the best!"

Tom snorted. "That's what you say about every one."

"Every one is the best," she said, her small body shaking with excitement. "Don't you think so, Tom?"

"I reckon so," he agreed.

"Lily, did you see that one?" Katie asked.

"Aw, Kate," Tom said. "Can't you see she's too busy lookin' at Joe?"

Jarrod glanced over at the young couple sitting pressed together from shoulder to thigh. Their hands were clasped tightly. Another time, it might have concerned him. Now, with someone following Lily, he was grateful for the young man's presence. In fact, he was counting on Joe Schafer not to let her out of his sight.

When Jarrod turned his gaze to Abby, he saw the worry in her eyes. His gut tightened a notch as anger flowed through him. He'd have given a lot to see her have a perfect day. Thanks to someone out there, it had been spoiled. He glanced at the children's faces and their rapt expressions as they stared at the sky expectantly. At least they were enjoying themselves.

A wave of protectiveness surged through him. He'd never felt anything so powerful. Without a doubt, he knew he would do *anything* to keep these children—his children—healthy, happy, and safe.

Through the smoke, he thought he caught a glimpse of a stranger wandering behind the spectators. Then there was another explosion and Katie stood up, clapping as she jumped around. When she sat again, there was no sign of the man.

"Did you see that, Uncle Jarrod?" the little girl asked, throwing her arms around him.

"Almost," he said, hugging her.

"I did. It was a fine one."

There were four outbursts in quick succession, followed by red, white, blue, and gold fire.

Katie stood transfixed. When there was nothing but darkness mixing with smoke and the smell of gunpowder, she turned to Jarrod, for once completely speechless.

He stood up and lifted her into his arms. "What did you think, Katie?"

"It was the most wonderful thing I ever saw," she whispered reverently. "Didn't you think so, Oliver?"

Abby stared down at the blond head resting against her breasts, his body completely relaxed in sleep. "It's been a long day. He's tuckered out."

"Must be, if he slept through that." Jarrod felt a tug in his chest, and emotion thickened in his throat. He cleared it and said, "Best get everyone to the boardinghouse now. I'll carry him."

Jarrod set Katie on her feet and lifted Oliver into his arms. As he snuggled the warm little body close to him, he remembered Tom saying on his birthday that it was the best day of his life.

Jarrod knew how the boy felt.

Sitting in her nightgown on the bed, Katie exclaimed, "I loved the fireworks. It was the best thing I ever saw. What makes the colors, Abby?"

"I don't know."

"Maybe Uncle Jarrod knows. I'll go across the hall and ask him." She started to jump down.

"No, Katie." Her voice was sharper than she'd meant for it to be. "He's not there."

"Not in his room with Oliver and Tom? Why would he leave them? Where'd he go?"

"They can take care of themselves for a little while. If they need anything, they just have to come across the hall."

"Where's Uncle Jarrod?"

"He had an errand."

"But it's late. Why would he do an errand so late?" Katie asked.

Abby sighed. It was the first time she'd ever felt short-tempered with the little girl's questions. Jarrod was out looking for the stranger who had trailed Lily all day. She couldn't tell Katie the truth, for fear of alarming her. "Don't worry," was the last thing he'd said. That was the dumbest thing she'd ever heard. How could she not?

Where was he? He'd been gone a long time. Hollister wasn't that big. He should have been back by now. Unless—

"Abby, did you hear me?"

She looked at Katie. "I'm sorry, sweetie. What did you say?"

"Don't encourage her to ask questions, Abby." Lily was beside her sister in the bed, and already under the covers. She yawned.

"Did you girls have a nice day?" Abby asked, trying to distract them as well as herself.

Katie nodded enthusiastically. "I liked the fireworks best. Didn't you, Lily?"

"Not me." The older girl flushed. "Joe held my hand. Not tight," she said quickly. "But he fitted his fingers between mine. It was wonderful."

Abby smiled. "I'm glad, sweetie."

Doubtful, Katie looked down at her sister. "You think holding hands with a boy is better than fireworks?"

Lily looked knowingly at Abby, then sent her sister a pitying glance. "You don't understand. Go to sleep, Katie."

Abby watched the friction between the girls. There were all kinds of ways to make sparks fly, she mused, thinking about her own run-in with Jarrod by the oak tree. She had felt the warmth of his body, seen the sizzle in his eyes. Please God, let him come back tonight unharmed, she thought.

There was a soft sound out in the hall and Abby jumped. Then she shot out of her chair by the window and hurried to the door, hoping it was Jarrod and praying that he was all right.

"Is that you, Jarrod?" she asked, listening carefully. She heard a muffled yes and yanked the door open. She gasped at the stranger standing there.

He held his hat in his hands. "Name's Rafe Donovan, ma'am. I've come for my brother's children."

# 13

*Abby stared at the stranger,* her heart pounding. "Rafe Donovan? Are you related to—"

"Reed was my brother." He lifted his hat, indicating the room behind her. "Those kids in there are blood kin to me."

"And me." Jarrod moved past the man and stood beside her in the doorway. The roar of blood in her ears had kept her from hearing his approach. Relief flooded Abby at the sight of him.

Jarrod's face was haggard as he scowled at her. "I thought you knew better than to open the door unless it was me."

Abby's eyes widened at the angry expression on his face. "I thought—"

"My fault, Blackstone. I told her I was you. She'd never have let me in otherwise."

"You tricked me into opening the door. I didn't let you in," she corrected. She looked up at Jarrod, glad to have his reassuring presence beside her.

Rafe Donovan was a big man, not as tall as Jarrod, but wide in the shoulders and chest. Deep-set blue eyes, nearly hidden by shaggy brown hair, dominated a face that was all angles and crevices and sharp lines. Whiskers dusted his upper lip and jaw.

"Who is it, Uncle Jarrod? Who's there?" Katie asked from behind them.

"Get her to bed," Jarrod said in a low voice rife with tension. He moved into the hall and shut the door as Abby stepped back into the room.

Satisfied that she could handle the children, Jarrod took the man's measure. The calluses on his hands indicated he worked hard for a living. Worn denim pants and a plaid shirt gave the same impression. Hard as he tried, Jarrod couldn't find fault with him. At least not on the outside.

"What do you want, Donovan?" he asked. "Only a man up to no good sneaks around. Why were you following my niece?"

"She's my niece too." He looked down for a moment, then met Jarrod's gaze. "I can't say exactly why I waited. Just wanted to see the way of things before I came forward."

"Now you have. Why'd you wait so long? I don't mean here in Hollister. Sally passed on over two months ago. Why are you only just showin' up?"

"Just found out about it," Donovan said. "I'm from New Mexico. Took a while for me to get the news. Soon as I did, I came for the kids."

Something tightened in Jarrod's chest. "No."

"Look, Blackstone, I think you ought to know I'm not like my brother. I didn't approve of him or his ways. It was liquor and gambling that took him down. Fact is, I tried everything I could to stop him. But because of his bad habits, I have clear title to the land we worked. I bought him out so's he could pay off gambling debts. What was left he used to move his family to Arizona."

"So you're a better man. I'm glad. But I don't see what that has to do with my sister's children."

"I was sorry to hear about Sally. Always liked her. I never favored the way my brother lived. Not that he cared what I thought. Soon's I met your sister, I knew if anyone could get through to Reed, it was her. He did change, at first. For her."

Surprisingly, that brought Jarrod some comfort. He was

glad to know that Sally hadn't completely misjudged her husband. That there had been some good in Reed Donovan.

"Are you married?" Jarrod asked him.

"Nope. Never did marry." Rafe shook his head regretfully. "Between the ranch and Reed, there was too much to do. We had a spell of bad luck on the ranch, a couple years after he married Sally. It sent him back to the bottle. In the end, he wouldn't listen to her any more than he did me."

"I don't give a damn about your brother. If he had acted like a man and faced his responsibilities to my sister and those kids, Sally would be alive today. You'll never convince me otherwise."

Donovan looked at the hat brim rolled in his hands, then back up. "Maybe. Maybe not. I'm not here to argue with you about the past. I'm here on account of those kids."

"Then things are real simple," Jarrod said. "They're with me."

The other man tossed his head to clear the hair from his eyes. "I'd think you'd welcome the chance to hand them over. It can't be easy taking care of 'em."

"It's not. Which makes me wonder why you want them. I should think you'd be grateful someone else has stepped in to do it."

"I am. But the thing is, I promised Reed if anything happened to him, I'd take care of his kids."

Jarrod sneered. "He didn't think enough of his children to provide for them day to day. Why the hell should I believe he cared enough to think about their future?"

"I reckon I can understand why you'd feel that way. But much as you want to believe otherwise, he wasn't all bad."

"Tell that to four kids who had nothing all their lives, including a father."

"I'm prepared to be that for 'em. My spread does a fair to middlin' business. They'd never want for food or shelter. Have to work, though." He shook the hair from his eyes again. "No gettin' around that. They'd have to earn their keep. Builds character, that's what my pa always said."

"God knows it worked for your brother," Jarrod said

dryly. "When I got those kids, they were hardly more than skin and bone. Clothes were patched and worn-out. Sally did the best she could, but it was your brother's fault that they were wanting. You think I can forget that? You think I can turn them over to the brother of the man who let that happen to them? Even if I wanted to give them up, why should I believe that you'd do better by them than Reed?"

Abby opened the door. "Keep your voice down," she whispered. "I just got Katie to sleep."

"Sorry," Jarrod said, drawing in a calming breath.

She slipped into the hall and quietly closed the door. "What's going on?" she asked, her gaze settling on the other man.

"Like I said, ma'am, I've come for my brother's children."

Jarrod grabbed the front of his shirt and shoved him against the opposite wall. "Maybe I didn't make it clear. The kids are staying with me. It'd be best for everyone if you'd go back where you came from and forgot about them."

Donovan looked him straight in the eye without flinching. "How come you never did anything for them before, Blackstone? You got more money than God. If they were in bad shape, you coulda helped out."

Jarrod knew he was right. Maybe he'd never wanted to see that things hadn't worked out for Sally and her kids. Maybe that's why he'd never gone to see her, using the ranch as an excuse. He tightened his grip on Donovan's shirt.

"What about you? How come you're just showing up?" His voice rose.

"Jarrod," Abby said, pulling on his arm. He hardly felt her touch as the rage squeezed out rational thought. "Let him go, Jarrod. This won't solve anything."

Rafe Donovan swallowed hard. Other than that, he didn't show fear. It made Jarrod madder when he found something to respect in the man.

"Your wife's right, Blackstone. It's late. Guess I was wrong to spring this on ya the way I did. I'd best go. We'll talk again in the morning."

Abby tightened her grip on Jarrod's upper arm. "I think that would be best, Mr. Donovan."

Jarrod dropped his hands from the man's shirt, not bothering to correct the man's mistake about him and Abby. "Don't bother to come back in the morning. We won't be here."

"You'd best be talkin' in anger, mister." Donovan's eyes narrowed on him.

"I'm tellin' you not to waste your time." Jarrod's gaze never left the other man's. "There's nothing more to say. I've got a ranch to run. So do you. I suggest you get back to it."

Donovan continued to stare at Jarrod. "I'll go when I get what I came for. Ma'am." He nodded to Abby. "I'll see you in the morning," he said to Jarrod. Then he turned and walked away.

Fists clenched at his sides, Jarrod watched him go. "Have the kids ready to travel just before first light."

"But, Jarrod—"

He glared at her. "Do it."

Abby finished washing up the supper dishes. She looked through the kitchen window and felt a tug at her heart when she looked at Jarrod. It had been two days since his run-in with Rafe Donovan. He'd been out there on the porch for over an hour, just rocking in that chair.

Now he sat forward, hands on his knees, giving her a clear view of his back. His strong shoulders, the ripple of muscles beneath the material pulled tightly across them, the broad expanse tapering to his narrow waist—the sight never failed to stir her blood and steal her breath away. What's he thinking? she wondered.

He'd hardly said anything to her since they'd returned to the ranch. She knew he'd directed the hands to keep their eyes open for Rafe Donovan. If the man showed up, she wasn't sure what they were supposed to do. The anger, worry, and danger she saw in Jarrod's face made her wonder if he'd ordered the man shot on sight.

Abby couldn't find it in her heart to fault him. One of the reasons he mattered so much to her was that he'd truly become a father to the children. That meant protecting them, which was what he believed he was doing.

She sighed, hoping the kids knew how lucky they were.

Abby wondered if things would be different for her now if her own father had been able to stay and hold the family together. Could she have stayed at the Blackstone Ranch and given in to the longings she felt for Jarrod? She shook her head. Things were what they were. She'd carried her dream around for too long. It was pointless to wish for something that couldn't be.

She set her cloth over the dishes drying on the drainboard and went outside. The sun hadn't gone down, but it wouldn't be long. Deep shadows crept closer to the porch. A pleasant breeze cooled her cheeks, which were warm from cooking and cleaning up.

Abby sighed and brushed the wisps of hair back from her face as she took the chair next to Jarrod. A small round table separated them. Still, she could smell the masculine scent of the soap he'd used to wash up before supper. In the weeks she'd been there, that smell had come to remind her of Jarrod. It never failed to stir the fluttering in her stomach.

She looked at him, deep in thought. "Jarrod? Sooner or later you have to talk about this."

He drew in a big breath. "Why? It's over as far as I'm concerned."

She noticed he didn't ask what "this" was. Rafe Donovan was on his mind whether he would admit it or not. And whether he wanted to or not, they were going to air what they were both thinking. "It's not over as far as he's concerned."

"How can you be so sure?"

"The man came from New Mexico. You think he's going to turn around and go home because you say so?"

"If he knows what's good for him, he will." He looked at her, and she flinched at the intensity of his gaze. But someone had to make him see that not only was it probable the man wouldn't give up, there was another issue to consider.

"Have you thought about what's good for the children? The fact that they might want to know him?"

"I have always thought about what's best for them. Have you considered the fact that the man might be up to something?"

"What?"

"Money. Reed Donovan was after it when he came sniffing around Sally. My father disinherited her. But her children stand to gain. Maybe he wants to get his hands on Blackstone land through them. What makes you think Rafe is any different from his brother?"

"Everyone deserves the benefit of the doubt."

"You're too trusting, Abby."

"You're too skeptical, Jarrod."

The ghost of a smile hovered on his lips for a moment, then vanished. "I wish I could see only the good in people like you do, but I can't. I don't trust him. And I don't understand why you want me to give him a chance."

"Because he's blood kin to them. They have a right to get to know their father's family. Maybe they have a need to know."

"No good can come of it," he snapped.

"You can't be sure of that. From what you told me, it sounds like he's a decent man."

"If he was telling the truth."

"Don't sell your sister short, Jarrod."

He frowned. "What are you talking about?"

"Sally was a Blackstone. That tells me she was nobody's fool. She would never have picked a man that she didn't see some good in." She sighed. "What she didn't see was that his weakness overshadowed the good. But Rafe Donovan has given you no reason to believe he's a good-for-nothing. He came a long way for those children."

"Doesn't that make you wonder why?" He stood and walked to the railing, leaning a shoulder against the support post. "He has a ranch to run. He left it to come after his brother's children. He's after something besides the kids."

"You don't know that." She decided to try another way

to get through to him. "Have you talked to the children about this?"

"No."

"Maybe they want to get to know him."

"They're kids. They don't know what they want."

"What if they resent you someday for keeping them from family?" she asked.

His eyes narrowed. "Having kin around doesn't make life perfect, Abby."

"I never said it does. It's just that closing your mind to possibilities can come back to haunt you. Could you live with their resentment if you deny them this opportunity, Jarrod?"

She felt his hesitation.

He scowled at her. "There's not much I could refuse them."

Abby thought he was weakening. "If he's like his brother, they'll see through him. He won't be able to hide it."

"Reed hid it from Sally."

"She was in love with him. They were both young. Give Rafe a chance to show his true colors. Just think about it."

"All right. If I decide there's some merit in what you say, I'll talk to the children and see what they want. If they agree, he can see them. If they don't want any part of him, that's how it's going to be. Will that make you happy, Abby?"

"It's not a question of my happiness, but what's best for the children. I just think they need family."

"I think that depends on who the family is." He looked out into the darkness that had descended while they'd talked. "There's one thing I won't change my mind about."

"What's that?"

"He's not taking those kids off Blackstone land, Abby. Not ever."

In the kitchen, huddling beneath the open window, Lily put her finger to her lips to shush the others when Jarrod stopped talking. He'd been acting funny ever since they'd come back from town. Abby too. Every time she asked what was wrong, they'd said nothing. They were lying. Lily knew it was to protect them. But she'd learned from living with Mama and Papa, when he'd been there, it was better to know what you were facing. She hated surprises, and if Abby and Uncle Jarrod wouldn't tell them anything, then they'd darn well have to find out on their own.

She motioned for them to follow her upstairs. When they were safely in her room with the door closed, she looked at them.

"What do you think, Tom?" she asked.

Katie threw herself on the bed and rested her chin in her hands. "Is this a family meeting, Lily?"

Tom glared at her. "Of course it is. What'd you think, knothead?"

Katie stuck her lip out. "We haven't had one in a long time. I was just askin', Tom. You shouldn't be so mean."

Lily noticed that Oliver stuck his thumb in his mouth. She hadn't seen him do that since Uncle Jarrod told him cowboys didn't. She didn't like the way things were going. Not at all.

She looked at her oldest brother. "Do you think Abby's right and we should give him a chance? You remember what Pa was like, same as I do. What if he's that way too?"

Lily had heard all the excuses for her father's behavior— bad luck, liquor, couldn't handle the responsibility of so many children. All she knew was that she'd been happy since they'd come to live with Uncle Jarrod. But not before that. Not even with Mama, although she still missed her all the time.

"Abby thinks we should get to know him." Katie looked from her sister to her brother.

"She's not always right," Lily said.

"That's fer dang sure," Tom agreed.

Katie sniffed. "You just don't like Abby, Tom. Right from the start you didn't. You wouldn't go along with anything she said."

"Katie's right, Tom," Lily said. "You haven't taken to

Abby same as the rest of us. But I like her. Right from the start I did."

"Better than Mama?" he shot back.

"Of course not. I'd give anything if Mama was still here. But she's not, and no amount of wishing will make it so. Besides, that doesn't mean we can't like Abby. Even if this time I think she's wrong. I don't want any part of Pa's side of the family."

Tom shot her a grateful look and nodded. "Me neither, Lil. So what do we do?"

That was a good question, Lily thought. When Uncle Jarrod had said that he'd never let the man take them off Blackstone land, it had made her feel like she finally belonged. The feeling was so big it had filled her up inside with happiness.

She looked around at all of them. "It's easy. Uncle Jarrod said he would ask us what we wanted to do. We'll tell him we don't want to see Rafe Donovan, and he won't make us. Simple."

"What if Abby pushes?" Tom asked. "She's got a bee in her bonnet about family. Uncle Jarrod listens to her more often than not."

"If that happens, I think we shouldn't do anything." Lily folded her arms over her chest and waited.

"What?" Tom cried. "We gotta decide somethin'. Else why'd you call this family meeting?"

"Yes, why, Lily?" Katie wanted to know. "We always figure out a plan."

Lily paced to the door then back to the bed and turned to look at her brother. "This time I think the plan is to do nothing."

"Why, Lil?"

"Uncle Jarrod said he'd never let that man take us off Blackstone land. So he won't. I don't think we have to have a plan. Except for all of us to agree that we don't want anything to do with that man. Right, Katie?"

"I don't know him, Lily. How can I tell if I don't want to meet him?"

Katie liked everyone and couldn't remember how bad

things had been with their father. They had to make sure
she would go along.

"Do you want to leave Uncle Jarrod?" Tom asked
harshly.

"No," Katie said in a small voice. "I love him."

"All right, then," Lily said. "When Uncle Jarrod asks,
we'll tell him we don't want anything to do with that man."

"Kidnapping?" Abby stared at Sheriff Zachary Magruder
with Rafe Donovan beside him. "Jarrod did no such thing."

"He says different, Abby. I have to check it out."

Abby looked at the other man, politely standing on the
front porch with his hat in his hand, almost the same way
she'd last seen him a week ago. "You know that's not the
way it happened."

"I don't want to think so, ma'am. But he took the kids
out of town—"

"He took them home," she said coldly.

Donovan shrugged. "Doesn't matter what words you use,
he took the kids out of town without so much as a by-your-
leave. When I tried to talk to him on the ranch, I was met
with guns. This was the only way."

"Does Jarrod know you're here?" she asked the sheriff.

He nodded. "We ran into him up in San Augustine
Canyon. He said to meet him here."

"Then come in." She opened the door wide and allowed
them entrance. "If you'll make yourselves comfortable in the
living room, I'll put on some coffee."

"Thanks, Abby," Zach said as she shut the door. "I'm
sure this is just a simple misunderstanding we can clear up
quickly."

She nodded doubtfully, then left them in the front room
and went to the kitchen. She had just put the pot on the iron
stove when Jarrod walked in the back door.

"Lord, I'm glad to see you," she said. "Why didn't you
tell me he'd shown up before this?"

He stood in the center of the room, boots braced apart,
as he stared at her. "The kids said they wanted no part of

him. Slim and Dusty sent him packing. There was no reason
for you to know."

He'd shut her out. For the first time, Abby felt like the
employee she was. She should have known better than to
listen to Jarrod. On Tom's birthday he had told her to let
tomorrow take care of itself. She'd done that. She'd let herself mother the children and begin to feel a part of this family. A reminder that she was nothing more than an outsider
was what she got for her efforts.

"I see." She turned away, reaching up to pull cups from
the cupboard.

She heard him come up behind her, felt the warmth of
his body before the touch of his hands on her arms. "I'm
sorry, Abby. I didn't mean that to sound as harsh as it did."

"There's no reason to apologize. This is your home. I
work for you and carry out orders like any of the ranch
hands."

"You're not like the others and you know it—" His voice
was tight with anger, frustration, and impatience.

"You've got more to worry about than my feelings. What
are you going to do, Jarrod? He's accused you of kidnapping
the children."

"Zach knows that's not true."

"Everyone knows that. The point is, Donovan's not
backing down. What are you going to do?" Abby pulled
out a tray and set three mugs on it along with the steaming
coffeepot and containers of cream and sugar.

"I'm not sure yet." He picked up the tray and started
through the doorway. He turned to her. "You coming?"

"I'm just the housekeeper. I didn't think you'd want me
there."

"Don't be that way, Abby. I kept his visit quiet to spare
you the worry. I know you love the kids."

"Of course I do."

"Do you think they should go with Donovan?"

"I never thought that. They love you so much, and
they've been through too many changes. The best thing for
them is to stay here." She shook her head emphatically. "I

only wanted you to be open-minded if the kids wanted to know him. That's all."

"That's why I want you in on this. I'm counting on you to say it just like that to Zach Magruder."

"If you think it will help."

"I do," he said. He put the tray on the table, then went to the cupboard and pulled another mug out. "You ready?" he asked, lifting the tray again.

When she nodded, he waited for her to precede him into the living room. The two men stood when she and Jarrod entered.

"Abby, Jarrod." The sheriff nodded to both of them.

"Let's all sit down," Jarrod said, setting the tray of coffee on the table in front of the sofa. "Will you pour, Abby?"

"Of course." She sat down with him beside her.

Zach settled himself into the wing-back chair by the hearth. He was a big man, over six feet tall, making that seat an uncomfortable fit. Abby smiled to herself. Maybe that would speed this along. Rafe Donovan stood in front of the fireplace, even after she handed him a cup of coffee.

"Now, then," Zach began. "What's this all about?"

"I've come for my brother's kids," Donovan answered.

"They're my sister's kids," Jarrod snapped. "They're staying here on Blackstone land where she wanted them."

"Their last name is Donovan. Reed wanted me to take care of 'em and that's what I aim to do."

Jarrod opened his mouth and the sheriff held up his hand for quiet. "We're gettin' nowhere fast."

Jarrod pointed to the other man. "What makes him think he's got more right to them than I do?"

"My brother wrote it in his last will and testament."

Zach shifted, trying to get comfortable in the small space. "I've seen it, Jarrod. Looks official to me."

"It's a piece of paper, Zach. He could have forged the signature. Even if he didn't, I've got a letter from Sally asking me to raise her children as Blackstones."

"Seems you both got a pretty good claim." Zach looked from one man to the other as each of them stared at him for a solution. He shook his head.

"I got an idea," Donovan said. "What about splittin' the kids up? A girl and boy apiece." He looked at them.

"Mr. Donovan! That's out of the question." Abby shot to her feet before Jarrod could stop her. "How could you suggest such a thing? Split up the children? Good heavens, until they came to Jarrod, all they had was each other. Why you can't—"

Jarrod touched her arm. "Hold on, Firecracker."

"But, Jarrod," she cried, looking down at him. "You aren't seriously considering it?"

"You didn't give me a chance to say anything one way or the other."

What he felt was a wave of relief. He knew how important family was to Abby. Still, when she'd expressed her opinion that the children get to know their other folks, he couldn't help questioning her loyalty. He smiled inside at her outburst. When Donovan suggested the compromise, he'd lost Abby's sympathy. Jarrod was glad to have her wholeheartedly on his side.

"How *do* you feel about separating the kids?" Zach asked Jarrod.

"'Bout the same as I'd feel if someone tried to take my land or livestock. I'd do whatever was necessary to stop 'em."

Donovan's blue eyes narrowed on him. "That a threat, Blackstone?"

"No. It's a promise."

"I have just as much right to those kids as you do."

"Mr. Donovan," Abby said coldly. "Are you really considering what's best for the children? Or do you want them because of some misguided notion of saving them since you couldn't help your brother?"

"A promise is a promise," he answered stubbornly. "I gave my word and I won't go back on it."

"Even if the children want to stay here with Jarrod and me?" she asked softly.

"No offense, ma'am, but they're just kids. They got no

notion of what's best."

"That's true," Abby said. "They need guidance. That's probably the one thing we all agree on. But you didn't see the children when they came to Jarrod. You can't know how much they've grown from a scared, skinny lot, into a happy, healthy family."

"What is it you're tellin' me, ma'am?"

"There's no easy way to say this, Donovan," Jarrod said. Fact was he didn't *want* to take the sting out of it for the other man. He just wanted him gone. But with Zach Magruder there, he thought it would look better if he tried to meet Donovan halfway. "I talked to the kids. Told them I'd go along with whatever they wanted. They don't want to go with you."

"You bad-mouth me to them, Blackstone?" His whole body went rigid with anger.

Abby moved around the coffee table and looked at him. "Mr. Donovan, Jarrod never said anything about you to the children until I convinced him you have a right to get to know them."

Donovan smiled a little. "Someone around here's got a brain in their head."

Abby gazed at him sympathetically. "The fact is, they made up their own minds. They don't want anything to do with you."

"You're lyin'," he said.

A flush of angry color blotched Abby's cheeks. "I'm going to overlook that because you're upset, Mr. Donovan. I don't lie. The children have nothing but bad memories of their father, and they want no part of anyone related to him. And after your willingness to tear them apart, I must agree with their instincts."

"Abby's right," Jarrod said. "The kids belong together. They've lost their father and mother. No call for them to lose each other too."

Donovan took a step toward Jarrod. "This has nothing to do with what the kids want, Blackstone. You think you're better'n me—"

Zach jumped out of the chair. "Everyone hold on. This

isn't getting us anywhere. My gut tells me neither one of you is gonna back down."

"You got that right," Donovan said.

Jarrod nodded his agreement.

"There's no choice then. You need to go before the circuit judge."

# 14

"*Lil, I think we better get us a plan.* Right quick." Tom closed the door of her room and leaned back against it.

Three pairs of eyes watched her, and Lily had never felt the weight of being the oldest as heavily as she did now. The four of them had hidden in the shadows at the top of the stairs, listening while the adults argued for a long time. When the sheriff left with the other man, Uncle Jarrod went out the kitchen door and slammed it, rattling the windows. He was mad as a wet hornet about that man taking them away.

It made her feel good inside to know Uncle Jarrod wanted them that much and was dead set against splitting them up. Mama would be sad if they weren't together. But their other uncle seemed just as bent on taking them away.

Now in her room, the other three were looking to her to figure something out. She had no idea what to do.

"Should we run away?" Oliver asked, taking his thumb out of his mouth.

Tom glared at the younger boy. "That's a dumb idea."

"We did it before, in the back of Abby's wagon."

"That was when Abby lived in town. And it's different. It's not boarding school," Lily reminded Oliver.

"I don't want to go with that man," Katie said, pouting. "I don't like him. Seems a good reason to run away." Her curls bounced as she flopped on Lily's bed and folded her arms over her chest.

"We're talkin' about the law," Tom said. "If the judge says we gotta go with him, I ain't sure running away will help."

Lily thought for a moment. "What if the judge says we get to stay with Uncle Jarrod?"

Tom sat on her bed, beside Katie, and let his shoulders slump and his long arms dangle between his knees. "What if he doesn't?"

"Are you willing to run away from the ranch and Uncle Jarrod and Abby and your horse? Do you want to give up our home if there's one chance that we'll get to stay?"

"What if we have to go, Lil? What if that old judge says we gotta go with him?" Tom asked.

Lily thought he looked real close to crying, something he hadn't done for a long time, not even when Mama died. "Then we run away," she said, nodding emphatically.

Jarrod stomped through the oak grove that stretched beyond the house. Rage and discouragement took turns churning up his insides. He wandered along the dry creek bed into Bulito Canyon for nearly a mile, not realizing where he was headed. Then he rounded a bend and came upon the falls where he and Sally had played as children.

He had nearly forgotten this place, until the kids discovered it the day after their arrival. They'd found it for the same reason he and his sister stumbled across it so long ago: no one had the time to be bothered with them.

The thought made him feel guilty. He remembered Abby telling him the children needed to spend time with him. Strange that he'd gotten her message after he'd persuaded her to come live at the ranch. Since then, she had gotten him to take time off for Tom's birthday and the Fourth of July. She'd made a difference to all of them.

He looked around, breathing in the scent of damp earth

and the poplar leaves that rustled in the breeze. The falls were smaller and more intimate than he remembered. Water trickled from a thin stream that skipped down the rock face from far above, a high ground of oaks and shrubs. Sunlight dappling the surface of the creek turned it to diamonds.

Memories washed over him. He and Sally had talked here for hours, sometimes until almost dark, and their mother had scolded them, out of fear, he knew now. He shook his head, remembering all the grand plans Sally had confided to him. Not once had they included dying too young.

For the first time since learning of his sister's death, he could clearly picture her face. He could almost hear her laughter echo off the rocks. He recalled her saying that if she ever had children, she wanted them to have a place like this for their own.

He knew why he'd instinctively come here. His memories. They were all tangled up with the land he and Sally had grown up on, the land she had loved as much as he did.

Now Rafe Donovan was trying to take Sally's kids away from him. No, they weren't hers any longer. Or Rafe's. They were his. Sally had given them to him, and he would fight with every last ounce of strength to prevent Rafe Donovan from getting them.

"Jarrod?"

Abby. He didn't have to turn around to know that she was here. Her soft voice, just saying his name, was a world of comfort. A vague thought slipped through his mind that her presence in this place felt right. She made his contentment complete somehow.

He turned to look at her. With a backdrop of greenery behind her, her fiery red hair gleamed. "How did you find me, Abby?"

"I followed you from the house. I was worried."

He gave her a small smile. "Why?"

"I'm not sure," she admitted. She sat on the rock beside him, her clear blue gaze intently fixed on his face. "I'd never seen you look that way before."

"What way?"

"Like you wanted to rip someone's head off and feed it to him."

"How do I look now?"

She hesitated a moment, carefully studying him. "Sad. Still mad. Determined too."

He nodded. "Did you see the kids?"

"No. Gib sent me after you. He said he'd look in on them."

"Do they know what's going on?"

"I don't think so. Lily took them upstairs when Donovan showed up with Zach. I'm sure they were in their rooms the whole time. They probably didn't hear anything."

They sat in silence for a while as Abby looked around.

Finally she turned to him, an angry frown marring the smoothness of her brow. "You can't let him take them, Jarrod. He was perfectly willing to split them up. He saw absolutely nothing wrong with that plan."

"I don't intend to let him have them."

Her gaze snapped to his. "What are you going to do?"

"It crossed my mind to pack them up and leave."

"Oh, Jarrod," she said, touching his arm. Her expression softened. "This is your home, and theirs. You can't just leave it. And what about the children? They're adjusting so well here. Sally wanted them to grow up on Blackstone land. I think it would break Tom's heart if he had to give up his horse."

"Have you got another suggestion?"

"Take your chances in court."

"I don't like relying on chance any more than I like running. It's a surefire road to failure."

"I can't see that you have any other choice. Zach said a judge will have to decide who's got the best claim to them. Seems pretty much equal to me. Each of you can give them a home, food, and shelter. You have just as good a chance of getting them as he does."

"I've been giving this a lot of thought since he showed up. I think there's a way I can tip the scales in my favor."

"What?" she asked eagerly.

"Do you remember the night of the Fourth when he first showed up?" She nodded, but the puzzled look on her face told him she had no idea what he was aiming at. "He's not married, Abby."

"Neither are you—" She stopped and her eyes grew wide. "You're going to get married?"

Her normally expressive face went completely blank. What was she thinking? he wondered. That he'd slipped over the edge into crazy? He waited a moment for her to say something. Finally he couldn't stand it.

"It would give me an edge. What do you think?" he asked.

He watched her mull this over. After several moments she said, "I think you're right. If you had a wife, you would look better to a judge."

"Good. I'm glad you approve," he said.

"You don't have much time. Do you have someone in mind?" she asked sharply. Her eyes narrowed and an angry flush slipped into her cheeks.

Was she having a typically jealous female reaction? Would it bother her if he married another woman? That thought pleased him.

"I have someone very much in mind," he said, looking at her intently.

For several moments she stared back at him. When he smiled, she looked surprised and stood up.

Abby backed away from him as if he'd just grown horns. "No! You know I'd do almost anything for those kids, but you can't ask me to do that."

"Didn't figure I'd *have* to ask after the way you reacted when he suggested splitting up the kids."

"Why me, Jarrod? There are any number of women who would jump at a proposal from you."

He enjoyed the way her eyes flashed when she said that. Whether she would admit it or not, she was disturbed that women seemed to like him. But he couldn't imagine proposing even a fake marriage to anyone but Abby.

"If I asked someone else, the kids would be suspicious. We don't want them to get wind of this and spill the beans. They have always wanted you, Abby. They won't question us getting married."

"They're not the only ones who might smell a rat. Donovan will accuse you of marrying just to keep the children. For that matter, why would a judge believe it wasn't a trick?"

"Because Hettie Schafer spread the word all over town that we were sparking."

Red blotches covered her cheeks. "I'd forgotten about that, what with everything that happened after. What will folks think?"

"Exactly what we want them to. That I'm a man. You're a woman. We're alone out here on the ranch. Nature took its course."

"But it's not true!" she cried. "We've done no such thing."

He grinned at her. "We could. Then it wouldn't be gossip, but the Lord's honest truth."

She pointed at him. "Don't you dare bring up honesty and the Lord while making such an immoral, indecent suggestion."

"Indecent? I don't think so. Besides, you wanted to that night I kissed you. You can't forget about it any more than I can."

"That's beside the point."

At least she didn't deny how she felt. That was something. He was going to need every ounce of persuasion he could muster to convince her to marry him and give him the advantage over Donovan.

"What is the point, Abby?"

"We have a strictly business relationship and an understanding that nothing further will happen between us."

"But if everyone thinks we've done the deed, no one will question it when we get married."

"When?" She put her hands on her hips and glared at him. "You hold it right there, Jarrod Blackstone. You're taking an awful lot for granted."

"Am I?"

"Most definitely. I have never made any secret of the fact that I don't plan to marry, and I'm leaving just as soon as I have enough money to see Clint through college."

"You can still do that as soon as I have clear custody of the kids."

She looked doubtful. "What about the marriage? You don't want it any more than I do. You said so."

And he'd meant it. After Dulcy left, he had made up his mind not to make the same mistake twice. But this was different. It wasn't for love. So there was no way he could fail Abby. Besides, now that he'd gotten to really know her, he found she was the strongest woman he'd ever met. The idea of marrying her wasn't so bad, though that didn't seem the kind of sweet talk that would convince her to say yes.

"After Donovan leaves town, we'll get the vows annulled. We can if we don't—"

"I know." She looked down as the blush deepened.

"It will work."

"What if he finds out we're not really married?"

"Once we've beaten him at his own game, he'll leave and never look back."

"Then you think he won't stay in touch with the children? That he doesn't really want them?"

"That's what I think." He shook his head thoughtfully. "I can't fault his sense of duty, but I can't shake the feeling that his reasons are partly selfish."

"What do you mean? Do you still think he's trying to get his hands on your land through the children?"

"No. I don't think he'd turn it down if it happened. But I don't believe that's his purpose. He said something that's been bothering me."

"What?"

"That the kids would have to work. Not that I'm against that. I agree with him. But after a roof over their heads, it was the next thing he talked about. He's not concerned about whether or not they're happy. He's looking for ranch hands."

"But they're just children," she cried. "Oliver's hardly more than a baby."

"I think it's more complicated than that. He's got no one to pass his land on to."

"You believe he's thinking about that?"

"I know he is."

"How can you be so sure?"

"Because it's important to a man."

Because he had thought a lot about what would happen to Blackstone land when he was gone. Because he and Rafe Donovan were on equal footing, Jarrod was pretty sure he understood what was going through the man's mind.

He couldn't swear that this was what drove Rafe to seek out the children, but it had occurred to him. He too had no children of his own, no heirs, but he wanted Blackstone Ranch to stay in the family. In fact, he had decided to divide the acres into parcels, one for each of the kids.

"So what do you say, Abby? Will you marry me?"

"I don't know—"

"You admitted it could work."

"Yes, but that was before I knew you meant marrying *me*."

"You don't want to see them split up."

"Of course not—"

"Would you rather they were uprooted to New Mexico?"

She shook her head. "That would be awful after everything they've been through already."

"Maybe you think Rafe Donovan would be better for them than staying here on Blackstone Ranch with me?"

"I've already told you I don't think that."

"Then it's settled," he said.

"No, it's not. I have to think about this, Jarrod."

He sighed. As dead set against the state of matrimony as she was, he should have figured on this. To him, it was the perfect solution, but he'd learned not to push Abby Miller. A gentle nudge was different. Under the circumstances, he felt he had no choice.

"All right. You think. But don't take too long. You said yourself there's not a lot of time to waste."

\* \* \*

The next day Abby was tired. Doing lessons with four out-of-sorts children was a discouraging task. In the kitchen, she meandered around the table, supervising them as they quietly did their sums. Oliver insisted on being given work. He said his uncle had told him a cowboy had to know how to count his cattle.

She'd hardly gotten a lick of sleep all night, thanks to that same uncle and his marriage proposal. It seemed like a good plan, but even the best laid plans had a way of going wrong. She was so close to realizing her dream of reuniting her own family. But how could she turn her back on these children?

More than anything, she feared her attraction to Jarrod. He was right when he'd said she wanted him the night he carried her into his room. If they were married, there was no reason on God's green earth why she shouldn't share his bed. Except if she did, she was stuck, and her dream would remain unfulfilled.

Tom slammed his hand on the table. "Why do we have to do lessons?"

"Are you having trouble, Tom?" Abby asked, leaning down to look at his work.

"You bet I am. I should be taking care of my horse."

Katie looked at him. "You haven't named her yet. What are you gonna call her?"

"That's right, Tom," Lily said. "What are you going to name her?"

Tom scowled at them. "Haven't thought of a good one yet."

Lily grinned at him. "Boys have no imagination."

"That so?" he said. "Maybe I'll call her Joe."

"That's a boy's name, Tom," Katie said. "What about Josephine?"

"Nah."

"I like it, Tom," Oliver said, bouncing from foot to foot.

"Don't you want to run outside and use the necessary?" Abby asked him.

"No'm. Don't hafta."

"All right." She looked around at all of them. "Why don't you think about famous historical people we've talked about."

Tom responded thoughtfully, "She's a girl horse. Ain't too many girls that are famous."

"Sure there are, Tom," Lily said. "Martha Washington, for one."

"Ain't callin' her Martha. Forget that, Lil."

"I know, Tom," Katie said. "What about Queen Elizabeth?"

"That's a little better," he admitted. "But I'm not sure. What about—"

"I know," Lily cried. "Cleopatra."

"Joan of Arc," Tom said.

"Cowgirl," Oliver said.

Tom gave his younger brother a small shove. "That's a stupid name for a horse."

"Is not. Right, Abby?" he said, looking up at her.

"What does she know?" Tom asked, standing up as he glared at her.

"That's enough, boys." Abby heard the kitchen door open, but kept her gaze on Tom.

Tom glared at her. "You got no right to take over namin' my horse."

"That's no way to talk to a lady, boy."

All of them turned to stare at the intruder. Abby was the first to speak. "Mr. Donovan. What are you doing here? How dare you just walk in."

"What you mean is how'd I get past the guns Blackstone has patrolling the place. Figured walking in was the only way, since I wouldn't be invited in."

Katie jumped up and stood by Abby. "Is he my uncle?"

"I am." He looked at the girl with a gentle half smile. Abby hadn't seen him look kindly at any of the children before.

Lily stood on Abby's other side. "You followed me in town."

"I did, miss. Wanted to get a look at you all before I introduced myself." For a moment he looked down at the hat curled in his hands. "Can't say as I much care for you throwing yourself at that Schafer boy."

"I didn't throw myself at him—"

"Shouldn't contradict your elders," he interrupted.

"Don't you talk to my sister like that." Tom jumped up and stood in front of the three of them, his stance challenging. He had taken to heart Jarrod's words about protecting women. Abby was proud of him.

"I gotta go," Oliver said, sliding down from his chair. He ran to the door.

"Hurry, Oliver," Abby said as he ran outside.

Donovan watched the little boy leave and scratched his head. "He ain't hardly housebroke yet? Seems kinda old t'be doin' that. Maybe he needs a good paddlin' to remind him."

Abby was outraged. The hand she placed on Tom's shoulder was trembling, and she hoped Donovan didn't see it. "Tom, I think you should let your Uncle Jarrod and Gib Cochran know that we have a visitor."

Without turning to her, he nodded. "Yes'm," he said, then left the kitchen through the door that led to the front room. Abby was glad he'd chosen not to pass Donovan. She didn't trust him as far as she could throw him.

He looked at her regretfully. "Wasn't any call to send the boy out like that. I don't mean any harm."

"No?" Abby asked, her voice rising. "You walk in here uninvited and advocate beating a four-year-old boy for something that will take care of itself with time, and expect me to believe you mean no harm? You have no right to do that."

"Beggin' your pardon, ma'am. I do have rights and I should have a say in how these young 'uns turn out. After all, their last name is Donovan. You said so yourself. The children should get to know their pa's folks."

"I was wrong, Mr. Donovan. The more I know of you, the more I think the children's decision to have nothing to do with you was correct. You have no business raising these youngsters."

His gaze narrowed. "Then it's a right good thing you ain't got nothin' to say about it."

She glared right back. "Don't be so sure."


Even though Donovan was gone when Jarrod came storming into the house with Tom on his heels, Abby was relieved to see him. She wouldn't put it past Rafe to slip around the ranch hands again. God help her, she wished she could throw herself into Jarrod's arms and ask him to hold her. She was still shaking. When his gaze held hers for several moments and darkened dangerously, she knew he noticed. He glanced at each of the children in turn, then asked, "Everyone all right?"

"Yes," they answered just as Oliver ran in the back door. He raced over to Abby and grabbed onto her leg.

"I don't like that mean man."

She put a reassuring hand on his arm. "Don't you worry about him, sweetie. He's not going to hurt you."

Jarrod lifted his hat and brushed his forearm across his brow, wiping the sweat away. "Gib, Dusty, and Slim are fixing beans and biscuits down at the bunkhouse. They asked me to invite you all down there to join 'em for the noon meal."

"Oh, boy!" Oliver said. "Can we, Abby?"

She took a deep breath to get control of her voice. "I think it would be downright unfriendly not to."

"Oh, good," Katie said. "I like Mr. Cochran. C'mon, Oliver." The two youngest ran out the door.

"You need me anymore, Uncle Jarrod?" Tom asked, obviously anxious to follow his brother and sister. His loyalty to Jarrod was unmistakable and heartwarming.

"No, son. You go on."

"Yes, sir." Tom was out the door faster than she could remind him to mind his manners.

Jarrod looked at Lily, standing quietly beside Abby. "Why don't you go on along and help them?" he suggested.

"You want to talk to Abby alone, don't you, Uncle Jarrod?"

He grinned slowly, sheepishly. It was the first time since he'd come in the room that he relaxed even slightly. He walked over to the young girl and tenderly rubbed the back of his knuckles along her cheek. "I guess when I can't fool you like the others, you're growing up and becoming a young lady."

"I am?" she asked, brightening.

He nodded. "I'm not sure I like it. But every day it's more clear that I can't stop it."

"No, sir," she said.

"Yes, I'd like to talk to Abby alone."

Lily tipped her head to the side as she toyed nervously with a strand of brown hair. "If I'm a young lady, why can't I stay and hear what you're going to say? I know it has something to do with that man."

"It does. But I don't want to upset you."

"Young ladies don't get upset unless they're sent out of the room."

"This is adult talk." He lifted her chin. "You're not past being a young lady yet."

"But—"

Abby folded her arms over her chest. "Lily, please don't argue. Your uncle asked you to help Mr. Cochran with the other children."

"Yes, ma'am." Lily heaved a big sigh as she shuffled to the door, proving beyond a doubt that she had one foot still firmly planted in childhood.

When the door was closed behind her, Jarrod gave Abby a serious look. "Do you know how to use a gun?" he asked.

"Yes. Mr. Whittemore wouldn't let me make deliveries for Hollister Freight until he was certain I could handle a rifle and pistol."

"Good," Jarrod answered approvingly.

"Do you think I'll need a gun?" she asked.

"I don't know. And I'd sure as hell hate to look back and say 'if only.'"

"You think he'd harm the children?"

"I wouldn't put it past him to take them at gunpoint. But no, I don't believe he would actually hurt them."

"Not unless it was in the name of discipline," she muttered, glaring at the back door as if it were Rafe Donovan.

"What was that?"

"He thought a good licking would stop Oliver's accidents on the way to the outhouse," she said, her tone full of disgust.

"If he lays a hand on those kids, ever, I'll—What are you grinning at?"

"I was remembering their first day here, when you took Tom into your study and I was worried that you believed in spare the rod and spoil the child. You'd never touch one of them in punishment. Would you?"

He shrugged, then gave her a grin that sent her heart skidding all the way to her toes. "Don't spread it around."

Her smile faded as the seriousness of the situation came back to her. "He hasn't any idea how to be a loving father. It would be the worst thing in the world for them. I couldn't stand it if—We can't let him have them."

"We?" His expression was intense, expectant.

"If you still want to—" She stood as tall as she could in front of him and met his determined look with one of her own. "I'll marry you, Jarrod."

# 15

*Two days later, Abby* waited upstairs in Reverend Taylor's spare bedroom. A bouquet of Henrietta Schafer's white roses filled her hands. She was grateful for her friend's flowers, and enjoyed their beauty and sweet, perfumed fragrance. But mostly she was thankful because holding them prevented her from nervously twisting her fingers together while she waited to go downstairs and become Jarrod Blackstone's bride.

She checked her appearance in the mirror mounted on the wall above the pine dresser. Her long-sleeved, high-necked, pale blue cotton dress was simple and plain. But she thought the color suited her. Bea Peters had helped with her hair, sweeping the red curls on top of her head with wisps at her temples and a few on her forehead. The style made her neck look long and slender and her blue eyes huge. Or maybe the dark circles beneath them did that.

She hadn't slept much since agreeing to this marriage.

"It's for the children," she said to her reflection. "It's temporary."

Jarrod didn't want any more than that, and she was in complete agreement with him. That's all there is to it, she told herself, hoping to silence the small, insistent voice that haunted her at night. The one that kept her awake, taunting her with thoughts of what a real marriage to Jarrod Blackstone might be like.

A soft knock on the door startled her, making her heart pound as if she'd run a mile. "Come in," she called.

Bea Peters and Henrietta Schafer walked into the room, beaming at her.

Henrietta pressed her clasped hands to her chest as her gaze traveled from the top of Abby's head to the hem of her dress. "You're pretty as a picture. I wish your mama could be here to see the way you look."

"And Clint." Tears gathered in Abby's throat and she didn't trust herself to say any more.

"Just wait until Jarrod sees you," Bea said.

"You don't think he'll be disappointed?" Abby asked anxiously.

She told herself the only reason she cared how she looked was because this marriage had to appear real to everyone. Her need to please Jarrod was nothing more than playing her part.

"Disappointed?" Henrietta laughed. "That man'll think he died and went to heaven."

"Everything's ready downstairs, dear," Bea said. "The reverend is waiting."

"Let's go," Abby said, taking a deep breath.

She left the bedroom after the two women and waited at the top of the staircase until they had descended. When she heard Mrs. Taylor playing the piano, she started down, holding her flowers in one hand and the railing with the other. Carefully, she took each step on shaky legs until she reached the wood floor at the bottom. From there she could see into the front room, where Bea and Henrietta had taken their places to the right of the clergyman.

The children were there and all dressed up for the occasion. Lily looked quite the young lady in her green organdy. Katie wore the same color and had matching ribbons in her blond curls. Tom and Oliver wore wool suits and looked terribly uncomfortable as they fidgeted and ran their fingers around their tight collars.

Then there was Jarrod.

He looked so handsome in his suit, Abby's breath caught. His gaze lifted to her hair then slid downward, taking in every detail of her appearance. He certainly didn't look disappointed. His expression, eyes glowing with admiration, filled her with elation.

No man had ever looked at her that way before. It didn't matter why they were here, or what would happen later. She wished she could freeze this moment in time and hold it forever in her heart. She pleased him. That made her unexpectedly happy.

While she stood in the doorway, hesitating, Jarrod came to meet her. With an approving smile, he held out his arm, and she placed her shaking hand in the crook of his elbow.

He covered her cold fingers with his own warm ones and squeezed reassuringly. "Thank you for doing this," he whispered, stirring the hair near her ear. Tingles raced down her neck and settled in her breasts. "Are you ready?" he asked.

When she nodded he led her into the room, stopping before the reverend. The children gathered around, the girls beside Abby, the boys next to Jarrod.

Oliver peeked past Jarrod's long legs and looked at her. "You look pretty, Abby," he said in a loud whisper.

Tom elbowed him. "Shhh."

He looked up at his uncle. "Is this like church, Uncle Jarrod? Do I hafta be quiet?"

"That's up to the preacher. Reverend?" he asked.

The balding man with twinkling blue eyes looked at Oliver over the half glasses resting on the end of his nose. "When I'm talking, you have to be quiet, or I can't marry your uncle and Abby. You want them to be married, don't you, Oliver?"

The boy nodded solemnly. "Yes, sir. Then I'll have a ma and a pa."

Abby must have jerked, because she felt Jarrod press her hand again. She glanced up into his gray eyes. Without words he told her not to worry. The most important thing was to keep custody of the children, no matter what happened later. They were doing the right thing.

"Abby? Jarrod? Shall I begin?" the reverend asked.

With Jarrod's reassuring presence next to her, Abby answered the cleric's question. "Yes, Reverend Taylor."

He opened the good book and began to read. "Marriage is a holy state, and not one to be entered into lightly. We are gathered together in the sight of God . . ."

Numbed by fatigue and anxiety, Abby didn't hear the words. But the warmth and scent of the man beside her made her feel safe for reasons she couldn't explain. Her stomach fluttered, a sensation that was starting to feel like an old friend. Jarrod already knew that she was attracted to him. She couldn't deny it to herself. The question was how she was going to keep her feelings from growing beyond her control.

"Do you, Jarrod Blackstone, take Abigail Miller to be your lawful wife?"

The sound of her name wrenched Abby from her thoughts. Jarrod's slow half smile sent her heart pounding against her ribs.

"I do," he said, his voice deep, confident.

Reverend Taylor looked at Abby, holding her attention. "Do you, Abigail Miller, take Jarrod Blackstone to be your wedded husband, for richer, for poorer, in sickness and health, till death do you part?"

She hesitated for a second, thinking carefully about what she was promising.

Beside Jarrod, Oliver shuffled his feet as he clutched his privates. "Hurry up and say yes, Abby. I gotta go."

"Abby?" the reverend asked.

She glanced at Jarrod, who nodded his encouragement. "I do," she said.

"Promises have been exchanged and accepted. Are there rings?" he asked.

Abby and Jarrod looked at each other. They'd had so much on their minds, they hadn't even thought about that.

Jarrod cleared his throat. "No rings. We'll take care of that later."

Reverend Taylor continued. "Then with the powers vested in me by the Lord and the great state of California, I now pronounce you man and wife. What God has joined together, let no man put asunder." For a moment he looked from one to the other expectantly. When nothing happened, he said, "You may kiss your bride."

Jarrod grinned down at Abby. "Mrs. Blackstone—"

The last coherent thought Abby had before his mouth claimed hers was that every last person in that room must be able to hear her heart thumping in her chest. Then his warm lips moved gently on her own, and she didn't think she'd notice or care if the roof fell in. She lost herself in the feel of his arms wrapped around her, pressing her tightly to his chest until she could hardly breathe. She could have stayed that way forever.

"Abby." Oliver tugged on her skirt. "I gotta go."

When Jarrod released her mouth, she blinked several times, struggling to regain control. "Tom?" she said, her voice hoarse. "Go with him, and be sure you watch him."

Thoughts of Rafe Donovan were never far from her mind. Since their arrival in Hollister, they hadn't seen him. But they knew he hadn't left town.

"I'll take 'im," Tom grumbled.

Katie tugged on Abby's skirt. "What did he mean by the last thing he said?" she asked, pointing at the cleric.

"What did he say, sweetie?"

"About putting us under. What's he gonna put over us?"

"He said asunder, Katie."

"What did he mean?" Worried green eyes met her own.

"That your uncle and I are together and no one should separate us." Something tugged hard inside Abby, a lump that settled in her chest somewhere between guilt and conscience.

"Good," Katie said, her curls bouncing as she nodded fervently. Her smile was radiant. "I like asunder."

"So do I, Katie."

Reverend Taylor put a hand on Katie's shoulder. "Would you like to come into the kitchen with Mrs. Taylor and me? We could use some help with refreshments."

"Yes, sir," the little girl said eagerly.

When Katie had left with the older couple, Lily stood shyly in front of Abby, then hugged her quickly. She pulled back, then said, "I don't know what to call you. Aunt Abby?"

Oh, Lord, Abby thought, glancing up at Jarrod beside her. She hadn't expected anything to change, especially not so soon. She had been wrong. Now she was family by marriage.

"You can call her Abby, just like you've been doing," Jarrod said. "That okay with you, Abby?"

"Fine."

"All right," Lily agreed.

Bea and Henrietta came over, each dabbing her eyes with a handkerchief.

"Congratulations, Jarrod. Abby," Bea said, looking from one to the other. "I had no idea when I cooked up that plan with the children that my matchmaking would actually be successful. I'm very happy for you two."

She hugged Jarrod for what Abby thought was a little longer than necessary.

Jarrod grinned down at Bea as his arm encircled Abby's waist and pulled her close against him. "It never would have worked unless we were meant to be together. Right, Abby?" He squeezed her until her breast pressed into his side.

Irritation flashed through her as she decided he was playing his part with far more fervor than she thought was necessary. Two could play that game.

"Yes, sweetheart," she said, noting with satisfaction the way he looked at her questioningly. "This marriage was meant to be."

Oliver and Tom came back into the room, and the younger boy ran over to them. "Abby, I wanna spend the night with the Shemanskis."

Abby bent down to meet his eyes. "We settled this earlier. We're going to stay in the boardinghouse, the way we always do."

Henrietta cleared her throat. "Abby, Jarrod, this all happened so fast, I didn't have time to get you a gift. So I took the liberty of makin' arrangements for the children to stay with friends. I'm givin' you a weddin' night. Best room in the boardin'house, on me."

As the words sank in, Abby's eyes grew bigger. She had two choices: refuse the kind offer and show everyone that the marriage was a fake, or spend the night alone with Jarrod.

Abby was grateful when Jarrod spoke up. Her own throat was too dry to form words.

"Thanks, Hettie. We appreciate that a lot. Don't we, honey?" he said, looking down at her.

"We sure do. But Oliver, I don't know if you can stay with Matt Shemanski. Doesn't he have the chicken pox?"

Bea Peters nodded. "Annie's had her hands full. First one got sick, and they've been dropping like flies ever since." She brushed the blond hair from Oliver's forehead. "You're going to stay with me."

"Aw, Bea. I don't wanna stay with you!"

"Don't be rude, Oliver. Wasn't it nice of Bea to offer to take you in?" Abby asked.

The little boy looked down at his shoes and mumbled, "I reckon. But she won't make a fort with me out of blankets 'n' stuff. Even Tom plays with me better'n she does."

Abby glanced apologetically at the older woman, who shook her head, indicating she understood Oliver's reluctance.

Abby looked at Jarrod. "I guess that settles it. He'll have to stay with us tonight."

"Not on your life." Henrietta frowned. "A couple only gets one weddin' night. It's gotta be special. That doesn't include having a willful four-year-old with ya. Y'hear me, Oliver? You can stay with me. In Joe's room. He'll build you a fort the likes of which you've never seen. You'd like that wouldn't you?"

"Yes'm," the boy said eagerly.

Henrietta smiled with satisfaction. "It's all settled, then."

"Where's Lily staying?" Jarrod asked, his eyes narrowing. "Joe doesn't have enough room for her too, does he, Hettie?"

Bea touched his arm reassuringly. "Lily and Tom and Katie are staying with me."

"Good."

Reverend and Mrs. Taylor came in with a bottle of champagne and glasses. He smiled at his wife. "Clara's sister sent this to us and we've been waiting for a special occasion to open it. We're very fond of Abby and decided this is the right time."

When the glasses were handed out all around, the reverend lifted his and cleared his throat. "To Abby and Jarrod Blackstone. May they have a long and happy life together."

Abby downed her drink in one gulp. The bubbles tickled her throat. The words pricked her conscience.

The night ahead would be punishment for her deceit.

Jarrod unlocked the door to their room and let Abby precede him inside. He was concerned about her. She'd gone from pale as a sheet after finding out the children wouldn't be with them tonight to pink as a rose from champagne. Now her back was to him as she walked to the quilt-covered bed. She was so tense, she walked like a board with feet.

He turned the key to lock them inside. In the silent room, the sound was as loud as a gunshot and he saw Abby flinch.

"I didn't know things would work out like this, Abby. I'm sorry." He lit the lantern on the dresser.

She turned to him. "It's not your fault. The question is what we do now. I'm too keyed up to sleep, and it's barely sundown."

"We could play cards." He looked at her sheepishly. "If we had a deck. I guess sending down to the Watering Hole for one wouldn't be such a good idea."

"Why not?" she asked innocently as she sat on the bed.

"Because folks don't expect us to play poker on our wedding night."

"Oh." She folded her hands in her lap and stared at them.

He wished she would get off that bed. It was far too easy to picture her lying back on that mattress, her red hair spread around her like fire. He could almost see her body—naked, soft, sensuous, the sheets caressing her skin as he longed to do. Curling his fingers into his palms, he reminded himself he had given his word that they would have a marriage in name only. He wouldn't go back on it. But how would he find the strength he needed to keep his promise when he'd wanted her since she brought the children to the ranch?

From that day to this all he'd been able to think about was how beautiful she was. How much he wanted her. But if he took her, he'd fail her. He couldn't do that. Not to Abby.

She looked up at him, then stood. "Jarrod? Are you tired?"

"Yes," he lied.

"Then maybe we should try to get some sleep. You take the bed. I'll sit up in the rocker."

"You've got circles under your eyes practically down to your—" His gaze dropped to the feminine swell of her breasts beneath the blue cotton bodice. The material hugged her, outlining the sweet curves. His palms itched to know the weight and texture of her. He swallowed, gathering the strength to talk. "I mean, you look like you're about to drop from exhaustion."

"I haven't slept very well lately. I must look awful—"

He shook his head. "You're pretty as a sunset, Abby. All fire and golden light."

Her eyes closed for a moment as she took in a shaky breath. "Jarrod, don't. Please—"

"I'm sorry, Abby. I didn't intend to say it. I mean straight out like that."

"Don't think I'm not flattered, because I am. It's just that we can't let ourselves get carried away."

"I have no intention of getting carried away," he said, his voice tight with irritation. "I was just stating a fact. I think you're pretty."

"Thank you," she snapped back, echoing his tone.

He didn't need her to remind him that they both had a lot

riding on their self-control. What fried him was that she looked so cool, so unaffected by him, when he was short of breath and hot all over. Because of her. He remembered her flash of eager innocence when he'd kissed her, and the way she'd wrapped her arms around his neck as if she never wanted to let go of him. If he kissed her now, would she go soft and clingy and weak-kneed? Was her indifference an act? If so, it was a good one. For all she seemed to care, he could have been her brother.

"There's no need to be irritated with me, Jarrod. This was your idea."

"My idea?" He crossed the distance separating them and stood close enough to smell her womanly scent, feel the heat from her body as it joined with his own and threatened to burst into flame. "It was my plan to get married, not to be cooped up inside the same four walls in this damn boarding-house."

"And what about this Aunt Abby business?"

"That wasn't my idea either. Lily came up with that on her own."

"I warned you that the children would become attached to me, to us. As a couple, I mean." She drew in a breath. "Oliver wants us to be his mother and father. Lily wants me to be her aunt by marriage. This was a bad idea. I never should have agreed."

"You can back out any time. But if you do, you might as well hand the kids over to Donovan."

"You know I don't want that." She turned away from him. "I just didn't figure on how dishonest and low-down I would feel."

"Just remember, Abby, the end justifies the means. We agreed this was the best way."

"I know, but—"

"Buts are a waste of time. We're married." He sighed. "I don't want to fight with you, Abby. Not tonight."

"Me either. You're my friend. I hope you always will be. No matter what happens."

"Count on it." He grinned at her.

Abby felt the heat of that smile all the way to her toes and back. She wasn't feeling exactly friendly at the moment. One touch and she would be in his arms.

"Since we agree that we're friends," he said, "I have a proposition for you."

"What?"

"We share the bed."

She blinked. "Share it?"

"Sure. Why not?" A teasing note crept into his voice. "You've got nothing to fear from me."

"I didn't think so, but—" A devilish expression lit his eyes. She knew she wasn't going to like this.

"I assume I'm safe from you?" he asked.

She laughed. "Of course."

That was a bald-faced lie. But if he could keep away from her, she certainly would do her darnedest not to embarrass herself by throwing herself at him.

"Then, it's settled. We share the bed." He pulled off his jacket and set it on the rocker in the corner. Then he unbuttoned his shirt and slid it off his broad shoulders.

"What are you doing?" She cleared her throat. "I mean, I know what you're doing. H-How much are you—I mean, what do you sleep in?"

"Nothing. It's too hot for clothes. What about you?" he asked, as cool as if they were talking about the weather.

"A—A nightgown." She tried to keep her voice as unconcerned as his. Except for that first slip, she thought she did a pretty good job. "I need to change," she said, looking around to see how she could manage it and maintain her modesty. More than anything, she wished there was a dressing screen in that room.

"I'll turn my back," he said, as if he could read her mind.

"Thanks."

She retreated to the shadows in the corner of the room with her lawn nightgown. Facing away from him, she started unhooking the tiny buttons down the back of her dress. The ones between her shoulder blades were impossible to reach. If Lily were there, she would have had the girl help her.

But she only had Jarrod. It was either ask him, or explain why she was sleeping in her clothes—and suffer the embarrassment when he teased her unmercifully.

"Jarrod? Could you help me with the back of my dress? I can't get the buttons."

"Sure. Come on over here, into the light."

She did as he asked and moved closer to the lantern on the dresser, presenting her back to him. As he worked, the backs of his fingers grazed her skin, sending sparks skittering through her. Her breathing quickened.

"There," he said. "All done."

"Thank you," she answered, clutching the front of her dress to the cotton chemise covering her breasts.

He didn't move away. He was so close, his breath stirred her hair. Abby's heart hammered in her chest. If she had a lick of sense, she would turn to him, throw her arms around him, and press her mouth to his. She would pour all the yearning stored up inside her into the kiss. She would do everything she could to make him care about her the way she did about him, and be a wife to him in every sense of the word.

In the end, she couldn't. She was afraid. Of him, of herself, but mostly of losing the dream she'd held on to for so long.

As she started to move back to her shadowed corner, Jarrod gripped her upper arms. Abby closed her eyes for a moment, drawing in a shuddering breath. He pulled her back against his chest, and the sprinkling of hair tickled the bare skin between her shoulder blades.

"Abby," he said in a hoarse whisper. He rubbed his cheek against her hair, then with one hand pulled out the pins until the heavy strands fell in waves around her face and down her arms. "I'm sorry, Abby. I couldn't help it. If I didn't touch you, I'd—"

She turned in his arms and cupped his face, loving the way the day's growth of beard was rough against her palms. He opened his mouth to say something, and she silenced him with the touch of her finger to his lips.

"Don't," she whispered. "Let's not think. I can't. Not now."

His eyes filled with passion as he slowly nodded and lowered his mouth to hers. That first soft touch released something wild and primitive inside her. In seconds her breathing turned rapid and harsh. Blood pulsed through her veins and raced to every part of her, heating her skin.

Jarrod sat on the bed and pulled her between the vee of his legs. The bodice of her dress pooled at her waist. He rested his hands on her ribs, brushing his thumbs across her nipples, which were taut through the thin cotton of her chemise. The exquisite sensation bolted clear to her toes. An appreciative moan slipped from her throat.

"Did you like that, Abby?"

"Yes." The one word was more of a satisfied sigh than anything else.

He reached up and untied the three blue satin ribbons between her breasts, then pushed aside the material until her skin was bared to him. "I knew you would be beautiful. I didn't know how beautiful."

"Really?" His compliment was too lovely to believe.

His gaze captured hers. "Really. Inside and out, Abby, you are the prettiest sight I have ever seen."

She sighed, reassured by his words as she let her eyes slide closed. When he captured the peak of her breast in his mouth, she gasped at the powerful pleasure that rocked through her. "Oh, Jarrod, I've never felt anything so wonderful."

He moved to her other breast and lavished attention on it. She threaded her fingers through the thickness of his hair, holding him to her as she arched into his touch. Between her legs, a strange tightening started. Her body trembled as tension built within her. This was just the beginning. She sensed it; she craved more. Leaning back, she opened her eyes and stared into his, dark with desire.

"Show me, Jarrod. I want to know everything."

He sucked in a breath. "Are you sure, Abby? There's no going back."

"I know. I'm sure."

Jarrod looped an arm around her waist and swept her onto the bed beside him. He brushed a hand down her body, pushing her clothing along with it. Abby lifted her hips, helping, pulling frantically at the material, eager to free herself to him. When she was naked, his gaze moved over her, caressing her as his hands had done just moments before.

He cupped her breast, gently. "I thought you were lovely when you came down the stairs at Reverend Taylor's. That was nothing compared to how beautiful you look now."

His fingers traveled over her belly, teasing and arousing as they went. With tender slowness he eased her legs apart and curved his palm over the mound of her womanhood.

"Oh, Jarrod—" She stopped and her body went still as he slipped a finger into her most feminine place. Pleasure rippled through her.

"Abby?"

"Don't stop, Jarrod."

More than anyone else she trusted him. His thumb brushed over the sensitive nub at the top of her womanhood. It was as if lightning crackled through her. He began to move his hand faster, rubbing, caressing, loving.

Almost of their own accord, her hips began to move in a rhythm that his hand set. She pressed herself into his touch, searching for—something. Tightness grew within her. When she thought she couldn't stand one more second of his tender torture, radiance exploded behind her closed eyes. Her body trembled with wave after wave of pleasure. She felt as if she had splintered into a thousand pieces of light, then come back together.

When the exquisite feeling subsided, she opened her eyes and looked at him. His gaze held supreme male satisfaction at her shattering experience. There was also something strained about him, a tightness around his mouth.

With his body pressed tightly to her, she felt the rigid length of his arousal against her thigh. He needed release too.

"What about you, Jarrod? There's more. Isn't there?"

He nodded as he shifted uncomfortably on the mattress beside her. "There's more."

"Show me. Let me give something back to you. That was the most"—she stopped, searching for a word grand enough to describe the sensation he'd given her—"incredible, extraordinary, unbelievable feeling I've ever known."

He shook his head. "That was my gift to you, Abby. It's all I can give you."

"No—"

He touched a finger to her lips. "Yes. I won't break my promise. As long as we don't consummate this marriage, we can have it annulled. That's what you want, isn't it? To be free, so you can leave?"

Was it? She couldn't think straight anymore. Not when she was in his arms like this. The thought of leaving him sat like a stone on her heart.

But he was right. She needed to be free. As much as she wanted to ignore that fact, she couldn't. Taking a deep breath, she looked at him.

Her chest swelled with gratitude at his unselfishness. Pain hovered around the edges, but she pushed it away. She wouldn't think about it now. Leaning on her elbow, she hovered over him and placed a light kiss on his lips.

"Thank you, Jarrod."

# 16

"*Wish ya didn't have to go off so soon, Jarrod.*" Hettie Schafer put a hand to her forehead, shielding her eyes from the early morning sun that was just peeking up over the boardinghouse roof.

"Got to get back to the ranch," Jarrod said, trying to tamp down his irritation with the woman. He knew her gift of a wedding night had been given out of kindness, but a kick in the head would have been more charitable than being alone with Abby. He felt about ready to explode even if someone only looked at him cross-eyed.

He was waiting for Abby to round up the kids so they could head back to the ranch. Couldn't be too soon for him. Another night in the same room with her would probably do him in.

He heard bootsteps on the boardwalk behind him. When Rafe Donovan stepped down into the dirt street beside him, Jarrod's morning went from godawful to downright stinking.

"What do you want, Donovan?"

Hettie started to say something, and Jarrod held up his hand to silence her.

Donovan scratched his chin thoughtfully. "Hear tell congratulations are in order. Everyone in town is talkin' about how you married that pretty little redhead."

"So?"

"Funny that no one told me you weren't hitched when I took her for your wife."

Jarrod shrugged. "Your mistake. What of it?"

"It 'pears to me that you got married pretty sudden like. Could be you think the judge'll favor you because of it?"

Hettie put her hands on her hips. "Folks who live in Hollister know Jarrod and Abby have been sweet on each other for a long time. They were bound to get married sooner or later."

"Maybe it happened sooner so's you'd get the edge on me."

Hettie pointed at him. "That's a lie. Jarrod and Abby got married because they're in love. I'm prepared to swear to that in a court of law, and so will everyone else in this town."

Jarrod was grateful for her support. But he was afraid if she kept it up, she would confirm what Donovan already suspected.

He turned to the small woman and bent low to kiss her cheek. "Thanks for everything, Hettie. You go on inside. You've got customers to see to."

"But—"

He gestured toward her front door. "Go on, now. I'll take care of this."

She reluctantly agreed and went to the door of the restaurant. After shooting Donovan a hostile look, she disappeared inside.

"It won't work, Blackstone."

"What?"

"This phony weddin' to get the kids."

"A couple is a damn sight better bet to make a home for them than a bachelor they never laid eyes on before."

"I talked to that lawyer fella here in town. He says the judge will look at custody of those kids like property. A man owns everything."

Jarrod's eyes narrowed. "What are you getting at?"

"I've got a will signed by my brother and duly witnessed. You got a letter from Sally. Married or not, the judge will see my side as the stronger."

"Like hell he will, Donovan. There's more at stake than the law. Like what those kids want. Where they want to stay. Where they'll be happy."

"It's like I told you, they're just kids. They need someone to tell 'em what to do."

"I don't care what that two-bit lawyer said. You won't be the one calling the shots. Count on it."

Donovan pulled his hat down on his head. "We'll just have to wait and see what the judge says. Won't we, Blackstone?"

"I reckon we will, Donovan."

The man started to walk away, then turned back, his blue eyes narrowed. "By the way, I just came from the sheriff's office."

"Glad to hear it. Too bad Zach didn't talk you into dropping your claim."

"He wanted me to know the circuit judge is due in two weeks."

Abby saw Rafe Donovan nod to Jarrod, then walk away. She briefly wondered what they had talked about, but she had other things on her mind.

She stopped by the wagon and looked up at Jarrod. "Have you seen Oliver?"

He frowned. "Isn't he at Bea's with the other kids?"

"No. Bea put him to bed, but he wasn't there this morning. All his things are gone." She lifted her chin in the direction Donovan had taken. "I saw you with Donovan. Do you think he might have Oliver?"

"I didn't get that feeling." He glanced over his shoulder, an angry scowl twisting his features. "He had other things on his mind."

Abby decided she would ask him about that later. Right now, she was going from concerned to frantic about Oliver.

"Where do you suppose he could be? He's so little, Jarrod. What if—"

"Don't go borrowin' trouble. He'll turn up." He tugged her against him and rubbed her back reassuringly.

She wanted to stay there forever. But she pulled out of his arms. "I can't wait. I'll go crazy if I don't look for him."

"Then start at the Shemanskis."

"But he was told not to go there. Matt's sick."

"Oliver doesn't care. He was sure disappointed that he had to stay at Bea's."

"But Annie would have sent him packing," Abby said.

"If she knew he was there," he answered.

"Let's go look."

They hurried down Main Street toward the mercantile, where the Shemanskis lived above their store. A staircase in the back led up to the rooms. When Abby knocked on the door, Annie quickly answered it, holding a year-old-baby on her hip.

The woman was taller than Abby, with hazel eyes and brown hair pulled away from her face and into a bun at her nape. "I'm so glad to see you."

"Is Oliver here?" Abby asked.

Annie nodded. "I just discovered him. Might not have noticed except my Sarah didn't have a place to sit at the breakfast table."

"He's all right, then?" Jarrod wanted to know.

"Fine as frog's hair," Annie said. "Now. Has he had chicken pox?"

Jarrod shoved his hands in his denim pockets. "Good question. Guess we're gonna find out."

The baby in her arms started to squirm and she shifted the infant to a more comfortable position. "He sneaked into Matt's room. The boys were so quiet we never knew. The damage is done. I'm sorry, Jarrod," she said, shooting Abby a sympathetic look.

"I apologize, Annie." Abby looked past her to where there was raucous laughter. "I never would have dreamed he'd sneak over here."

The other woman laughed. "He certainly wasn't any trouble." She looked from one to the other. "I hear congratulations are in order. I'm real happy for both of you."

"Thanks," Jarrod said, sliding Abby a glance. "We're real happy about it too."

He didn't look or sound very happy, Abby thought. The lines creasing his face beside his nose and mouth, and the circles beneath his eyes, made him look like he'd been awake all night. At least that wouldn't give away their secret. After the exquisite things Jarrod had done to her, she could understand why a man and woman newly married would stay up all night. A shiver raced through her as she recalled the feelings Jarrod had elicited from her.

"You've got your hands full," Jarrod said. "So we'd best take our little fella on home. I'd say he needs a lesson in learning to mind what he's told."

"Don't be too hard on him," Annie said.

Abby smiled up at Jarrod. "I wouldn't worry about that."

In her own room the following morning, Abby smoothed the quilt over her mattress one last time. It wasn't quite sunup, and she had to fix breakfast for Jarrod before he began his day. The children were still asleep. They didn't get up until after he had gone, including Tom, who stayed for lessons before joining his uncle for chores.

Abby opened her door and heard voices in Jarrod's room. Just as she stepped into the hall, Tom did the same. When he saw her, he froze.

"What are you doing up so early?" she asked.

"What are you doin' sleepin' in your old room? You married Uncle Jarrod. Married folks sleep in the same bed." His voice rose a notch.

"Quiet, Tom. You'll wake everyone else."

The last thing she needed was trying to explain this to all the children. It would be hard enough telling Tom. She wasn't sure what to say. It had been late when they'd arrived at the ranch. She had bedded the children down, then gone straight to her own room without a thought about how it would look if anyone found her away from her brand-new husband.

"What's wrong?" Jarrod stopped in the hall beside his nephew, and his eyebrows rose when he saw her standing there. He put a hand on the boy's shoulder. "Let's go down to the kitchen and have some breakfast."

Tom shook his head, and straight brown hair fell over his eyes. He angrily brushed it away. "I wanna know what she's doin' in her old room now that she's married to you."

Abby saw the love in his young eyes when he looked at his uncle. Then his gaze rested on her and it was filled with hurt and betrayal. This bargain she had struck was getting worse all the time.

"Let's go down to the kitchen and talk about this before we wake everyone else."

"Yes, sir." Tom stomped past Abby without acknowledging her and went downstairs.

Jarrod followed and stopped beside Abby, a concerned expression on his face. He hadn't shaved yet, making him look more intense. "I hadn't thought further than speaking the vows, Abby."

"Me either. What are we going to say to him?"

He shook his head. "Wish I knew. At the reverend's he was downright cheerful. I was beginning to think he was warming up to you."

"I know. The same thought crossed my mind." She bit her lip as she studied the spot where the boy had been. She took Jarrod's arm and moved him away from the other children's rooms. "I think we have to tell him the truth. Maybe you can convince him that dishonesty is all right sometimes."

He looked at her sharply. "What does that mean?"

She touched a finger to her lips, shushing him. "I'm sorry, Jarrod. But a twelve-year-old boy sees everything in black and white. To him we're lying."

He ran a hand through his hair. "You're right. We have to tell him what's going on and hope he'll understand."

"You have to do the talking. He looked at me as if he wished I'd disappear."

"You're exaggerating."

She shook her head. "You didn't see the expression on his face."

"No matter. We can't put it off."

She nodded, then led the way downstairs. Tom was sitting at the table, and Abby took the chair across from him, while Jarrod sat to his left.

"Tom, do you have any idea how much I've come to care about you and your brother and sisters?"

Tom looked at his uncle. "Really?"

Jarrod smiled. "Really. I'd do anything to keep the four of you here with me."

"Includin' marrying Abby?"

"That's right."

"Don't see what that's got to do with anything."

"I'm going to try to explain it." Jarrod took a deep breath. "Your father left a paper saying that you would live with his brother if anything happened to him. Rafe wants to honor that wish and take you back to his ranch in New Mexico."

"I don't want to go. Neither will the others."

Jarrod squeezed his arm reassuringly. "I don't want you to. Neither does Abby. We have to go before a judge and let him decide who you should live with. All I have is your mother's letter giving the four of you to me. I don't want to take any chances that the judge won't see things my way. Your uncle Rafe isn't married. So—"

"You married Abby?" There was such distaste in his voice that Abby flinched.

"It was my idea." Jarrod met her gaze, and she saw that he hadn't missed the venom in the boy's tone. "Abby didn't think it was a good one. But Donovan wanted to split you up. And the day he was here, the way he was with all of you convinced her that you'd be better off with me."

"Married folks stay in the same room together." Tom sat up and folded his arms over his chest, staring down at the table.

"That's true. In this case, Abby's doing me a favor. She's my wife in name only. Do you know what that means?"

"Means she's pretending." The boy shot her a glare.

"That's right. When the judge says that the four of you can stay with me, then we won't be married anymore."

"I thought it was real. Reverend Taylor is a real preacher. You said real words. You kissed her real hard. Why isn't it forever?"

Jarrod sighed and rubbed his chin thoughtfully. "When Abby agreed to be our housekeeper, she did it to help me out, but she made sure I knew it was only for a short time."

"Why?" Tom's eyes narrowed, but this time he didn't look at her.

Abby spoke up. "I can't stay because I have to find my father. He went away when I was about your age, Tom, and I promised myself when I was big enough I'd find him and live with him. Can you understand what that means to me?"

"So you're tricking everyone."

"Not exactly," Jarrod said. "We're really and truly married. But when everything is settled and you can stay, we're going to annul it as if we never said the vows. Do you understand, son?"

The boy looked at Jarrod without saying anything.

"I know it's dishonest, and I wouldn't blame you if you lost respect for me. That would hurt me a lot, but not as much as losing you. That's all I have to say. Except that it would be best to keep this from your brother and sisters. If word gets back to the judge, it wouldn't look good."

Tom shifted on his chair. "Can I tell Lil? Katie and Oliver got big mouths. But Lil won't say anything."

Jarrod glanced at Abby. "What do you think?"

Her heart went out to Tom as she studied the bewildered look on his young face. He needed someone to talk to. "As long as she knows how important it is to keep this quiet. Let's tell her together—"

Tom jumped up so fast his chair went over backward, startling Abby. "I don't want to do anything with you. You're nothin' but a fake."

Jarrod stood up quickly. "Don't speak to Abby that way, Tom."

The boy turned a look on him full of youthful fury and resentment. "What difference does it make? She's leaving."

He turned and ran out of the kitchen just as the rays of the sun peeked through the window.

Frowning, Jarrod turned back to Abby. "I'm sorry."

"I know." She looked down at her clasped hands for a moment, trying to control their shaking. Then she met his stormy gaze. "The question is, what are we going to do now?"

"About what?"

She sighed. "Tom noticed our sleeping arrangements. You think Katie and Oliver won't? They're the ones who are most likely to let something slip in town."

"So what do we do?" He rubbed his cheek thoughtfully. When a gleam stole into his eyes, she held up a hand to stop what she knew was coming.

"I am not moving lock, stock, and barrel into your bedroom. It's out of the question."

"Why, Abby? What are you afraid of?" His tone was as smooth and soft as silk.

"I'm not afraid of you, if that's what you're implying. It's just not proper."

"The hell it isn't. We're married, legal *and* proper."

"I'm not going to argue with you about this. I will not jeopardize my plan."

"So I'm a threat to you." He smiled that lazy smile that stole her breath away. "I believe I'll take that as a compliment."

As Jarrod moved closer, Abby stood up and backed away from him. "You can take it any way you darn well please, just keep your distance, Jarrod Blackstone."

"Why, Mrs. Blackstone?" He stopped in front of her and touched one finger to her neck, the exact spot where her pulse fluttered wildly. "I think you liked sharing my bed and you're afraid you could get so used to it you might not want to go chasing shadows."

Abby figured she would take the truth of his words to her grave. "I think maybe we can work out a compromise."

"Such as?"

"I will move my things into your room and retire there until we're sure the children are sound asleep."

"Then?"

"I will sleep in my room and get up before they do so no one will suspect a thing."

"Seems a lot of sneaking around to me."

"Maybe, but I can't think of any other way."

He rubbed the back of his neck. "Won't be for long anyhow."

"Why? What's happened?"

"I didn't want to upset you or say anything in front of the kids until they have to know. Donovan told me yesterday the judge will be in Hollister in two weeks."

"Two weeks?"

Abby's stomach clenched.

That night, Jarrod was restless. The house was quiet. Abby had left him and gone to her room as soon as she figured the kids were asleep. He wished he could find that peace. The truth was, he was worried about the upcoming custody hearing. Even more, he missed having Abby beside him. She felt right in his bed. Without her body beside his, the sweet sound of her breathing, her movements rustling the sheets, it was as if a part of him was missing.

He'd never felt that way before. Not even with Dulcy. He was fighting like hell against it, but more and more he feared that Abby had the power to hurt him like no one else ever had.

After tossing and turning for what seemed hours, he got up. He was warm. The house had held in the heat of the day. Maybe if he sat on the porch and cooled off he could get some rest, get Abby out of his thoughts. He put on his trousers.

Stepping out into the upstairs hall, Jarrod automatically glanced toward the kids' rooms. When he noticed a light coming from under Lily's door, his brows drew together in concern. Was she all right? Had Tom upset her with the news he'd learned that morning?

Quickly, he moved across the hall and was about to knock when he heard voices. Lily wasn't alone. He heard Katie, Tom, and Oliver. Jarrod grinned as the latter was shushed repeatedly. Poor Oliver couldn't keep his voice down if his life depended on it. He sobered instantly, wondering what was keeping them awake.

After knocking softly, he opened the door. Tom was poised in the doorway between his room and Lily's, apparently trying to escape. Katie and Oliver burrowed beneath the covers on Lily's bed, to hide. As if two big lumps on the mattress could be overlooked. He stifled a smile.

"What's going on? Why aren't you all asleep?"

Dressed in her white, cotton nightgown, Lily stood by her bed, trying to block his view. "Uncle Jarrod, I—"

"She couldn't sleep. I came in to talk," Tom said.

He nodded toward the two mounds beneath the covers. "I suppose Katie and Oliver couldn't sleep either?"

"You can't see me, Uncle Jarrod." Oliver's muffled voice came from the bed. "I'm hidin'."

Katie threw back the covers. "How did you know where we were?"

"It wasn't easy," Jarrod said. "I almost missed you." He looked at the four of them. "Now who wants to tell me what's going on?"

"Are you mad, Uncle Jarrod?" Katie asked. "We were having a family meeting."

"A meeting?" he asked.

"We used to do it with Mama, to figure things out. She always talked to us when she needed to decide something," Lily said.

"We helped 'er," Oliver said, sliding out from his hiding place and sitting cross-legged in the center of the bed.

"Is that what you're doing now? Trying to make a decision?" Jarrod asked, looking pointedly at Tom. He hoped the boy hadn't spilled the beans to Katie and Oliver. If he had, as soon as they hit town for the hearing, everyone in Hollister would know his marriage to Abby was a fraud. Including the judge.

"We're just talking about things." Tom shook his head slightly, indicating he hadn't said anything to them.

"What things?" Jarrod asked.

"Do we have to go with our other uncle?" Katie asked.

Oliver pulled his thumb out of his mouth. "He's mean. Wanted t'wallop me when I went t'the outhouse."

Lily sat on the bed. "We don't want to go with him. Mama said we should be raised as Blackstones on the ranch where she grew up, with you. She talked to us about it and we all decided it was best. Don't make us go. We like it here. We want to stay with you, Uncle Jarrod."

His chest tight with emotion, Jarrod slowly sat down beside her. He draped an arm around her shoulders, and she leaned against him. Tom sat down on his other side, just before Katie and Oliver jumped on his back. They threw their chubby, loving arms around his neck. The weight of those warm bodies felt good. He closed his eyes for a moment as he drew in a deep breath to compose himself. No way was Rafe Donovan, or anyone else, taking these kids from him.

Jarrod swallowed hard. "I would have talked to you sooner if I'd known you knew what was going on with Donovan."

"We eavesdropped when he was here with the sheriff," Katie said. "Are you mad? Your voice sounds funny."

He shook his head. "I'm not mad. Just wish you'd let me in on this sooner, is all."

"Really? Why?" Oliver asked.

Jarrod took a deep breath. "Your mama was a smart lady. These meetings are real important. I'd like to be part of your family if you'll let me. What do you say?"

"Of course," Lily said.

Oliver threw himself backward on the mattress. "Yippee," he hollered.

"That was yes," Tom said. "Goes double for me."

"Me too," Katie added. "Are you gonna come to all our family meetings from now on, Uncle Jarrod?"

"Yes, I will. But it's late. From now on, I think we should have them at suppertime."

"Goody," Oliver said. "Then Abby can be there too."

"She's not part of the family," Tom said, a note of bitterness lacing his words.

Katie leaned over Jarrod's shoulder and looked at him. "But aren't you married?"

"Yes," he answered.

"Then isn't she part of the family?" Katie persisted.

Tom shrugged sheepishly when Jarrod glared at him. "Tom just meant that she's not related by blood. Right, Tom?"

"I s'pose," the boy said grudgingly.

Katie hugged him around the neck. "Uncle Jarrod, don't you think Abby should come to our family meetings?"

"That's up to her."

If she wanted to stay and be a part of the family, he wasn't opposed to the idea. But that wasn't likely to happen, and he wouldn't count on it. After one failure with a woman, he wasn't about to set himself up for another.

He released Lily and pulled Katie's arms from around his neck, then tugged her over his shoulder. The little girl squealed with delight at the sudden somersault. "I think it's getting late and you should all be in bed and asleep."

"Will you tuck us in?" Katie asked.

"Sure."

He'd do anything for them.

In the hallway outside Lily's room, Abby pressed her back against the wall as she brushed her knuckle across the tear trickling down her cheek. Half asleep in her own bed, she had heard one of the children cry out and awoke with a start. Hurrying to Oliver, she had seen the light from Lily's room and stopped. When she heard her name, she froze outside. Tom's words had knocked the wind from her as surely as if he'd socked her in the stomach.

*She's not part of the family.*

True enough. Still, that didn't make it hurt any less. The fact was, she didn't fit anywhere. Not until she found her father.

From Lily's room, she heard the bedsprings groan and

figured Jarrod was about to settle the children. She started for her room, then decided since they were all still awake, she should go to Jarrod's.

Lordy, she would breathe a sigh of relief when this was over.

A few minutes later Jarrod entered the bedroom and shut the door. Silvery moonlight streamed in through the window, right where Abby was sitting. He started when he turned around and saw her.

"Did the kids disturb you?" he asked.

"I heard them, if that's what you mean." They had disturbed her, but not in the way he meant. And she wasn't about to tell him. "I heard you with them and knew they were in good hands. But I figured until they're asleep again, I should wait in here. That's all right, isn't it?"

He nodded, folded his arms over his bare chest, then leaned back against the dresser. "It would probably be for the best. They're restless. Seems they've known about Donovan since he came to the ranch with Zach. The little scoundrels eavesdropped."

She smiled briefly. "They're developing a bad habit of doing that."

"I can't blame them for wanting to know what's going on. Too many things have happened to them that they have no control over."

"Now they're facing another change. I wish that man could see what he's doing to them."

"Me too." There was something in his tone that drew Abby's attention.

"You're not worried that he might actually get custody?"

He sat beside her on the bed, his bare shoulder brushing against her cotton nightgown. "That's exactly what I'm concerned about."

"Even though we're married? As far as everyone else knows," she added quickly.

"It could go either way, Abby. There's no way to predict how a judge will rule." The misery in his voice touched something deep inside her.

She put her arms around him. Just for comfort, she told

herself. When she buried her face into the hollow between his neck and shoulder, he let out a shuddering breath. Then his arms came around her, hugging her tightly.

He nuzzled her hair. "You smell so good, Abby. So sweet, so right."

She lifted her face, and before she knew it, his lips were on hers in a crushing kiss. All his frustration and concern poured into her, and she accepted it, pleased to be there for him. She was glad too for the touch of his mouth to hers and all the glorious things he made her feel.

Her rapid breathing joined with his until all she could hear was a roaring in her ears. Jarrod pulled her across his lap and laid her on the bed, settling himself half over her.

Her breasts were crushed to his chest and she rubbed against him, delighting in the feel of him against her—hard to soft, rough to smooth, man to woman.

"Abby." Her name, just a whisper on his lips, told her of his inner turmoil. "Let me love you, Abby. I want you so much."

He kissed her neck, finding a sensitive place just beneath her ear. She writhed against him, moaning at his sweet torture.

"You want me too." He continued to stroke her neck. "Don't you? Tell me you want me, Abby."

"Yes," she said. "I want you."

He took her breast in his palm through the material of her nightgown. As he caressed the tender mound, her nipple grew taut. His hand slid over her abdomen, down to the hem of her nightgown. He started to draw it up and over her head.

The bedroom door opened. "Abby? Uncle Jarrod?"

Both of them sat up on the side of the bed, breathing hard. Katie stood in the doorway, rubbing her eyes.

Abby recovered enough to speak first. "What's wrong, sweetie?"

"I had a bad dream. That mean man was trying to take me," she said sniffling.

Abby went over and lifted the little girl into her arms. "No one is going to hurt you. I promise."

Jarrod rubbed his chin, an agitated movement clearly indicating his frustration. "I thought she wasn't having bad dreams anymore."

"She wasn't," Abby said. "But I'm not surprised at this, what with everything going on."

"Uncle Jarrod?" Katie looked at him from the security of Abby's arms.

"What, Katie?" he asked.

Abby hoped the little girl wouldn't notice how hoarse his voice sounded, or understand the reason for it.

"Can I stay here? With you and Abby? No one will get me then."

His gaze met hers, and Abby knew he was leaving the decision up to her. She drew in a long breath, thankful that the interruption had saved her from making a big mistake. This was exactly what she had been afraid would happen if she spent any time in Jarrod's bed.

"Katie, how about if I take you into my old bed so we won't disturb your uncle? It's late and he has to be up very early in the morning."

"No," she said, her tone whiny and tired, and on the edge of unreasonable. "He's stronger'n you. I want to sleep here with you and Uncle Jarrod."

Fearing the little girl would wake the other children, Abby knew she had little choice but to agree. "All right, Katie. You can stay here with us."

Abby put the little girl on the bed. "Scoot over, Katie," she ordered.

Katie did as she was told and Abby climbed in beside her, putting her arms around the little girl as she tried to make her feel safe.

In turn, Katie would protect her from Jarrod. Abby stared at the broad expanse of his bare chest as he stood on the far side of the bed, bathed in a shaft of moonlight. He was the most incredible-looking man she had ever seen. Instead of weakening over time, her attraction continued to grow stronger.

"It's going to be a long two weeks," Abby whispered.

# 17

*Two weeks later, at exactly* ten in the morning, the six of them stood in the Watering Hole before Judge Douglas. Abby was amazed that so many people in Hollister had come to offer Jarrod their support.

The judge was a small gray-haired man in his early sixties. His most imposing feature was the thick, iron-gray mustache he continually smoothed over his upper lip. He sat at a table in front of the mahogany bar which was closed until after court. Jarrod, Abby, and the children stood facing him on the right. Donovan was on the left.

Judge Douglas looked from one to the other. "Mr. Blackstone. . ."

Katie tugged on Jarrod's pants. "That's you. Right, Uncle Jarrod?"

He nodded, then put a finger to his lips to silence her.

"I'd like quiet in my court, young lady," the judge said.

"Why?" Katie wanted to know.

"So you can hear the decision I've made."

"Are we gonna get to stay with Uncle Jarrod?" Katie asked hopefully.

Judge Douglas cleared his throat loudly and shifted uncomfortably in his chair. "I'm afraid not, little lady.

Reed Donovan was head of his family. He knew what he was doing when he made out that will, and it takes precedence over a personal letter from Sally Blackstone Donovan."

"No!" Jarrod shook his head, unbelieving.

Donovan grinned. "Looks like you lost, Blackstone." Conversation buzzed around them. Oliver and Katie grabbed onto Abby, their arms locked about her waist. Stunned, she put a hand on each child's shoulder, holding tightly to them.

"I'm not goin' with him!" Tom shouted.

"We want to stay with Uncle Jarrod," Lily said, tears filling her green eyes.

"Don't wanna go with him," Oliver said, then stuck his thumb in his mouth.

"Can he make us go?" Katie asked, looking from the judge to Abby.

"You bet I can, little lady," Judge Douglas said. He glared at Jarrod, his pale brown eyes narrowing. "Don't go getting any notions of taking those kids anywhere. That would be foolish. You'd wind up in jail, son."

"You don't give a good goddamn about what's best for these children."

"Hold on, son—"

Jarrod pointed at him. "You hold on. These kids want to stay with me. Any idiot can see that."

"You calling me an idiot, Blackstone?"

"If the shoe fits, Judge." Jarrod's eyes turned dark and stormy with anger.

"I'd say he just called you an idiot, your honor."

Jarrod pointed at him. "You stay out of this, Donovan."

The man held up his hands in a peaceable manner. "I'm not stirrin' things up."

"Then keep your damned mouth shut."

"Don't you tell me what to do—"

Jarrod had grabbed Rafe by the shirtfront almost before anyone saw him move.

The judge's gavel pounded the table. "Order in this court!"

Zach Magruder and two other men pulled Jarrod off Donovan and held him back until he calmed down.

Rafe Donovan stepped forward. "I believe I'll take the children now, your honor."

Oliver and Katie started to cry. Sobbing, Lily ran to Jarrod and grabbed him around the waist. Katie and Oliver followed.

"I ain't goin' with him!" Tom shouted. "Can't none of you make me!"

Judge Douglas hit the table again.

The noise snapped Abby from her stunned silence. She stepped forward. "Will you stop banging that stupid little hammer? Can't you see it's upsetting the children?" Glancing heavenward, she directed a wry look to a higher power. "Silly me. Of course you can't see that you're upsetting the children. If you knew anything about them, you wouldn't have made such a stupid decision."

"Young woman, are you calling me an idiot too?"

"Yes."

"By God, one more word from either of you and I'll have you removed from these proceedings and tossed in jail!"

"No!" Katie and Oliver wailed together.

"Ya can't do that, Judge," Tom said.

Lily wept into the front of Jarrod's shirt. He looked at the judge. "I apologize for my outburst, your honor."

"Jarrod," Abby cried. "Don't you dare apologize to this—this—arrogant ass."

The judge pointed at her, gavel in hand. "Sheriff Magruder, remove that woman from my courtroom."

Zach shifted uncomfortably. "Now, your honor—"

"Do it!" he bellowed.

Zach moved over to Abby and took her arm. "Sorry, Abby."

She yanked and tried to pull away. "I'm not going, Zach."

He looked over to one of his deputies and motioned him over. "Sorry, Abby," he said again. "It's my job."

The deputy took her other arm and the two burly men

lifted her bodily. As they carried Abby out the door, she hollered at the top of her lungs just exactly what she thought of justice in general and Judge Douglas in particular.

"Is this a family meeting, Uncle Jarrod?" Katie asked, unshed tears glistening in her eyes.

Jarrod glanced across the room at the judge, who was talking to Rafe Donovan. He didn't have much time, just enough to say good-bye to the kids, and he had to make every second count.

"Yes, Katie. But this time I want you to just listen."

"Do you think he'll let me be a cowboy?" Oliver asked, glancing uncertainly at the man across the room.

"If you'll all listen, I don't think you'll have to worry about it," Jarrod said. He went down on one knee and gathered them all close.

Tom's eyes glowed with anticipation. "You got a plan, Uncle Jarrod?"

"Yes. Now here's what I want you to do. . . ."

In a few minutes he outlined for each of them what their job was. It was all he could come up with on short notice. "Do you all understand?"

They nodded solemnly.

"Do you think it'll work, Uncle Jarrod?" Tom asked.

"Yup," he answered with more confidence than he felt. "But don't you worry, no matter what, I won't let him take you off Blackstone land."

Jarrod glanced up and saw Donovan approaching.

He stopped just a foot away, with his hat in his hands. "Time's up, Blackstone."

The tears Katie had been crying began to trickle faster down her cheeks. "Will we ever see you again, Uncle Jarrod?"

"Count on it." Jarrod hugged her. Then he pulled Oliver onto his knee. His throat tightened with emotion. He saw moisture gathering in the boy's eyes. "Remember, cowboys never cry."

"Don't wanna be a cowboy." His small body trembled as Oliver threw his arms around Jarrod. "Won't never get to see the Specific Ocean now."

"It'll be all right, son. You'll see." He set the boy on the floor. He stood up and looked at Tom, then stuck his hand out. The boy put his smaller one in Jarrod's palm and gravely shook hands. Then he threw himself against Jarrod.

"Will you take care of my horse for me?"

Jarrod nodded. Then he looked at Lily. She was on the brink of womanhood, and he might never see her blossom into the fine lady he knew she would be. Sally's daughter. He swallowed hard. That lump seemed to be getting bigger all the time.

Donovan cleared his throat loudly. "I haven't got all day. The judge gave you time to say all this—"

"Donovan—" Jarrod glared at him. One more word and he would knock the son of a bitch from here to kingdom come. He took a calming breath. "Hold on. This isn't easy."

Lily gave Jarrod a wavering smile. "Uncle Jarrod, will you tell Joe good-bye for me?"

"I will. I'm counting on you, Lily," he said, looking at her intently.

"I won't let you down," she said, determination strengthening her voice.

Jarrod looked at Donovan. "Take care of them. If I ever hear you're not—"

"Don't worry. I'll do right by 'em."

"See that you do."


Abby sat glumly on the scratchy wool blanket covering the single mattress in her cell. With her elbows propped on her thighs and her chin in her hands, she tried to summon the anger that had landed her here in the first place. In the cell beside hers, Bernie Rumson was sleeping off the effects of too much liquor, and snoring to wake the dead while he did it. He didn't smell too sweet either.

"Hey, Magruder," she called out. "You running for reelection this year?"

"Nope," came his answer from the front of the jail.

"Hmph."

"What was that?"

"I said it's a good thing," she called out. "In fact, if you run again, don't count on my support."

"I'll keep that in mind." She could hear his chuckle loud and clear.

She sure had him worried, she thought miserably. How in the world was she going to get out of here? She had to help Jarrod. He must be devastated. She stood up and studied the bars over the window. If she had to dig and claw her way out, she would get to Jarrod.

A chair scraped on the wooden floor in the other room. "Looks like ya got help on the way."

Eagerly, she moved to the bars blocking her exit and gripped them tightly. "What's going on?"

"Jarrod's here to get you out."

"Lucky for you, Magruder." She heard him chuckle again. The door opened, then she heard the sound of voices speaking quietly. "What's going on out there?" she called.

"Hold on, Abby," Zach said. "I'll have you out as soon as I take care of the paperwork."

"You can take your paperwork and—"

Then Zach walked into the room, with Jarrod right behind him. "And what, Abby?"

She smiled sweetly. "File it."

When she and Jarrod were outside, she turned to him and put her hand on his arm. "The children?"

"Gone with Donovan."

"You let him take them? How could you? Why—"

He gripped her upper arms, his eyes full of anger. "What was I supposed to do? Pull a gun and kidnap them?"

"I don't know. I just thought you would think of something."

"I did. It's not much, but we have to hurry."

"What do you want me to do?" Her heart pounded.

"Let's go. I'll explain on the way."

\*　　\*　　\*

Donovan took a spoonful of beans and made a face. He glared at Lily. "These're burned again, girl. Thought you said you could cook."

"They are cooked, just a little too much is all." Lily met his gaze squarely. She would never let him know that she was afraid of him, like she'd been of her father. So far, though, Donovan hadn't been mean like Pa. But he wasn't anything like Uncle Jarrod either. She missed him terribly, and Abby too.

"I like 'em like this," Tom said, defending her cooking.

Lily stole a glance at Donovan. They'd been on the trail three days and he was cross and irritable, but not bent on letting them go.

Katie set her metal plate on her lap. "When are we gettin' to your ranch, mister?"

"Keep tellin' you girl, it's Uncle Rafe."

"How much longer, Mr. Uncle Rafe?" Lily hid a smile as he let out a long breath.

"We're still on Blackstone land. If we hadn't had to stop for your stuff—" Donovan stopped to drink his coffee, then spit it out. He scowled as he brushed the back of his hand over his mouth. "There's grounds in here. Didn't no one ever teach you how to make this stuff right?"

Lily shrugged. "I'm doing the best I can. If I'd had more time to learn—"

"I gotta go!" Oliver jumped up and clutched his privates, but not before a dark stain showed on the front of his pants.

"Jeez, boy! Can't you tell when you gotta go?"

Oliver stuck his thumb in his mouth and shook his head. "I'm jus' liddle, mister."

Donovan sighed. "I ought to—"

Tom jumped up. "I'll take 'im, before it gets real dark."

The man waved them off with a flick of his wrist.

Lily smiled. She knew Tom gathered whatever bugs and critters he could find while he was out there with Oliver. Donovan wouldn't like it tonight any better than he had the last two.

Katie looked up at the sky. "How many stars are up there, Mr. Uncle Rafe?"

"How the hell should I know?"

"Don't you know you shouldn't say those bad words? Didn't anyone teach you that it's not polite, especially in front of children?"

He spoke through gritted teeth. "Did anyone ever teach you not to ask so many questions?"

"Abby says it's good to be curious and the only way to find things out is to ask."

"So I have Abby to thank for the fact that my nerves are as raw as a greenhorn cowboy?" He stared at Katie, who just looked right back at him. Finally he said, "I wonder where those boys got to? They been gone an awful long time."

Lily glanced off into the brush, hoping he wasn't getting suspicious. "Oliver sometimes takes a while."

"Hell, he let most of his water go right here," Donovan said with a snort.

"He's only four years old." Lily stood up. "I'll wash up the dishes before bed."

He glared at Katie. "You gonna sleep all night this time?"

"I'll try," she answered. "Can't always tell when that bad dream will come. Uncle Jarrod—"

"Don't say it." He held up his hands to stop her. "Not one more time. I don't want to know how Blackstone does things. You're with me now. We're gonna do it my way. You got that?"

"Yes, mister," Katie said, thrusting out her lower lip.

He pointed at her. "Don't you pout, girl."

The brush rustling nearby told them Tom and Oliver were returning. Tom burst into the clearing. "Lily, Oliver's got spots."

Donovan agitatedly rubbed the back of his neck. "It won't work, boy. I know what you're tryin' to do and I ain't gonna fall for it."

"Where are they?" Lily asked, studying the boy's face. As much as she hated agreeing with Donovan about anything, she didn't see anything either.

"Look at his back," Tom said.

She pulled Oliver by the fire and lifted his shirt. A covering of small red dots went from the waist of his trousers to the base of his neck.

"Tom's right. He's got spots. If you don't believe me, look for yourself," Lily said.

"You think I don't know you want to go back with Blackstone?" Donovan stared in turn at each of them. "This is just a trick. I'm not fallin' for it."

"Oliver hasn't felt good all day," Lily pointed out.

The man threw up his hands. "I don't want to hear any more. Get to bed, all of you. We're gettin' up early tomorrow and I want to move. This time tomorrow night, we'll be off Blackstone land."

As worry about Oliver settled over her, Lily finished washing up, then settled her brothers and sister. Donovan was already in his bedroll. Everything was quiet for a while. Then Donovan let out a yelp, threw his covers aside, and jumped up.

"There's somethin' in there," he hollered. "It was crawlin' on me."

They sat up and looked as a snake quickly slithered from the man's bedroll. Tom eyed the markings on the creature's back and laughed. "That's just a harmless ol' garter snake. Gib showed me how to tell which are dangerous. He won't hurt you, mister."

Donovan pointed at him. "You put it in there, you little son of a bitch. And the ants the night before and the crickets the night before that."

"What makes you think so, mister?" Tom looked innocent as a newborn babe, and Lily wondered how he'd learned to lie so well.

Katie covered her ears. "You shouldn't call Tom bad names, Mr. Rafe."

Oliver started to cry, and Lily gathered him onto her lap. "My head hurts," he wailed. "I itch all over."

"Talk to your brother. He probably put ants in your bed," Donovan replied.

"I did no such thing," Tom said angrily.

"Doesn't matter if ya did or didn't. Go to sleep. All of ya. I don't want to hear another word from anyone."

Oliver whimpered, and as Lily cradled him against her, she felt the heat from his body. Something was very wrong with him. Donovan could deny it all he wanted, but Lily was really worried.

Oliver wasn't faking.

Abby crouched in front of the campfire and poured Jarrod a cup of coffee. He accepted it gratefully and blew on the steaming liquid before sipping. He looked tired. Night was turning to gray dawn, and day four of following Donovan and the children was about to begin.

Until now, Abby had had no idea how large the ranch was. When she'd finally asked, Jarrod told her it consisted of 39,000 acres, five ranches in one. They could ride for a long time and not leave Blackstone land. But she knew he was worried.

Jarrod had hardly slept during the last three days. She knew that because she hadn't either.

"Jarrod?"

"Hmm?" He cradled the cup between his palms and stared into it.

"What if your plan doesn't work? What if he doesn't give them back?"

"He will." There was a deadly certainty to his words.

Still Abby wasn't convinced. The more time that went by, the harder it was to keep her doubts from creeping in. "What if he doesn't?"

"He will, Abby," he snapped. He turned blazing eyes on her. "Don't do this. I don't want to hear it—" He stopped and gritted his teeth. The muscle in his cheek jerked as he got his anger under control.

"I'm sorry." She stood up and busied herself folding her bedroll.

Behind her, Jarrod kicked the ground. Rocks and dirt scattered. "Oh, hell," he said.

He came up, then, and put his hands on her shoulders. "I'm the one who's sorry. I had no call to yell like that." He turned Abby toward him and stared into her eyes, which were brimming with unshed tears. "Especially not at you, Abby. I wouldn't have gotten this far without your help."

He held her close. As she rested her cheek over his heart, she heard its steady thumping. A small sob escaped her before she could stop it.

"Don't cry," he said. "We'll get them back even if I have to give him everything I own to do it."

She looked up at him, astonished, because he sounded like he meant it. "Would you really do that?" she asked.

"Damn right I would." His mouth thinned in determination.

"Let's hope it doesn't come to that. Don't you think it's time to break camp and pick up their trail?"

"You're right. They're only about mile or two ahead of us. I scouted them before I joined you last night."

Jarrod saddled the horses while Abby packed up. He could have kicked himself for the way he'd treated her. But he was worried. He'd made a promise to the kids, and if he didn't get them back before nightfall, it would be broken.

He helped Abby up into the saddle, then swung onto his roan. They headed in the direction of Donovan's camp. Before traveling far, he spotted a dust cloud on the road ahead of them.

He pointed. "Look at that."

Abby reined her horse, then stood taller in the stirrups and shaded her eyes. "It looks like a big farm wagon."

"Donovan." His chest tightened. "Why would he circle back like this, unless. . ." Jarrod looked at her, afraid to hope.

"Let's wait and see," she said cautiously.

They stood their ground right there in the road. Jarrod figured it was time for a showdown with Rafe Donovan no matter the reason the man had changed his course. Their horses shifted restlessly as they waited and watched.

He saw Tom point in their direction, then the kids in the

back of the wagon jumping up and down. As he looked closer, he saw it was just the girls.

"Where's Oliver?" he asked sharply.

"I don't see him," Abby answered, turning to look at him with concern.

"If anything's happened to that boy, I'll—"

"Don't borrow trouble, Jarrod." She kneed her mount and the restive animal leaped forward.

Jarrod followed, and they stopped beside the wagon as Donovan pulled back on the reins.

"Hi, Uncle Jarrod," Tom said.

"Where's Oliver?" Jarrod demanded, his gaze quickly traveling over the three children he could see.

Before Donovan could say anything, Lily leaned over the wagon seat between Tom and Donovan. "He's here in the back of the wagon, Uncle Jarrod. He's sick."

Without a word, Abby quickly slid off her horse and hurried over to the wagon. She climbed inside and hunched down until she disappeared.

Katie peeked around Tom's other side. "Are you glad to see us, Uncle Jarrod? Were you following us the whole time like you said?"

"You bet, honey. I was never far behind."

Jarrod looked at the other man, loosely holding the reins. "What's going on, Donovan? Why'd you turn around?"

"Like she said," he indicated Lily, "the kid took sick. He said somethin' last night, but I thought he was fakin'."

Abby stood up, a worried frown on her face. "It looks like chicken pox. He's got a fever."

"Is he gonna be all right, Abby?" Katie asked. "He don't look so good, does he?"

Abby put an arm around the girl's shoulders. "He'll be fine. He just needs some looking after," she said pointedly.

Donovan glanced at her, then looked back at Jarrod. "Like I was sayin', this mornin' I could see he was sick. We were on our way back to the ranch, where he can be looked after proper. No way I want a sick kid on the trail."

Jarrod nodded, a grudging respect for the other man

beginning. "That's good. Let's get him back there." He started to wheel his horse around.

"Blackstone?"

"What?"

"Just thought you should know I believed I was doing the right thing by these kids."

A spurt of hope cut loose inside Jarrod. "What are you saying?"

"I'd never deliberately bring harm to these young'uns. When Oliver there took sick, I figured maybe I'd bit off more than I could chew."

"And?" Jarrod prodded. He watched Abby walk back to her horse and mount up. Expectation glowed in her eyes, and he knew she was thinking the same thing he was.

Donovan met Jarrod's gaze directly. "They'd be best off with a pa," he looked at Abby, "and a ma. I can't give them that."

"So you were bringing them back to the ranch for good?"

"Yes. My brother wanted me to see that his children were taken care of. It's clear to me now that leaving them with you and Mrs. Blackstone is the best way to see that done."

Jarrod grinned. "I think I might have to change my opinion of you, Rafe."

The other man returned his look. "Maybe not, after I tell you what I think of you for siccing those kids on me the way you did."

"You figured that out?"

"Three nights in a row of critters in my bedroll was a sight more than coincidence. Lily burned every meal. My stomach's wearing a hole clear to my backbone. Katie had dreams every night and kept me up. I'm so tired I can hardly see straight. And Oliver—" He shrugged. "Blackstone, I don't know how you do it. Didn't seem like lookin' after four youngsters would be so dang hard."

"I had help," he said, glancing at Abby. "You get used to having kids around."

"Maybe. If they had nobody, you can bet I'd have 'em

with me. But I got awful dang sick and tired of them singing your praises. They went to a heap of trouble to get me to take 'em back. After a spell it dawned on me that you were the one they wanted. That's where they'd best be."

Saddle leather creaked as Jarrod leaned over with his hand outstretched. Donovan took it.

"Thanks," Jarrod said.

Donovan nodded, then picked up the reins again. "Let's get this young'un back where he belongs." He slanted Jarrod a wry look. "Bet we can make it in half the time now that everything's as it should be."

"Maybe."

Donovan flicked the reins over the backs of his team of horses. "Giddyap," he called.

Jarrod and Abby rode ahead of the wagon. He looked over at her, emotion squeezing his chest until he could hardly breathe. "It didn't happen, Abby. I kept my promise."

"What?" she asked.

"He didn't take them off Blackstone land."

# 18

*Jarrod stood on the front porch* along with Gib Cochran, watching the big farm wagon until it lumbered out of sight.

"Rafe Donovan turned out to be a right nice fella," Gib said.

"Yup, he did," Jarrod agreed.

"A relief to me, I can tell ya."

"How's that?"

"It's good t'know those young'uns got sound blood from both sides of the family."

"I suppose," Jarrod said.

"Mighty nice of him t'stay till Oliver was fit as a fiddle and fixin' t'paint chickens again."

Jarrod grinned. "Amazing how fast kids bounce back."

Gib scratched the gray-and-black stubble on his chin. "Donovan spent a good bit of time watching after the other kids while you and Abby tended to the little fella."

"Did he? I wasn't aware of that."

"Didn't think ya were. Had your hands full with that boy, gettin' his fever down 'n' all."

"He gave us some anxious times, that's for sure. If it hadn't been for Abby—"

"Always comes back to the Firecracker, don't it?"

Jarrod slanted him a sharp look. "What do you mean?"

"More'n once she's turned you around to her way of thinkin'. She said all along those kids should get to know their pa's folks. I don't know about you, but I feel a dang sight better now that they have."

"You already said that."

There was a point here somewhere. He'd known Gib for a long time. Eventually he would get to it. From experience, Jarrod knew whatever the man wanted to tell him would be worth the wait.

"While you were gone, a letter came from San Francisco," Gib added, his coal-black gaze intense.

With all that had happened, Jarrod had forgotten the wire he'd sent. "It must be from Luke Brody. I asked him to—"

"Ain't from him."

Jarrod's eyes narrowed. "You opened it?"

"Nope. Says right there on the outside. It's from Sam Miller, care of Luke Brody."

"Luke must have found Abby's father."

"Can't figure you out, boy."

"What's that supposed to mean?"

"You can't let her go any more than you could them young'uns. So why in tarnation did you make it easy for her to leave?"

"You said it yourself—she sets a lot of store by family." Jarrod shifted his shoulders, trying to ease the tension in his neck. He couldn't deny that he would have trouble letting Abby go. "She's bent on finding him. I wanted to help. Abby's my friend—"

Gib laughed. "She's a dang sight more than that, and if you can't see that by now, you're dumb as a post."

"I see it." Putting that thought into words opened the way for the pain that followed.

He loved her.

"I can't stop her from leaving, Gib."

"The hell you can't—"

"She agreed to stay until things were settled with the children."

"I thought she planned to save enough for her brother's schoolin'."

"I'll see that Clint has enough money to finish his education. It's the least I can do for Abby after everything she's done for me." He ran his hand through his hair. "If living with her father is what she wants, there's nothing standing in her way."

"'Cept you." Jarrod stared at him, and Gib shook his head, exasperated. "If you don't know that she's sweet on you—"

"That's the damnable part. I know she cares. But if I stand in her way, she'll never forgive me. She's one stubborn, bullheaded woman."

"Them's the worst kind." Gib grinned. "And the best. 'Specially for you."

"I have to give her the letter, Gib. I couldn't keep it from her."

"Why don't ya at least read it first. See if—"

"You know I can't do that."

Just then the front door opened. Tom raced outside, his face white as a sheet, gray eyes fearful. "Uncle Jarrod, come quick."

"What's wrong?"

"It's Abby. She passed out cold."

"What?" Jarrod said, alarmed. "Fainted?"

"Yes, sir. She was fryin' bacon for us and just dropped like a stone."

Jarrod turned and ran into the house. In the kitchen, he found Abby with her head in Lily's lap as Katie stroked her hand. Both girls were crying.

"Help her, Uncle Jarrod," Lily demanded, her voice trembling.

Fear tightened in his gut. Abby wasn't a swooning kind of woman. Jarrod went down on one knee beside her. He touched a hand to her forehead and felt the heat. Her face was flushed and her eyes closed. "I need water."

"I'll get it," Tom said.

Jarrod scooped Abby into his arms. "Bring it up to my room. And cloths," he ordered, staring at the girls.

"Yes, sir," they answered.

"What's wrong with her?" Katie asked.

At the doorway he stopped, gathering Abby more tightly to his chest.

"My guess is Abby never had chicken pox."

For three days Jarrod stayed by Abby's bedside. When the spots came out, they covered her from head to toe. Dusty had brought the doc from town, for all the good the old sawbones had done. He'd said fever was the most dangerous part of the disease. If they could get that to break, she'd be nothing more than uncomfortable from the itching.

Beside him, Abby moaned. He'd covered her in cool, damp sheets. Oliver had rested easier after they'd done that for him. But Abby was so much worse than the boy had been.

Worry gnawed at Jarrod as he remembered the doc saying adult cases of chicken pox were almost always worse than children's. He hadn't said Abby could die, but Jarrod had seen that possibility in his eyes.

"Fight, Abby," he said, sponging off her face with cool water. Her cheekbones were prominent because of the flesh she'd lost. He had struggled to get water into her. Food was impossible. "Dammit, you fight this. I won't lose you."

There was a knock at the door, then it opened. "I brung ya more water, Uncle Jarrod," Tom said.

"Put it there on the nightstand," Jarrod ordered, not taking his gaze from the delicate woman in the bed. It tore at him to see his vibrant Abby—Firecracker—so deathly ill.

"Yes, sir."

Something in the boy's tone caught at Jarrod. He looked at Tom staring at Abby, and saw his fear.

Jarrod dropped the cloth into the basin and said, "Come here, son." He opened his arms.

Like a shot, Tom was in Jarrod's embrace and buried his face in Jarrod's neck. His whole body shook.

"You're worried about Abby, aren't you, Tom?" he asked gently. He felt the boy nod. "You care about her a lot more than you let on."

Tom lifted his tear-streaked face. "I do care. I like her a lot, right from the start I did. But I was afraid—" He rubbed a knuckle beneath his runny nose. Then his gray eyes took on a haunted, frightened look. "Is she gonna die? Mama got sick and the doc couldn't help her. She died. Is Abby gonna die like Mama?"

Oh, Lord. What could he tell this poor boy to take away his agony? Abby would know what to say. She always did. But Abby was too sick right now, and he didn't know if she would get well.

Jarrod swallowed hard. "I don't know, Tom."

The boy didn't meet his eyes. "I never cried for Mama, not even once. I never did 'cuz then it would be real. Do you think Mama was mad that I didn't cry for her?"

"No. Your mother understood. She wouldn't want you to be sad. She'd want you to grow into a good, kind man."

He hung his head. "Haven't been very good to Abby. What if I never get to say I'm sorry? I am, Uncle Jarrod. Real sorry for all the mean things I said to her."

"You'll get a chance," Jarrod said, with more certainty than he felt.

"You think so?" Tom said hopefully.

Jarrod searched for words to help Tom, no matter what the Lord had in mind for Abby. "Son, I'm doing my best to keep her with us. But if it doesn't work out that way, we have to be thankful that we had her for the time we did."

"She was always nice to me. Even when I wasn't so—"

Jarrod squeezed his shoulder. "She knows you've been through a lot with your ma."

Tom brushed his tears away. "Oliver got better."

"Yup. No reason Abby can't too." Jarrod drew in a deep breath, steadying his voice. "But it wouldn't hurt if you did a little praying."

He nodded. "Abby taught us one. Well, she learned everyone else, but I was bein' a knothead. I listened, though. When she wasn't lookin'. I learned the prayer."

"That's fine, Tom." Jarrod was so tired his whole body hurt, right down to the roots of his hair. "I'm going to get a cup of coffee. Would you stay here with Abby?"

"Yes, sir."

Jarrod stood up. "I won't be long. If anything happens, anything at all, you hightail it straight to me. You understand?"

Tom nodded.

In the doorway, Jarrod glanced back. Tom was on his knees beside the bed, hands clasped, head bowed. "Now I lay me down to sleep. I pray the Lord my soul to keep. . . ."

Must have been lack of sleep, Jarrod decided, that caused everything to waver in front of his eyes.

Jarrod lifted his head from his arms and looked around groggily, wondering where he was. In front of him was a mug of coffee, cold now. It took a few seconds, but finally his head cleared and he remembered. He had put his head down on the kitchen table, just for a few minutes, while Tom stayed with Abby.

He stood up so quickly the chair toppled backward. He ran upstairs, taking the stairs two at a time, stopping outside the bedroom door to catch his breath. He heard someone talking.

"You look fine, Abby." That was Tom.

For a second he'd thought he had heard Abby's clear voice, but was afraid to believe it. For three days, she hadn't done more than mutter incoherently. Jarrod slipped into the room and saw the boy sitting on the bed talking to her.

"Ya gotta get better soon, Abby. We got lots to tell you. Joe Schafer took your job at Hollister Freight. You should see Lily lookin' through all them catalogs to order stuff so's he'll deliver it. Katie's wakin' up at night again. Lily and me take turns 'cuz Uncle Jarrod's takin' care of you. Oliver's not havin' accidents no more, but he's taken to stickin' that thumb in his mouth again." Tom plucked at the sheet as he stopped for breath. "So you see, Abby, ya gotta get better. Even if ya decided to go to find your pa, maybe you'll decide to come back. We love you, Abby."

Jarrod moved into the room and Tom looked up at him. "Was it all right I told her that?"

"Yup. Just fine."

"Jarrod?" The voice was hoarse, but it was Abby's.

His gaze shot to her face. Her eyes were open. "Abby?"

"What happened to me?"

This was the first time she had looked at him lucidly. He felt her forehead. It was blessedly cool. "You have chicken pox. The doc said you—"

"The doctor was here?" she asked. Her voice was weak, but Jarrod heard the astonishment.

She was going to be all right. Leaning back as he stared heavenward, Jarrod took a deep, shuddering breath. "Thank you, Lord. I owe you."

Jarrod stood beside Tom. "How do you feel, Abby?" the boy asked.

"Like I've been run over by a wagon," she said, rubbing her forehead.

Jarrod looked at Tom. "Why don't you find your brother and sisters and tell them the good news?"

He glanced at Abby, reluctant to leave her.

"Your uncle's right, Tom. The others will want to know I'm feeling better."

"Yes, ma'am," he said. "Take care of her, Uncle Jarrod."

"Count on it."

Then the boy was gone.

Abby struggled to sit up. Jarrod moved to help her, and the sheet fell away, exposing her nakedness. She quickly covered herself.

"I had to," Jarrod said. "It was the only way I knew to keep the fever down." He pulled her cotton nightgown from the dresser and handed it to her. Then he turned away as she slipped it over her head.

"How long was I sick?"

"You don't remember anything?"

"Not much. You can turn around now," she said, leaning back against the pillows. "The last thing I recall was making breakfast. Rafe Donovan left that morning. My head hurt and I was so cold my teeth chattered."

"You didn't know the children were in and out?" She shook her head. He pointed to a vase of wilting wildflowers that Katie had brought. Pencil drawings that she recognized as Oliver's were tacked up on the wall opposite the bed. A big sign beneath it in Lily's handwriting said, *Get well, Abby.*

"The next thing I remember was hearing Tom's voice. He said, 'We love you.'" That puzzled her.

"Tom carried water up and down the stairs for three days." He smiled at her shocked expression. "Yes, Tom. When he met you, he had just lost his mother and never grieved for her, he finally admitted. He was afraid to care about anyone because it hurt too much when they were gone. He's always liked you, Abby."

"I'm glad."

Jarrod sat on the bed beside her. His muscled thigh brushed hers and a spark of awareness charged through her.

"How do you feel?"

She thought for a minute. "Much better. I'm hungry."

He laughed. He threw his head back and kept laughing until he had to wipe the tears from his eyes.

"Are you all right, Jarrod?" What she'd said wasn't that funny.

"It's just so good to see you"— he stopped as if searching for the right word—"normal."

She gingerly touched her cheeks and felt the bumps and scabs. She recalled the redness and scabs Oliver had suffered when he was recovering. It was dreadful. "You call this normal? I must look a sight." She started to hide her face in her hands.

Jarrod took them in his own. "You're beautiful, Abby."

*  *  *

Three days later Abby felt so much better, she dressed and went downstairs for breakfast. Jarrod had already fed the children. They were cleaning up when she walked into the room.

Oliver's face brightened when he saw her. "Hi, Abby!"

He ran over and hugged her around the legs.

Katie ran to her, but there was a serious expression on her face as she looked up. "Are you all right enough to get out of bed? You were awful sick and Uncle Jarrod said it would take time for you to feel better and we musn't disturb you. So are you better enough that we can disturb you now?"

Abby smiled and tucked a blond curl behind Katie's ear. "I'm almost back to normal, and you never disturb me."

The little girl jumped up and down. "I knew it! She's all better, Uncle Jarrod."

Jarrod stood at the washbasin, his long sleeves rolled to his elbows, revealing strong, tanned forearms. He grinned at her. "That's a relief. It would be easier to hold back an over-flowing river than the likes of this group." Wiping his hands, he said, "Have a seat and I'll rustle up some flapjacks for you."

"They're real good," Katie said.

"Uncle Jarrod's a good cook," Oliver added.

"Your uncle is a man of many talents," Abby said. Then her gaze locked with Jarrod's and she knew he was thinking about abilities other than cooking. Heat warmed her neck and cheeks.

Quickly, Abby took the chair at the table beside Tom. He smiled at her shyly.

"So, how's your horse?" she asked, making conversation to cover the awkwardness.

"She's fine," the boy answered.

"Have you found a name for her yet?"

"No'm."

The back door burst open and Lily raced inside, hair

windblown from running, eyes sparkling. "Joe's here, Uncle Jarrod. He brought that saddle you ordered for Tom."

"Tell Gib," he said. "He'll know what to do with it." The girl nodded, then stopped at the door. "Mornin', Abby. Glad to see you up."

Before Abby could answer, Lily was gone.

"Funny," Tom said. "We were just talking about my horse. Can I go see the saddle, Uncle Jarrod?"

"Me too!" Katie and Oliver said together.

"Sure, you go on." Just before Tom closed the door, Jarrod called out, "Tell Joe to see me before he leaves so I can pay him."

"Yes, sir."

"So, Joe took my old job," Abby said. "I vaguely remember Tom telling me that."

"Yup, Gib told me he was here a couple weeks ago with—"

Jarrod looked at her for a long moment, his expression sad.

"What is it, Jarrod? You look funny, like you lost your best friend."

"Just before you got sick, Gib told me there was a letter for you."

"From my father?" she asked. Excitement chased away her irritation that he'd forgotten about it. She so loved hearing from her father.

"Before I give it to you," Jarrod said, his voice sounding strange, "there's something I need to explain." He drew in a deep breath as he crossed the room and set the hand towel on the back of a chair. "When we were in town on the Fourth of July, I sent a wire to Luke Brody, a friend of mine in San Francisco. I asked him to see what he could find out about your father."

"The letter's from him?"

Jarrod nodded. "It's from your father, and Luke sent it along. I'll get it."

Anticipation bubbled inside Abby. Maybe her dream was just about to come true. Jarrod returned with the letter and handed it to her.

With trembling hands, she tore it open and read.

> *Dear Abby,*
> *I'm afraid in trying not to hurt you, I've done you a terrible disservice. You cried so when I told you I was leaving, it broke my heart. God help me, I had to go. But I led you on in believing I planned to come back. The truth is, I remarried. I have a little girl. Emma is nine years old. They don't know about you and Clint and your mother. I tried to love your ma, for your sake, and your brother's. But I couldn't. She deserved a better man than me. I left for both of us.*
>
> *I'm begging you, Abby, don't try to find me. It could destroy my family and I can't risk that. For the first time in my life, I'm really and truly happy.*
>
> *I do love you, Abby. Believe that. I'm sorry I hurt you. I'm certain you can't forgive me so I won't even ask. I wish you the same happiness that I've found.*
> *Love,*
> *Father*

The information stunned her, and she had to read it three times before the words made sense.

"What's wrong, Abby? You're white as a sheet. Are you sick again?"

She handed him the letter. "My father doesn't want me to see him, let alone live with him."

Jarrod scanned the page. "He has a family."

She nodded numbly. "They don't know about Clint and me. My brother was right all along. He said if Sam had cared about us, he would have stayed. My father doesn't want me to jeopardize his new life."

"I don't know what to say, Abby. I'm sorry—"

"It's not your fault. He didn't love my mother. He left because he wasn't happy. But he is now."

"He loves you, Abby. He's stayed in touch all these years because he cares about you."

All these years. She had waited, and worked, and prayed

that she could reunite her family. But he had made another home and another family. Bitterness welled up inside her. If only he had told her. For years, he'd let her believe her fantasy because he didn't have the guts to tell her he didn't care.

She shook her head. "He doesn't love me. It was guilt, pure and simple. And it was cruel and heartless. I've been planning and hoping and dreaming all these years. For nothing."

"I shouldn't have meddled. I'm sorry—"

She stood up. "Don't be. I'm glad you found him for me. Why should I waste any more time on him?"

"That means you're going to respect his wishes?"

"Yes. His daughter—my half sister—is younger than I was when he left. I won't hurt her the way I—" Her voice caught and she bit her lip.

Jarrod pulled her into his arms. The last thing she wanted to do was cry in front of him, but she couldn't stop the tears. Maybe it was all that had happened in so short a time, or maybe the toll her illness had taken on her. She hid her face against his chest and cried her heart out. A small corner of her mind was grateful for his strength, the haven he provided. The comfort was too wonderful to ignore.

She *needed* him. It frightened her how much.

"It's going to be all right, Abby," he crooned. He held her tight and rubbed her back as sobs wracked her. He talked, but most of the words didn't penetrate the blackness of her shattered dreams.

As evening approached, Jarrod found Abby at the waterfall. It pleased him that she sought comfort in the place he and Sally always had. Abby looked up when the sound of his boots on the rocks caught her attention.

"If you want me to go, I will," he said. "But I've left you alone all day and I thought maybe you were ready to talk now."

"I'm not very good company, Jarrod."

"I didn't come here to be entertained."

She smiled. "That's good."

"Have you come to any conclusions?"

"Yes. I'm a fool," she said grimly.

"Abby, don't—"

"What?" she asked. "Say the truth? Why not? It wouldn't be anything everyone else doesn't already know. He didn't leave to find work. He left because he didn't want us, mother and Clint and me. Everyone tried to tell me, including you. I wanted to believe his story about making us a better life. But the truth is: a man doesn't walk out on his family."

"I'm sure there's more to it than that."

She shook her head. "Look at you. Four children came into your life out of the blue. Did you walk away from them?"

"No. But that was thanks to you. If you hadn't made me see that they needed guidance and caring, I might have. Your father's a weak man. His daughter is a strong, wonderful woman, in spite of what he did. Maybe because of it. The important thing is getting on with life."

She sighed. "I've put mine on hold for years."

"It's your time, Abby. What are you going to do with it?" he asked.

He held his breath, hoping for a sign of how she felt.

"I don't know," she admitted. "It's as if I don't know who I am anymore."

"You're my wife, Abby."

"Don't be offended, but—I forgot." She shook her head. "Nothing has gone as we planned, has it?"

"No."

"You didn't want to get married any more than I did, and here we are. Married, and we didn't even need to be. Donovan dropped his claim to the children, I have no reason to look for my father—We can have it annulled as soon as possible."

That wasn't exactly the sign he was hoping for. He hoped this was only her bitterness talking. She was wrong; he hadn't wanted to be married at first. But he did now.

"What will you do if we get the annulment?" he asked.

"I'll go back to Hollister. Find a job. Seems mine's been taken. Henrietta may have work for me. There's always chores to do in the Watering Hole—" She stopped and looked at him thoughtfully. "What do you mean 'if' we get the annulment?"

"Stay here."

She looked at him, her blue eyes wide. "What?"

"You just said there's no reason to leave. Your job's been taken. Stay here."

She stood up and her stubborn little chin rose a notch. "I don't need your charity, Jarrod Blackstone."

"It's not charity."

"I don't need your pity either," she snapped.

"You're the last person in the world I'd pity." Jarrod took a deep breath. "I want you to stay and be my wife."

"Your wife? You mean—your *wife*?"

He nodded. "And a mother to the children. We all need you, Abby."

"Aha." Her eyes narrowed. "You still need help looking after the children. If I stay as your wife, you don't have to pay me to be the housekeeper."

"You know that's not it. I'll see that your brother finishes his schooling—"

"Don't bother. It's not your responsibility. I'm not your responsibility. The kids are. And I suggest you start looking for another housekeeper. As soon as I can, I'm going back to Hollister and getting that annulment." She tapped her chest. "I have a place to go. Don't think I don't."

She turned on her heel and walked away.

Jarrod sat on the rock she had just left and scratched his chin thoughtfully. He wasn't sure what he'd said that had lit her fuse. He did need her. Not for the children, for him. Whatever happened, she would always be in his heart. He wanted her in his life, in his bed. He couldn't imagine going on without her.

He'd come here to say straight out that he loved her.

He'd been trying to find the right moment, not wanting

to burden her while she was dealing with her father's rejection.

He had to remember not to be sensitive again, he told himself.

Abruptly, Jarrod stood up. By God, he hadn't gone through hell just to do nothing and let her walk out of his life. Abby had shown him how to give himself to the people he loved. He knew now why Dulcy had left. Not because of the isolation of the ranch, but because he hadn't cared about her enough to be there for her. He wouldn't make the same mistake with Abby. He couldn't. Every moment away from her was a moment without color and light. His gut told him her decision to leave was rooted in pride. All he had to do was convince her that he loved her more than his own life.

It was time for action.

Time for the one thing that would keep her from getting that annulment.

# 19

*"Abby, Gib's takin' us to see the Specific Ocean!"* Oliver ran into her room as Abby folded her clothes and set them on the bed. Her carpetbag was on the floor and she kicked it underneath the mattress. She didn't want the child to see her packing. The boy looked at her pile of clothing, then back up to her. "Are ya comin' with us?"

She shook her head. "I can't. I have to—"

"Here you are, Oliver." Jarrod leaned one broad shoulder against the doorjamb. His gaze drifted from her to the evidence that she was leaving, then back again.

"What's this about the Pacific Ocean?" she asked.

"Oliver wants to see it."

"Gib's taking him?"

"Gib and Slim are taking all the kids. They're camping out for a few days."

"Why aren't you taking them?" she asked suspiciously. "When did all this happen?"

"Gib and I decided last night. After I got back from the waterfall."

What she wanted to ask was why no one had told her. But she figured she had given up that right when she informed Jarrod she was leaving. Tears burned her eyes, but she'd rather walk naked in a hailstorm than let Oliver, and especially Jarrod, see her cry.

Oliver climbed up on the neatly made bed and swung his legs back and forth. "Uncle Jarrod gots lots of work to catch up on, on account of you 'n' me bein' sick and him takin' care of us."

"You can't put the trip off until you're free to take them?" she asked Jarrod.

Oliver jumped down and folded his arms over his chest. "I been waitin' t'see the Specific Ocean forever. I can't wait no more."

"Anymore," Abby and Jarrod corrected him together.

They looked at each other and smiled. Then Abby's amusement faded as a wave of pain washed over her. She hadn't known how difficult it would be to leave. She loved the children.

And she loved Jarrod, more than she'd thought it was possible to love a man.

As much as she cared for the children, it would hurt too much to stay, knowing she was nothing more to him than a housekeeper. He had only married her to keep the children; he'd never planned for the situation to be permanent. Abby knew Jarrod didn't like to take chances—a surefire road to failure, he'd once called it. Love was the biggest risk of all. He'd been burned once. Would he put himself in a position for it to happen again? Despite his assurance that he wanted her as a wife, she was afraid he only said it because he felt sorry for her. She wouldn't be able to bear seeing the pity in his eyes grow day after day.

And it would, even though she knew he cared about her.

He'd awakened her to passion on their wedding night. But he hadn't said a single word about loving her. Because he would never let himself love any woman. She was afraid another rejection, especially from Jarrod, would be more than she could take.

Feeling sorry for her would be just as bad. He was too good a man to send her away. But pride wouldn't let her chance that she would never be more to him than someone to care for his children.

Tom raced into the room. "Abby! I got a name for my horse."

"Tell me," she said, trying to pretend an excitement she didn't feel.

"I gotta ask you something first. Would you mind if I called her Abby?"

Her gaze met Jarrod's amused one. Ordinarily she might be offended at having a horse named after her. But coming from Tom, it meant so much. Another wave of tears rushed into her eyes, and she fought to hold them back.

"It might be sort of confusing with two Abbys. Don't you think?" Then she remembered she was leaving. "If you want to name her that, it's fine with me, Tom."

The boy scratched his forehead thoughtfully. "Hadn't figured on it bein' confusing. Guess I'll think on it some more." He tugged his brother toward the door. "Gib sent me to find you. We gotta put our stuff in the wagon. He's ready to go."

"Oh, boy!" Oliver exclaimed.

It was early afternoon when Jarrod stood beside Abby in front of the house and said good-bye to the children. He saw the pain etched on her face and knew the effort it took her not to release the tears she'd been holding back since that morning.

Abby kissed Oliver's cheek. "Remember to go before you get in your bedroll."

"Yes'm," he said, giving her a hug.

Katie wrapped her arms around Abby's neck. "I'm gonna miss you," the little girl said. "What if I have a bad dream?"

"I'm sure you won't," Abby said. "But if you do, Gib will know what to do. He'll take good care of you."

As Jarrod lifted the two youngest into the back of the wagon, Abby gave Lily a hug and a kiss. Then she turned to Tom, hesitating. She stuck her hand out to shake his. The boy took it, then leaned over and kissed her cheek. "I'll bring you back something special," he said.

She merely nodded, and Jarrod knew it was because words would destroy her shaky control.

When everyone was in the wagon, Gib nodded to Jarrod. "You know where we'll be. That stretch of shore just above Sanchez Canyon."

"I know it," Jarrod said. "You'll be gone two days?"

"Any longer and we'll get word to you."

"Take good care of them, Gib."

The old man nodded, then flicked the reins and the horses started forward. Jarrod and Abby called out good-byes and waved until the wagon was out of sight. Jarrod looked down at her. A whole world of hurt hovered in her blue eyes.

So far his plan had gone ahead like clockwork. Out of all the plans he'd made since Abby came into his life, it was the only one that had. A good thing, since this was the most important.

He watched her as she strained for a last look at the children. Jarrod knew the precise moment when she realized they were completely alone. She looked toward the house, then up at him, and her body tensed.

"Jarrod, I'm going to finish packing my things and then I'm going back to town."

"All right," he said. "I'll go with you and see you safely there."

"No!" Her hand fluttered near her throat. "I mean that's not necessary. I've made the trip so often, I could do it in my sleep. If you'll loan me a horse, I'll see it's returned."

He decided not to deal with that. Instead he went straight to her heart. "Do the kids know you won't be here when they get back?"

She bit the corner of her lip. "No. It would spoil their trip. I couldn't do that." She turned and went into the house.

Jarrod caught her at the bottom of the staircase and gripped her upper arm to stop her. He turned her to face him. "How can you leave without saying good-bye to them?"

"It's better that way—"

"For who? Not them. It must be better for you. Your

father may be weak and selfish, but at least he had the guts to face you when he left."

"That's not fair, Jarrod," she cried.

"Damn straight. Like father, like daughter. You're running away from the kids."

"I'm not—"

"What are you afraid of, Abby?" He held up a hand to stop her protest. "You love the kids. You've never held back with them."

"Of course I love them. I'd never hurt them deliberately."

"Then it must be me you're afraid of."

"That's ridiculous."

"Is it? You won't let yourself care. You're afraid of being hurt again."

She pulled her arm from his grasp and stepped on the first stair. They were almost eye-to-eye, and hers were sparking like kerosene-fed flames.

"You're not going to talk me out of leaving, Jarrod."

"Talking wasn't what I had in mind," he said with a wry smile.

"I knew it!" She pointed at him. "You deliberately sent the children off with Gib so you could—So that—To try and—"

"Have my way with you? Seduce you? Love you? Give you a dream to replace the one you lost?" he asked, lowering his voice intimately. "Guilty as charged. And not a bit sorry."

She shook her head and started backing up the stairs. "Don't come near me, Jarrod," she warned.

"Why?" He smiled, and saw the pulse in her throat beat faster. "Because you don't trust yourself?"

"I don't trust you."

"If you tell me no, I'll stop. I'd never hurt you."

They were at the top of the stairs and she was still backing away from him down the hallway.

"Then I'm telling you no. Stop. Right now," she added when he kept moving toward her.

"I haven't started anything yet." That was a lie. The

moment the children were out of sight, he had begun stalking her with every intention of making her his.

"Don't you lay a hand on me, Jarrod. Not one finger."

He moved quickly, before she could sidestep him, and backed her against the wall just outside his bedroom. This time when he took her in there he would make sure they finished what he started.

Putting his hands on the wall, he trapped her without actually touching her.

"I'm warning you, Jarrod."

"I haven't laid a finger on you. But I have very specific plans for my mouth—and yours," he said, grinning at her gasp of outrage.

Before she could duck away, he pressed his lips to hers. Her body tensed, but she didn't move to escape. With his tongue, he gently nudged her lips apart. She allowed him into the sweet recesses of her mouth. He caressed her until she reluctantly relaxed and then sighed with pleasure.

He continued his assault. Her defenses were crumbling and he couldn't give her an opportunity to shore up her resistance. He gently kissed the corner of her mouth, her delicate jaw, then took her earlobe into his mouth and bit lightly. When she groaned and squirmed restlessly, he lowered his mouth to the spot below her ear that he knew would make her surrender.

She drew air in between her teeth, and the small, feminine noises she made sorely tested his own restraint. His breathing grew ragged. The waiting for her had seemed like a lifetime. Now that it was over, he was afraid he would disappoint her.

Her skin was silky and smooth to his touch. Her full, soft lips slightly parted in unknowing invitation, shiny from his moist, tormenting kisses. Yearning, as elemental and desperate as the need to draw another breath, took hold of Jarrod and tore him wide open. He was fully aroused, aching from the need for release. But the pain of losing her would be far greater. Instinct told him she shared his desire. But if he was wrong, if she didn't want him as much as he wanted her, he would respect her wishes and back off. Although it would be the hardest thing he'd ever do.

Abby stared into the intensity of Jarrod's gray gaze, took in the way his eyes darkened when his mouth moved over hers. Her body had betrayed her, as she'd known it would if he touched her. She could hardly catch her next breath, but the sensations running through her had nothing to do with survival and everything to do with being a woman.

She saw the uncertainty in his eyes. He was giving her the opportunity to walk away. She had to choose: a lifetime of loneliness, or perfect happiness in his arms. In the end, the choice was easy.

She had already lost her heart to Jarrod. She would lose her soul if she didn't love him now.

Abby lifted his hand from the wall beside her cheek and pressed a kiss into his palm. He closed his eyes as a groan tore from deep in his throat.

She laced her fingers through his and drew him into the room with her. Starting to close the door, she laughed nervously. "We're alone. I forgot."

"I didn't." He took her face in his hands and stared deeply into her eyes. "Are you sure about this, Abby? Really sure? I don't want you to feel I pushed you—"

She stopped him with two fingers on his lips. "You did push, make no mistake about that, Jarrod. But I'm glad. I want this and I've never been more sure of anything in my life."

He smiled. "I'm going to take you at your word because, frankly, I don't think I could stop now."

The room was cool and an afternoon breeze slipped past crisscrossed lace curtains and out the windows on the other side. The sun shone on the front of the house, leaving this side shadowed.

He led her to the bed and pressed lightly on her shoulders until she sat on the mattress. The bedclothes were neatly folded at the foot. She smiled. He had certainly planned ahead, *and* been awfully sure of himself. She sighed, not finding it in her to care. She wanted him. How could she be angry at him for feeling the same way?

Jarrod slowly slipped off Abby's shoes and stockings. Her heartbeat increased as he took lovely liberties while he performed the task. Then he took her hands in his and tugged her to a standing position as he unbuttoned her split skirt and let it fall to her feet. Soon she stood before him in chemise and pantalettes.

He reached out and touched the tip of her breast with one finger. Her nipple puckered and hardened. Her breath caught in her throat as that one light touch created a powerful hunger that swept through her.

Emboldened by the approval she saw in his face, she released the ribbons at the front of the garment. With both hands, Jarrod parted the sides and slid the material off her shoulders. He brought her hands to his mouth and kissed each in turn. "You are more beautiful than I imagined. And believe me, I've been imagining a lot lately."

She reached for the buttons on his shirt and began unfastening them. "I want to see you."

When he shrugged the shirt off, she pressed her palms to the mat of hair covering his chest, loving the way it tickled. Even better was the way her bare breasts tingled against his skin when he drew her against him. She could feel every beat of her heart. The closeness was so exquisite, a tingling sensation rose all the way from her toes.

"I want to see all of you," he said, slipping his hand between them to release the tie of her pantalettes. When they were removed, she stood before him without a stitch of clothing.

His hands—big, warm, rough—swallowed hers and held them in a loose grip. "You're perfect," he whispered.

"I'm glad you think so." She shivered.

"Are you cold?"

She shook her head. How could she tell him that it was the way he looked at her? His gaze was like a warm current that spread through her body in waves. The feelings were so powerful, she couldn't keep them inside.

Jarrod lifted Abby, placed her on the mattress, and pulled the sheet over her. Then he removed the rest of his clothes.

As he stood before her, her heart lurched wildly. Wide shoulders and powerful chest tapered to a flat midsection. The mat of hair narrowed on his abdomen and dipped lower, nestling his aroused manhood.

"You're perfect too," she said, her voice husky.

He grinned. "I'm glad you think so," he answered, echoing her own words. He slipped into bed and pulled her into his arms. "You're so small, so fragile. You make me feel awkward, and afraid."

"Of what?" she asked, surprised. She was the one who'd never done this before.

"I don't want to hurt you." His voice, warm and sweet, touched her everywhere.

"I know."

"I've never felt this way before. You bring out new feelings in me—the need to protect, the desire to please."

"You do please me."

That was when she felt her heart slip out of her grasp and her last traces of control shattered. The tenderness was more than she could bear. The force of her love pushed her to him and spun her like a leaf in a twister. No words could express what she was feeling. She could only show him.

Her hand slipped around him, exploring his tough body. The muscles rippling over his back moved beneath her fingers as he cradled her against his strength. So strong, yet so gentle.

Her breathing quickened as he trailed little kisses over her neck, shoulder, and lower. When he took the tip of her breast between his lips, she arched her back, offering herself more fully to him. At the same time, his hand slipped over her abdomen and between her thighs. He performed an exploration of his own, until his thumb stroked the bud of her femininity. She gasped as tremors of pure pleasure shook her and her hips arched against his hand. Her body melted into his and she couldn't tell where hers left off and his began.

He stroked her. Each touch fueled the fire inside her, making it burn hotter. Heat surged through her; passion branded her. A throbbing began between her legs, sending ribbons of sensation through her stomach. As he continued to take her higher, a frantic, frenzied, desperate need for liberation built within her. Finally, she gave a strained cry as her body clenched and surged wildly and release rolled through her in wave after wave of pleasure.

Limp and gasping for breath, she looked up at him. She curved her hand to his jaw, wanting to know what it would be like to cradle him within her body, to feel his strength inside her, to give him the same pleasure he'd given her.

He smiled and nodded when he read the look in her eyes.

"You're my bride, no question about that," he said hoarsely. "Now it's time to make you my wife."

"Yes."

"I'll try not to hurt you, honey."

She kissed him. "I'm not made of glass. I won't shatter."

He still looked worried as he positioned his body over hers. Gently, he eased into her. He filled her near to bursting, yet she welcomed him. She felt a tearing sensation and one quick, sharp pain. He held himself still for a few moments as he watched her carefully. When she drew him down for a soft kiss, he looked relieved. Then he began to move within her, slowly at first.

Ripples of almost painful delight spiraled from her abdomen outward. Jarrod's face grew intense with concentration. The sensuous sounds of their bodies coming together mingled with his ragged breathing and her own soft sighs of pleasure.

As tension built within her again, she knew she'd been wrong before. She just might shatter into a million pieces.

Then Jarrod went still for a moment, his eyes closed. He gave a harsh cry, a rough sound that burst from his throat as he thrust into her. One last lunge, then he shuddered.

Jarrod lowered himself into her, rolled onto his side, and gathered Abby against him. His face turned toward her and his warm breath stirred her hair. They lay like that, spent and content, for a long time. His breathing grew even, telling her he'd fallen asleep.

Abby sighed, brushing the hair from his forehead. Loving Jarrod had been even more wonderful than she'd thought. And more terrible. Now that she knew the ecstasy of being with him, how could she go back to the desolation of being alone?

But she knew she had to. He hadn't said he loved her, and she couldn't settle for less. That's what had destroyed her own family. She wouldn't do it to herself, and especially not to Jarrod.

Abby looked up from the bowl of eggs she'd been stirring when Jarrod entered the doorway to the kitchen. He was wearing nothing but denims. The sight of his bare chest covered with a dusting of hair made her catch her breath. He had loved her thoroughly all afternoon, until the shadows of twilight had crept into the house. Then he'd dozed again and she had come downstairs to think.

"What are you doing?" His voice sounded uncertain, but with a note of anger.

She understood his uncertainty. She felt the same thing. As well as sad and wistful. If only things could have been different. But she didn't know how to go back. "I'm hungry." That wasn't a lie. "Aren't you?"

"I suppose."

"What's wrong, Jarrod?"

"I woke up and you were gone. I was afraid you'd left for good."

She looked down at the eggs she had broken into the bowl and sighed. "You were right when you said I was being a coward with the children. I can't leave without telling them good-bye. They deserve to know what's going on."

Even though that meant the pain of staying on alone with Jarrod until they returned from their trip.

He laughed, but there was no humor in it. "I don't know what's going on. How can I explain it to them?"

"I can't say what's going on with you, but for myself, I'll tell you one thing—I'm finished running away." Before she left him, she wanted to make sure he knew one thing. "I love

you, Jarrod Blackstone. You've never said how you feel.
And I'm not asking for anything. I just needed to say it
once."

A surprised expression crossed his face before he shook
his head. He moved forward and caught her in his arms.
"You're my wife. Stay with me, Abby. The family you've
always wanted is right here. All you have to do is reach out
and take it."

"You said you wanted me to stay for you and the children. But you haven't once said how you feel about me."

"I thought I just showed you how I feel."

"I'm not in the mood for teasing." She tried to pull away,
but he tightened his grip.

"Neither am I. Don't let your pride tear us apart. Don't
leave me, Abby." His expression was anything but playful. "I
love you."

"Why didn't you tell me before?"

"I was waiting for the right time. So much has happened.
I almost lost you when you were sick. Whether I said the
words or not, the love was there. I should have told you. I
won't make that mistake again. I'll say it, and go on saying it
while we grow old together. I love you, Abby."

She released the breath she'd been holding. She studied
his face for several moments. His eyes were full of intensity.
She believed him.

"All right, then." She pulled away from him and started
stirring the eggs again. "Do you want biscuits and bacon
with your eggs?"

"Abby?" Puzzled, Jarrod scratched his chin. "What does
that mean, 'All right, then'?"

"It means that was all I needed to hear. If you'd told me
that yesterday, you'd have slept better last night and saved
yourself and Gib a lot of trouble." She shook her head and
tsk-tsked him. "Scheming, and plotting to get rid of the children. All you had to do was tell me you loved me."

"I planned to tell you, there by the waterfall. You never
gave me a chance. That temper of yours—"

When she grinned, he pulled her to him in a fierce grip

that would have convinced her even if his words hadn't. "No way on God's green earth would I have let you walk away from me, Abby."

"Good. If I'd known that, *I'd* have slept better last night." She reached a hand up to smooth the frown lines on his forehead. "I love you, Jarrod."

Holding her face in his hands, he stared into her eyes. "Are you still hungry?"

"Yes," she said breathlessly.

"For me?"

"Yes," she said again, then pulled away. "And as soon as I cook up these eggs and replenish my strength, I plan to have *my* way with you."

"Hot damn," he said grinning. "Firecracker sure fits you."

# Epilogue

*Abby pulled her shawl* closer around her shoulders as she rocked on the back porch after dinner. The nights had turned cool, as it was getting on toward fall. These six weeks since Jarrod had told her he loved her had been the happiest of her life. He'd made sure to show her every night exactly how he felt. She smiled as a shiver of anticipation rippled through her. How she looked forward to bedtime, and a night in his arms. The children had come back from their camping trip, and if they noticed the intimate changes between her and Jarrod, they never said anything. They went about their day, happy and normal. She loved every minute of watching them grow. Well, almost every minute. Oliver did manage to get dirtier than any two four-year-olds. Katie never stopped asking questions. And Joe Schafer found a lot of errands to bring him out to the ranch—and Lily. How that girl would fret every time he left.

And Tom.

She smiled as she thought of him. Since he'd let go of his grief, his loving nature had shone through. He was forever bringing her something—a flower, a rock he thought was pretty. She sighed, glad that Jarrod hadn't let her pride ruin everything. Truth to tell, it was Jarrod who had left her no pride. Thank heaven.

The kitchen door opened and her husband walked onto the porch.

"I thought I'd find you out here," he said.

"It's lovely, isn't it?"

"Yup. Have you had enough for tonight? The children sent me to fetch you."

"Is something wrong?" she asked, bolting out of her chair. Dizziness hit her and she swayed on her feet.

Jarrod steadied her with his hands on her shoulders. "Are you all right?"

"Fine. I think I just stood up too fast." She suspected it was more than that.

"Come off it, Abby. You move like a whirlwind and never get light-headed. When are you going to admit to me that you're probably in the family way?"

Abby looked surprised. "How did you—"

"I know every inch of your body. I've been noticing changes."

"Why didn't you say anything?"

"I was waiting for you. When did you plan to tell me?" Jarrod asked.

"I wasn't sure how you would take the news. This makes five children, Jarrod!"

He put his arms around her and lifted her feet off the ground. She laughed when he swung her in a circle. "I couldn't be happier." He set her on the ground and looked at her seriously. "My parents built lots of bedrooms in this house. They intended to fill it with children. Sally did her part. Now we can do the rest."

She grinned up at him. It *was* a big place, with enough room for a lot of love and lots of children. What fun they'd have filling the house with noise and laughter and all the family she'd ever dreamed of.

"Speaking of children, you said they sent you to get me. I take it there's nothing wrong?"

"I don't think so. This is a family meeting. I found out a

while back that it's something Sally did with them. They let me in on it about the time we went in front of the judge."

"I know," she said, remembering how miserable she had felt about being left out. "I heard you that night."

"You never said anything."

"It was family. I wasn't part of it."

"You are now."

She smiled up at him. "What are we waiting for?"

Jarrod led her upstairs to the open door of Lily's room. Katie and Oliver sat on the bed dangling their legs back and forth. Lily stood in front of the dresser, and Tom leaned on the wall beside the door leading to his room.

"I thought you'd never get here," Oliver said.

"What took you so long?" Katie asked.

"This is real important," Tom said.

"Quiet everyone." Lily held her hands up. "Abby, we wanted you both here at this family meeting because we have something we want to ask you."

"I was hoping you'd include me."

Tom took a step forward. "Is that why you wanted to go look for your pa? Ya never said nothin' more about it, and I just wondered."

Abby sighed. "Yes. I wanted to reunite my family, and nearly missed out on being a part of this one. Thanks to your uncle, that didn't happen."

Tom cleared his throat. "In that case, Abby, I wanted to tell you that I finally decided on a name for my horse."

"Tom," Lily said, "this isn't the time for that."

"Yes, it is. I decided to call her Abby."

Katie clapped her hands. "Do you like that, Abby?"

"I like it just fine," she said, looking at Tom. "You're sure it won't be too confusing with two Abbys?"

"Not if we call you Ma," he said. He flushed as he looked from her to Jarrod. "We wondered if you'd mind if we call you Pa."

Jarrod's hand squeezed Abby's waist as he pulled her against him. She pressed her cheek to his chest as a lump of emotion caught in her throat.

Four pairs of eyes stared at them. Finally Tom said, "Why don't ya say somethin'?"

Jarrod swallowed hard. "Abby and I would be pleased for you to call us that and think of us as your parents. Right, Abby?"

She nodded, too full of emotion to speak.

They held their arms out and the children rushed into them.

Oliver pulled away first. "Ma, are you sure you like that name for Tom's horse? I think Lady would be better."

"What do you know? You're just a baby," Tom said.

"Am not." He looked up at the two adults, his head tipped so far back Abby thought he might topple over backward. "He keeps callin' me baby 'cause I'm the youngest. Ma? Pa? Can't you make him stop?"

Jarrod looked at Abby and smiled. "I reckon we can. In about seven or eight months."

Oliver frowned. "Huh?"

"We're going to have a baby, Oliver," Abby said. "Then you won't be the youngest anymore."

"Good," he said, nodding emphatically. "I'm gonna be a *big* brother."

Lily smiled and hugged Abby again. "A baby? Really?"

Katie jumped up and down. "We're gonna have a baby. Right, Uncle—I mean, Pa?"

"That's right," he said. "This means you'll all have to help Abby when it gets here. That's what families do."

They nodded solemnly and swore they would.

Abby studied the contented children around her and the warmth and strength of the man at her side. Love, support, family—the things she had craved all her life. Happiness bubbled up inside her and tears trickled down her cheeks.

Her dream had come true the moment she became Jarrod Blackstone's bride.

# Let HarperMonogram Sweep You Away